PRAIS EXPLORING HOME BY A. AMERICAN

Angery American has done it again. Another great installment of his HOME series, *Exploring Home*, fulfills our desires for more of Morgan and the crew. AA's gritty dialogue and visual prose paint a masterpiece for us post-apocalyptic junkies. This book may be my favorite in the series since the first.

—**David Crawford**, *Lights Out*

Chris Weatherman, widely known as Angery American and hailed as the master of post-apocalyptic fiction, has once again astounded readers with his latest masterpiece. Book 12 of the acclaimed Going Home series lives up to every bit of its hype and exceeds all expectations. With Morgan Carter and his loyal crew at the helm, the story paints a vivid and heart-pounding depiction of life in the aftermath of the cataclysmic event. Prepare to be engulfed in an enthralling tale of survival and intensity.

—**Pete Robertucci**, *Three Days to Eden*

Angery American became a driving force in the post-apocalyptic genre with his number one book, *Going Home*. I remember when I first was introduced to Morgan and Sarge over a decade ago and Book 12 is an amazing continuation of the storyline. As his co-author in the *Charlie's Requiem* series, a number one spin-off set in the *Going Home* world, I am constantly astonished at his creativity. Rest assured that this next installment is one of his best works. *Exploring Home* pulls on your heart, whether it is the joy of new life, or the pain of a country ripped apart. Old characters and new will touch your soul as they struggle to survive. Take the time to read or listen to the continuation of this epic tale. The only downside is that it will leave you wanting even more.

—**Walt Browning**, *Charlie's Requiem*

My absolute favorite book series of all time! From the moment I started reading the first book, I couldn't put it down. Chris is a great author who has a unique way of telling a story that not only entertains and keeps you hooked, but he also sprinkles knowledge, information, and ideas throughout the series. I highly recommend!

—**Matt Tate**, Netflix series *Snowflake Mountain* co-host, American Survival Co. owner

In his latest foray into dystopian fiction, Angery American brings the heat with his book, *Exploring Home*. Whether new to A. American's world gone sideways, or a returning participant in the trials and tribulations of Morgan and crew, you won't be disappointed. In addition to Morgan, Thad, Sarge, Mike, Ted, and other story arch mainstays are back in the thick of it.

As with all his books, A. American's talent for crafting a believable, action-filled, post-apocalyptic world draws you in. That and his well-developed characters make this a must-read for preppers, dystopian fiction lovers, and his raving fans. Don't miss it!

—**Brian Duff**, *Mind4Survival*

BOOKS BY A. AMERICAN

The Survivalist Series™:
Going Home (Book 1)
Surviving Home (Book 2)
Escaping Home (Book 3)
Forsaking Home (Book 4)
Resurrecting Home (Book 5)
Enforcing Home (Book 6)
Avenging Home (Book 7)
Home Invasion (Book 8)
Conflicted Home (Book 9)
Home Coming (Book 10)
Engineering Home (Book 11)

Charlie's Requiem Series
by A. American and Walt Browning:
Charlie's Requiem: A Novella (Book 1)
Charlie's Requiem: Democide (Book 2)
Charlie's Requiem: Resistance (Book 3)
Charlie's Requiem: Retribution (Book 4)
Charlie's Requiem: Contagion (Book 5)

Other Books:
Cry Havoc
Ramblin' Man
Decline and Decay: Strategies for Surviving the Coming Unpleasantness by A. American and Alan Kay
Hope by A. American and G. Michael Hopf

EXPLORING HOME

BOOK 12 OF THE SURVIVALIST SERIES

A. AMERICAN

EXPLORING HOME. Copyright © 2023 by Angery American Enterprises Inc. All rights reserved. Printed in the United States of America. Except as permitted under the U.S. Copyright Act of 1976, no part of this publication may be reproduced, distributed, or transmitted in any form or by any means, or stored in a database or retrieval system, without prior written permission of Angery American Enterprises Inc.

This is a work of fiction. Names, characters, places, and incidents either are the product of the author's imagination or are used fictitiously, and any resemblance to locales, events, business establishments, or actual persons (living or dead) is entirely coincidental.

ANGERYAMERICAN.com

ISBN: 978-0-9966960-7-4

Publicity requests: 2911 Media, Jeremy Westby, jpw@2911.us

Managed by HB Entertainment, Holly Bonnette, hbeartists@gmail.com

Cover Design by Brad Harris

Editing by Lori Lynn Enterprises

Formatting by Transcendent Publishing

CONTENTS

Chapter 1 1

Chapter 2 37

Chapter 3 71

Chapter 4 89

Chapter 5 101

Chapter 6 125

Chapter 7 149

Chapter 8 191

Chapter 9 223

Chapter 10 237

Chapter 11 261

Chapter 12 289

Chapter 13 315

Chapter 14 335

Chapter 15 359

About the Author 377

Angery American Online 379

EXPLORING
HOME

CHAPTER 1

Chaos. That's the only word for it. The old man was screaming into the radio at Mike and Ted while Jamie got the MRAP ready to roll. He called Wallner and told him to bring Red and come to his place.

"Who is Rhino One?" I asked Sarge, following behind him as he headed for the door.

"It's the convoy. They're early."

"We headed to the school?"

"Damn straight. Get your shit together. We're leaving soon."

"What about Fred?" The idea of childbirth in our current situation scared the shit out of me.

As he was climbing into the Hummer, Sarge asked, "You a doctor, Morgan? You a pediatrician?"

I didn't answer, just gave him a *fuck you* look.

"Then you can't do shit about that situation. Control the controllable. You *can* get your shit together and come with me to town."

"Yeah, yeah. I'll get my shit."

"Meet me at my place." Then he paused, and a serious look crossed his face. "And bring that Aaron with you. We need to have a talk with him."

"About?"

"Tabor."

I was confused. "Why?"

Sarge wasn't looking at me. He was staring off at some indistinct point. "We'll talk about it in town."

As I turned to walk away, I heard Dad call out, "Morgan!"

I stopped to wait for him. "What's up?"

"What's going on? Seems like a Chinese fire drill right now."

I ran my hand over my face. "Good comparison. One of Fred's babies is breech. Doc and Erin are doing their best to deliver it. The Army convoy is here, or nearly here, and we're running reconnaissance on a group of assholes we need to kill. So, yeah, pretty much a Chinese fire drill."

"Anything I can do?"

"Nothing I know of. I'm headed to town with the old man. I'm not sure exactly what is going on."

"All right, will be here if you need me."

>—||||||—<

Doc grabbed Erin's hand, placing it on Fred's belly. "Hold the head; I'm going to try and push from this side."

Sweat poured down Doc's and Erin's faces. Fred was also dripping in sweat and screaming. Kay sat by her head with Jess, and the two women were doing their best to comfort their friend. It was a futile effort, and Fred screamed out with each contraction—contractions that weren't doing what they were supposed to, which is to move a baby down the birth canal.

"Mel!" Doc called out. "Come over here and trade places with Erin."

Mel moved quickly. Doc demonstrated what he wanted her to do, and she placed her hands in the appropriate spots. As soon as Erin was free, Doc started giving her orders.

"Get the O2 SAT monitor out of my bag and get it on her. I also want a BP, Ricky-Tick."

Erin was a professional and quickly placed the monitor on Fred's finger as Jess held Fred's arm out to get her blood pressure. While the situation was critical, there was no panic. Just the painful agony Fred was enduring. The only person who seemed panicked was Mary. She stood beside Thad, both of her arms wrapped around one of his. Her eyes were wide and she barely drew a breath.

When Fred let out a particularly loud wail, Mary jumped. Thad looked down at her sympathetically. "Come on," he said, getting her attention. "Let's give them some room to work." Mary's head bobbed up and down and he took her outside where they sat down on the steps to the porch. Mary sat with her hands folded between her knees, rocking back and forth.

Thad put his arm around her and pulled her in tight. "It's not always like that," he said, as he leaned away a bit to look into her eyes. They were wet with tears and fear contorted her face.

"I'm so scared," she said, dropping her head onto his shoulder. "I was scared before, but now I'm *really* scared."

Thad put his hand on her head and caressed her hair. "I know this looks scary, but as I said, it's not normal. When little Tony was born, Anita did amazing." He stared off into the distance. "The labor wasn't long either." He chuckled. "I was a mess. I was so nervous and scared. But not Anita. She was strong." He paused and leaned away again. "Like you."

Mary looked up at him and wiped the tears from her face. "I don't know." She looked over her shoulder when Fred cried out again.

Thad gently cupped her chin, lifting it to face him. "You'll do fine." He stared into her eyes for a long moment. "You're going to be a great mother, and I cannot wait for your child, *our* child, to get here. You're a strong woman, Mary. Everything you've lived through. You're tougher than you think."

She dropped her gaze for a moment, then rested her head again on his shoulder. "As long as I have you," she said, looking up at him. "As long as I have you. I know everything will be ok."

"You have more than just me. You have everyone here. Just look at everyone that's in there helping. We have an amazing family here. A family of circumstance and choice, but more of a family than most people will ever have. They love you, and they will all be here for you. For us."

"Just like we are for them," Mary whispered.

Thad patted her knee. "Exactly." They sat quietly for a minute before Thad said, "Let's go find Aric. He's probably about to go crazy."

Mary stood up, the tears now gone, and held out her hand.

>—⫻⫻⫻⫻—<

Dalton stretched and yawned. "Any change?"

Karl was sitting on the hood of the Jeep, rubbing his eyes. "No." He pointed at a stainless coffee pot sitting on a small folding table. "That's fresh. Nothing really going on. Lots of skinny dipping over there, though."

"Probably trying to get a damn bath," Dalton said as he filled his titanium cup from the pot.

"Maybe," said Karl, "but what they're going to get is sick. I've watched them fill all kinds of containers with water from the lake right there where they're all soaking the stink off their asses."

"In my visit to their camp, they were pretty studious about boiling it."

Karl hopped off the hood. "Maybe so. But if they're using that water to wash their hands or dishes or anything, they're gonna get sick."

"Very likely. Have you seen any sort of a latrine set up?"

"No." Karl pointed toward the lake. "But over there by the boat ramp is a shitter. I've seen a pretty steady stream of people headed over there."

CHAPTER 1

"One shitter for that many people isn't going to cut it. We need to let the folks in town know to be very diligent about boiling any water they need to use from the lake. These fuckheads over here will make everyone on the other side of the damn lake sick."

"They should already be boiling it. This is Florida, home of stagnant surface water," Karl said and laughed. "Florida surface water, the stuff diarrhea is made of." He laughed again, proud of his little joke.

"I hate this state," Dalton complained. "You have no idea how pissed off I was to be here when all this shit went down. The water is full of uh-LIG-ga-tors. One walk in the woods and ticks are hanging off your nutsack like grapes. You can't sleep on the ground. Fuck this state."

"Don't hold back," said Karl. "Tell me how you really feel." Karl laughed.

Dalton climbed up on the Jeep hood and got himself in position behind the spotting scope. "I would," he said as he slid his ass across the hood, "but I'm a Christian."

Karl looked the big man up and down. "Yeah, like the Crusades. Imri is up after you," he added with a yawn.

"Get some sleep," said Dalton as he settled his eye behind the optic.

>⫸⫷<

We were in quite a convoy. Sarge was driving the Hummer with me in the passenger seat and Aaron in the back. Jamie and Ian were in the MRAP with Red and Wallner. Mike and Ted each in a war wagon. I had no idea why we were taking so many vehicles.

"Where are we going?" Aaron asked from the back seat of the Hummer.

"To the high school in town," I replied.

"What for?"

"There's an Army convoy coming in. They're bringing supplies with them and they'll be operating out of the school," Sarge answered.

"Oh, I was wondering what was going on. Everyone was running around and all," Aaron said. "But why am I here?"

"We'll get to that later." Sarge's reply seemed to make Aaron nervous, so he sat back in his seat and stared out the window.

"Are we planning on bringing a bunch of stuff back?" I asked Sarge as nighttime Altoona raced by.

"Some, probably. Right now, I just want to get these boys settled in for the night, and we'll come back tomorrow and start getting things set up."

It wasn't long before we turned onto Bulldog Lane, named for the Umatilla Bulldogs. The school was lit up, all the exterior lights were on, and Baker stood in front of the entrance with a couple of people in uniform that I didn't recognize. A couple of M-ATVs sat in the parking lot. These were the smaller MRAPs, not the big ones like we have. I liked the smaller ones and wished I had one.

"Doesn't look like much of a convoy," I said.

"It's out on the ball field, dipshit," the old man snapped.

"Wow," said Aaron, "you got the power onto the school."

"Damn skippy!" said Sarge as he pulled into an empty spot.

The rest of our little convoy pulled in and parked as well. We all got out and Sarge waved Ian over. He leaned over and whispered into his ear and Ian nodded.

As Ian walked away, he called out to Aaron, "Hey man, come with us."

Aaron didn't blink. He simply followed Ian.

We walked over to Baker and the men she was standing with. Seeing the old man, Baker said, "Here he is now," motioning at Sarge. "Colonel Merryweather, Colonel Mitchell."

CHAPTER 1

"Knock that shit off, Baker," Sarge snapped, then looked at the other man and offered his hand. "Colonel, good to meet you."

Merryweather took his hand. "Good to meet you as well, Colonel. We've heard a lot about you."

"Probably all bullshit," Sarge quipped back.

"Probably wasn't enough bullshit," I said, and the old man cut his eyes at me.

Merryweather looked at me. "You must be Morgan," he said and held out his hand.

I shook it. "That's me."

"So, you're the governor of Florida?" he asked with a smirk.

I just shrugged. "I have no fucking idea. But rumor has it."

Merryweather opened the door. "Let's go inside and talk."

We went into a conference room in the school. It was kind of surreal to walk into a room like this. I hadn't been in a conference room in over a year. Hell, I hadn't really been in a commercial building for over a year. Not one that wasn't looted out and fucked up.

We all filed in. Baker, Ted, and Mike were with us, as well as Wallner and Red. Several soldiers also joined us. Our group was a stark contrast to the soldiers we were meeting. While relaxed grooming standards were now common in the Army, from the looks of things, we were something else.

Baker wore her hair in a long ponytail and seldom wore any armor or even carried a rifle. Mike and Ted looked the part of Special Forces guys with pieces of uniform mixed with civilian clothes and the obligatory *cool-guy* beards.

Sarge was usually in uniform, though even his beard was beyond any standard. As for myself, I probably looked more like some deranged militia leader or Civil War general than anything else. Once everyone sat down, Merryweather stood at the head of the table and introduced his people.

7

As the conversation started, I was struck by the room. While my home had power, there wasn't much we used it for. Here, in a commercial building, I could hear the sixty cycles of the A/C power coursing through the building. I could hear fluorescent lights that so brilliantly lit the small space. It seemed incredible.

"This is Lieutenant Simmons." Merryweather named everyone as he pointed to them. "Sergeant Roberts, Warrant Officer Daniels, and Sergeant Mottishaw. Can you guys all introduce yourselves?"

Sarge held his hand up. "First Sergeant Mitchell."

"That's actually Colonel Mitchell," Merryweather corrected him to his staff.

Mikey raised his hand. "Mike."

"What's your rank?" Simmons asked.

"Just Mike."

Then Ted spoke up. "Ted. Just Ted."

"Teddy is a CW3, and that snot nose over there is an E-5," Sarge added.

Wallner and Red introduced themselves. Baker had already covered this, and it came to me.

Raising my hand, I said, "Morgan Carter. No rank, I'm a civilian."

Roberts grunted, "You don't look like one."

"He's not," Sarge interrupted. "Colonel?" Sarge asked, prodding Merryweather.

"Right." Merryweather looked at his people and continued, "Morgan is the civilian governor of Florida and the sheriff of Lake County. He's been appointed and has been doing some really good work around here. Colonel Mitchell is the Military Governor. These two men are the ultimate authority for the state of Florida."

I noticed a large map of the state hanging on the wall when I came in and Merryweather turned to it now.

"While the state lines have not changed, for your purposes, they have. You two are responsible for everything south of I-10, on the peninsula. We will handle everything above that to include the panhandle. Mayport and NAS Jax are operational, as well as Eglin. Umatilla will be the furthest south FOB in the state."

I raised my hand again. "Civilian here. I don't speak Army."

"Forward operating base," the Colonel said, then continued. "From here, we need to push south as well as east and west. We need to survey both coasts. Aerial surveys have been conducted, but we need a detailed survey from the ground. As you proceed, we will be standing up new FOBs. It will be your responsibility to identify those locations for us."

I raised my hand again. "Why are we doing this?" I looked around the table. "We're a small group here. You obviously have more resources than we do. Why aren't you guys doing this?"

Merryweather listened to me, his hands on his hips and nodding slightly in what I can only imagine as true *officer posture*.

"Sure. The reason, Governor, is that we simply do not have the manpower. We are stretched thin. And frankly, you're a victim of your own success. What you've done here is impressive to many. I'm sure you've worked hard for it, but none of it came easy. This community has overcome a lot and prospered far more than most places.

"Don't get me wrong. There are others like you out there, and they're all getting the same treatment you are. Those that stepped up and made a difference, did the hard thing, and thought about more than themselves, are all being supported. That's how you need to think about this; we're going to start supporting you. You just keep doing what you're doing, and we will provide you with all the support we can."

"Like what?" I asked.

"Excuse me?" Merryweather sounded surprised.

"What kind of support?" As I asked the question, my radio crackled. There was no transmission, just a break in the squelch. I held my hand up and plucked the radio from my plate carrier.

"Jess, how's it going with Fred?"

The room was quiet, as well as the radio, for a brief moment. Then she said, "*Uh, the baby isn't doing too good. Ronnie is working on her.*"

"The baby was born?"

"*Yeah.*"

"How's Fred?"

"*Ok. Exhausted.*"

"Wait," Mottishaw interrupted. "*Fred* is having a baby?" The look on his face was one of total confusion.

"Fred's a woman," Sarge explained.

"Do you guys need anything?" I asked Jess.

"*Ronnie says we could use some oxygen.*"

I looked at Merryweather. "Is oxygen on your support list?"

"We have O2," said Simmons.

Sarge looked at Mike. "Mikey, get some O2 and have Ian and Jamie run it back to the ranch ASAP."

"We have a flight surgeon with us," Merryweather said. "You want them to go with you?"

I replied before the old man could. "Yes, please."

Mike jumped up and Simmons followed him out of the room.

"Your group has a new baby?" Merryweather asked.

"Hopefully two," I said with a smile.

He smiled back. "That's amazing."

I gave him a nod. "Now, back to this support."

"Right. A lot has changed in the year since The Day."

Hearing him use the term, I smirked.

"Everything all right?" he asked.

"You just called it 'The Day.' That's what I've been calling it too." As I said the words aloud, I could almost see *duh* written across his face.

"That's what everyone calls it." He paused for effect. "As I was saying, a lot has changed. We are now being supported in a major fashion by many of the world's governments. Every imaginable resource is pouring into the country. We've been utilizing NAS Jax and Mayport here and need an inspection of the port at Canaveral as soon as possible. That will enable us to start moving cargo there and reduce transport times. We will also want one in Miami."

"You need us to go all the way to Miami?" I asked.

"We do. Boca Chica will be coming back online soon. But we need to get some Marines down there first to make sure the Cubans are gone. We'll be conducting an amphibious operation in the coming weeks to secure the facility."

Before I could ask, Sarge looked over and said, "Naval air station in Key West."

"Gotcha," I said.

"If and when Boca Chica comes back online, it will aid in taking some of the pressure off you guys here. We know it's a long way and honestly expect to have it back in our hands before you could ever make it down there. Your main task is the central part of the state. Canaveral, Orlando, and Miami are top priorities on that list."

"That's all well and good," I said, "but what about the people here? I really don't give two shits about the military side. What are *you* going to do for the people? And Miami is not Central Florida."

"Glad you asked," Merryweather replied quickly. "Food, clothing, medicine, and even fuel are coming in. We will be adding capacity to each of the FOBs as they develop. In other words, the more you need, the more we'll send you. As for Miami, I know it's not easy. But it's important. Really important."

"We need to give these people something to do," I said. "They're just sitting around most days with thousand-yard stares, stewing in their skin."

"Yes," said Merryweather.

Simmons walked into the conference room with a stack of folders.

"Hand me the militia folder." Merryweather held out his hand as the young officer handed it over, and Merryweather passed it to me. "This authorizes you to stand up a militia."

Taking the folder, I opened it and looked without actually seeing the contents. "We've already done that."

"You have?" Merryweather asked.

"Yes. They've received rudimentary training," said Sarge.

"How did you arm them?"

I shot a glance at Sarge. He cut his eyes toward me and quickly continued, "With whatever we could find. We've salvaged some hardware from various places." He didn't bother to mention we had enough Russian hardware to arm a small nation.

"And that, gentlemen, is why you two are in the positions you're in. The population is a fraction of what it once was. Those that simply couldn't do for themselves perished. The people that are left are pretty hardy stock. Which brings me to another item, LT?"

Simmons stood up, opened a folder, and cleared his throat. "Under the terms of Martial Law, the Department of Defense is instituting a policy of conscription."

"What the fuck?" I nearly shouted.

"Sorry?" Simmons asked.

"Not even a draft? Straight to roll 'em up and drag 'em off to the Army?" I asked.

"Governor—" Merryweather started before I cut him off.

"Just call me fuckin' Morgan."

"Alright, Fuckin' Morgan," Sarge shot back with a shit-eating grin.

I glared at the old man. "Don't be a dick. Nobody likes a dick."

The other men in the room were silent, unsure of just what was going on. Sarge relieved the tension for them. "Don't worry about him. He gets a little bitchy when he hasn't had his bottle before bed."

"Yeah, and he's an ass all the time," I said.

The LT was still unsure what to do, so Merryweather nodded for him to continue.

"Ok then," said the LT, "conscription was deemed the appropriate action. There is no way to notify people of a draft."

I looked at Sarge briefly as my leg bounced like a jackhammer under the table. "What are the conditions for conscription?"

He read from the folder he was holding, cleared his throat again, and began to nervously speak. "All able-bodied residents of the country between sixteen and fifty years of age are now eligible for conscription. Each conscript will be interviewed to determine if they possess certain high-priority skills."

I shot the old man a look. He didn't bother looking over; he knew I was glaring at him and spoke up. "Morgan has three daughters. He's worried about them being wrapped up in conscription."

"Four," I quickly added.

"Four," Sarge agreed.

"Well, uh," Simmons stumbled for words.

Merryweather came to his rescue. "Morgan, no one is going to ask you to give your daughters up for conscription. You and your family are doing enough for the country."

I breathed a sigh of relief. "Good. That's good. I mean, if they want to volunteer, that's one thing. I just don't want them voluntold."

With a dour look, Merryweather replied, "Completely understandable."

"What about my militia people? Can they be conscripted?" I asked.

"No, if they are in the service of the militia, they cannot be," offered Merryweather.

"What about my deputies, judge, police officers, and medics?"

"You have a judge?" Simmons asked.

"Of course. It wouldn't look right for the representative of law enforcement to be meting out punishment, judge, jury, and executioner style."

"Now that," Merryweather interrupted, "is a first."

"What?" Sarge asked.

"Someone actually thinking this through. Thinking ahead, looking at the long game, and appointing a judge. Who is it?"

"His name's Mitch," I said. "He had no real connection to any sort of law enforcement, and that is why we asked him to."

"We'd like to meet him," said Merryweather.

"You will."

"More importantly, what about my people?" Sarge interrupted.

"Say again?" asked Merryweather.

"The people presently under my command are to remain under my command." It was a statement, not a question.

"Of course. As I said, you are the final military authority."

"Good," Sarge shot back. "Do you have those files I requested?"

Merryweather nodded and looked at the LT, who handed him two file folders. It seemed surreal to me to be dealing with files again. *What a waste of time*, I thought.

"Morgan, can you go get Aaron and bring him in?" Sarge asked.

Unsure of what he was up to, I said, "Sure."

I found Aaron outside with the soldiers loading supplies into our vehicles. "Hey Aaron, come inside for a minute," I called out and waited as he walked over.

"What's up?" he asked.

I shrugged. "No idea. Let's find out together."

The reply did not instill any confidence in him. With slouched shoulders and keeping his gaze on the ground, he followed me back into the conference room. When we walked in, Sarge introduced Aaron to everyone and laid one of the folders on the table before him.

"Aaron, you were inside the camp of the marauders headed this way, correct?" Sarge asked.

"Yeah, I told you that," Aaron answered.

"And you saw the man that was heading up this little sideshow?"

"Yeah, they call him Chuck."

Sarge opened the folder to reveal a photo of a man in a DHS uniform. "Is this the man?"

Aaron stepped over to get a better look. "Yeah, that's him. He looks different now. But that's him."

Sarge grunted and I asked, "What's up?"

"I didn't think it was true."

I was confused. "What's true?"

Sarge jabbed a finger into the photo. "Because I choked this son-of-a-bitch to death with my bare hands and left him in a fuckin' burning building. He must have more lives than a damn cat in Chinatown."

"Shoot him in the face next time," I suggested. "Kind of removes this sort of possibility."

"It does effectively resolve the issue," said Simmons.

"Next time I see this asshole, there will be no doubt," said Sarge. Taking another photo out of the file, he asked, "You recognize this character?"

Aaron looked at it. "No. Never seen him before."

"You said there was a Jap with them. This isn't him?"

Aaron shook his head. "Nope. That's not him. This guy isn't as wiry and his face is round. Not him."

"Shane shot Niigata in the head. That's a fact," I said.

Sarge slid the photos back into the folder. "Maybe so. But it looks like we're already dealing with one ghost." Then he looked around the room. "We'll have plenty of time to get to know one another and play grab-ass later. It's getting late, and we have a couple of babies to go check on."

"We've loaded your vehicles with some supplies," said Simmons.

As everyone was shaking hands, I paused at Merryweather. "None of your people fuck with the civilians. If they are giving you a hard time, do what you have to, but let me know immediately. You're a curiosity, and people will be wandering around, wanting to know what you guys are up to. We've not really seen any official presence, at least most of them haven't. Just go easy."

"No problem, Sheriff," he said with a smile and gripped my hand firmly. I squeezed it tighter and pulled him into me.

As I stared into his eyes, I said, "And your people are not above the law here. If they do anything wrong—*anything*—they will be held accountable."

"I understand your concern. But our people will be the least of your worries. If they get out of line, we'll deal with them."

"*I'll* deal with them," Sarge said from the door. "And the arm of justice around here is long, swift, and decisive. If there are any shitbags in your ranks, send them back up north." He turned to walk out the door and added, "It'll be one less hole you have to dig here."

Several soldiers were piling boxes and crates into the back of the Hummer. Mike and Ted were kind of supervising the operation with the help of Red and Wallner. With new soldiers around, there was much shit-talking, laughing, and general fuckery going on. I'm sure the guys were happy to see new faces and have someone new to talk to.

Sarge took a look around. "Where's Ian and Jamie?"

"They haven't come back. Left with the O2 and the surgeon," answered Ted.

"Call 'em on the radio and tell them we're RTB."

"Roger that, boss."

"What the fuck is RTB? Ride this bone?" I laughed.

Sarge shot back, "How about right through your brain? That work for you?"

"Means return to base," Mike called out, adding, "fucking civilian!"

"Come on, Aaron," I said as I headed to the truck.

The rear section of the Hummer was stuffed with shit, but the backseat was open, and Aaron took his previous position. I climbed into the passenger seat as the old man got behind the wheel.

"Let's get the fuck out of here," Sarge grumbled as he started the truck.

I stared out the windshield as too many thoughts ran through my head. The truck was moving now. I continued staring as Umatilla blurred by in the blackness.

"This is going to be a fucking nightmare," I said aloud.

"I fear you are correct, Morgan," Sarge said, his voice low. "I didn't want any of this. I wasn't asked."

"Can we just not do it?"

"I was wondering that same thing, to be honest with you. Can't we tell them to take their ball and go home," he looked over at me, "but I was told in pretty certain terms we'd been *voluntold*."

"I mean, they could try and make us. Or we could go home, get what we need, and come back and eliminate them."

"Kill the soldiers?" Aaron asked.

"They'll send more," Sarge said, and nearly whispered, "a lot more."

I looked over my shoulder at Aaron. "It's not like that's what I want to do. I just don't know if I'm ready to start having to answer to anyone just yet. And this Governor shit, I really don't like that. Never have been a fan of politicians. What the fuck have I done to qualify me to govern an entire state? Especially in the current situation!"

"Look at it this way, Morg," Sarge said. "At least we'll have an impact on restoring the country. I mean, someone is going to. It might as well be us."

"Great. Now, what are you thinking?" I asked.

Sarge let out a long breath. "I think I've done my time in the Army, and I really don't want to do any more." He looked over at me. "I retired for a reason."

"Looks like both our plans have changed," I said. "Besides, what the hell else have you got to do?"

"I've got a pretty big pile of abso-fucking-lutely nothing I been meaning to get to. Thought that was a lock after the balloon went up, and there's Kay. I'd love to spend a little more time with her." He gave a sheepish grin.

"You think any of this shit was on my to-do list?" I laughed back at him.

"Guess we're just fucked." He smiled a wide, shitty smile at me.

"I need new friends," I said, shaking my head.

Sarge stifled a laugh. "Who the hell said we were friends?"

"You two are not right," Aaron said from the backseat, causing Sarge and me both to start laughing.

"I wouldn't know normal if it hit me in the face," I said.

We backed the MRAP up in front of Danny's house, and Miss Kay was there, directing the unloading of all the supplies. Some boxes were being piled off to the side. They were clearly marked with the orange diamond of ordinance. We didn't need that in the house. Sarge parked the truck and we walked over to the porch.

"How're the babies?" Sarge asked Kay.

Kay smiled and her face brightened. "They're doing wonderful!"

"How's Fred?" I asked.

"She's very tired. The delivery was hard on her, but Ronnie is still there with her. And Mel and the other doctor that came in."

Sarge looked around for Mike. "Mikey, you got a handle on this?"

Mike nodded.

Sarge turned back to me. "Want to walk down there with me?"

"Sure." I looked at Kay. "Where are the girls?"

"They're at your house, I think. Your mom had them, last I saw."

Just then, we heard the raucous sound of the four girls approaching. As they came into the light of the porch with Mom and Dad bringing up the rear, it was quite the sight to behold.

Little Bit had Ruckus with her, of course. The little squirrel was her constant companion.

Taylor and Tammy were both girly girls and often wore dresses. The two spent time searching the closets of abandoned homes to create new outfits, and fashion shows were now common.

Lee Ann had recently asked Mel to cut her hair. Unlike her sisters, she never was a fan of long hair and now sported a cute pixie style.

Before anyone could say a word, Little Bit started to carry on. "I want to go see my babies!" She ran over and hugged my leg. "I want to go see them, Daddy!"

I roughed her hair. "Not yet, kiddo. Fred needs a little time to rest. You can see them tomorrow, maybe."

She stomped her feet and balled her hands at her sides. "I want to go now!"

It was unlike her to behave like this, so I knelt down to be at eye level with her. "And I said you will wait until tomorrow. Fred needs to rest. If you want to keep acting like a little snot about it, we can go home and discuss it."

Her little fist uncurled, and her head dropped. "I jus' wanna to see my babies."

I pulled her in with one arm. "I know you do, and you will have all the time with the babies in the world starting tomorrow. Fred will need big girls to help her, I promise." Defeated, she retreated to Grandma.

"How'd it go in town?" Dad asked.

"Remains to be seen, I reckon. They say there's going to be more supplies coming in. Maybe more people as well."

"That's a good thing. The supplies, at least. And I don't think any place is really crowded anymore."

"True," I said. "But I don't know if I want to deal with everything that comes with it."

Dad's head cocked to the side. "Like what?"

CHAPTER 1

"Like he's the governor of Florida now, Butch," Sarge chimed in.

Visibly surprised, Dad asked, "What?"

I shook my head. "What he said. They said we've done such a good job here, and that's why."

"The military made the call? They just what? Told you?"

"Pretty much sums it up. He didn't get away either," I said, motioning toward the old man. "He's the military Governor."

Dad stood there for a minute, thinking about what he'd just been told. "Well, I guess it's a good thing that we're moving in the right direction and help is finally showing up. But damn."

"Yeah," I echoed, "damn."

"Come on, Governor," Sarge teased me, "let's go check on Fred and those babies. We can talk about all this at supper."

"I'll pitch in here." Dad turned to help with the unloading.

Sarge and I walked out the gate at Danny's place and onto the road. It was dark, and the air was cool. Neither of us spoke for quite a while and simply walked in silence. My head was spinning, and I felt nauseous. Fortunately, it was one of those crystal clear nights where you could see the Milky Way, and that helped me feel better. That was one thing about the change I didn't mind. The skies were so clear, and you could see more stars than you could imagine.

"It ain't gonna be all bad," Sarge said. His voice was low.

"What?"

"Don't be a dumbass. You know exactly what I'm talking about."

I stuffed my hands into my pockets and shrugged. A useless gesture in the dark. "I don't know. I mean, it's been hard, ya know. But we're getting by pretty good now, and I don't know if I want the system to come back."

"I can relate to that. Especially about the old system." In the darkness, he bumped into me and gave me a slight elbow.

21

"But you know, with us being in the positions we're in, we can help make sure none of the bullshit comes back. There's plenty of good things we could bring back and more than enough shit we don't want to. Well, we get to decide which is which."

I thought about what he said. It did make sense, and it got me thinking. "They know we have the Bradley, right?"

"It's not a Bradley, dipshit! It's a Stryker. And yeah. They sent ammo for it."

"Stryker, Bradley, tank, what's the difference?" I rolled my eyes in the dark.

"All the difference! Damn, I hate civilians."

"Call it whatever you want. I don't give a shit. You just have to make sure we keep it. Don't turn it over to them."

"Already thinking that. We're also going to expand the militia."

I clapped my hands. "Exactly! I'm all for things improving. And we will do everything in our power to make that happen. But, I want to retain the tools to be able to say *no*, and have it mean something. We have enough weapons to stand up to a hell of a force."

Sarge slapped my back. "Glad to hear we're on the same page. Let's just keep this little piece of info to ourselves for now. We can talk about it with our people, but we need to make sure we never talk about this around Wallner's people. Not that I don't trust them. Just with Big Green back in town, they may get a little nostalgic for the old Army ways."

"Agreed. We need to have a meeting with all of our people this evening. After we eat and Wallner's people get gone, we can talk."

"We have to figure out what to do with this flight surgeon, too," said Sarge.

We found Mel and Erin sitting on the front porch when we walked up. Sarge greeted them. "You two look worn out."

CHAPTER 1

Erin blew a strand of hair out of her face. "I never wanted to do labor and delivery."

"How bad was it?" I asked.

"Not like any of mine," Mel said and laughed.

"Thank the Lord," I said. "A C-section would be a nightmare right now."

The front door squeaked open and the flight surgeon walked out. We surprised him. Two new faces, not quite in uniforms, and armed. "Uh," he hesitated and looked at Mel and Erin. The man was huge, almost as big as Thad, and his complexion was darker.

"They're with us," said Mel.

Sarge held his hand out. "Colonel Mitchell."

I almost, *almost* started to fuck with him. But I knew it wouldn't end well, so I didn't. After shaking Sarge's hand, the man looked at me.

"Morgan." He shook my hand. "Tech Sergeant Joiner. Call me Harvey."

"I thought you were a flight surgeon," Sarge said, looking at the man's uniform.

He laughed and looked down at the wings on his chest. "You know, the Army can't tell Air Force insignia from one another."

Sarge stuck his hand out again. "I have mad respect for the PJs. You guys are consummate professionals."

Harvey shook the old man's hand a second time. "Thank you. It's been an interesting ride."

"How's momma and them babies?" Sarge asked.

He took a deep breath. "Doin' well, all things considered. It was a rough delivery." He wiped the sweat from his face.

"We'll get you a ride back into town in a bit. We'll feed you first if you'd like," Sarge offered.

"Something to eat would be nice."

"We've got supper down the road. Let us check on these babies and we'll get you down there and fed up before getting you back to town."

Harvey laughed. "Supper? Where are you from?"

"I'm a Florida Cracker," Sarge replied, "born and raised. But I prefer to be called a Saltine American."

Harvey doubled over in laughter. "Saltine American, that's priceless." He laughed for a minute and straightened up, wiping tears from his face. "I just haven't heard anyone call it *supper* in a long time. I grew up in Mississippi, we called it supper."

"Gotta stay away from them Yankees, Harvey," Sarge said as he stepped into the house.

"Hey!" Mel shouted, "I'm a Yankee!"

"No, no," I corrected her, "you're a *damn* Yankee!"

We went back into the room where Fred and Aric were lying on the bed with the babies. Fred was snoozing and Aric was holding one of them, just looking at the infant while he gently caressed the fine hair on the baby's head.

Sarge leaned against the frame of the open door. "The picture of fatherhood."

Aric looked up and smiled, then looked at Fred. The other baby was lying on her chest. Both momma and the baby were sleeping. "If this is what it looks like, I'm all in."

Sarge walked over and looked down at the baby. "They're so cute when they're new."

"You want to hold her?" Aric asked, raising his arms slightly.

"No, no. She's sleeping." Sarge cocked his head to the side. "She?"

Aric smiled and nodded. "Little girl."

I stepped up beside the bed to get a look at the newest member of the family. "Oh yeah, cute as a button. So, is that a brother or a sister?" I asked, pointing at Fred and the baby.

A smile spread across Aric's face. "A brother. I have a son." He looked down at the baby in his arms. "And a daughter."

"You got the set on your first try. Good job." Sarge returned a broad smile.

I patted Aric's shoulder gently. "Congratulations, Dad."

"Thanks. Looks like things are about to change for me."

"Has Fred tried to nurse yet?" I asked.

"Oh yeah," Aric quickly replied. "She nursed both babies. It was the most amazing thing to see."

Hearing the babies were nursing was a relief. It was something that was always on my mind and the biggest fear I had about babies being born in our new world. I kept it cool on the outside. "That's great. Best thing for them."

"Thad said he's going to get the barn built soon though. Just in case," said Aric.

"We could use the milk for a number of things," said Sarge.

Mel and Erin walked in as we talked. Mel came up and put her head on my shoulder. "Aren't they just the cutest little things?"

Putting my arm around her, I said, "They sure are."

"Makes me want one." Mel said with a sniffle.

I squeezed her. "Not a chance in hell. You'll just have to borrow Fred's from time to time."

"Oh, I know. It just really makes me want a baby." She wiped tears from her eyes. "Not that I really would. Not now."

"Or could," I said.

"You've been fixed?" Erin asked.

"Oh yes. An even more worthy investment in light of current events, if you ask me."

"No one did," Sarge shot back. "Aric, you four get some rest. You need anything?"

"Not right now," said Aric. "Nothing I can think of."

"If you need anything, just let us know, and we'll get someone down here for you."

"I think Mel and Erin have already made a plan for that," Aric replied.

"We have," Mel said. "There will be someone here to help them pretty much around the clock until they get a routine established. We're working out a schedule."

"Good call. I like a woman that can take charge," said Sarge.

Mel looked at me. "I'm staying here tonight with Erin. Can you get the kids home and in bed?"

"Sure. Little Bit really wants to see the babies. I told her maybe tomorrow."

"I'll bring her down here tomorrow," said Mel. "All the girls."

"We're out," Sarge said. "Let momma and daddy get some rest while they can. They're gonna need it."

"Yeah, they are," I added.

"Why does everyone keep saying that?" Aric asked.

I laughed softly. "You'll see."

We left the house with Harvey and chatted as we walked back to Danny's. "You staying here in town or were you just here for the trip down?" Sarge asked.

"I'm staying," Harvey said. "Part of this program is to put medical personnel in each community if we can."

"We've already got a few, but more are always welcome," said Sarge.

"Seems like a nice little place here. I've heard a lot about you guys. All the things you've done here."

"Just trying to keep the wheels down is all," Sarge said.

"Well, I've been around parts of the country and can tell you for sure you guys are doing one hell of a job."

"Is it that bad everywhere?" I asked.

CHAPTER 1

"It is. Worse than you can imagine in some places," said Harvey. "The big cities are indescribable, hellish. We won't even go into them anymore. We tried early on and it was disastrous. We lost valuable men and equipment. We won't try that again until our forces are up to snuff."

"I knew they would be a shit show," said Sarge.

"What I expected, too," I added.

"It's like something from a dystopian movie. Shit you would never imagine. Cannibalism and all."

"No shit?" I asked.

"For sure," Harvey answered. "They are hell holes now. Gangs run the cities, and they look at people as property and livestock. It's terrifying, really."

"What sort of weapons do they have?" Sarge asked.

"Guns. Lots of guns. And they're pretty creative. I've seen medieval siege weapons hurling flaming barrels. They know the ground and are harder than hell to root out. As I said, we stopped even trying for now."

"Put a perimeter around them and keep 'em on the inside," Sarge scoffed.

"About all we're doing. It's helped in places where we can maintain it. Keeps them from raiding the nearby settlements. In the northeast, there are free-fire zones where any moving vehicle is destroyed. Some of the groups are Mad Max-like. They wear weird shit, masks and whatnot, and terrorize everyone around them. Some are straight-up slavers. Then there are the racial gangs where it's only about the color of your skin."

"That was to be expected," said Sarge.

"It was. But the brutality of it shocked us."

"Not me." I got a look from both men. The moon had risen, so I could see them turn their heads. "I told people it would be like that. That it would be worse than anything they could even imagine."

"If so, you were on point," said Harvey.

"You hear folks say they believe people are inherently good and will rise to the occasion. I always said people are just base animals and will do whatever it takes to survive. We're just another predator on this rock. We just have bigger brains and thumbs."

"You're right about people doing whatever it takes to survive. I've seen some crazy shit. But there's worse than just trying to survive out there," Harvey added, shaking his head.

"Sure there is," Sarge interrupted. "With the way the country was going, getting soft on crime and looking at animals like pedophiles as just suffering from mental illness, and even the later attempts to normalize them, it only makes sense that once the zookeepers were gone, the animals would run amuck."

"That's why I said you guys were lucky here. You haven't really seen that yet."

"We've seen enough," I said.

"Yeah, but you folks took a different path. We've heard about much of what you've done. You have the material and manpower to be the most epic warlords in the country. But you're not."

"Too much responsibility," I shot back.

"What is?" Harvey asked.

"Being a warlord. Too much responsibility. It's hard enough dealing with people that actually kind of like us. I couldn't imagine trying to conduct operations to capture areas."

"From what we've seen, they move around a lot. Hit an area and stay there until all resources are consumed, then they move on."

"Sounds like a hard way of making a living," said Sarge.

"How do they keep their numbers up?" I asked. "I mean, they have to take losses. You can't just go on forever."

"Give 'em a choice," said Sarge.

"Exactly," said Harvey. "They come in and take an area, then give the people an opportunity to join them. If they don't, you probably have an idea what happens to them."

"Shit, I'd say yes, and when they gave me a weapon, I'd disappear one night and become their worst fucking nightmare," I said.

"After they kept you in a cage for a week or so, and you got to watch them butcher your friends or family and roast them on a fire, you would do whatever it took to get out of there," said Sarge.

"Like you said, Morgan, people will do anything to survive," Harvey added.

"I guess some people are just weak. Like all those bleating sheep in The Before that wanted Uncle Sugar to do everything for them," I said. "Some people simply do not possess the skills to survive."

Kay was in the kitchen cleaning up when we walked in. Thad and Mary were on the porch with several others. Sarge called out to Kay as we came in.

"Miss Kay, I know it's late, but could you rustle up some supper for Harvey?"

"Way ahead of you, Linus," Kay replied and pointed at the bar top. "Harvey, you have a seat. I have a plate for you in the oven."

Harvey sat down, and Kay retrieved the plate and slid it across the bar to him. "Here you go. Thank you so much for your help today. We really appreciate it."

"I'm just glad I could help. This looks delicious." Looking up, he asked, "You folks eat like this every day?"

"Oh, I'm sorry Harvey. It's been a busy day. We just had to make do today," said Miss Kay.

"If this is make-do, I can't wait to see what a normal day is like!"

Looking around, I asked Kay, "Where are the girls?"

"Your mom took them home with her."

"Ok, good." I looked at Sarge. "Hey, tomorrow we need to run up to Juniper to get with that Vincent guy."

"You got everything together for them?"

"I need to run to Altoona in the morning and get the shoes from Kelly. But everything else is ready. I was thinking with their medical issues that maybe Harvey could go with us. Give Doc a hand."

"You got any plans for tomorrow?" Sarge asked.

"Whatever you tell me to plan for. I guess I work for you now."

"Well then, why don't you just stay here tonight? Don't make sense to drive you back to town just to have to get you in the morning. I'll let Merryweather know you're staying."

"Danny's on the back porch," I said. "I'll get with him and get Harvey a place to crash for the night. Harvey, when you finish your supper, come out back here and I'll introduce you to some of our folks." Harvey saluted me with a fork as I went out the door.

I dropped into a spot on a picnic table beside Thad and clapped him on the shoulder. "What's up, big man?"

"Hey, Morg. How're the babies doing?"

"They're good. Gonna be a little crazy around here for a few days, I would imagine. Mel and Erin are staying down there tonight to help out."

Thad looked at Mary, who sat beside him. "You should do that too, some nights. Gonna need the practice."

Mary smiled and bumped him with a shoulder. "Stop it," she laughed.

"I'm still right," Thad laughed.

"In that case, you should do it as well," I interjected.

CHAPTER 1

The smile left his face as he realized what was coming his way. "That ain't funny."

"I'm still right," I shot back, getting everyone to laugh.

Danny pointed at Thad. "He got you, Thad. Can't argue with him,"

"Hey Danny, can Harvey crash here tonight?" I asked.

"Sure. Spare room is ready. But who is Harvey?"

"He's a PJ that came in with the troops today. We have to go to Juniper tomorrow. He's going with us to help Doc out."

"What's a PJ?" Danny asked.

Just then, Harvey came out the door. I pointed at the man and said, "That is."

Harvey stopped and looked around the porch. "Is what?"

"You're a PJ," I said.

Harvey smiled. "Yes, indeed I am."

"I still don't know what a PJ is," Danny interjected.

"Air Force pararescue," said Harvey. "Basically, a really dangerous medic."

"PJs are a hell of a lot more than that," Sarge barked out from behind the man. Harvey looked over his shoulder and stepped aside for the old man. "A lot of people have no idea who these guys are. But I can tell you from experience when the shit hits the fan, these are the guys you're hoping will show up."

"Everyone, this is Harvey. Harvey, this is everyone." I stood up, preparing to leave.

"Where the hell you going?" Sarge asked.

"Home."

"If you guys don't need us tomorrow, we're going to the sawmill. We need to get some lumber going," Thad said.

"Soon," Danny added.

"You boys get on that," said Sarge. "We can handle this little project tomorrow."

"Alright then, I'll see you guys at breakfast in the morning."

As everyone who hadn't met Harvey was making their introductions, I left the porch and cut through the fence. Aaron's tent was illuminated by dappled moonlight that broke through the canopy of trees, and I could hear light snoring, so I assumed he was sleeping and didn't bother him. The dogs trotted out to meet me as I walked across the yard. Stopping, I knelt down to scratch Meathead and Drake on the ears.

"Must be nice to be a dog," I said as I gave them each attention. "You idiots ain't got shit to worry about."

The house was dark, which meant the kids must've been over at Mom and Dad's. Looking at my watch, it was only about 8:30—they could hang out over there a little longer. I went into the house. Getting a glass of tea, I plopped down on the couch and put my feet up. This new development was really bothersome. I wasn't one to look for responsibility or leadership, and it was eating at me.

Draining my glass, I levered myself off the couch and headed for the door. Meathead and Drake were nowhere in sight. Probably out for their nightly patrol. I could see soft light and hear the sounds of laughter coming from Mom and Dad's place as I walked over. Stopping in the yard, I could see through the front window. The girls were all busy building some sort of fort.

Dining room chairs had been pulled out and sheets were being draped over them. It always made me smile to see them do this. I thought Taylor and Lee Ann would have outgrown such fun. But they clearly hadn't, as they were both engaged in securing sheets in place. Stepping up on the porch, I knocked on the door as I opened it.

"Anyone home?" I asked as I stepped into a chorus of laughter.

"Daddy!" Little Bit shouted as she ran to me, wrapping her arms around me.

CHAPTER 1

>∺∺≺

Imri was on watch, boring during the best of times. Much worse when you know nothing is going to kick off. Imri was Israeli and their military, the IDF, is not known for their patience when dealing with an adversary. Not to mention he was out of smokes. In the group's travels around the country, he was constantly on the lookout for cigarettes, and it had been quite some time since he'd come across any. It made staying awake that much more difficult.

He got up and paced around for a bit, stretching his back, arms, and legs. After getting the blood flowing again, he went back over to the Jeep where there was the last remaining luxury—coffee. As much as Imri missed smoking, he simply couldn't function without coffee. And while this wasn't Turkish, his favorite, it was coffee. Pouring himself a cup, he lit his small Primus multifuel stove to warm it up.

The little stove had been a permanent piece of his kit since he'd acquired it. It was always convenient to be able to use gasoline, which they always seemed to find. Not to mention the occasional can of white gas they came across when searching remote locations. Cabins in the mountains were some of their best resupply stops.

While people had built these places as vacation homes—a place to get away to, and in many cases, a bug-out or retreat location—many never made it to them. Some of the locations were well stocked with food, fuel, medical supplies, and even weapons and ammunition. Many of them had safes, even the ones that were already looted when they arrived. However, those safes had never faced a skilled Israeli breacher. The skill had kept the group in ammo and provided additional NVGs and thermal optics and weapons. Imri rather liked this new world.

Once the coffee was steaming, Imri shut the stove off, took a small plastic container out of his ruck, and shook a little of his precious sugar into the cup. As he stirred the sugar, he eyed the pack. Still stirring, he reached in and took out a can of condensed milk. The label was gone now, but it had the Borden label on it when he found it in a cabin. It might not be champagne, but he'd been saving it for a special moment.

"Fuck it." He pulled his knife from its sheath and pierced the top with a twist of the blade. Adding a small vent hole, he poured some of the sweet milk into his coffee. A smile spread across his lips as he did. After stirring it in, he took a sip.

"Ahh, damn. Now that's a good cup of coffee." Taking another sip, he added, "I hope they can milk that damn cow."

"Is that coffee?" A voice came from behind Imri.

As he glanced over his shoulder, Imri quickly moved the can of milk into his ruck. "Yeah, I was just heating some up."

Chad came up wiping a mug out with the bottom of his T-shirt. "Good. I can't sleep. You can go get some rest if you want. I'm up anyway."

"You'll have to heat the coffee. I'll leave you the stove."

"Thanks, bro." Chad filled his cup. Once it was on the flame, he looked back at Imri.

Imri was staring out across the road at the boat ramp. "I wish we could get a look in there. See what they're up to."

"They ain't doing shit. Probably looks and smells like Woodstock over there. Bunch of dirty hippies swimming and washing their asses in the lake."

Imri drained his coffee. "And drinking the same water."

"I wish we had a drone. That would make this shit so much easier."

"The good ole days, when you could kill a motherfucker you couldn't even see." Imri let out a sigh.

"These guys do have mortars," Chad said with a smirk.

"Yeah, but Morgan doesn't want any of the civilians with them hurt."

"Fuck 'em. If they're running with a crew like that, they're not innocent." Chad turned to face Imri. "Besides, what was the motto of the Mossad? *If you're not part of the solution, you're part of the problem?* Or something like that."

"Something like that."

CHAPTER 2

A blue haze hung over the yard of Sarge's place. The two-ton truck, an LMT, sat idling as we loaded more supplies into the bed. It was early; we hadn't even had breakfast yet. But we had a busy day ahead of us and needed a head start. I looked up into the sky. The sun was not yet over the horizon, but almost. There wasn't a cloud in sight. It was going to be a beautiful, clear day. There was just enough chill in the air to raise the hair on your arms if you weren't active, and it felt amazing.

"Morgan!" Sarge barked.

"What?" I asked over my shoulder as I hefted a fifty-pound bag of rice to Mike in the bed of the truck.

"We'll get the rest of this. Run to town and see if Kelly is there and get those shoes so we can get this damn gypsy convoy on the road."

"The damn sun ain't even up yet. He won't be there."

"Maybe not, but you'll be there the moment he shows up. Take this with you," Sarge said as he handed me a box.

I looked in, and there were several MREs. A one-pound bag of sugar—I didn't even know they made it in that size—some coffee, cans of tuna, toothpaste, and all manner of other stuff.

"I'll add it to what I already have for him," I said as I carried it over to the war wagon.

"Hey, Butch!" Thad called out.

Dad was in the bed of the truck with Mike. "Yeah! You ready to go?"

Thad gestured with his chin in the direction of the road. "Here comes Danny."

I walked over to the truck as Dad climbed down. "You guys headed to the sawmill?"

"Yeah. We're going to pull the grapple over there this morning and get some logs onto that saw. Me, Danny, Travis, and Thad drew up the barn last night. This'll be fun."

"You guys find any screws or nails?" I asked.

"We found the mother lode of screws," Thad said as he clapped me on the back.

"The hardware store?" I asked. What we called the hardware store was a house on the corner. The old fellow who lived there died in his recliner. I still had the 1911 he'd ended it with. But he had a shop that was a real wonder. It was stocked with so much material that we endlessly raided it, and yet we never failed to find in that cavernous building what we needed when we needed it.

"We even found enough tin for the roof, too," Dad added.

"Nice. Y'all have fun with that mill and be careful. Let's not lose any digits or appendages," I said. "Come back home with all yer parts."

"That's the plan," Thad replied seriously. "Doc gave us a med-kit too. Just in case."

Danny honked the horn and Dad and Thad said goodbye and climbed in. I hopped into the war wagon, fired it up, and pulled out behind them. I waved at the guys at the bunker as I passed and followed the Hummer until I got to the market where they made the left to head to the mill.

The market wasn't quite awake yet. But a couple of people were pulling the tarps off their little stalls or setting their wares up for the day. I decided to get out and wander around while I waited for Kelly.

I stopped at the booth of a very old woman, bent over with age. She looked ancient and wrinkled, and her furrowed face reminded me of the apple-head dolls my granny used to make when I was a kid. Her skin was nearly the same dark burnished color, and here she was setting out beautiful baskets made from a variety of materials.

"Mornin' ma'am," I said as I picked up one of her works of art.

She half-turned, cutting her eyes up at me, and smiled. "Mornin' Sheriff." She set a pine needle basket on the table and turned to me. Reaching out, she took my hand in both of hers. "It's so nice to see you."

"Is there something you need? Something I can do for you?" Her statement had worried me.

She patted my hand. "Oh, no, no. You do enough for all of us. I just wanted to tell you."

I gripped her small, frail hands in mine. "I appreciate that. But I don't think I do all that much for everyone."

Still looking up at me, she said, "You do far more than you know. There's no real trouble here. And when there is," she shook my hand firmly, "you deal with it right quick and proper. It makes everyone mind their Ps and Qs, having a lawman around that will do the right thing when it needs doin'."

I was in a constant state of wonder about what the people of the area thought of me. I didn't really have much interaction with them unless there was an issue. Unless they asked or we happened to find trouble, I left them alone. And maybe that's what they liked about me. Maybe they respected the fact I respected them, didn't interfere in their lives, and was always trying to improve them.

"Besides," she added, jabbing a crooked finger at me, "you got the power back on. We know you have them Army folks here doing most of the work. But everyone knows it was you that did that."

"Well, there's about to be a lot more soldiers around here. And it wasn't just me that got the power back on. There were a lot of folks involved. We still need to get it on for more of the families here. But thank you, ma'am."

She waved a hand at me and patted my arm. "Call me Birdie. You're too old to be calling me ma'am."

I smiled. "Yes, ma'am. If you say so, Miss Birdie."

She smiled and cackled in laughter. "You're a good boy, Sheriff. A good boy."

"Things are going to get a little better around here. Those soldiers that came in brought a lot of stuff with them. Things everyone here needs. Is there anything you need, Birdie?"

She wore a simple threadbare dress in a small floral pattern with an apron over it. She moved about her stall barefoot, and I expected her to say she needed some shoes. If that was the case, she could have easily traded Kelly for a pair. Instead, she reached into her apron pocket and took out an old corncob pipe. Clasping it between her few teeth, she said, "I sure could use something to put in this."

I smiled so wide I thought my face would split. "Well, Miss Birdie, you are in luck."

She took the pipe from her mouth and looked at me expectantly.

"I'll be right back."

I walked over to the war wagon and rummaged around in the box for Kelly. During my cursory inspection of its contents, I thought I saw a bag of tobacco. And sure enough, there was a bag of some British loose tobacco in the box. *Looks like Kelly isn't getting this,* I thought. Stuffing the bag into my pocket, I walked back over to her. She was still there, leaning on her table, watching me.

"It may not be pipe tobacco," I said as I pulled it out of my pocket, "but will this work?"

Her eyes went wide and her nearly toothless mouth fell open. "Sheriff, that will do just fine," she said as she gently took it as though it was as fragile as a bubble. Looking up, she asked, "Where in the world did you find this?"

"I told you things were going to be changing around here. We're going to be receiving regular shipments of supplies. Food, clothes, all kinds of things."

"And tobacco?"

I smiled. "I guess so. It must have come in with the other supplies."

Spreading her arms, she stepped toward me, wrapping me in a hug. "Bless you, Sheriff. Bless you."

"It's nothing, Miss Birdie. Really. Hope you enjoy it."

Holding the pipe and the bag, she stared at each, finally saying, "Now if I can only find a match." Then she looked up at me with a sly grin.

I nearly laughed out loud. "Now that would certainly be a bad day! New bag of tobacco and no matches! I ain't got any matches," I said, and her face fell. Opening a pocket on my plate carrier, I reached in. "But I do have this," I said as I produced a Bic lighter.

Her face brightened immediately. Taking the lighter, she gently placed it on the table. With extreme care, she opened the bag of tobacco and stuck the pipe in it, using one finger to pack the bowl while being careful not to drop a single piece. Once packed, she took it out of the bag and delicately set it down on the table before sealing the bag and rolling it up. Then she put the pipe in her mouth and struck a flame.

Her eyes were closed as she puffed the pipe to life. Light gray smoke drifted from both the pipe and her mouth. Satisfied it was lit, she took a long pull, holding it for just a second before exhaling a cloud of smoke. Keeping the pipe between her lips, she began to laugh a cackling, raspy laugh. Using the table to steady herself, she made her way to the opposite end of it and picked up a large basket with a hoop handle.

"Here, Sheriff. I want you to have this."

"Miss Birdie, you don't have to do that. It made my day just seeing you enjoy it."

"Well, you take it anyway. I'm sure that pretty wife of yours can use it in the garden. This—" she held the pipe out, "is the best thing I could ask for." She took another puff from it before continuing. "I'm an old woman and I know there ain't that many sunrises in my future. And I sure do love to smoke this old pipe. You've given me the best gift in the world, Sheriff."

"In that case, you are most welcome."

I hung out chatting with Birdie as she smoked her pipe and laid out her baskets that truly were beautiful. I asked about some, how long they took to make and the like. Some took many, many hours to complete and she would trade those for food mostly. The hours she spent making them really made the trades lopsided affairs with whoever she was trading with. But, like she said, she was just too damn old to go out and get it herself.

Mario and Shelley showed up and began setting up their stall. I walked over and we greeted one another with handshakes.

"How's business?" I asked.

"Not setting the world on fire. But, it's something to do," said Shelley.

"How about you?" Mario asked.

"Busy. Way busier than I want to be."

Mario straightened up and looked around. "What? Is there trouble?"

"No. Well, I don't really know yet. The Army sent a unit down here. They brought a lot of supplies with them and personnel. Some equipment as well. We met with them last night."

"That can't be all that bad then." Mario sounded relieved.

"Can't say I'm real excited about someone else telling us what to do. Not that they have yet. Just the idea of it irks me."

"What are they here for?"

"They're muscle, I guess. We set them up in the high school. Power is on there and the kitchen will be producing one hot meal a day here soon. Anyone will be able to get a meal. They've also brought in doctors, lots of food, and general supplies we haven't seen in ages."

"Like what?"

I pointed to Birdie smoking her pipe. "All kinds of shit. Even tobacco."

Mario looked over. "No shit. That made her day, then. All she talks about is smoking that old pipe."

As we chatted, I saw Kelly roll in on his three-wheeled bike.

"I gotta run," I said. "If you guys need anything, let me know."

The big basket on the back of the trike was full of shoes, almost overflowing. Kelly rolled up beside me and stopped. Looking back over his shoulder, he said, "Here's yer shoes."

"They look good." I picked up a pair. "Crazy you came up with this idea."

"I figured one thing everyone was gonna need was shoes. It took a while to figure it out, but once I did, it was off to the races."

Pointing at the war wagon, I said, "Roll over there and we'll load them in. I've got some stuff for you as well."

After piling the shoes into the buggy, I dropped a full case of MREs into the basket of the bike and handed Kelly the other box.

"This one has a little of everything in it."

He opened the box and looked in. "Holy shit! Coffee? Where the hell did you get coffee? And *sugar*? *Tooth*paste!" He looked up in astonishment at me. "Where did all this come from? You guys been sitting on this stuff all this time?"

"Oh no, it just came in. The Army came to town and are here to stay. They brought it all. And a lot more."

"No shit?" Kelly asked as he pawed through the box. "This is really amazing." Snatching his hand from the box clutching a can of tuna, he shouted, "And tuna!" He looked back up at me. "What are they going to do?"

"There's a few things on their list. Part of it is just to make life better around here."

My radio crackled to life with the old man's voice booming through it, *You done ratchet jawing yet?*

Kelly looked at the radio. "Who's that?"

Grabbing the mic, I replied, "A pain in my ass." Keying the radio, I said, "Headed back now."

"Hurry the hell up. Everyone is waiting on you."

"Go ahead and roll out. I'll catch up."

"We're already moving."

"Be there shortly."

"You taking these up to Juniper?"

"Yeah," I said, "those folks need some help."

Kelly looked at the box he still cradled. "Looks like I'm taking the day off." Looking up and smiling, he said, "I'm gonna go have a cup of coffee. A cup of *coffee*!"

I slapped him on the back. "Get to it, then, ole buddy. Thank you for your help here."

"Shit, I'll help any time you need me, Sheriff," he said, then another smile spread across his face. "Fucking *coffee*!"

I laughed at him as I climbed into the buggy and fired it up. I waved to Mario as I pulled out onto Highway 19. With nothing but open road in front of me and knowing the trucks were already en route, I floored the old war wagon. While it wasn't really all that fast, it was the fastest I'd gone in some time, and it was exhilarating. The air whooshed by the open cab and the speed made it feel even colder than it was. I loved it.

I thought about Kelly's reaction to the coffee and Birdie's to the tobacco. While we'd gone without many things, we'd managed to stay in coffee. I liked coffee, but wasn't a fanatic about it like some. I preferred my tea. Which I'd also been fortunate in maintaining a supply of, although it was very low now. But so many more hadn't had the small luxuries we'd been afforded, and to see their reactions really drove that home.

Thinking about Birdie and her bag of tobacco made me think of something I'd grabbed right before walking out the door. The last can of Copenhagen. I'd put it in the freezer at some point and forgot about it. It was less than half full, but it was Copenhagen and I hadn't had a dip in months. And having a pinch while driving was as good as it gets!

With the wind whipping around me, I slowed down until it was manageable. I wasn't about to lose the last of my Cope to a sudden gust. Running out is one thing, seeing your last few dips disappear in a brown cloud before your very eyes would be shitty compounded. Once I had the pinch in, though, I stomped on the accelerator, continuing with renewed vigor.

Passing the house where Perez was killed, I looked over. From the outside, it appeared the place was now empty. Though nowadays, most places looked like that, so it was hard to tell. I made a mental note to come back and stop in and check on those people if they were still there.

It didn't take long to catch up to the trucks. Cresting a hill, they came into view. I keyed my radio. "Got eyes on you."

"I see you back there."

I fell in behind the LMT. The Hummer was riding point, and I could see someone in the turret, though I didn't know who. The only thing that would have made the ride better was some tunes. Damn, I missed music! With the wind in my beard, AC/DC's "Thunderstruck" would be awesome right about now. That made me think. I was going to have to talk to our new arrivals and see if anyone had an iPod or any kind of player they might be willing to swap. We just happened to be sitting on a mountain of Russian hardware I bet they would love to trade for.

As we made the turn onto Highway 40 headed west, I looked for the motorcycle we crushed near here and it was nowhere to be seen. They must have recovered it. Can't imagine what they would do with the thing. It was pretty well fucked after Mikey ran it over. But then, it isn't like they're making new ones, so even a crushed one could have salvageable parts.

I hadn't seen a soul since leaving Altoona. The long ride down Highway 19 was lonely until I saw a deer on the side of the road. It was up toward the tree line, looking at the big trucks. It was the first deer I'd seen in some time. Maybe they were making a comeback after the initial decimation by hungry people. It was a little glimmer of hope. Seeing the deer buoyed my spirits more than the soldiers coming to town that maybe things would get back to normal. Maybe someday we would look back at this time and share the memories of how we all survived the hardships. Maybe.

The turn into Juniper was as I remembered it, only the gate was closed, and several men came out of the brush to greet us when we pulled up. I sat watching, the diesel engine humming, as whoever was in the turret of the Hummer talked with the men. In a moment, the gate was swung open, and we were waved through.

I kept a little distance from the LMT in front of me. While Vincent seemed like a nice enough guy, I just didn't know him that well and didn't trust him. I hoped today would change that. The park looked as peaceful as ever as I passed by the old booth where you used to have to pay for the privilege of using public land. Not that I really minded except it was run by a contractor, which means it was being operated at a profit, and in my opinion, that's bullshit.

CHAPTER 2

The little building had been turned into a home by someone. It was obvious from the accumulated *stuff* scattered about. Not that it was a mess, just that whoever it was had hauled in all manner of salvaged material. Mounted on a post beside the building was a large cast-iron bell and a woman came out and began ringing it. Passing by the structure, we moved into the parking lot of the park and the trucks rolled to a stop right in front of the walkway down to the springs.

I'd split from the others and drove in the exit to the area so I was able to pull right up to the LMT. People were coming up from the spring. Alerted to our arrival by the bell, they walked out with nervous looks on their faces. They were all armed with a wide assortment of firearms. Everything from AR-15s to single-shot shotguns. While they may have been nervous, there was no apparent threat from any of them.

I saw Vincent come trotting out with a smile on his face. As I was getting out of the buggy, I saw him look over his shoulder with an apparent *I told you so,* for someone. Sarge was out of the Hummer and intercepted him on his way.

"Morning, Vincent," the old man barked.

"Good morning to you!" he nearly shouted back in reply. He looked at the truck and added, "We're really glad to see you guys."

Sarge looked at the truck. "Well, get your folks out here. We've got some stuff for you."

Vincent looked back and waved his people forward. "Come on, let's unload all this!"

While they walked to the back of the truck, I stopped at the Hummer. Ian was up in the turret manning a SAW.

"Whatcha think?" I asked.

"They look kind of pathetic."

"Shit man, they've been living in a damn swamp for a year. I think they look pretty good."

Ian clucked his tongue. "I guess that's true."

"Let me go over and help, I guess," I half moaned as I pushed myself off the Hummer.

"Go get 'em, Governor!" he shouted. I turned as I walked and gave him the finger.

>―▓―<

Little Bit sat on the bed next to Fred, a tiny baby cradled in her lap. She had a smile so wide you'd think her face was going to split open. She cooed at the baby and stuck her small finger in the baby's even smaller hand.

"She grabbed my finger!" she nearly shouted.

"Not too loud, sweetie. You don't want to scare her. You have to remember, everything is new to her. Sounds, sights, smells, everything," Mel gently admonished her.

"I know," Little Bit said, her eyes glued to the infant. "She's so cute. She's so little. I love her so much!"

Just then the baby started to fuss. Little Bit quickly became worried. Looking up at Mel, she asked, "Is she ok? What's wrong with her?"

Fred reached over and gently picked her daughter up. "Nothing is wrong, honey. She's just hungry."

Fred brought the baby to her chest and opened the button-up shirt she was wearing. Cradling the baby in her arms, she brought the tiny infant to her breast, and she immediately started feeding. The crying stopped.

"See?" Fred said. "She's happy now."

Little Bit giggled. "She's sucking on your boobie."

"That's how you feed babies," said Fred.

"I know. That's what mommy did for me."

Mel ran her hand over Little Bit's head. "I sure did. Your sisters, too. Speaking of them, where are they?" she asked as she stepped to the door.

She found them on the front porch. They sat on the edge with their feet dangling over. "Hey, you guys want to come in and see the babies?"

Tammy was the first one to her feet. "Yes!"

Lee Ann and Taylor quickly joined her, and Mel followed the girls into the house. When Tammy stepped into the bedroom, she froze.

Lee Ann and Taylor pushed past Tammy to get to the bed where Little Bit made attempts at baby talk with the infant lying on the mattress beside Fred.

"You ok?" Mel asked Tammy. Then she scanned the scene. Seeing Fred's exposed breast, she wondered if that was what stopped Tammy in her tracks. Mel leaned in and whispered, "It's totally natural. It's just a baby." Tammy's face was unreadable, so Mel waited for her to say something.

Tammy looked at Fred and then Mel before she finally spoke up. "Yeah, um, she's just feeding the baby. Can I go in?"

"Of course you can." Mel placed a gentle hand on Tammy's back.

"Come over here, Tammy." Fred patted the bed beside her.

Tammy sat down on the bed. The infant was nursing, and Tammy placed her finger into the tiny hand. The baby closed her fingers around it and Tammy smiled.

"It's so small," said Tammy.

"We all were at one time," Fred said with a smile.

They chatted about the babies while the little girl nursed. After a little while, Tammy asked, "Have you given them names yet?"

Fred let out a long sigh as she took the baby girl from her breast and closed her shirt. "Not yet. Aric and I can't decide."

Putting the baby over her shoulder, Fred patted the baby's back until she burped, then laid her out on the bed. Little Bit was quickly lying beside the infant as she kicked her tiny legs and moved her hands. Suddenly the baby tensed, and the unmistakable sound of a diaper being loaded filled the room.

Little Bit went wide-eyed and quickly pinched her nose. "That really stinks!" Then she started to laugh and the rest of the girls joined in.

"Looks like it's time to change her," Fred said.

Little Bit quickly jumped off the bed. "I'm not doing that!"

"I'll help," Tammy said.

Fred looked at her and smiled. "Okay. We need a diaper from over there."

"I'll get it," Taylor said as she got up.

>⊫⊫⊫<

Dad deftly reached out with the grapple, picked a log up, and gently swung it over to the mill. They quickly discovered the grapple wasn't the best option for this job, but, as it was the only one, it had to work. The loading process had to be done very carefully. The grapple was designed to load logs on a trailer, not precisely place them on a sawmill. But it could be done.

Thad gave hand signals as Danny steadied one end of the log. Thad signaled and Dad slowly lowered it into the rail. Thad waved and Dad released the log. As soon as it was in place, the dogs on the mill were engaged and Danny set to cutting it up. The process was going smoothly, and Thad stacked the finished lumber as it came off the blade. By the time the log was cut up, Dad had a new one ready. In this process, they moved quickly and efficiently.

Thad was tossing a bark slab off to the side and shouted to Danny, "We might have enough lumber today to get going on the barn!"

Danny was reversing the log to make another cut when he pointed to his ear protection and shrugged. There was no way he could hear Thad. The saw was loud, and ear protection was absolutely necessary. Thad just smiled to himself, muttering, "We'll have enough today."

>⊱〰〰〰⊰<

The park at Juniper had been turned into quite the camp. The concession stand was now someone's home. Several someones, from the look of it. The big pavilion, the newer of the two, had also been turned into housing. The sides had been closed in with palm fronds. The other pavilion, the old wood one, had also been closed in on three sides.

Scattered around the spring were several shelters constructed from all manner of materials. There was a large pile of junk out behind the concession stand. It appeared to be material the group had scavenged. There was vinyl siding, wire, lumber, and rolled plastic sheeting. All kinds of stuff.

I was walking beside Vincent as I took it all in. Pointing to the pile, I asked, "Your hardware store?"

With a frustrated wave, Vincent said, "Back when we had fuel, we would go on scavenging runs. Whatever we found, we'd bring back here. Never really know what you need."

"Ain't that the truth."

"I wanted to show you something," he said and started walking toward the old water wheel. "Let's walk over there."

The water wheel at Juniper Springs was built in the thirties by the CCC. I never knew what it was originally for or what the wheel turned. Long ago any machinery had been removed and all that remained was the buildings and the wheel. The building was large with a high ceiling and in remarkably good condition.

I followed Vincent into the structure, which he told me was his home.

"I've been thinking about this for a while," he said as he walked over to a window facing the spillway from the spring.

He motioned for me to come over. When I got close, he pointed out the window. "See that shaft?"

Looking out, I saw the three-inch shaft that served as the wheel's axle. "I do. What are you thinking?"

"Do you think we could get a generator hooked up to that?" he asked.

I leaned out and looked at the shaft again. Obviously, it had come through the wall in the past, but that hole had been sealed up a long time ago. "I'm sure we could." I leaned back in and asked, "You wanting to get power on out here?"

"It would make life easier. We could have some lights and the well would run so we wouldn't have to haul water from the spring to the bathrooms to flush the toilets."

"The toilets still work?" I asked.

"There's a septic system here, so yeah, they work."

"Not to mention it might give you access to the kitchen in the concession stand."

Pointing, Vincent stared down his finger at me. "Exactly."

"I've got a guy that is pretty crafty like that. I'll get him and some of the engineers out here to look at this. I'm sure we can get you some power on."

We walked back to the concession stand and chatted as we did. Doc and Harvey, the Air Force PJ, were using the picnic tables behind the concession stand for a med check. All the kids in the camp were lined up there. Jamie was handing out shoes to the parents who were helping the smaller ones put them on. They were all excited about the shoes.

Seeing the kids running around and looking at the simple carpet shoes on their feet as though they were Air Jordans in '85 made me smile. Something as simple as a pair of shoes made them so happy. It was also a statement about our situation. The fact you couldn't come up with something we'd taken for granted for so long demonstrated how far we had to go.

"I really appreciate you bringing the doctors out here. The kids really need it," Vincent said as he walked through the breezeway that connected the restroom and concession stand.

"No worries. We're trying to get things organized, but we still have a lot to do."

As we walked, I could hear the old man shouting.

Vincent chuckled. "He's a real people person, huh?"

"Oh yeah," I laughed, "he loves people."

"Some of the guys here were pretty pissed at you guys," said Vincent. "They wanted to get even for crushing the motorcycle, but I managed to talk them out of it."

"I'm glad you did," I said. "That would have ended badly for them."

"That's what I figured."

I turned to look at him. "Didn't stop them from wanting to steal fuel though, did it?"

Vincent shook his head. "No. I tried to talk them out of that nonsense. But they wouldn't listen. Said you guys had more fuel than you needed and should share it."

I stepped in front of him and stopped. "I want to make one thing crystal clear. Share this with your people. In times of strife, everyone quickly becomes a good little socialist. Thinking those that have more than they do should *share* it. That's bullshit. Would your people here like it if we came in and kicked you out of here because we wanted the water?"

"Well, no. But that's different. This is where we live."

"Only because you moved out here. This was a national park. You came in, occupied it, and I'm sure you've had to defend it to one degree or another. The only thing that you can really claim is yours is what you can defend. And trust me, we can defend what's ours. With that said, we're not greedy people and will help if we're asked, for damn sure. Just don't think you're somehow owed anything by us."

"I see where you're coming from. We've all taken things. We always try to make sure no one is living in a place before we salvage from it. We're not trying to steal from anyone."

"Exactly. And in today's world, there's plenty to salvage. Lots of stuff laying around and few people to use it. There's no issue with that. Just remind your folks here—if they need something, just ask for it." I held out my hand. "Deal?"

Vincent shook my hand. "Deal. Now, let's go see what he's hollering about."

All the shouting was over the unloading of the fuel. We'd put the drums on the truck with the tractor. Getting them down was proving more difficult. But the old man had planned on it and brought some large timbers and a couple coils of heavy-duty rope. The timbers were laid up on the bed of the truck and barrels were rolled to the edge. The rope was looped over them with one end tied off. Four men were in the bed of the truck lowering them by letting rope out.

The process wasn't going particularly smoothly, as the first barrel fell off the timbers about halfway down. Fortunately, the drum didn't rupture, but Sarge was pissed about it and was letting everyone know.

"You booger eaters need to control the descent! You have to match one another! What kind of a shit show do you people have here? This is common fucking sense!"

"Alright, alright! We get it!" one of the men in the truck shouted.

"Well, excuse the shit outta me!" Sarge barked back. "I couldn't tell that from your first attempt! I'm from Missouri, fuckin' show me!"

The men were now pissed and set out to show him. The ass-chewing had the desired effect, and the next barrel made it to the ground without issue. Save for the one guy that thought it would be a good idea to get between the timbers to offer some help from the ground until the old man barked at him.

"That damn barrel slips, you're a dead man! Get yer ass outta there!"

Others joined in. "Yeah, that's a bad idea man. You saw the other one fall. No way you could do shit about that."

The man stepped out and realized the mistake he was making. "Yeah, that wasn't real bright."

Everything was unloaded, and Vincent's people started carrying it into their camp. There was a lot of chatter about some of the items we'd brought. It was primarily focused on the food. There was quite a bit of cornmeal. We'd also taken some of the provisions the Army brought in, like rice, beans, flour, sugar, and cooking oil. The hygiene items were also a big hit; toothbrushes and toothpaste were excitedly received.

We'd also brought some clothes and boots for the adults, which were being divided up. But the biggest surprise was yet to come for them. Sarge walked up to Vincent with a large box and dropped it on the ground at his feet.

"Alright," Sarge started, "don't plan on a resupply of this too often. But there will be more of it around."

"What is it?" Vincent asked.

Sarge pulled the top of the box open and took out a black bag. Holding it up, he said, "Coffee!"

"No shit?" Vincent practically shouted. "Kicking Horse? Where is this from?"

"Canada," Sarge replied. "It's pretty good, too. I made some this morning."

Vincent opened the bag, stuck his nose in it, and inhaled deeply. "Oh, my Lord, that smells good!"

"I know, right?" Sarge smiled. "Mikey is getting your ammo. Where do you want it?"

"We'll put it in the concession stand. That's the most secure place we have."

"Do you have a lot of people coming out here?" I asked.

Vincent shook his head. "Not anymore. We did in the beginning. Some of them became part of the group here. Others were just looking for a place, or when they realized people were here, thought they would come in and steal from us."

"I'm guessing the thieves were properly dealt with?" Sarge asked.

"They were," Vincent answered flatly.

"You have fuel now for both your truck and motorcycles. I would suggest you guys come into town once a week or so. At least send someone in. There will be hot meals daily here soon and we're working on a plan for distributing supplies. We're not in a complete vacuum anymore," I said.

"That's good to know."

"One thing, though," I added, looking around. "Send in older guys or women. Don't send in young fighting-age males."

Vincent seemed surprised by this. "Why?"

"The Army has reinstituted the draft," Sarge answered.

"Sorry," Vincent leaned in, "come again?"

"You heard him. Actually conscription, which is worse," I said.

"We're not sure just what they're up to yet. So it's just some friendly advice."

"You guys, you uh, don't trust the Army?" Vincent asked.

"Not yet," I said.

"Not until we see just what they're up to," Sarge added.

"Well shit. Like we didn't have enough to worry about," Vincent sighed.

"We're not saying they're doing anything wrong," Sarge said as he scooted the box of coffee over with his foot. "We just want to keep an eye on them. There's a lot of work to be done and they're going to need bodies and they gotta come from somewhere."

"Yeah, I get it. There are no more free meals, ya know?"

"Oh, how we do," I said.

"Well, we really appreciate what you've done for us. If there is anything we can do to help, just ask," Vincent said.

"Thanks, Vincent," I said. "We're happy to help."

"Maybe life will start getting a little easier now," Sarge added with a smile. The old man looked around and continued. "Looks like we're about done here and there's plenty we still need to do, Vincent."

"No problem. You guys have been a big help," Vincent said. As he spoke, we heard a motorcycle crank up.

"Sounds like they've got some gas now," Sarge observed.

"Yeah, we have a couple of places we want to check out. They've been waiting on the gas. I think they're more excited about that than anything else."

Taking a look around, I said, "Alright then. I'm out." Looking at Sarge, I said, "I'm going to run back into town before heading home."

"What's up?" Sarge asked.

"Nothing important. I want to talk to Audie and check in with our militia guys."

"Good idea," he said. "Make sure they don't get conscripted."

"Exactly."

I was walking back to the buggy when Jess ran up. "Where you going?" she asked.

"Running back to town to take care of a few things."

She looked back over at Doc and Harvey, who appeared to be wrapping up their clinic. "Can I come with you? Ronnie is going back to check the babies and I don't really have anything to do."

I shrugged. "Sure, why not? Let's grab Harvey there, too. I'll drop him off at the school."

"I'll get him. I'd like to see the school too," she said and ran off.

I climbed in, started the machine up, and waited. I watched Jess as she and Harvey walked toward me. They chatted easily, with Jess even laughing and Harvey smiling. *Damn, I hope these guys aren't up to no good*, I thought. I liked some of them already.

As they approached, Harvey pretended to look at his empty palm. "You don't look like the Uber driver in the picture."

I ran my hand through my beard. "Yeah, haven't had time to shave in a couple days."

"A *couple* days!" he shouted and laughed. "You're going to look like Father Time before long."

"I feel as old as him," I said as they climbed in.

"Don't let Morgan fool you, Harvey. He's just a big Teddy bear."

"A tactical Teddy bear," retorted Harvey. "Where the hell did you guys get all this gear?" he asked as I put the buggy in gear and started to drive away. "I mean, you guys have some top-shelf stuff. Also see some of the newer Russian gear floating around."

"I'm a scrounge of the first order," I said as we turned onto Highway 40 and headed east.

Harvey was in the front seat. He had his weapon pointed out the open side of the war wagon and looked over at me. "You know, I've been around this country a fair bit and I gotta say we really haven't seen anything like this. Some places close to it, but nothing like this. You have law enforcement, and a clinic, even if it is rudimentary. A judge? I mean, that's just crazy."

"Just because the world fell apart didn't mean we needed to," I said.

"Morgan here is modest and doesn't like to take credit for anything," Jess added as she leaned forward between the front seats. "If it wasn't for him, I don't know what things would be like here. I know it would be a lot worse for me."

Harvey looked at her. "Why?"

Jess looked at me, putting a hand on my shoulder. "He saved me." Then her head snapped to face Harvey. "Don't get me wrong, he didn't *want* to." She looked back at me. "But he did."

Harvey watched this exchange without saying anything. After a moment of riding in silence, he spoke. "It's impressive. I don't care if you want to take credit or not. What you've done, all of you, is really something." He looked over at me and waited until I glanced over at him to continue. "There's been a lot of talk about you guys in meetings I've been in."

"Why? We're not doing anything special. Besides, how the hell did they find us to begin with?"

Harvey laughed. "Oh, that would be Colonel Mitchell. He is … *famous* isn't the right word, and *notorious* just doesn't do it justice. The best way to describe what I've heard about him is this: he was a pain in the ass in the Army. Officers hated him. Soldiers loved him. And I personally heard General Fawcett say he was hands down the best man to be here. They were actually pretty damned excited to find him."

"How did they find him?" Jess asked.

"Oh, he called in on a radio." Harvey broke out into a belly laugh. "That was a hell of a day when they realized they had such a valuable asset down here. Then we found out there were other DOD assets here. There are files on all of you now."

That statement didn't sit well with me. I looked over, my face obviously painted with my annoyance. "Files for what? Why?"

"Just about each of you. You know, basic shit. Plus skills, things you've all done. That sort of thing."

"They have a file on each of us? Everyone?"

"Just about. Not the people in town. But all the people in your group. Except for one guy, Dalton. That guy has them pulling their hair out. They can't find shit on him. One of our tasks, while we're here, is to interview him."

"What for? He's not a threat to anyone that doesn't deserve it."

"I know you weren't in the military, Morgan, so I'll let you in on a secret about them. They don't like surprises—or unknowns—and he is certainly an unknown."

I looked over at him. "To you people. He's known to us. He's family, like a brother to me. You guys try and fuck around with him and it won't end well." I glanced back at the road then back to him. "For you."

"Dalton is a sweetheart," Jess added. "A big scary sweetheart, but he's never done anything to anyone except help."

Harvey held his hands up. "Hey man, we're not here to mess with your program. They just want to know more about him. It sounds like he has skills that could be very useful in rebuilding the country."

"You let your captain know that he doesn't *interview* any of my people without me present. Period. Not open for discussion."

"I'll pass the word."

I looked over, this time waiting on him to look at me. When he did, I added, "We have a substantial capability. Probably more than you guys realize. I know you're here to help with getting life back on track. But if it turns out to be anything other than that …"

"We're well aware," said Harvey. "But I promise you, there are no dirty tricks here."

Jess leaned in again. "Ignore him, Harvey. Morgan can be a little intense." She looked at me. "Too intense most of the time. Like the weight of the world is totally on his shoulders."

Harvey smiled broadly at her. "We're all on the same side. Promise."

Jess smiled and looked at me. "See, Grumpy? Relax."

I didn't reply, just hoped it was all real. But I wasn't about to trust them until they demonstrated the fact. People seldom tell you what they really think. But to get what they want, they will always tell you what they need to. People: our greatest liability and asset at the same time.

We were approaching Umatilla when I started to slow. "Harvey, would you mind checking on someone for me?"

"Sure, that's what I'm here for."

As I turned off the road, Jess shouted, "We're going to see Gena!" She leaned forward to talk to Harvey. "You're gonna love her, and Batman."

Harvey looked at me. "Batman?"

I just shrugged and laughed.

Dylan was on the porch when we pulled up in front of the house with a smile and wave. When I shut the buggy down, he called out, "Hey Morgan, Jess, good to see you!" We got out and I introduced Harvey. The two men shook hands.

"Where's Gena?" I asked.

Dylan jabbed a thumb over his shoulder. "She's back there in the greenhouse." He turned and started around the house. With a wave over his shoulder, he said, "Come on. We'll find her."

Gena was in her greenhouse, tending to her "medicine." The plants were enormous. But that wasn't all that was in her verdant jungle. There were veggies of several varieties, as well as several beds of various herbs. Harvey took it all in as we moved through the light humidity that gave the place a tropical feel.

"Morgan!" she called out and ran over, standing on her toes to wrap her arms around my neck. "What are you doing here? It's so nice to see you! And Jess! Hey sweetie! How are you?" she asked as she wrapped her arms around Jess.

Still in a hug, Jess replied, "It's so good to see you!" She stepped back and looked at Gena. "How are you feeling?"

"I feel great!" It was obvious she was having a good day. She practically beamed.

"Gena," I interrupted, "this is Harvey. He's an Air Force doc. I just asked him to check on you since we were driving by."

"I don't really need checking on. I feel great!"

"You didn't two days ago," Dylan interjected, getting a dismissive wave from Gena.

While we chatted, Harvey looked around at the enormous marijuana plants that occupied a substantial portion of the greenhouse. I pulled him back to the moment, "Harvey, Gena has MS. Just wanted you to take a look at her."

Harvey looked at Gena as he rubbed a leaf of one of the marijuana plants, asking, "You treating it with this?"

Gena reached out and gently ran her hand over the leaves of a large plant. "These are my babies. They provide my medicine. They're the only thing keeping me going."

"How are your symptoms? Seizures, coordination, fatigue, tremors? You experiencing any of them?"

"I haven't had a seizure in …" Gena paused to look at Dylan.

"It's been a couple of weeks, and it was a mild one," he offered.

"What about the other symptoms?" Harvey asked.

"A little from time to time. I get dizzy if I work too much outside."

"Now Gena," Dylan interjected. "You have tremors from time to time and you get headaches and vertigo."

She gave him a dismissive wave. "Oh, that's only if I overdo it out here."

"Well, I don't have any drugs for MS with me. But would you mind me just taking your vitals and doing a basic exam?"

"She wouldn't mind at all," Dylan replied for her.

"I'm fully capable of answering for myself, thank you very much," she scoffed at Dylan. Looking at Harvey she added, "Sure, you want to go inside?"

"Wherever you're the most comfortable."

Harvey and Gena headed for the porch with Jess in tow, leaving Dylan and me in the greenhouse. I looked around. "It amazes me every time I come in here."

"Shit, it's all we have to do nowadays. It should look like this." He looked off in the direction of the porch. "What's with this guy?"

"The Army has sent a detachment here. They set up shop at the high school."

"Thought you said he was Air Force."

"He is," I said, "but they are simply having to use what they have. Part of the reason I stopped by here is to give you info on this."

"What's up?

"It looks like they're here to help. But they've started conscripting people into the military. On the one hand, I disagree with that. But on the other, we need people to be productive and all working toward fixing this. So, I'm in a wait-and-see position."

"Well, it will give people something to do, ya know?" He looked at me, squinting one eye. "Not to mention, if they are in the Army, they'll get fed, clothes, boots, and a place to sleep. I mean, it's not really a bad thing."

"You're right about that. I considered the same thing. It just depends on how they do it. Who they want to roll up. We're on the same side. I'm just wary. Which brings me to another thing. Can we bring some stuff over here to store?"

"Sure. Like what?"

"Weapons and ammo. Maybe some other gear. They know where we live and that we just happen to have enough ordinance to overthrow a small nation. I don't want them showing up to *requisition* it."

"Morgan, you can store anything you want to here. Anything we can do to help, we will. You know that. There's a spare bedroom in the house that you can stack to the rafters with whatever you want."

I gripped his shoulder. "Thank you, ole buddy. It'll be better to store them in there since the AC is working here."

Dylan smiled. "Man, of all the things that have happened, getting the power back on was amazing. Our central air doesn't work. But I had three window shakers in the shed for hurricane season, and they're doing a fine job of keeping the house comfortable."

"We'll probably move the stuff over here at night, so no one sees it."

"We have a little bit of stuff in that room. I'll get it all cleaned out today, so when you show up it's ready."

I held my fist out and he bumped it. "You are the man."

Dylan laughed. "I'm not the man. But I know him. *Sheriff.*" It made me laugh. We could hear Jess prattling on about something as they came back into the greenhouse, and that ended our conversation.

"For a woman her age," Harvey said and looked at Gena, "no offense," then back at Dylan and me, "she's in really good shape. I'm going to see if we can source some drugs for her." He looked at Gena and asked, "You said you were on Lemtrada before?"

She nodded in reply.

"I think I can get that. It may take a while, but I will make it a priority."

Gena smiled and caressed one of her plants. "That's fine. My babies are doing a good job. I make tinctures and several things from them. I don't like to smoke it."

Her statement got a laugh out of Dylan as he reached into his pocket. Removing his hand, he held it out, saying, "Here's your pipe."

Gena snatched it. "You hush." Then looked at Harvey. "I only smoke it if I'm having an episode."

Harvey laughed. "Miss Gena, I don't care how you take it. Not like it's illegal." With a look of curiosity on his face, he looked at me and asked, "Or is it?"

"Shit no! I don't care about this. Should'a never been outlawed in the first place. I believe in personal liberty, Harvey. As long as what you're doing doesn't infringe on the liberty of another, do you, boo boo."

With an affirmative nod, Harvey said, "If more people thought this way we wouldn't be in the mess we're in."

"Well, Harvey, we're getting a Mulligan. We have the opportunity to correct all the mistakes of the last two hundred plus years. The government needs to be small, limited in scope and power, and local. That's how it's going to be here in Florida."

"You have my vote, Governor," he said.

"Governor?" Gena asked.

"Oh yeah, Gena. Ole Morgan here is now the governor of Florida," Jess quipped.

"Would you knock that shit off," I shot back. "Not my idea, not the right guy for the job."

"No," Dylan added. "You *are* the right man for the job in this moment. The fact that you don't want it proves it. You're not in it for yourself. You've done more for people around here than anyone has."

"Maybe, here in this little town. But I don't have all the answers and being responsible for the entire state is just more than I think I can handle."

Harvey reached out with a huge hand and gripped my shoulder with more than casual force. "You're not going to be doing it alone. We're here for you, too. And whether you realize it or not, we work for you."

"I know you, Morgan," Jess added. "I know you can do it and you'll do it right. It makes me feel better knowing you're the one that will be in charge."

I looked around. "Do we sing Kumbaya now? Or are you guys done blowing smoke up my ass?"

"I think that about does it," Harvey said with a smile. "Besides, I don't sing."

"Then let's load up. I need to get you back and I have other shit to tend to," I said.

We said our goodbyes and were back in the war wagon, pulling out onto the county road. But almost as soon as we were moving again, I pulled off the road.

"What are we doing here?" Jess asked, anxiety thick in her voice.

Harvey looked at the brick house and asked, "What's with this place?"

I stared at the house, looking for signs of life. "We lost a man here. A good man. It was a terrible mistake that took two lives. I want to see if the people that were living here are still here," I said as I got out.

"I'll cover you," Jess said as she hopped out.

Looking over my shoulder, I said, "No shooting unless I do. Got it?" She nodded, and I added, "I don't want another tragedy here."

Harvey got out as well, his M4 at low ready. "I'll go with you."

"No, just stay here and keep an eye out. I don't want to scare them."

He didn't protest, and I walked up the overgrown sidewalk to the front door. I made sure my rifle wasn't in my hand and knocked on it. The force of the knock was enough to cause the unsecured door to yield and it cracked open. I pushed it open, staying outside, and called out, "Hello! Anyone here? Hello?"

An empty house has a presence about it. Almost as if you can feel there's no life. This is harder in homes with power. All the appliances that make life so simple in modern times create a frequency that, even if you don't realize it, your body senses. This place felt … *dead* isn't the right word. It was *hollow*. I could tell it was devoid of life before I ever stepped in.

Harvey came up behind me, his rifle at the ready, and gripped my shoulder, giving it a squeeze. Knowing it was unnecessary, I raised mine as well and stepped through the door. Harvey and I cleared the house in no time. It was quite obvious that it had been abandoned for some time. How long ago was that?

We were standing on the landing at the top of the stairs when Harvey asked, "What happened here?"

I gave him the cliff notes version of what took place. He listened as only a warrior that has also lost brothers to senseless encounters can. When I finished, he shook his head. "Damn, that's brutal."

"Yeah. It's one thing to die for something. It's another to die from a terrible mistake that should've never happened."

I took a minute to go through the house. There wasn't so much as a morsel of food to be found. Clothes were missing from the master bedroom. But in another bedroom, there were a little boy's clothes and toys still littering the floor. A sense of sadness came over me. The thought that this family had made it that long. Managed to keep their son alive for a year, only to be killed in a stupid accident.

Coming out of the bedroom, I said, "I'm done," and I started down the stairs. Harvey followed me out of the house without saying a word.

As we approached the buggy, Jess was standing beside it with her carbine at low ready. She was quite the sight compared to that first day I saw her. Now she wore a plate carrier and carried a rifle. That innocent little college girl was long gone. In its place was a very capable, dependable woman. I couldn't help but crack a slight smile. That's what having a tribe does for you.

"How was it?" she asked, looking nervously at the house.

"They're gone. I can't blame them. I wouldn't have stuck around here either." Then I thought about that. "Actually, I would have. Just long enough to kill everyone involved."

"I wonder where they went."

"Doesn't really matter," I said. "Hang out here for a minute. I want to go look at something."

"I'll come with you," Harvey said.

I waved him off. "I'm good, man. Just hang out here. I'll be right back," I said and walked off.

———※———

Harvey leaned against the buggy and watched me walk away. "What's his story?" he asked Jess.

"Morgan? You guys have a file on him, you said. You probably know more about him than I do."

"We know the stale bullshit. The facts. But we don't know *who* he is, if you know what I mean."

"Morgan is a good man in the purest sense of the word. He's always looking out for everyone else. He will do for others before he does for himself. He's smart. Comes up with all kinds of crazy solutions to problems. Morgan is the glue that holds all this together. It's like he has gravity and people are just drawn to him," Jess laughed and looked at Harvey. "Funny thing is, he hates it. He really does."

"What? Helping people?"

"No, like, the responsibility. So many people looking to him for answers. He really feels that and will always do his best for them."

Harvey jutted his chin in the direction of the house. "What about what he said about how he'd have killed everyone involved in this? He doesn't have military training."

"Maybe not, but he was a quick study. Morgan is the fairest man you'll meet. But he's killed plenty of people. He was shot by a guy in town and Morgan killed him with a knife. He's one of those men that's hard to kill. Not because he's some super badass. There's just something about him."

Harvey sounded surprised. "He's been shot?"

An anguished expression twisted Jess's face. "Yeah. Twice."

"How did the other one happen?"

Jess looked up at the bigger man, her face the picture of painful sadness. "I shot him. In the head."

Harvey was stunned. "Uh, I mean, you said he didn't want to help you. Is that why?"

"No, no. We were with Thad at the time, and things were really good. Some people showed up and Morgan tried to help them, but they were just looking for people to rob. He knew it, and we ran in the middle of the night. But there was a bunch of them. They found us and started shooting. I'd never fired a gun before. Morgan gave me a pistol. I panicked and went to cover my head and pulled the trigger."

"That the scar above his ear?"

Jess nodded as she wiped a tear from her eye.

"And yet, you're still here."

Sniffling, Jess said, "That's Morgan."

>―||||||―<

Walking back up to the buggy, I asked, "You guys ready?"

Jess wiped her eyes. "Yep."

I looked at her. "You okay?"

She nodded and climbed in.

"She was just telling me what happened. Sad, man," Harvey added.

"Yes, it was. Let's get you back to the school."

"Shit, I'd rather stay with you guys," Harvey laughed.

We dropped Harvey off at the school and quickly left. He asked if we wanted to come in and talk to the Captain, but I passed on the offer. I didn't have anything to talk to them about, and I wasn't in the mood for a social call. Instead, we headed over to the plant.

CHAPTER 3

"How much longer are we going to have to be out here?" Chad complained, looking at the camp on the lake.

"You want cards or not, Woodchuck?" Karl asked.

Chad sat back down on one of the milk crates the men were using as seating. They were gathered around a rotted piece of plywood serving as a card table. Chad looked at his cards and tossed them down. "No, fold."

Karl looked up. "I was thinking about that. I know they want to get rid of these guys, but they seem pretty comfortable where they are. Like they have no plans on leaving."

"Maybe we could get them to leave. You know, offer them something to chase," Imri added.

Karl rubbed his stubbled chin. "That is an idea."

"I bet they would be interested in anything that rolled past them," Dalton added. Then he half turned to look at the Jeep. "You know, a shiny red Jeep with a trailer on it would be hard for anyone to resist today."

Karl looked incredulous. "You want to risk my Jeep?"

"I don't think it would be a risk. Just have our people in position to ambush them. We could pick the place and time. I doubt they would even consider the chances of an ambush."

"I don't know," Imri cut in. "These guys know who they're dealing with and the capabilities you guys have."

"Maybe. But they've never seen this thing. Not to mention, we're still a decent distance from town. They may not put it together," Dalton said.

"I think it's worth a shot," Karl said, slapping his cards down on the table. "I'm going to send a message in. Let's see if we can set this up. I'm tired of being out here bored out of my mind."

"I second that," Imri added.

"Third," Chad said.

Dalton rapped his cup on the makeshift table. "Motion carries."

Karl went to the back of the Jeep where the radio was set up. Using the trigram list and OTPs they'd created, he drafted his message, encoded, and encrypted it. Wallner was on the radio when he made the call and copied it all down.

Wait one, came the reply. After ten or so minutes, the radio crackled, *copy all*.

Karl came back to the table and sat down on his crate. "Now we wait and see."

"I think he'll do it," Dalton said as he stretched. "The old man likes to control the narrative. He's not one to let his adversary dictate the terms of a fight."

"As any good mission planner should!" said Karl.

>―⧫―<

Audie and Cecil were busy milling corn. The men worked well together and had a process that the two of them alone could handle with ease. Terry was back there helping out of sheer boredom when we walked in. Cecil looked up and smiled.

"What a pleasant surprise. Hello, Jess!" he called out.

Jess ran up to him and wrapped her arms around the older man. "It's so nice to see you, Cecil!" She stepped back and looked him up and down. "Are you getting enough to eat? You look good."

"Yes ma'am! I'm doing just fine." He pointed back to the pile of corn and added, "Easier to get some dinner these days."

While Cecil and Jess chatted, I walked over to Audie, who was manning the mill using a shovel to keep the discharge clear of ground meal.

"Hey Audie, how's our town miller doing?"

He smiled as he always did. Audie was one of the most affable people I'd ever met. He always smiled when greeting someone and never had a negative word to say. He was one of my favorite people. Maybe because I envied his disposition.

"Doing great! How about you?"

"I have another project for you. If you think you can do it."

"I'm all ears. What's up?"

I leaned against an old conveyor line. "I was just up at Juniper Springs. You ever been there?"

"Long time ago."

"You remember the water wheel there?"

He nodded. "Vaguely."

"Well, it's just that. An old water wheel built in the thirties by the CCC. There's the building that housed whatever they were doing there, but it's empty now. The wheel is still there and it works."

"I don't think it's worth moving this out there. Seems like we'd just be shooting ourselves in the foot, so to speak."

"No, no. I don't want to do that. I was wondering if there would be a way we could attach a generator to the wheel for power."

Audie stabbed the shovel into the meal; I had his attention now. "Depends. I'd have to see the wheel and determine what RPM it's operating at. We'd have to find some gear boxes to step that up, and of course a generator head."

"Let's go find Baker and talk to her," I said, then looked over at Terry who was using the tractor to fill another tote with whole corn. "Hey! Terry!" I called out. When he looked up, I waved him over. He shut the machine off and climbed down.

"What's up?"

"Let's go talk to Baker," I said.

Baker, Scott, and Eric were in the control room of the small power plant with a drawing spread out on the table. They all looked up when we walked in, smiles all around.

"Hey! Morgan," Baker said. "To what do we owe the pleasure of the governor himself stopping by?" This naturally got a laugh out of Scott.

"Stick that governor shit up your ass, Baker." I didn't discriminate between the sexes. It actually got a loud laugh and a clap out of her.

"Ok, ok, what's up?" she asked.

"We may have an engineering project for you guys up at Juniper Springs."

"What the hell do you want to do up there?" Scott asked.

"I want to see if we can turn the water wheel up there into a generator."

"What for?" Baker asked.

"There's quite the village up there now. We were just there, delivering supplies to them. Doc and the PJ that came to town held a little clinic as well. Plus, we could use it as an outpost. Put a radio in and maybe get those people trained up as militia."

Baker started to nod. "A COP, combat outpost. That's actually a good idea."

"I think you guys need to take Audie up there and look at the wheel and see if we can figure this out."

"I'm always up for an adventure," Audie added.

"Road trip sounds fun to me," Scott added.

"You guys know where it is, so go up there when you get a chance and take a look. Just let them know you're with us. They won't cause you any trouble," I said. "I need to run. Let me know what you think after you get a look at it."

CHAPTER 3

I left Audie and the engineers and found Jess and Cecil still chatting. "Come on, Jess. The man's got work to do."

"You're fine," Cecil laughed. "It's always good to see Jess."

Jess smiled, looked at me, and stuck her tongue out. "Maybe because there is such a long interval between your visits," I said with a chuckle.

Jess had a look of shock on her face. "What?"

Now I was laughing. "You know that whole, 'distance makes the heart grow fonder' thing and all?"

Jess turned back to Cecil. "Sorry, Cecil. Every party has to have a pooper and Morgan is the resident pooper."

I shrugged. "I do what I can. But I do have to go look for someone."

"All right, you two get out of here. This corn ain't gonna grind itself," said Cecil.

As we walked back to the war wagon, Jess asked who I was looking for. "I want to find Bubba or Matt, one of the new militia folks. Need to have a chat with them."

"About the Army?"

We'd reached our ride, and as I climbed in, I looked over the top roll bar at her. "About the Army."

Leaving the juice plant, I drove down to the old Kangaroo that was now the center of life in Umatilla, the store served as a market of sorts as well as where the locals hung out for most of the day. The store was a lot different now. Tables were set up under the canopy over the pumps. All the windows and the glass doors were busted out. At first, when I saw it, I thought it was just vandalism. Then I discovered it was intentional.

The glass was broken out to keep the inside of the store cooler. Some folks used the store for their table of wares, and some just to sit out of the sun and play checkers. There was also more than one chessboard set up, not to mention dominos and a couple of card tables. The power had been restored to the store in the early days of getting it back on. This allowed the use of fans, and they were everywhere.

It reminded me of my childhood. I grew up in Florida before air conditioning. I think I was in middle school before I lived in a house with central air. When I looked back on those days, I wondered how in the hell we did it. The summers in Florida can be brutal! Sweating is all but useless because of the humidity in the air; it never evaporates, so you'd be soaked in sweat and still hot. But a fan would at least dry the sweat and cool you a little.

With the restoration of power there wasn't that much demand. In many of the homes the AC didn't work. Capacitors and compressors were fried on The Day. Fans were making a real comeback. As a result, there were fans of all kinds with extension cords crisscrossing the parking lot.

It wasn't hard to find who I was looking for. Bubba Linton and Ronald Mangnum were sitting on the porch of the store when I pulled in. Seeing the buggy roll in, both men got to their feet. I was happy to see both were carrying their rifles.

"I'll only be a minute," I told Jess as I climbed out.

"I'm going to look around," she said as she got out as well.

"Hey Morgan," Bubba greeted me as I stepped up on the porch.

"Bubba, Ron. How you guys doin'?"

"We're good. Just hanging out," Ronald answered.

Looking around, I motioned with my chin for them to follow me. We walked away from the front of the store for a little privacy.

"What's up?" Bubba asked.

"I'm sure you guys have heard the Army is in town."

"We have. Haven't seen any of them yet. Ron and I walked over to the school earlier and there seemed to be a lot of activity there. But they're staying put for now," Bubba said.

"Got guards put up around and not letting anyone on the property, too," Ron added.

"That should all change soon. You'll start seeing them around. We're also going to be opening the cafeteria up for one hot meal a day soon."

"Well shit, that'll be nice," Bubba said with surprise.

"We wondered what they were doing here," Ron said.

"Here's the thing. They are here to help. At least so far, that's the way it looks. However, there is another purpose they have that I want to protect our folks from."

Bubba snorted then spat on the ground. "I knew there was a catch. Always is."

"Because of the condition the country is in and the enormous numbers of people that have died, they've instituted conscription."

"You mean like the draft?" Bubba asked.

"More like getting clubbed over the head and waking up in a uniform," Ron countered.

"I don't think they're gonna club anyone. But they are looking for conscripts here. I've already told them anyone in the militia is exempt. I need you guys to find a sheet or something, a colored piece of cloth, and wear a band of it on your right arm to signify you as militia."

"What color?" Ron asked.

"I don't care. Just so everyone has the same color."

Morgan, where the hell are you? Sarge barked over my radio.

"I'm in town. What's up?"

Need you to get back to the ranch. We've got an opportunity to deal with our unwanted guests.

"I'll head that way in a minute."

Hurry up every chance you get, princess.

"He talking about the Army?" Bubba asked.

"No, these are the folks we were training you to fight. Find a cloth and get the others rounded up. Make sure they have the band as well. I might need you guys shortly. Either way, I'll get up here to let you know. I'm also working on getting some radios for you guys to make all this easier."

"We'll be around here," Ron said as I headed back in the buggy. Jess heard the radio call and met there.

"What's up?" she asked as she climbed in.

"You heard as much as I did. Guess we'll find out together."

We drove back to the old man's place without talking. I was moving fast. If there was a chance we could bring an end to this shit today, I was all about it. The old man's place was crowded with people. The Stryker sat idling along with our MRAP. People were gathered around the open garage door and I walked around and slipped in.

Seeing me, Sarge shouted, "Now that Morgan is here, let's go over this operation. This crew seems pretty comfortable at the lake. Karl came up with an idea to lure them out. He's going to use the Jeep as bait and see if they'll chase it. I'm sure they will. Karl will lead them to us, and we'll destroy them."

He turned to a whiteboard set up on a stand. "Lakeshore Drive," he said as a pointer slapped onto the crude map. "We're going to set up an ambush here, on this curve. On the lake side there is a significant elevation drop that vehicles can't traverse. On the other is a fence with a mound behind it, a perfect funnel."

He moved the pointer down the line that represented the road. "The Stryker will sit here, backed off the road. When we initiate the ambush, the Stryker pulls out and hits the first vehicle in the column." Moving the pointer back down the road, he added, "Ian and Jamie will be in a house here and will hit the last vehicle with Kornet. They'll probably give up at that point, but we will have people all along here. If they do anything other than put their hands up, kill them."

The Kornet is a Russian wire-guided anti-tank rocket. The weapon system has a variety of rockets that can be used with it, from high explosive to anti-tank, with a range of up to ten thousand meters depending on the ordinance in use. The weapon operator has to maintain visual contact with the target and guide the warhead to it. They are simple to operate and reliable.

"What do you want my people to do?" Wallner asked.

"You're going to be held in reserve, just in case. Mike and Ted will be in the Stryker," he paused and looked at Ted. "You'll be able to pull out and make that shot, correct?"

Mike answered, "Oh yeah. I'll have the muzzle on them as they come down the road. I'll probably take the shot before we stop."

"Make sure that damn thing isn't jammed up when you get on target. That would be a problem."

"It'll be ready," Ted said.

"The rest of you will be placed down the line of the ambush. You do not fire unless told to," Sarge paused and looked everyone in the eye. "We clear on that?"

As the old man talked, Mel came up beside me and wrapped her arm around me. I looked down at her to see the Minimi hanging from her shoulder. "Nice gun," I said with a smile.

She looked down at it. "What can I say, I like big guns and I cannot lie." I couldn't help but laugh.

"Everyone clear on this?" Sarge asked. There was a murmuring of replies and the old man shouted, "Alright, let's load up!"

Sarge walked over to me. "Ride with me," he said, with a jerk of his head in the direction of the Hummer.

Doc intercepted Mel. "Hey Mel," he greeted her with a smile. "Morgan, I wanted to tell you about the folks up at Juniper."

"What about them?"

"They are pretty infested with lice. You may want to make mention of that. It's something I should have thought of a long time ago, but it slipped my mind."

"Oh, that's not good," Mel said.

"What can we do about it?" I asked.

Doc shrugged. "I'm not sure, honestly. We don't have access to the normal stuff to treat them. You know of anything?"

"Kerosene," I suggested.

"Anything else short of soaking people's heads in diesel?"

"Turpentine would do it. But we'd have to make it."

"How do you make turpentine?" Mel asked.

"A lot of work," I replied.

"Let's just put the word out and see if there's a major problem or not," Doc said. "I just wanted you to know about it."

"I appreciate the heads-up."

"Ick, lice," Mel muttered.

We climbed in and while we waited for everyone to get loaded up, I asked, "So, when did this come about?"

"Karl radioed in earlier. Looks like they're pretty comfortable on the lake and may not venture out. He thinks if they see the Jeep they'll chase it."

I wasn't convinced. "You really think they'll go for it? Follow them straight to Eustis?"

"I don't see why not."

"Would you? If you were him?" I asked.

"No. But he's not me. Besides, if this doesn't work we'll figure out another way." He looked over at me. "But I think it will work."

"Let's hope," I said as he put the Hummer in gear and pulled out at the head of the column.

We rode in silence until we came to Umatilla, and I told him to stop at the market.

"What for?" he asked.

"You want any of the militia on this?" I asked.

He thought about it for a second before answering. "Sure. More guns the better."

I hopped out and waved Bubba over. He, Matt, and Ron came running over. "What's up?"

"Jump on one of these trucks. We've got some business to take care of."

The men didn't hesitate and ran back toward the two trucks. As they were loading, I looked over and saw a Hummer coming out of the school. "Shit," I muttered as I walked back. "You see 'em?" I asked Sarge.

He looked over his shoulder. "Yeah, I see them. Let's see what they want."

LT Simmons and Sgt. Roberts were in the Hummer and pulled up beside us. They looked at the file of vehicles and asked, "What's up?"

"We've got some business to deal with," Sarge replied.

"What sort of business? Looks pretty serious," Simmons asked.

"Old business. Got nothing to do with you guys."

"You need some help?" Roberts asked.

"No. I think we can handle it."

Simmons stepped out and looked at the Stryker. "We were wondering if you really had it."

"We do," I said. "It belongs to the State Militia."

Simmons laughed. "I thought it belonged to the Army."

"It used to. Now it belongs to the State Militia," I said in a tone devoid of any emotion.

Simmons looked at me and stepped back, holding his hands up. "Hey, didn't mean it that way. That thing is yours; we're not trying to take it or anything."

"That's good cause we're keeping it," said Sarge.

"Shit, I don't blame you. Must be some bad shit if you're taking it out," Roberts said.

Sarge wiped invisible dust from the conference table, saying, "They have a couple MRAPs. This is just to ensure it's an unfair fight."

Simmons snorted. "It will be, then. They don't stand a chance against that thing."

"We gotta run, boys," Sarge said. The two men stepped back, and our column started to move out.

As we passed the juice plant, I asked, "You think they're gonna try and take it?"

"They can't, can they?" asked Mel.

"Well, Miss Mel, it's like this," Sarge said. "Possession is nine-tenths of the law today. I don't think they will. They know we have it, and if it's needed, it will be there."

We drew some curious looks in Eustis as we quickly rolled through town, but it wasn't long before we were turning on Lakeshore. Lakeshore Drive is a winding road that parallels Lake Eustis along its southern shore. In normal times, it was always a pretty drive, with old oaks draped in Spanish moss hanging over the road, and towering pines growing above them. The lake was close in places but never more than a handful of meters from the road at any point.

We were pretty far down the road when Sarge stopped and stepped out. The column halted and he walked back to the Stryker. Ted poked his head out and Sarge pointed and shouted to Ted to indicate where he was to back in. Ted nodded and gave a thumbs up. Sarge paused at the truck with Wallner's people and spoke to him. Wallner and his men jumped out of the truck and walked toward the Stryker.

We pulled down the road a little further before making a left turn. Sarge wound his way into a new subdivision built across the road from the lake and stopped. He got out as everyone piled out of the trucks. Ian and Jamie had the Kornet, and Sarge pointed to a house and told them to set it up where they had an open view of the road.

"The rest of you, come with me!" Sarge barked.

We walked between two houses and came to the mound on the drawing. There was a decorative fence between us and the road, and I asked the old man about it.

"How are we supposed to push through the ambush with this fence?"

"I don't think we're going to need to. I'm pretty sure as soon as we take out the pissants running the show, the rest will lose their stomach for a fight. If not, we'll kill 'em from here."

Sarge walked down the berm, putting people in place, two to a position, and identified their fields of fire and what their limits were to the left and right. This is a point that most people forget about when planning an ambush. You have to know exactly where your people are and have limits on fields of fire so there are no accidents. This is a hard discipline for soldiers to get correct, let alone a bunch of civilians.

"Morgan, you and Mel come with me," Sarge said as we made our way to the center point of the kill zone. "We'll hang out here. That way we can get to wherever we may need to quick." He plucked the mic from his plate carrier. "Mikey, you got that gun up?"

Cocked, locked, and ready to rock!

"Ian, is the Goose in place?"

Roger that. We're in position.

"Fire Star, Fire Star, Swamprat," Sarge called into the radio.
Send it, Swamprat.
"Time to get your rabbit on!"
Roger that!

Karl and the guys were already loaded up. Imri sat on a tarp that covered the pile of gear in the trailer. Dalton was in the passenger seat and wore a Multicam balaclava to hide his face, as he had spoken with Tabor and some of his people while in their camp and might be recognized. Not that they planned on getting close, just close enough to encourage a chase.

Karl pulled out onto Highway 19, also called South Duncan Ave, and headed toward the lake. As soon as they came to the intersection with Highway 441, the camp was in view, and so were they.

"Clear right," Dalton announced. Old habits die hard.

"Here we go!" Karl called out as he made the turn at moderate speed.

"They're moving," Dalton called from the passenger seat.

"What are they doing?" Chad asked, as he tried to get a view by leaning forward.

Karl put his elbow on Chad's forehead. "Sit back, Chadster, I need the room."

People were indeed moving in the camp, and it was only a few seconds before heavy blue diesel exhaust started to swirl over the area as trucks started up. Karl slowed as the two MRAPs and pickups started maneuvering to get out of the camp.

"They're taking the bait," Dalton said as he checked the chamber of the AR between his legs.

"Oh yeah, they're coming," Karl added.

The men had already discussed what to do when the pursuit began. From the trailer, Imri would fire on them, just enough to make it look like they were trying to get away but not enough to cause any damage. The exception was he would take out any shooters that came up. As the convoy pulled out of the camp, Karl slowed and did a U-turn, making a show out of looking at them nervously.

Now headed toward Mount Dora, he started to pick up speed as the trucks were coming on hard.

"Damn, these guys are serious." Karl laughed as he shifted through the gears of the Jeep.

Imri started to shoot at the trucks. His first shots were wild and didn't hit anything. Then he fired a couple of shots into the windshield of the lead MRAP. The driver jerked the wheel slightly before getting the big vehicle back under control. A few more wild shots. Then Imri shot the rearview mirror on the driver's side. He laughed to himself when he did.

At Lake Eustis Drive, Karl swung left onto the road that would become Lakeshore Drive. It was less than a mile to the ambush site.

"They're still coming!" Chad called out.

"Come on, come on," Karl muttered.

"They're slowing down!" Imri shouted.

Looking in the mirror, Karl saw the trucks were indeed slowing and he slowed as well, trying to keep the game up. But it was to no avail. At Ann Rou Road the trucks stopped and slowly made the turn onto the small street that ran up behind the hospital.

"Shit!" Karl barked. "They're gone."

>──≻───≺

Sarge stomped his feet and let out a string of impressive cussing. He finished with, "Sons of bitches!"

I so, so badly wanted to fuck with him. But he knew it, and when he made eye contact with me he gave a look that told me he knew and that it wasn't a good idea. It wasn't long before the Jeep pulled up and stopped. Imri was sprawled in the trailer with a big grin on his face. Dalton climbed out as he pulled the balaclava off his head. Sarge immediately stormed off in their direction.

"What happened?" Mel asked.

"They turned around."

"Why?"

I shrugged. "I don't know. Maybe smarter than we're giving them credit for."

We started to walk toward the road and Mel took my hand and asked, "What's this mean? What's going to happen now?"

"No idea," I said with a smile. "Let's go find out."

"I was afraid they wouldn't follow us in here," Karl said as Sarge approached.

"I really thought they would." Sarge wiped the sweat from his forehead.

"It is pretty confined in here," said Karl. "I mean, it's the perfect place for an ambush." He paused and looked at the old man. "But I guess they could see that too."

"It's almost too perfect," Dalton added.

"That's why I wanted it here," said Sarge. "I didn't think they would be tactically proficient enough not to drive into it. That's on me. Underestimated them."

Mel and I walked up and asked the obvious question, "Well, now what?"

Sarge looked around. "Ain't no sense in staying here. Let's head back. We'll come up with a new plan."

"We have enough people," I said. "Why don't we get the soldiers from town, our people, and the militia together and just roll up on them? We hit them hard and fast, have the Bradley there to help get the point across. I don't think they would be stupid enough to try and fight it out."

"It's a Stryker, dipshit," said Sarge. "We may have to do something head-on. But I want to make sure there's no other way."

"I don't think they would fight," Karl offered.

Dalton took a drink from his canteen and wiped his beard. "After being in their camp, I don't think they would either. Not most of them, anyway. There's a couple in there, maybe ten or fifteen that could. But if we make it obvious they have no other choice, a heavy presence that moves in fast, I think we could take them."

Sarge squinted an eye and looked at Karl. "You think it would work? Little risk to it."

"I think it would work. We roll up with the Stryker, Hummers with weapons mounted, MRAPs, everything we can get our hands on and a lot of people to go with it. I think the show of force alone will persuade them to surrender."

Sarge thought about it. While he was rubbing his chin and staring at his boots, Imri spoke up.

"Or," the word immediately got Sarge's attention, "you could just let me and Dalton go in one night and eliminate the problems. There are not that many of them. Little work with a blade and it's over."

"Fuck that!" I nearly shouted. "You two aren't going in there alone like that. Dalton went in once and got out. We're not risking that again."

"Yeah, Imri," Karl started to speak with a smile, "as much as I know you would like to do that, that ain't happening."

"Shit," Imri complained, "you never let me do anything I want to do."

Karl laughed. "Besides, these aren't Arabs."

Waving his hands with a look of pure innocence on his face, Imri said, "Hey, I don't discriminate! I don't care who they are. Some people just need killing."

"Not that way, Imri," I said. "I want to kill them without them killing any of us."

"All right, let's get everyone loaded up and head back," said Sarge. "We're wasting time here."

CHAPTER 4

Thad tossed another two-by-four into the truck. The smile he wore looked as though it would split his face. "I can't believe we cut this much lumber today!"

Danny added a board. "I know! Once we figured that saw out, there was nothing to it."

"There's something to be said for machinery," Dad added.

"Come on," Thad said, nodding at the end of a huge six-inch by six-inch post, "you two grab that end."

"Thad," Dad said, "I can load these with the grapple. Be a hell of a lot easier on all our backs."

"Well, Butch, I forget we have machinery now." Thad laughed.

"Hang on," Dad said, "let me jump up there, and I'll swing over here and get 'em."

Dad climbed up into the cab and swung the boom over in a smooth, fluid motion. The grapple didn't even sway back and forth as he lowered it onto the pile of six-bys and gently closed it so as not to damage any of the precious lumber. Picking them up, he gently placed them into the truck, opening the grapple and allowing them to slide slowly into the bed.

"I like Butch's way better," Danny said with a smile.

"I do, too." Thad smiled back.

Dad shut the grapple down and climbed around the cab. "Thad! Come over here and grab this battery."

Thad ran around the machine and took the big battery when Dad slid it out onto the little catwalk. With a grunt, Thad took the weight on his shoulder. "Damn, this thing is heavy!"

"Yeah, it is!" Dad called out as he hopped down. "I couldn't carry it!"

Thad put the battery into the bed of the truck with the lumber. He looked at the long boards sticking out past the tailgate. Danny came up with the battery from the generator and put it in the truck as well.

"You think this'll stay here for the ride home?" Thad asked.

"There's a lot sticking out," Danny said.

Dad came over to the truck and looked at the lumber. "We can help it a little with the batteries," Dad said, looking around until he found a piece of scrap wood that nearly spanned the bed and laying it on top of the lumber next to the cab. "Slide that battery up here, Thad. Danny, put that other one on the other end. This isn't much, but having more weight up here will help a little."

Danny hopped into the bed. "I'll sit back here too. Just go slow."

"Oh, we goin' slow." Thad laughed as he climbed into the truck. Dad got in beside him, and they headed out the gate to County Road 439.

Danny was sprawled in the bed with his rifle laid down between his legs. He had a hand on each battery to ensure they didn't slide. It was necessary to pull them out so no one could take the equipment. It wasn't foolproof, but there weren't that many operating vehicles around anymore, and a good twelve-volt battery is something that would not be overlooked by anyone.

Tomorrow they would have the Hummer, hopefully, and could bring the generator back with them. The only thing anyone could do with it right now was steal the fuel out of it, which could be replaced. At the moment.

As Thad turned onto the highway, he said, "I'm going to go straight to the pasture with the cow."

"Might as well unload it where we're going to use it," Dad said.

"That's what I was thinking."

It was a slow, uneventful ride home, and it wasn't long before they pulled up in front of the gate.

"Look at that," Dad said with a nod.

Thad looked over to see Travis drop a set of post-hole diggers into a hole. Thad smiled and looked at Dad. "Look at that," he repeated.

The two climbed out, and Dad said, "Looks like he's got it all laid out."

Travis had laid out string lines with stakes and was busy digging the holes for the posts.

"Yeah, we talked about it last night," Danny said. "The layout. Didn't know he was going to do this. He didn't say anything about it."

The men walked over to where Travis was hard at work. "Hey, Travis!" Thad called out as they approached.

Travis looked up and smiled, dropping the tool into the hole again. "Hey!"

"Damn, you've already dug all the posts?" Danny asked.

Travis nodded and inspected his work. "Yeah. After talking to you last night, I knew what you wanted to do and just came over and got started. Figured it would save some time when you got back with the lumber."

"All we gotta do now is drop them in the ground," said Danny.

"We really should coat them with something. This isn't ground contact pressure-treated wood we're dealing with," Dad said.

Travis held up a finger. "I thought about that and found this." He walked over to the fence where his shirt hung, and a water bottle sat on the ground next to a couple of paint cans.

Picking one up, he walked back over. "I went looking for something to do that with and found this," he said, holding out a bucket of cold tar.

"Oh, that's perfect," Dad said. "A thick coat of that above ground level will help."

"I've got some brushes and a couple rollers, too. And I found some sawhorses earlier. We need to get them over here," Travis added.

"Let's toss this stuff off the truck and go get them," Thad said.

"We need a ladder and some other tools," Danny said, adding, "I have a set of DeWalt tools in the shop. I'll get those if you guys want to get the other stuff."

"We're going to need to bring that generator back to run saws and charge batteries out here," Dad said.

"We'll have the Hummer tomorrow," Thad confirmed.

Dad pulled a leather glove on. "All right then, let's get this off here. We got plenty to do."

>⸻⟨

As we came into Umatilla, I asked Sarge if he was going by the school to talk to the Army. "Nah," he said, "no reason to yet."

"Good. I don't feel like dealing with them."

"Linus," Mel said.

"Yes, ma'am?"

"We need to let everyone who went to Juniper Springs know they should do a lice check if they were close to those people."

"Lice?" Sarge barked back.

"Ronnie said they were pretty infested with them," she said. "It's probably a good idea."

"We don't need that shit running through our people. Let's do it at supper tonight. I don't want them youngin's getting damn lice."

Mel caught his eye in the mirror. "That's what I was going to suggest."

"Glad we're on the same page, Mel," he smiled back at her.

We stopped in town to unload the militia. While they were getting out of the truck, I asked Sarge if we had a radio I could give them.

"Sure. What for?"

"Well, it might be a good idea for them to have one. They can call us, or us them."

The old man nodded. "Oh, you mean just in general. I thought something was up."

I shook my head. "No. Just think they should have one."

"We do, and they should."

I opened my door and said, "Alright, I'll give them mine and grab the other one when we get back."

I walked over to where Bubba and Matt were talking. Seeing my approach, they smiled.

"Hey, Sheriff," Ronald said.

"Knock that shit off, man. It's Morgan."

He just continued to smile. "Whatever you say, Morgan."

"Here," I said, holding out the radio, "you guys take this. I'll bring you a battery charger tomorrow probably. Just keep it on this channel. If you guys need something, call us. And we'll do the same."

Bubba took the radio. "Will do, Boss."

"What was the deal back there?" Ronald asked.

"We were trying to ambush some assholes. They didn't take the bait, so we'll have to do it the hard way now."

"The hard way?" Bubba asked.

"Direct assault." That got a look of concern from him. "Not really direct. We're going to roll up on them heavy, all of our people and even some of the Army here. There aren't that many fighters in the group; most are civilians. If we roll up with a bunch of people, armor, machine guns, and a tank, they probably won't want any of that."

"Shit," Matt snorted, "I'd surrender!"

Pulling my bandanna out, I wiped my face. "That's the hope."

Sky Sommerfeldt ran over to us. "They're going to start giving out meals tomorrow!"

I was surprised. "Really? They said they were going to, but I didn't expect it this fast."

She handed me a piece of paper. It was an announcement informing the folks in town that at four PM every day, a hot meal would be provided. It instructed people to line up orderly and have their IDs with them if they still had them.

"Hmm," I muttered.

"What?" Bubba asked.

I looked around to see who was close by. "Don't take your IDs if you have them. Just inform them you're militia. Make sure you have the armbands on as well."

"Why?" Sky asked.

"Why do they need ID to feed you? They're obviously going to take down names and run them against some sort of database. That's my idea, anyway."

"For what?" Ronald asked.

I shrugged. "I don't know. But remember what I told you, they have instituted conscription. They may be able to look up info on what you did or your history. Since we don't know exactly what they're up to, let's be careful."

"Have they done something?" Sky asked.

I shook my head. "No. Just suspicious, is all. As a matter of fact, I'll come down as well. We'll be here too."

"Why are you coming?" Bubba asked.

I held the paper out and pointed to the last line on the page. "No weapons. That's what is really bothering me." I stared at the paper for a minute before adding, "You guys bring your weapons. You're militia and not under their command."

"Whose command are we under?" Ronald asked.

"Mine," I answered, looking up. "You do not answer to them. If Sarge tells you something, it's as good as coming from me. Other than that, you tell anyone trying to give you orders to talk to me, clear?"

Ronald's eyes narrowed and he nodded slowly. "Sure thing."

"I'll be back in town later for supper."

Aric and Fred sat on the porch, each with a baby wrapped in a blanket on their lap. A gentle breeze caused the leaves in the trees to sway lazily as a grasshopper buzzed across the yard. Both babies were sleeping peacefully. Rocking slowly as he stared at his son, Aric said, "They're just amazing."

Fred gently touched her daughter's nose. "I know. They're beautiful. So tiny." She looked up at Aric, who met her eyes. "We created two people." Looking back down, she began to cry.

Aric reached out and placed his hand on her forearm. "What's wrong, honey?"

Smiling through her tears, she looked up at him. "Nothing. I just thought, you know, after everything happened, that I would never have the chance to be a mother. That I would never fall in love." The tears began to flow harder. "But I did. And here we all are," she said, looking down at her daughter.

"I hated that camp. I hated what I was doing and that I allowed myself to do things I disagreed with. That I knew were wrong. But I was scared and alone and thought it was the right thing to do. But now, now I don't regret it. Because I found you in that camp." He stopped speaking and smiled. Then, patting her arm, he said, "You probably don't know, but I was watching you for a long time in the camp. I did what I could to keep you off the worst of the work details."

Surprised, Fred asked, "Really? I mean, I just thought they didn't think I could handle it. That I wasn't useful."

He laughed. "No, that was not the reason. I wanted to keep you in the camp where it was safe. You heard some of the stories from women that went out on work details, what happened to some of them, and there was never anything done about it. So many of those guards were sick fucks, and I was so happy when they were dealt with."

"I wonder how things went today."

"They wouldn't let me go," Aric muttered. The disgust was clear in his tone.

"Baby, you're a new daddy. They're just looking out for you."

"I don't need them to look out for me. I can take care of myself. I want to do my part around here."

Now Fred gripped his hand. "They aren't looking out for you, Aric." As he looked at her in confusion, she assured him. "They're looking out for us." She pointed from herself to the babies. "We need you. Forever. Your son and daughter need a father, and they're just trying to keep you out of danger."

"I need you and them. But I also have to start doing my part. All of it, and everyone needs to understand that."

"This does bring up another question," Fred said as she stroked the fine hair on her daughter's head. Looking up at Aric, she said, "We need to give them names."

Aric looked at his daughter cradled in Fred's lap. "I've been thinking about that. A lot, actually."

"You have?"

He smiled and looked Fred in the eye. "I want to call her Winnifred. So we can call her Fred too."

She immediately began to cry. "I never thought of that. Is that what you really want?"

"I do. I only know one woman called Fred, and she's amazing." He looked at his daughter. "She will be too."

"Then let's name him Aric, after you."

"I thought of that, but I don't want to."

Fred wiped her face. "Why not?"

"If it's okay with you, I'd like to name him Wyatt. It was my dad's middle name." He paused. "You would've liked my dad. He was a great man, the best man I've ever known."

Fred smiled as tears ran from her eyes again. "Winnifred and Wyatt." She lifted her daughter up to look into the baby's face and said, "Hello, Winnifred."

With tears now running down his face, Aric looked at his daughter and said, "Hey, Fred." Then he picked his son up in the same manner, looked him over, and said, "Hello, Wyatt."

"Hello, Wyatt," Fred echoed. Looking at Aric, she added, "But I might just call her Winnie. I think it's so pretty."

At that moment, Wyatt woke and began to cry. At the sound of the fussing, his sister also woke up and echoed the crying. Fred and Aric both laughed. "Well, I guess that's our fault," Aric said as he propped his son over his shoulder and began to gently pat his back and rock just a little harder.

"That's not what he wants," Fred said as she unbuttoned her shirt, bringing Wyatt's sister up to her breast. Baby Winnie immediately stopped crying and began to nurse. Fred rocked gently and cooed at the nursing infant.

Wyatt's fussing had subsided some when Aric looked at Fred and said, "You're beautiful. That is beautiful. You nursing her, it's just amazing."

Once Danny returned with some tools and the sawhorses, the men got to work on coating the bottoms of the six-by-six posts with tar. They coated four feet of one end of each of them, laying them crosswise on a couple of two-by-fours to dry.

"I think we shouldn't drop them in the ground until tomorrow," Dad said. "Give this time to dry all the way."

Thad wiped his forehead, smearing some tar on it when he did. "I think you're right. Besides, I don't know about you guys, but I'm hungry, too!"

"Hear that?" Danny asked.

"I do," Travis replied.

"I don't hear shit," Dad added. "Helicopter turbines and M-60s are hell on hearing." The joke got a laugh out of the guys.

"Sounds like the Stryker and MRAP," Danny said. "Let's go see what happened."

Collecting their tools, they climbed into the little red truck. Thad drove, and the rest of them sat in the bed, talking and laughing as young men would do on any sunny afternoon.

***

I saw the truck coming as I talked to Mel beside the Hummer. Dad's head stuck over the cab, and he smiled and waved when he saw me. I waved back, and Mel and I walked toward the truck as it rolled to a stop.

Dad slid over the side of the bed. Looking at the armor that was still moving around, he asked, "What happened?"

"Nothing," Mel huffed, adjusting the sling to the Minimi on her shoulder.

"We were going to try and ambush some assholes we've dealt with before. But they were smarter than the old man thought," I said.

Dad looked at the machine gun. "Damn, what I would have given for that little bastard in Vietnam. Would've been a hell of a lot easier to use in the back of the Loach."

Mel patted it. "I like it."

Dad looked around at the people dismounting trucks and at Mike as he hopped off the Stryker. "What sort of assholes are you after that you need all this?"

"They have some armored vehicles. We wanted to make sure we killed them all."

Ian walked by, carrying the Goose toward Sarge's garage. "Damn!" Dad said, "Rocket launchers too?"

"That's a recoilless," I said. "But we have RPGs, some wire-guided anti-tank rockets, and some other shit too."

Dad laughed. "I love it! All that bullshit about taking guns from us, and now look!" With a sudden realization, he looked at me. "Does the Army know you have all this?"

"Some. They know what we want them to know. We looted the shit out of the Russians after destroying their asses. We have a fuck ton of hardware."

"And that?" he asked, pointing at the Stryker.

"Yeah, they know. They also know they aren't getting it back. Even brought us some ammo when they came down."

Mel leaned in and put her hand on my shoulder. "He's the governor of Florida, which also makes him the head of the State Militia. No one can tell us what we can and cannot have."

"That's how it ought to be," Dad said with a sharp nod. Then realization spread across his face. "Governor?"

"Yeah," I said, "not my idea."

"Hey, Butch," Sarge said as he walked up.

"Missed 'em, huh?" Dad asked.

"Yeah. They're smarter than I gave them credit for. So, we'll just do it the hard way."

"The hard way?" Dad asked.

"Direct assault. But it's not like it sounds. We're going to roll in on them hard and heavy. I don't think there will be much resistance. But we'll be ready for it, just in case. We'll have enough firepower with us to level Tavares if we need to. I'll get with the boys in town; they're probably dying for an opportunity to shoot something."

CHAPTER 5

"They're serving the first hot meal this evening," I said and looked at Dad. "You want to go to town and have supper? Bring Mom?"

Sarge asked, "You going down there?"

"Yeah," I said. "I want to go see what's up."

Mel turned and started toward the house. "I'm going to go get the girls ready then."

"I'll be there shortly," I called to her.

"Think I'll go with you," Sarge said.

"I'll go get da momma ready," said Dad, standing up and stretching.

"How'd the sawmill work out today?" Sarge asked.

"Works like a charm. We cut a lot of lumber; amazing what you can do in a day's work with the right machines. Travis already had string lines laid out when we got back, and the holes dug for the posts. We're coating the bottoms of them with cold tar before putting them in the ground. We'll start building tomorrow."

"Well, hot damn!" Sarge shouted, then smiled. "I love being surrounded by can-do people. Folks that just get shit done when it needs doin'."

Dad made a show of looking around. "I would guess that's about all that's left these days."

I laughed. "You'd be surprised!"

"Y'all go get ready and meet me back here," Sarge said, looking around to make sure everything was being done to his standard. "We'll take the MRAP into town."

I walked to the house with the thought of changing clothes and decided against it. I was going like I was, full kit. The girls were laughing and carrying on in the bedrooms when I walked in. A trip to town was a big deal to them. It was kind of interesting to see things change like that.

In previous centuries people were born, raised, and lived in the same communities. Seldom did they venture out, except out of necessity. For the children of such families, a trip to town was a big deal. People would dress in their Sunday best and make a day of it. That's how the girls were acting now.

Mel was in the shower when I came in. I stepped in and pulled the curtain back. She was rinsing her hair when I did and yelped, smacking me with a wet hand.

"What are you doing?!" she shouted at me.

Laughing, I replied, "Just saying hi."

She jerked the curtain closed, and I reached around it to give her ass a wet slap. The curtain flew out wildly as I ducked out of the bathroom.

"Knock it off!"

Like music to my ears, her laughter followed me out the door.

I went to the fridge and filled a stainless-steel bottle with tea. I doubted they would have anything other than water. Lord knows I drink enough of that! My tea was my little escape—that one thing I was determined to cling to from the past, at least for as long as I could.

With the bottle full, I went into the living room and flopped onto the couch. It wasn't long before the girls started coming out. The first was Little Bit. She climbed up and rested against me. Ruckus was with her, naturally, scurrying all over the couch, me, and her. The little limb rat's antics made her giggle.

"Ruckus is getting big," I said.

She snatched the rodent up on one of its laps around the couch. Holding it close to her face she said, "Yes she is! She's a big girl now." For her part, Ruckus fought to free herself from Little Bit's grip, finally succeeding and jumping onto the blinds on the window. I'm sure from the outside it looked like there was a brawl going on. It made us both laugh, and she ran over to the blinds, ordering the limb rat to come down.

I sat smiling at what was going on. Tammy came out of the bedroom in a sundress. Seeing me, she stopped and twirled, the dress flaring out. "What do you think, Morgan?"

"Cute dress, kiddo. You ready to go to town?"

The smile faded from her face. "Yeah, I mean, kinda."

I stood up and walked over to her. Putting a hand on her shoulder, I said, "Don't worry. No one is going to hurt you." Looking up, she smiled in reply before wrapping her arms around me.

Lee Ann and Taylor were the last ones to come out. Taylor was wearing a dress as well. Lee Ann was in jeans and a T-shirt. Taylor walked over to the blinds Ruckus was using as a perch and put out a hand, and the little critter climbed right into it. Flipping onto its back, it play-fought with her hand as she walked over to Little Bit.

Taylor was giggling as she tickled the squirrel's belly. "She is so cute! Look at her!" she shouted as the little rat kicked with its back feet. She handed the little animal to her sister just as Mel came out of the bedroom. She was in jeans and a nice blouse.

"You look amazing," I said.

"You look like crap," she shot back. "Go change your clothes."

"I'm going like this."

"What? Why? We're all dressed nice."

"Just making a point."

"Daddy looks like Daddy always looks," Little Bit added without looking up from her rodent.

"I think he looks kind of cool," Tammy offered with a smile.

"Well, thank you, Tammy. You girls all look good too. Lee Ann, Taylor, you two get your weapons."

"Why?" Taylor asked. "Aren't we going to the Army's place? We should be safe there, shouldn't we?"

"It's not about safety, it's about sending a message, baby girl." Looking at Mel I added, "Get your baby, too."

She cocked her hip out and said, "I have my Glock."

"I know. Bring more guns." I gave her a smile and a wink.

Mel turned to go to the bedroom. Over her shoulder she said, "I'll get it. You girls get in the truck."

"We're walking down to the old man's place. We're taking the MRAP."

"Oh, wow," Tammy nearly shouted. "We get to ride in the big Army truck?"

I laughed. "Yes we do, kiddo. You guys wait outside for Gramma and Poppie."

"Yay! Gramma and Poppie are coming!" Little Bit shouted.

"Come on, let's go, Ashley," Lee Ann said as she steered her little sister toward the door.

I followed the kids outside. The dogs came running up, tongues lolling from their mouths. The girls made sure they received plenty of scratching and rubbing, but each of them insisted on coming up to me and demanding I do likewise. The dogs always made me smile. They lived a carefree life. Nothing changed for them when our society collapsed. Every day is just another day for them. I envied their ignorance.

"Hey Little Dude," Dad called out from the other side of the fence. It cracked me up that he called me that. I was easily six inches taller than him.

CHAPTER 5

"Hey Old Dude!" I had one for him too.

The girls took off at a run toward them as Mel came out the door with her Minimi slung over her shoulder. When I looked over at her, she struck an Instagram "gun bunny" pose.

"Does it match my outfit?" she asked.

"Baby, it *is* the outfit," I said with a smile.

The kids ran ahead of us with the dogs trailing them as we walked to the old man's place.

"You all look so nice," Mom said to Mel.

Mel cut her eyes at me. "Most of us. He wouldn't change."

Dad looked me up and down. "Shit, looks fine to me."

Giving him a look up and down, I said, "Not too bad yourself, old man." He wore BDU pants and a checked button-down shirt tucked in. He also had his pistol on his hip and rifle across his back.

I elbowed the rifle. "You getting used to carrying these again?"

He grunted. "Like riding a bike, little buddy, some things just stay with you. I actually like it. The days after everything went to shit, I learned quick I didn't have enough guns or ammo. I see now why you always had AR-15s."

"They are the best tool for the job."

Mel interrupted me. Patting her machine gun, she said, "I think *this* is the best tool for the job."

Dad laughed. "Well, I can tell you from personal experience, when you need a machine gun, you really need one, and nothing will take its place."

When we walked up, the MRAP was idling in front of Sarge's house. Jamie and Ian were there, along with Mike and Ted, who stood beside the War Wagon. What struck me was the trailer connected to the MRAP.

Seeing us, Sarge called out, "Y'all ready for supper?"

He was met with a chorus of cheers from the girls. All of them ran over to him and he spoke to each in turn, patting heads and tugging on the pigtails Taylor put in Tammy's hair. The old man certainly was an interesting character. He was one of the hardest sons-of-bitches I'd ever met, yet capable of tenderness with the young and vulnerable. Being in the presence of such men—and women for that matter, as our women were all far more capable than the average—it gave a sense of confidence and peace knowing they were looking out for me as I was for them.

"Butch, Karen, good to see you two. Ready to go see what the Army has cooked up today?" Sarge asked.

"Hey, free hot food is a wonderful thing," said Mom.

The corner of Sarge's lip pulled up. "Yeah, but it won't be nothing like what you and Miss Kay do around here. You two settled in?"

Dad swallowed his coffee before answering. "Pretty much."

"I'm still doing a little cleaning. It's nice, just doesn't feel like home yet. But it does a little more every day," Mom said.

"What's with the trailer?" I asked.

Sarge looked at the truck. "I figure we'll find people walking to town. Might as well offer them a ride."

"That's a really good idea," I said.

"Very nice of you to think of others," Mel added.

"Someone around here needs to," Sarge barked back, looking at me.

"We'll meet you guys there!" Ted called out as Mikey started the War Wagon.

Sarge waved at them, and I asked, "Where are they going?"

"Going to get Crystal and Janet."

"Ooh, date night," Mel cooed.

"This ain't no date!" Sarge barked.

Mel stepped over and I wrapped my arm around her. She looked up at me and said, "It is for some of us."

CHAPTER 5

"This is a date?" I asked. When she smiled, I asked, "Am I gonna get lucky?"

Mel glanced at the girls, who were oblivious to the comment, before issuing her rebuke. "Keep talking, and you won't."

"Shuttin' up," I quickly replied.

"Shut up, shuttin' up!" Sarge shot back. He looked at me, waiting for the reply he was certain was coming. When it didn't, he added, "You're pathetic," and shook his head.

Mel squeezed my arm. "No, he's smart."

"All right," Sarge shouted, "you youngin's load up!"

As we passed through Altoona, I looked at the market to see it deserted. It was still rather early, so I assumed people were headed to town for a hot meal. The suspicion was confirmed when we started passing people walking. The first was a group of four that turned out to be a family. They were shocked and grateful for the ride, and Dad quickly helped everyone into the trailer. And that was how the trip to town went. Picking people up in ones and twos and sometimes more. The trailer was loaded by the time we got to the school.

"Damn," Ian said from the passenger seat. "Look at that line of people."

"I didn't know there were even that many people around here," Jamie said as she slowed the big truck approaching the throng of people.

I leaned forward and looked out at them. "Shit," I said.

"Where have they all been?" Mel asked.

Little Bit hopped down from the bench she sat on and walked to the front as Ruckus clung to her back. She stood on her toes as she tried to look but was too short to see and fussed about it. Ian spun around and grabbed her up and dropped her into his lap.

"Ian! What are you doing?" she squealed.

"Now you can see," he answered as he roughed her hair. Jamie looked over at him and smiled. He caught her eye and winked at her. Ruckus decided Ian's hat was a better perch and immediately climbed up the side of his head to sit on her haunches atop it. The entire truck was laughing as he looked around, and the little limb rat just sat there.

Little Bit inhaled sharply and looked back. "There's kids!" She turned to look again. "Lots of them!"

This piqued the interest of Lee Ann and Taylor, who both strained to see. Tammy didn't. She actually sank back in her seat a little. I was sitting across from her and noticed a change in her demeanor. Catching Mel's eye, I nodded my chin at Tammy. Mel looked over at her and leaned in to whisper in her ear.

"What's wrong, sweetie?"

Tammy shrugged her shoulders but didn't reply. Mel put an arm around her and asked again. Tammy wiped her nose and quietly said, "I'm afraid I'll see bad people there."

Mel lifted the girl's chin. "Honey, look around here. You see all these people? They're not going to let anyone hurt you. Ever. If you see someone that hurt you, you tell me. You'll never see them again. I promise."

A tear ran down Tammy's cheek, and she wrapped her arms around Mel. Her face pressed into Mel's shoulder, she added, "I don't want the kids to make fun of me, either. Some of them know what happened. Some of them are really mean."

"Let me tell you a secret, Tammy," Mel said, and the girl looked up at her. "You have three sisters now. Two older ones and a younger one. Look at them."

Tammy looked at Lee Ann and Taylor. Both had their MP-5s laying across their laps. After giving the girl time to see it, Mel added, "They're not going to let anyone tease you. I don't think anyone will bother you if you're with them. They won't let it happen, either."

CHAPTER 5

Tammy threw her face into Mel's chest, tears soaking Mel's shirt. Then, while it was muffled, Mel distinctly heard Tammy say, "I love you, Mom."

Mel gently stroked the girl's hair. "We love you too, sweetie. Never forget that."

Tammy sat up, wiping her face. When she looked at me, I handed her my handkerchief and gave her a wink. She wiped her face before handing it back to me with a big smile. "Thank you," she started before cutting herself off and leaning into Mel again and whispering to her. Mel smiled and nodded, then looked at me and gave me a wink.

Tammy looked at me again. "Thanks, Dad."

It made me smile. "You're more than welcome, kiddo. We got you. Forever and always. You're family now."

There were easily a couple of hundred people lined up down the sidewalk in front of the school. Jamie applied the air brakes with a *whoosh* and I opened the back door and hopped out so I could help everyone down from the truck. Our passengers in the trailer were already climbing out as well. The father of the first family we picked up walked up as I was helping Mom down.

He held his hand out. "Just want to say thank you for the ride, Sheriff."

Shaking his hand, I said, "Not a problem, friend. We'll give you guys a ride back if you need it."

He looked at his family, a young boy who was obviously emaciated. His little belly was swollen along with his knobby joints. A girl, a couple of years older, held the child's hand. "We'll wait on you. They just can't make the walk. But we really need the food."

I looked down the street at the line. "Tell you what, you guys come with me. I'll get you guys in to eat, but first, I want the doc to take a look at your family. We have medicines and doctors now." I nodded at the little boy. "I'm worried about that little guy."

"I've done the best I could, Sheriff. But I was an insurance agent. Wasn't really an outdoors kind of guy. I wasn't prepared for this, and they're paying the price."

I gripped his shoulder. "You don't have to do it alone. Grab them up and follow me."

I told Mel to go with Sarge, and I would find them in a bit. "Where are you going?"

I jutted my chin in the direction of the family. "Taking them to see the doc. That little boy doesn't look too good."

There was a perimeter fence around the front of the school. The soldiers had been busy constructing sandbag bunkers and gun emplacements. A sign in front of the controlled entry point to the school campus read: ABSOLUTELY NO WEAPONS. Two men covered the position, and I was genuinely curious about how this would go.

So I was surprised when we approached and they stepped aside. One of them nodded as we stepped through. "Evening, Governor."

The other soldier looked at me questioningly. "Governor?"

"It's a long story," I said and looked at the soldier. "Where is Doc Harvey set up?"

Jabbing a thumb over his shoulder, he said, "He's in the nurse's office. Go in and take—"

I cut him off. "I know where it is, thanks."

I took the family into the office and found Harvey talking to some of the officers. Then, seeing me, he smiled. "Hey, Morgan."

"Hey Harvey, can you take a look at these folks for me? I'm worried about the little guy," I said, indicating the boy.

Harvey's smile faded when he looked at them. "Of course," speaking to the family, he said, "If you will come with me, I'll give you each a quick exam."

Harvey led them down the hall to the nurse's office and showed them in. Leaning in the door, he said something to them before walking back over to me. "I'm seeing a lot of kids that are starving, suffering from nutritional deficiencies and parasites. The distended belly is a dead giveaway."

"All we need to do is feed them up, isn't it?"

"We have to put them on a feeding schedule, and they have to be monitored. Allowing them just to eat what they wanted would kill them. Their stomachs are shrunk, and it takes time to get them back to normal."

"Well, do what you can for them. If you need anything from me, just let me know."

"I'll take care of them, Morgan."

I left them in Harvey's capable hands and went outside to see how the feeding operation was going. I bumped into Sgt. Mottishaw in the hall and asked him about Colonel Merryweather.

"He's gone. Back to Eglin."

"He didn't stick around long," I said, a little annoyed.

"He'll be back. Did they tell you about the trucks?"

"Trucks?"

Mottishaw's face brightened. "Oh yeah, we're getting some Hiluxes."

I laughed out loud. "Are you serious? They wouldn't let them be imported before. Guess the rules have changed?"

He laughed in reply. "I guess so. There's a car carrier coming into NAS JAX full of them. They're going to bring some of them here. He's out getting that organized."

"I've always wanted one. Very cool."

"Be better on fuel than what you have now, that's for sure."

I nodded. "And, I can put more asses in seats and be able to show our presence more." Then, looking around, I asked, "Where's Simmons?"

"Kitchen. He's overseeing the food distribution."

"How's that going?" I asked.

Mottishaw took his hat off and scratched his head. "Man, these people are hungry."

"I know, I'm glad you guys showed up. I'm gonna go back there and see if I can help."

Slapping me on the back, he said, "I'll go with you."

The kitchen was buzzing with people. The food being prepared was essentially squad meals: the same sort of entrees contained in MREs, except in large foil pans. The pans rested on stands, with a Sterno burner under them like you'd expect to see at any buffet. The people waited in an orderly line, picking up paper plates and plastic forks and spoons before moving down the line to load their plates with whatever they chose. There were no limits, and no pushing or shoving. There were, however, looks of amazement on some of their faces.

I walked down the line, acknowledging each person, shaking the occasional hand, and exchanging words with those I knew a little better. In every case, I was thanked by whoever I was speaking to. In every instance, I made sure to let them know it wasn't me but the Army that brought the chow and that they will continue to provide it daily.

After filling their plates, some would take a seat at the tables in the cafeteria. Others took their food and left. Some went outside to eat. As I walked through the tables, a man looked at me. His plate was completely covered in something that looked like Salisbury Steak, mashed potatoes and green beans. He held a piece of cornbread in one hand and a fork in the other.

"Sheriff, they're going to do this every day?"

I stopped and looked at him. He was probably in his sixties. Not a tooth in his head, and his eyes were sunken. *Weary* is the only word I could come up with to describe him.

Nodding, I replied, "Sure are. Things are changing. Only getting better from here on."

Tears ran down the man's cheeks. Then, setting his cornbread aside, he reached out and grabbed my hand, "God bless you, Sheriff. God bless you."

"Thanks, but it wasn't me, old friend."

Picking his cornbread back up, he took a bite and gestured at me with the remainder, "That's where you're wrong, Sheriff. If it weren't for you, they wouldn't be here." Then, laying his fork down, he picked up a styrofoam cup and held it up. "There's even coffee! I ain't had coffee in over a year!" His eyes shined as he said it, smiling the sunken smile of a toothless man that was honestly happy.

As he took a sip, I smiled. "Enjoy it. There's more coming."

I left him to eat and wandered around the room. There were so many kids it was surprising. Nearly all of them had the telltale belly. Those that didn't were the exception and not the rule. Their parents, who had struggled and worried for so long about how they would feed them, sat watching their kids while they ate. Relief would be an appropriate description.

I saw Harvey come in with the family. He escorted them to the line and spoke to one of the soldiers manning the serving line. He spoke into the man's ear, who nodded and went back into the kitchen. I walked over to them as the soldier returned and handed some prepackaged meals to Harvey. Harvey led them to a table and gave them each a meal, checking to make sure the little boy got the correct one.

"Remember what I told you, you have to eat slow. Your stomachs are shrunken, and if you eat too fast, you'll just get sick and throw up. Trust me, we have plenty. So eat this, and I'll come check on you in a bit."

The mother reached out and seized Harvey's arm. "Thank you, thank you so much," she said as tears ran down her face.

Harvey patted her hand. "You're welcome. Help is here now, eat. I'll be back in a bit." Then Harvey had a thought. "One more thing, hang on."

He walked over to a table against the wall, took a styrofoam cup, filled it from a cooler, and carried it back over. He set the cup down in front of the kids. "Be sure and drink your milk too."

The boy snatched the cup up and began to gulp it down, spilling more than he actually got into his mouth. His mother admonished him to slow down, and he got it under control enough to finish it. Setting the cup down, he wiped his mouth with the back of his hand, letting out an audible, "Ahhh!"

It made both Harvey and me laugh. Then, finally, the little boy looked up with a snaggle-toothed smile. "You want some more?" Harvey asked. The boy nodded his head vigorously.

"He loves milk. Drank nearly a gallon a day before," his mother said.

Harvey leaned down to talk to the boy. "You can have more, little buddy. But you have to eat this first, okay?" The boy nodded and dug into his meal.

I patted Harvey on the back and wandered outside, where people were still lining up. Finally, I found my people in line like the rest and joined them.

"What are they serving?" Mike asked, his arm wrapped around Crystal's waist.

"Looks like Salisbury steak, mashed taters, and green beans."

"Oh, hell yeah!" Mike shouted.

"Doesn't matter what it is!" Sarge barked at him. "You'll eat anyway."

Mike patted his stomach. "Mikey likes it." Naturally, Crystal laughed at this. Sarge simply rolled his eyes.

"I can't wait till you grow up and move out," Sarge said.

"But, I don't want to grow up. I'm a Toys 'R' Us kid."

"You've spent a lot of time short of oxygen, haven't you?" Sarge asked.

Mike shrugged. "Yeah, I mean, you can't really control autoerotic asphyxiation."

Shaking his head, Sarge said, "Holy mother of everything holy. You're just broken, fuckin' broken."

This got everyone laughing. Then Tammy asked, "What's autoerotic—"

Mel cut her off, putting her hand over the girl's mouth. "Nothing you need to worry about, sweetie."

Mike was smiling, but red as a fire hydrant. Mel cut him a look he understood immediately. Even Crystal slapped his arm.

"Hey," Mike said in his defense, "I forgot about the kids."

"Smooth move there, Ex-Lax," Ted said.

Sarge pointed at Ted. "I blame you!"

"Me?!"

"Yeah." Sarge pointed at Mike. "You're his handler. He's your responsibility."

"No, no, no, no." Ted held his hands up. "You can't blame me for that. He needs to be in a cage if he's my responsibility."

Mike scoffed, "You can't put me in a cage."

Sarge's back stiffened, and he propped his hands on his hips. "You wanna make a wager on that?"

"Calm down; I'm only playing," Mike said. Then added, "I wouldn't want you to break a hip or something."

The corners of Sarge's mouth curled up. Then, through clenched teeth, he said, "Keep it up, Mikey, and you'll be FUBAR."

Mike leaned toward the old man and said, "DILLIGAF."

Ted burst out laughing at the same time I did.

Sarge rocked back on his heels. "That's alright; you're just showing your ass 'cause there's company around. That's alright, I know where you lay your head at night. Ya little shit."

Mike looked at Crystal and asked, "Can I crash at your place tonight?"

"I was going to stay with you tonight," she answered.

Mike looked at Sarge. "Looks like I'll have company. So no fun and games tonight." Then Mike looked at Crystal. "Not for you, though," he said and gave her a wink.

"Oh, for fuck's sake," Sarge blurted out. "Come on Butch, let's get some coffee before I choke on my own vomit."

"Sounds good to me. Coffee is way better than vomit."

"This is quite the operation," Mom said, looking around.

"It is," said Crystal. "I haven't seen this many people in one place since The Day."

"I don't think anyone has," said Mel.

Some of the other kids noticed Ruckus scurrying around on Little Bit, and she was soon swarmed by them, asking her questions and all wanting to hold the limb rat. Finally, one of the soldiers working the serving line saw it and elbowed the woman beside him, jutting his chin in the direction of the swarm of kids. They smiled and shared some words.

It wasn't long before we got our plates loaded up in the serving line. The food was hot and looked good. I had my bottle of tea under my arm so I was ready. When we came to the two that had seen the squirrel, the woman couldn't help but ask questions.

"Is that a squirrel?"

Little Bit held Ruckus up. "Yep! Her name is Ruckus, and she's my bestest friend."

The woman leaned over to look at Ruckus. "She even has a little harness. It's so cute." Just then, Ruckus jumped onto her. She let out a little gasp but was immediately petting the rodent and smiling. "She is so cute!"

But Ruckus wasn't interested in making friends and ran down the woman's arm and jumped into the pan of mashed potatoes. The woman yelped, and the guy beside her laughed. "Oh no!" Mel shouted and scooped Ruckus up, now covered in mashed potatoes. "Ashley, keep control of her. Now we have to throw those away."

"I'm sorry, Mommy. You know she loves everyone."

"Looks to me like she loves mashed potatoes," Lee Ann added.

I held my plate out. "You ain't got to throw it away. Just dump it on here. I'll eat it. I've had far worse in my mouth."

Sarge was standing beside me, and his head turned slowly to face me. "I bet you have."

"Fornicate thyself, Blanket."

An evil giggle came out of the old man. "Oh, you're wanting an ass whoopin' too, huh? That's alright. You two smart asses, keep it up."

"If you can't play the game, stay on the bench, Old Man."

Sarge didn't reply. Instead, he kneed me in the thigh—hard. "Shit," he said after landing the blow, "got a twitch in my leg," and he grinned.

Rubbing my thigh, I smiled back at him. "Keep it up. The head trauma will give you a permanent twitch."

Mel pushed me down the line. "Enough peacocking. There's people behind you waiting to eat."

"Yeah, act like an adult," I said to Sarge as I moved with the line of impatient diners.

I could hear Sarge talking to Dad. "Butch, you drop him on his head a lot or something?"

"Oh, he got knocked in the head a lot. But, remember, he grew up not wearing a helmet."

Sarge snorted. "And eating paint chips."

"Only the lead ones," said Dad, getting a hearty laugh out of the old man.

We finally herded Little Bit away from the other kids and got her to sit down to eat. Our group took up a couple of tables, and the people around us were all keen to chat. They had lots of questions and asked them in rapid-fire succession. There wasn't much of a break in it until an old woman stood up at the table beside us and admonished the room for pestering us.

"Y'all need to leave the sheriff be and let him eat supper with his family," she announced.

"Sheriff?" a man's voice said. "I thought he was the governor."

The old woman looked at me. "Well, which is it?"

Looking at Mel, I rolled my eyes. She squeezed my hand and smiled. I stood up and looked around the room. All eyes were on me. "Well, it's both, I guess. For now, that is. I don't believe I should hold both positions, and we will be naming a new sheriff."

It wasn't a planned statement. I hadn't even considered such an action. It wasn't until I stood in front of those people that I suddenly realized the ethical issues with me holding two titles.

"What the hell do we need a sheriff for anyway?" a voice called from the back of the cafeteria.

"Or a governor?" another voice shouted.

"Because this isn't the end," I quickly replied. "Yes, our world is different. But the law still matters." I looked around the room, trying to make eye contact with as many people as possible. "There are consequences to your actions in this new world. And that's what the sheriff is for. As for a governor, someone needs to take point to repair our lives."

"Who the hell voted you in? I don't remember an election taking place," a man at a table near the back wall said. He'd been the first one to speak up.

"I wasn't voted in; the Army appointed me."

"So, the fucking Army runs the country now?"

"As a matter of fact, they do," I explained. "I have been appointed the interim civilian Governor. Let me introduce you all to your military Governor," I turned and looked at the old man. He took a sip of coffee and, hearing me, closed his eyes and slightly shook his head. "This is Colonel Mitchell."

Sarge stood up and gave a little wave. "Folks, I'm here simply to be the liaison between Governor Carter and the Department of Defense. Therefore, you shouldn't have any dealings with me directly. However, feel free to talk to me if you need something." With that Sarge sat back down before anyone could say a word to him.

"Great, now we got *two* unelected assholes," one of the men at the table said.

Mel's head popped up. "Watch your language. There are children here."

"Fuck you, bitch. No one's talking to you."

What happened next happened fast. Mel jumped to her feet, as did all of my people, and even the soldiers on the serving line dropped their spoons and stepped forward. She walked toward the man and leaned over his table on her palms.

"I'll show you a bitch," she said.

The man leaned back and smiled at her. "I bet you could."

I walked up behind her and whispered in her ear, "Easy, babe, you're giving him just what he wants. Calm down."

Through gritted teeth, still staring at the man, she said, "I'll show him a bitch."

"Come on, sit down. We got this."

She locked her eyes on mine. "I don't need you to have this."

"Look around. Everyone is looking. We have to be diplomatic about this."

She sat down, still glaring at the man, who slumped in his chair, an arm hanging over the back. Ian and Jamie were standing very near the men as I turned to talk to them.

"Gentlemen, you can have any opinion you want of me or how things are being done here. But you will have civility when you do so. We haven't hurt anyone; we're not meddling in your lives. We're simply trying to make all our lives better."

"Yeah," the man sniggered at me, "we sure as hell ain't seen much help. We've seen you people driving around in cars. None of you look hungry. Your clothes are clean, don't look to me like you're suffering much."

I didn't reply to the man directly. Instead, I turned to the room at large and asked, "Folks, do you all agree with him? Hmm? Remember that you're sitting in a cafeteria right now, having a hot meal provided by the Department of Defense. I'll also remind you of the food we've handed out previously and those people we dealt with on behalf of some of you sitting in this very room. Does anyone remember that?"

"The Sheriff is right," a woman said.

"I remember you executing a murderer," another man said.

"You've done more than anyone around here," an old black woman said, then she stood up and looked at the men at the table. She pointed an accusatory finger at them and continued. "People like you is never happy, is all. So what? You thought the government would come riding in here and save your worthless ass? Sheriff Carter here didn't want to be Sheriff, and I bet he don't want to be no Governor either."

She turned to look at me, and I shook my head with a "Nope."

Looking back to the table of belligerents, she continued, "See. He don't need to be messing with none of this. You right about his people looking healthy. They is because he took responsibility and prepared for his people." She turned to me again. "You prolly don't remember me. I used to see you at Publix all the time. I was a cashier there."

"Oh, I remember you, Miss Betty."

She brightened immediately. "You do? You is so sweet." Then, turning back to the men, she added, "You should be grateful. Try being part of the solution and not part of the problem."

The room erupted into claps and cheers, catching Miss Betty off guard. She blushed and looked at the room as a huge smile spread across her face. Then she waved meekly to the room before taking her seat. The men rose to their feet once it was clear they were the minority and headed for the door. But they weren't done just yet.

"Come on boys, food tastes like shit anyway," one of them said.

I started toward them. "I'll see you boys out."

Claps burst out once again with shouts of, *get out!* The men walked out of the cafeteria, and I stepped outside with them. Mike and Ted were already there, and I heard someone catch the door behind me and looked back to see Dad and Sarge following me. Seeing the group, the men looked around.

"You need all this muscle? This how it works now?"

"No, sir, I don't. We're just making sure there isn't any trouble." I stepped toward the man that called Mel a bitch and held out my hand. "Look, no hard feelings. I get it. Times are hard."

The man hesitated, but I stood there smiling, looking harmless as hell. When he finally took my hand, I gripped his with all my strength and quickly pulled him into me. I wasn't paying attention to anyone else, but I heard a lot of boots scraping the concrete. Then, face to face with him, I spoke into his ear.

"You ever call my wife a bitch again, I'll kick you to fucking sleep. Understand? You are free to have your opinions. But with that freedom comes the consequences of being an asshole." I let his hand go, and he jerked it back. "Are we clear?"

"Big talk from a man with a gun in a place where I can't have one."

I quickly slipped out of my rifle, handed it to Dad, removed my Glock, and handed it to Sarge. "No guns now. If we need to settle this right now, we can."

He looked at the guys. They were all ready to disappear the bastard and he knew it. "I ain't stupid. You ain't suckering me into a one-sided ass whoopin'."

"I'm not looking for one. But if you have a beef with me, be a man about it. Stack the fuck up, and let's settle it."

His friends were quickly losing heart for his bullshit. "Come on, man, it ain't worth it."

"Yeah," another added, "now isn't the time."

"That's where you're wrong. Now is the time," I retorted.

"Naw, you're right, boys. Now isn't the time," he said and licked his teeth. "I'll be seeing you, Sheriff."

"Oh shit," Sarge muttered.

"What?" the man asked.

"Well, the last man that told Morgan here that he *would be seeing him again* is in the dirt."

"If you're simple enough to think you're going to intimidate or threaten me, you really need to reconsider that."

"Ain't no one threatening anyone here," one of the more sensible of the group said. "We don't want no trouble, Sheriff."

The man I'd been talking to smiled at me. "Tell that pretty wife of yours hi for me."

"Your mouth is writing checks your ass can't cash, son," Sarge stated flatly. "If you think this is some sort of dick-measuring contest, think again. This is life and death, serious shit, son."

Mike took a step toward the man. "Morgan?"

"No, Mike, let 'em go. There's been nothing but words exchanged here." I looked the man in the eye and added, "Words do have consequences, though. Remember that. In the old world, the powers that be didn't want us settling our own issues. Those days are gone. This new world is all about fuck around and find out."

The men walked off into the night, murmuring to one another as they went. Mike stepped up beside me and said, "I can take care of this right now if you want me to."

"Nah, I don't think they're really a problem. Just a couple assholes is all."

"Come on, let's get back and finish supper. I want to get the hell out of here," Sarge said.

Unconsciously, Dad thumbed the 1911 on his side. Something he hadn't done for decades. "Damn good idea, Linus."

You can take the man out of the war. But you cannot take the warrior out of the man.

CHAPTER 6

Imri stared at the contraption in stunned silence before erupting. "Dude! This is brilliant!"

They were in the backyard of a house Dalton had decided to take over. He used it chiefly as a base of operations and a place to work on projects. Dalton was one of those guys that simply cannot sit still long. It was his nature to be busy with something. In The Before, he'd had a farm he maintained between contracts. Sitting on the couch watching TV wasn't his style. The still was an addition to the forge he'd built.

Imri did not fail to miss the small foundry, which naturally led to a conversation on knife building. Something both men were fond of.

"It works," Dalton mentioned as he picked up a jar and shook it, holding it up to check the bubbles out. "Coming out pretty good. Anything can be turned into a still. The only obstacle is your imagination."

"You have some done already? Come on, gimmie." Dalton handed the jar to Imri, and he took a long sip. Holding the raw liquor in his mouth for a second, his eyes went wide before he swallowed it. Then, letting out a loud breath, he said, "Shit! That's got to be one-ten-proof!"

"Yeah, it's a little hot yet. Aging it would really help."

Imri looked at the jar. "Like that's gonna happen," he said and took another sip.

Dalton said in a brisk British accent, "Strictly medicinal of course, Govna!"

Imri nodded and gestured with his hand at his stomach. "Of course, of course. I think I have worms or something."

Dalton laughed and held his hand out. "Me too."

Imri passed the jar to his friend, and Dalton took a tug.

Letting out a little whistle, Dalton said, "Damn sure puts the lightning in the white lightning."

Imri snorted and snapped back, "You made it!"

"Where's Karl and Chad?" Dalton asked, changing the subject.

"I think they were looking for food."

"Sounds like a fine idea," said Dalton. "Let's go see what Miss Kay has cooked up."

"Morgan and them all went to town, didn't they?"

Screwing the top back on the jar, Dalton said, "Yeah. Guess DOD is doing the first supper tonight."

"First supper!" Imri laughed.

As they walked around the side of the house and out to the road, Dalton said, "Beats the hell out of a last supper!"

Imri grunted back, "Yeah, but I'm not that kind of Jew."

"What kind is that?" Dalton asked.

"A good one." Imri laughed and Dalton laughed at Imri.

"You've been around here for a while, haven't you?" Imri asked.

"Yeah, several months."

"So, what's with this group? They seem to have their shit together pretty good. Definitely live better than anyone we've seen so far. With a couple of exceptions."

"They're just good people. I wandered for a long time, avoiding people at all costs and living off the land. So whenever I found people, I would watch them for a while and see how they behaved. This was the first group I approached."

"You were alone before you got here? You didn't have any contact with others in all that time?"

"Oh, I had plenty of contact. Just not the friendly variety."

"Us too. It's crazy how many people would just shoot first, immediately."

Dalton snorted. "It would seem everyone forgot what a parlay is."

"How did you contact these folks?"

Dalton laughed. "You'll think I'm crazy. The bunker they have back there wasn't here at the time. They had log barricades up at the end of the road and they kept it manned 24/7. One night I walked out into that field across the road and sauntered across the pasture with my rifle slung."

"At night? You're out of your mind!"

"Well, I knew they had some form of night vision. It turned out to be a cheap commercial piece, but it did its job. Morgan saw me, and we met on the side of the road. His people were a little nervous when I told them I'd been watching them for several days. But Morgan kept calm, and we chatted for a while. He invited me in, and I stayed once I saw what they had going on."

Imri looked around. "How did they get so tied up with the military?"

"The old man. From what I've gathered, Mike, Ted, and Doc were inserted to do some spook shit somewhere but didn't care for the smell of it. So instead, they went to his place. Morgan was there recovering from a gunshot wound. That's how they all met. Sarge was retired and when it was discovered he was out and about, he was reactivated and promoted to Colonel. He coordinates all the DOD work."

"So how did Morgan end up a sheriff and governor? Which is just batshit crazy to me."

"From what I have gathered, he was simply the right man in the right place. He was capable, did a lot to assist as many as he could. Hell, they got the power plant back up and running. There was also a National Guard unit in town he hooked up with early on. But the Russians came in and pretty well destroyed them."

Imri rubbed his beard. "We haven't seen any Russians; we did come across some Chinese. They were pretty well fucked when we found them. Stranded, no logistics support. I think sheer attrition will thin them out."

"We've had some Cubans as well. But they weren't much of a threat. They conducted a mortar strike on the park in town when Morgan was there giving out supplies. Danny's wife was killed there and Morgan's oldest daughter was wounded pretty bad."

"Shit," Imri muttered.

Dalton drew his kukri. "They didn't get away, though. I found them before they could displace."

Imri sniffed the air. "Damn, something smells good."

As the two men turned into Danny's gate, Dalton said, "That Miss Kay is a fine cook."

Rubbing his hands together, Imri said, "There is a fascinating group of people here."

When we finally returned home, Danny's house was a welcome sight. There were people on the front porch gently rocking in the chairs. Soft light filtered out the windows, casting long shadows on the yard. We all decided to go inside because everyone wanted to know how things went.

I got out and helped Mom down from the truck. The girls came bounding out and asked if they could go home.

"Yes," Mel said, "we'll be home in a little bit."

Thad and Mary sat on the porch with Aric and Fred, each holding a baby.

The rest of us started up the stairs when Thad asked, "How'd it go?"

CHAPTER 6

"Come on inside for the full story, Thad," Sarge said.

Mel stepped over to Fred. "Oh, let me see the baby!"

Fred lifted the blanket from the baby's head. "I just fed him. He's sleeping."

"Have they been fussy?"

Fred stroked the baby's forehead. "Not really."

"Fred's being modest," Aric said. "They're little angels."

I stood in the yard talking to Dad for a minute about what went down in town. He believed that I should have just shot the guy, but understood the situation and that I had made the right call.

"If he's going to be trouble, I'll deal with it then," I told him.

"I'm sure you will. But you can't always see trouble coming."

"This is true, did have one asshole put a bullet in me already."

Dad looked surprised. "What?"

With a dismissive wave, I said, "It was a while ago. Some fat asshole came into town and decided he was the new honcho. He had a small crew and tried throwing his weight around. We disarmed them, but he had a damn pearl-handled pimp gun, got close to me, and managed to get a round past my armor."

"What happened?" asked Dad.

I pulled my knife from my plate carrier. "I put this into him a couple of times. He leaked like a son of a bitch."

"That would do it," Dad said.

Sarge came out on the porch with a cup of coffee in his hand. "Y'all coming in here? I only want to do this once! Come in and get some coffee, Butch."

"Quit your bitchin'; we're coming," I said.

Even though I'd had supper in town, it was nothing like Miss Kay's cooking, and the house smelled wonderful. As usual, the back porch was full of people, and I followed Mel, Fred, and Aric to a table and took a seat. Mom was already in the kitchen helping Kay. The place had a natural rhythm where everyone took on tasks that needed tending without being asked and was always ready to pitch in and help.

"Alright, let's get this over with," Sarge said, putting a foot up on a bench. He went on to describe the events in town, focusing on the actual meal provided by the Army and the estimated number of people we saw. There was a brief mention of the altercation with the locals, and Mel shot daggers at me.

"We had to hold Mel back," Sarge said, smiling at her.

"No, you didn't. I could've taken care of that myself."

"I have no doubt," said Sarge. Then he added, "And I mean that." Looking at me, he asked, "What's this 'appointing a new sheriff' shit?"

"Seems unethical for me to hold both positions." All eyes were on me when I answered.

Sarge smiled at me and stood up straight. "I understand what you're saying, Morg. But here's the deal. You are and will remain the sheriff. You can moonlight as the governor, which is the DOD's official position. You're the man for the job. Period."

"What if I don't want to?" I asked.

Sarge scowled at me. "You think I want to be a fucking Colonel? I hate officers! I wasn't asked and you're not being asked either."

"What do you guys think?" I asked those gathered as I looked around.

Karl stood up. "I know we're new here, Morgan. But we've been around the country a little bit. You truly do not understand just what you have here. And if you are what is holding it all together, then you keep doing just that."

"That's just it, it isn't about me!" I stood up and looked around. "It's all of you, all of us working together. No one of us is more than the rest. If I disappeared tomorrow nothing would change. You guys would all carry on as usual. Life continues, no matter what. We've had losses aplenty and yet here we all are."

"That's true, Morgan," Jess piped up. "But you are the nucleus that brought everyone sitting here together. Could we go on without you? Yes, we could—"

"Speak for yourself," Mel interrupted.

Jess met her eyes. "You would too, Mel. It'd be hard, but you would." Jess turned her attention back to me. "And that's the point. Yes, we could, but it would be hard." She stood looking at me, shaking her head. "I simply do not get you, Morgan. You do so much, and yet you always underestimate yourself."

Thad rose to his feet. "Let's make this real simple." Everyone turned to look at the big man. "Everyone who thinks Morgan should remain Sheriff, raise your hand." The response was unanimous. "Everyone who thinks Morgan should be the governor, raise your hand." The reply was the same.

"There you go, Morgan, you've been elected," Sarge barked at me.

"I don't think that's what they meant," I said.

"I don't give a shit! This isn't, and never has been, a democracy. And it's about time we all started acting like it. But, I told you before, we have the opportunity to effect change. To make this country, or at least this state, a true republic that works the way it should. Where individual liberty is the law of the land. Or would you rather someone else do that job?"

"Yeah, Morg, what else you got to do?" Thad added with a laugh in an attempt to lighten the mood.

With a sigh, I said, "I know." The old man was right, after all. Smiling at Thad, I added, "Not a damn thing."

"Good!" Sarge barked. "That little shithead LT wants a meeting tomorrow."

"Why did they leave a Lieutenant in charge of the mission here?" Karl asked. "Should be a Major at least."

"Shit," Mike shouted, "we got a Colonel!"

Looking at Ted, Sarge quietly said, "Ted, muzzle your mutt, will ya?"

"Could just be a staffing issue," said Sarge. Then turning to look at Fred, he asked, "Fred, have you come up with names for those beautiful babies yet?"

"Oh, I was wondering that too," said Kay. "We can't just keep calling them *the babies.*"

Fred looked at Aric, and he nodded. She looked back to the infant in her arms and spoke. "Yes, we have." She held her son up and said, "His name is Wyatt. Named after Aric's dad."

There was a round of muttered approvals. Everyone was keeping the babies in mind and trying not to wake them.

"Well, Aric?" Kay asked.

Aric stood up and said, "I'd like to introduce you all to Winnifred." He looked around the porch at everyone gathered and added, "We're going to call her Little Fred, like her mother."

Fred smiled at Aric and said, "Or Winnie."

Kay immediately teared up, dabbing at her eyes with a dish towel. "That is the sweetest thing," she said.

Everyone whispered their congratulations to Fred and Aric, who were all smiles. While that was going on, I found Travis and Erin at a table with their kids and sat down.

"Hey guys," I said.

Erin smiled and Travis asked, "What's up?"

"How long do you think it will take to get that barn built?" I asked.

"It's pretty basic. Shouldn't take more than two or three days at the most, if I have help. Danny, Thad, and your Dad are milling the lumber. If I had help while they were doing that we could be done sooner."

"How many you need?"

"I'd think three or four would be enough."

"All right, I'll have you some help in the morning. I want to get to milking that cow. Anything you need, let me know, and I'll make it happen."

"Travis is pretty good at scrounging," Erin added.

I tapped the table and smiled. "I think most of us are these days."

Travis laughed. "Ain't that the truth."

Ted stood up and cleared his throat. "Hey y'all, can I have your attention?"

The porch quieted down and all eyes were on him. With the attention he requested now on him, he started to blush. Janet, who was sitting beside him, rose to her feet as she discreetly elbowed him in the side. Ted looked at her and stammered, "Uh, yeah. Um—"

"Cat got yer tongue?" Sarge barked, getting several laughs.

Janet patted him on the shoulder. "What Ted is trying to say is, we're moving in together." There was some light clapping and lots of thumbs up.

"Where?" I asked.

Ted looked at me, confused for a moment. "Here, Janet is moving here."

Mike leaped to his feet. "Not trying to steal your thunder," he said, looking at Ted, "but so are Crystal and me." Now there was more applause, and this time little Wyatt woke up and began to fuss. Fred quickly put the little boy to her breast, and he immediately quieted.

"You better hope Little Fred don't wake up," Ian said to Aric. "I'd like to see you try that!"

Jamie elbowed him so hard that he fell off the end of the bench he was sitting on, much to the delight of everyone.

"Oh, this is so nice!" said Kay. Then with a coy look, asked, "Is there a dual wedding in our future?"

"Let's not get ahead of ourselves, Miss Kay," Crystal said. "This one isn't housebroke yet."

Mike snorted. "Maybe not. But I do use the litter box."

With his cup nearly to his lips, Sarge said, "Crystal, you're either an angel or certifiably insane."

Mel got up and walked over to the two women. As she passed by Sarge, she turned sideways to squeeze between the old man and Thad. In doing so, her holstered Glock knocked the old man's cup out of his hand, spilling the coffee all over the table.

"Oh, Linus, I'm so sorry. I didn't mean—"

He held up a hand. "You're fine, Mel. At least the cup survived." As he spoke, he used a hand to scrape the coffee off the table and back into his cup. "See," he said as he raised it to take a sip, "all's good."

Before the cup touched his lips, Miss Kay was on her feet. "Oh no, you don't, Linus Mitchell!" she admonished him as she snatched the cup from his hand and headed for the kitchen.

Mike started to howl in laughter, that is, until all eyes on the porch suddenly focused on him. He cupped his hand over his mouth just as Crystal delivered a smack to the back of his head.

Sarge propped an elbow on the table, resting his chin on his hand, and said, "I don't think he heard you, Crystal, say it again." Naturally, this got everyone giggling.

"This is fun and all," I said, "but I'm tired, and I'm gonna head home."

"Sounds good to me," Mel said as she stood.

Sarge looked over. "Be at my place in the morning," he said, then added, "Early."

I glanced over at Thad. "Can you come with us? I can drop you off at the mill afterward."

As always, he replied with a smile. "Sure."

Dad got up and looked at Mom. "You ready, Momma?"

"I am. Been a long day," she said and looked around the porch. "Goodnight, everyone."

"I'm with Miss Karen," Thad said as he stood up. Looking at Mary, he asked, "You ready, beautiful lady?" Mary smiled and held her hand out, Thad helped her up, and we all went out the screen door into the yard.

"That was kind of crazy, what happened earlier tonight," Mom said.

Mel glanced over at me. "I'll show you crazy if I see that asshole again. You should have let me hit him."

Putting my arm over her shoulder, I said, "Baby, he probably wasn't just gonna sit there and let you slap him."

She pushed my arm off and snapped, "I wasn't going to slap him. I was going to punch him in the nose! I can take care of myself."

"From the way you went after him, I have no doubt about that," Dad said.

"He was just a rude ass," Mom added.

"Baby, I know you're pissed at me. But we have to think strategically. We can't be seen as throwing our weight around. Being heavy-handed just because we can. Now, because of the way it was handled, if he starts any shit in the near future, no one will question what happens to him. See where I'm going with this?"

"Yeah, yeah, I know. But I'm still pissed."

Dad patted Mel on the back. "Well, honey, from personal experience, I can say this kind of thing sorts itself out." He squeezed her shoulder and added, "Just be careful about getting a taste for violence. It can be tough to get out of. Believe me, I know all too well."

We said goodnight to Mom and Dad, and they went over to their house. We could hear the kids in the house laughing when we went in. They were watching a movie on the TV. Lee Ann and Taylor had made it their mission to find a TV that worked and had carted many of them home in their efforts.

Using a garden wagon, they'd gone from house to house taking the TV, bringing it home, and trying it out. Taylor had asked if we could turn the power back on to all the houses to make it easier. I told her that wasn't happening and that they had to do it the hard way.

After they piled the first couple of rejects on the front porch, Mel told them they had to get rid of them. I was impressed with the system they came up with. If the TV they tried didn't work, they would load it into the wagon and go to another house, where they would leave it and take a different TV. They are pretty smart kids.

However, they weren't content with just a TV. They also now had a PlayStation and an Xbox and all the games they could find, as well as a Blu-ray player. It was their new hobby, and we allowed them ample time to play games, though there were limits to it. They had chores and responsibilities as well, and as long as they were getting done, we allowed them to escape into a digital world that was all but dead.

They were in the middle of *Beetlejuice* when we came in. Piled on the living room floor were all the cushions from the couch and all the pillows from their bedrooms. Ruckus scampered about between them, giving each a turn to play with her. We stood just inside the door, watching them for a minute. I put my arm around Mel, and she leaned her head on my shoulder.

CHAPTER 6

In The Before, parents would have to fight to get their kids away from the TV and games. Here, it was a nostalgic vision of seeing the kids behave as they used to. And the best part was that it wasn't an obsession to them. It was generally an evening activity with the benefit of keeping them occupied and giving Mel and me some time to ourselves.

When we came in, the girls greeted us without looking back. "What'cha watching?" I asked, knowing the answer.

"Beetlejuice, Beetlejuice, Beetlejuice!" Tammy shouted, getting the others all laughing.

"Hmm," I grunted. "Guess it doesn't work."

Little Bit looked back. "It's just a movie, Daddy!"

"I'm going to grab a shower," I said to Mel.

Tammy looked back and asked, "Can we finish the movie?"

"Of course," said Mel. "Just don't stay up too late."

"We won't," said Taylor.

>—⊞⊞⊞⊞—<

Thad and Mary were getting ready for bed when Mary asked, "Why do you think Morgan wants you to go with them tomorrow?"

"Don't know. But he asked, so I'm going."

Mary got undressed and slid under the covers. Seeing her, Thad smiled. "Oh," he said as he did the same.

Putting his hand on her bare belly, he asked, "How do you feel?"

"I feel fine. Can you feel it? The bump?"

Thad ran his hand over her belly as a smile spread across his face. "I can." Looking at her, he added, "It's small. But he's in there."

Mary smiled. "What if it's a girl?"

"Then she's in there," he said and kissed her tummy.

Mary reached down, cupped his face in her hands, pulled him up to her, and kissed him. Running her hand over his head, she said, "You're getting fuzzy. Go to the bathroom, I'm going to shave your head."

"You don't have to do that, baby."

"Yes, I do, I have to touch it and look at it, and I like your head when it's smooth. Now go on. I'll get my robe."

Thad went into the bathroom and took out the straight razor. Having been nearly a lost art, a straight razor was now a treasure. Sure, there was a bit of a bloody learning curve, but once mastered, it was a valuable skill and one Mary proved adept at. She would shave anyone who asked, and did so often. As Thad ran the razor over a broad leather belt he used as a strop, Mary ran the sink full of hot water.

"Is it ready?" she asked.

"Almost."

She looked at him expectantly. "Sit down."

Mary soaked a hand towel in the hot water and wrung it mostly out. "This is hot," she said as she wrapped it around his head.

"Feels good," he said as he slipped an arm around her.

Mary fidgeted. "No funny stuff. You gotta sit still."

"Yes, ma'am," Thad replied but didn't move his arm.

While the hot towel softened the stubble on his head, Mary took out a cake of soap and placed it on the sink. Removing the towel, she lathered his head and took up the razor.

"Now, sit still, mister man."

It didn't take long for Thad to have a shiny dome that Mary wiped with the towel and pronounced him done. Thad stood up and looked in the mirror, running his hand over his head.

"Looks great, baby. Feels good."

"That's my man." Mary smiled.

"Well, this man wants to take his woman to bed."

Dropping the towel, Mary said, "Then what are you waiting for?"

>―||||||―<

Sarge sat at a table on the porch with Karl, Dalton, Imri, and Chad. Mike and Ted sat at the table beside them with Crystal and Janet.

Sarge spoke up. "I want you boys to come to this meeting tomorrow."

Karl leaned back and crossed his arms over his chest. "Ah, I don't know. I spent enough time in the Army, and they've shown they will reactivate you. I'm not looking to get tossed back into the Green Machine again."

"That's easy," said Sarge. "You're all part of the militia. You can't be."

"Linus, you and I both know if they find out who I am, who these guys are, that will not stop them," said Karl.

"Karl, I give you my word it will not happen. I am in overall command here, me. As for General Fawcett, he will back me up. You're already here and doing your part. Which brings me to another question: what are y'alls intentions?"

"What do you mean?" Imri asked.

"Do you fellers plan on sticking around here, or are you going to move on?" Sarge asked.

Karl looked at Chad and Imri.

"I'm good here," said Imri. "Place feels … normal."

"There's electricity, hot food, and showers. Why the hell would we leave?" Chad added.

Karl chuckled. "It seems they're pretty happy here. For me, I've been looking for a place where we could make a real difference. Where we could have an impact. I don't want to live a Mad Max existence for the rest of my life. You and I are a lot alike; we're getting old. I'd like some peace and quiet for a while. I've spent my entire adult life surrounded by chaos and violence. I've got a belly full. But that doesn't mean I'm ready to quit. We're here and will do whatever is necessary to bring security back."

Sarge said, "Good man, Karl. Chad, you and Imri too. Officially you're under Morgan's command. But anything tactical that needs doing, I handle. So, you really work for me."

"I was wondering about that," Karl said. "Morgan being in charge of the militia. Does he have combat experience?"

"He never served, but he's had plenty of OJT since The Day. I've been with him, and he's solid. He knows his limits and doesn't argue."

"Much," Mike interjected.

"Hell of a lot less than you, shithead!" Sarge barked back.

"You guys can trust Morgan," said Ted. "Like Top said, he's solid. I'll go into a fight with him any day."

"Agreed," said Dalton.

"That's good enough for me," said Imri.

"If you guys all vouch for him," said Karl, "that's enough for me too."

"Would you boys like any more coffee?" Kay asked.

"No, thank you, Kay. I think I'm about to head home and hit the rack," said Sarge.

The others all politely declined as well and excused themselves. Kay came out and took the old man's cup and leaned down and kissed him on the cheek. A devilish smile spread across Mike's face, but before he opened his mouth, Ted flicked his ear. Mike's head snapped around to see Ted shaking his head at him.

Mike looked back at Sarge and Kay, who were talking quietly to one another, then turned back to Ted and said, "You're right, man."

"I'm always right. Thought you would know that by now."

Sarge looked over. "What are you two idjits up to?"

CHAPTER 6

"Nothing, Boss. Headed home," Mike said without the usual smartassery. "Come on, Crystal. Let's go home."

"We're out too," Ted said as he got up.

"One thing," Sarge said as he spun around on the bench. "Does Dave know what you four are up to?"

"He does, Linus," said Janet. "Mike and Ted did the proper thing and came to the ranch and asked for his blessing."

Sarge looked stunned. "Really?"

As Mike passed the old man, he gripped his shoulder. "I know I act like I don't pay attention, Boss. But I have and do, and you've taught me a lot."

Kay teared up immediately. "That is the sweetest thing."

Then Mike leaned over and whispered in Sarge's ear, "Just don't get used to it, old man. Gotta keep you on your toes."

Sarge palmed the side of Mike's face, pushing him away. "Get your snot-nosed ass out of here. See you in the morning. 0800. And don't be late!" He paused. "One more thing—if you guys are staying here, we need to find you a house. So, take a look around and find one you want. Morgan is the electrician around here, and he'll go over the place and make sure it's good to go. That goes for you four as well."

"Will do," Karl replied with a nod.

"I have an idea on that," Kay said as she tossed her dish towel over her shoulder and returned to the kitchen.

>=||||||=<

The living room was reminiscent of Jonestown the next morning when I came out. The girls never did go to bed. The TV was still on with the start screen for the movie *Shrek* stuck on it. I picked up the remote and turned it off, and stood there for a minute just looking at the remote in my hand.

So much had changed since The Day. But the more things change, the more they seem the same. But that wasn't right either. Nothing was the same, and if we are really lucky, they never will be the same as before. Our country and society were sick. They'd been on their deathbeds for a long time. But things were starting to look up, and hopefully, this time, we could make them what they should have been.

As I was pouring my morning glass of tea, I was startled when Ruckus jumped on my back. I spilled tea all over the counter and nearly shit myself. She ran up onto my shoulder and sat on her haunches.

"Morning, Ruckus," I said. Her reply was to take a seat and scratch her ear. Then she jumped onto the counter and sniffed around. I opened the fridge to see what might be in there for her breakfast. There were a couple of biscuits in a container, so I broke a piece off one and handed it to her. She took it and immediately started to eat. Picking her up, I took her to her cage and put her in, never interrupting her nibbling.

Stepping out on the porch, I checked my watch. 6:45, and the sky was cobalt. It was going to be a beautiful day. Sipping my tea, I listened; that was always the best indication of what was going on in the neighborhood. This morning was quiet. There were no engines running. No voices, nothing. Just the sounds of the natural world waking up. Birds calling, and squirrels moving stealthily through the canopy of trees.

Going back inside, I grabbed my pistol belt and put it on. Mel was still sleeping, and I leaned over and kissed her. She wormed around under the blanket but didn't wake, and I left her that way. I always liked to see her asleep for some reason, and I smiled as I picked up my boots and left the room. Back out on the porch, I slid my feet into them without lacing them up and headed for the gate.

CHAPTER 6

"Morgan!" I heard Dad call out and turned to see him headed in my direction, coffee cup in hand.

"You manage to talk the old man out of some coffee?" I asked.

"Wasn't too hard; he recognizes a friend when he sees one."

I laughed. "Took pity on you, huh?"

"I reckon," he said, taking a sip. "Where you off to so early?"

"Some days I wake up early. Hell, most days really. I'm going to see if Red or some of the guys can help Travis today. You and Danny will be milling lumber and I'll drop Thad off after our little meeting in town this morning."

"We really need three people. It'd be pretty hard with just the two of us."

"Ok then, let's find you a helper for the day. And I know just the guy."

We walked down to the bunker, talking about the weather and other trivialities. I found Red and Stinness there. Red smiled as we approached.

"Morning, Morgan, Butch. What's got you two out so early?" Red asked.

"You know, man, lots to do," I said.

"Need some help?"

"As a matter of fact, we do. I need a couple guys with some carpentry skills."

"I can do that for sure," said Red.

"I can swing a hammer," Stinness added.

"Awesome. When do you guys get relieved?"

"0800," Red replied.

"Soon as you are, come on down to Danny's place and get with Travis. We need to get that barn built."

"We'll be there," said Stinness.

As we chatted, Thad walked up. He probably saw us from the kitchen window since the bunker was practically in his front yard. He greeted us with, "Morning, fellas."

"You ready for a ride to town?" I asked.

"Sure am. What's this about?"

I shrugged. "No idea. Old man didn't say."

"Guess we'll find out together."

Mary came out of the house and walked out to where we were. "I don't know about you men, but I'm hungry."

"You are eating for two now," I said with a smile.

"Let's go see what Miss Kay has for breakfast," Thad said. "Oh, that reminds me. We need to slaughter a couple hogs."

"Hogs?" Dad asked.

Looking at him, I said, "Oh yeah, we have some hogs. Guess I never mentioned that."

"How many are there?"

"A dozen now," Thad answered.

"No shit?" I was surprised. "I didn't realize there were so many. How the hell are you feeding them?"

"Me and Danny move them around with hot wire. They're used to it now and don't test it anymore. We just rotate them around by cutting new lanes through the woods to string new wire and push them into it."

"The weather is cooling down some. Be a good time to do it," Dad said.

"Let's pick a day and we'll do it," I said. "Let's get with Miss Kay about it so she can be ready." Looking at Dad I said, "We cut all the fat off them we can—they're pretty lean—and use it to make soap."

"I wondered where you got it from. It's good soap."

"We'll catch up with you guys as soon as we're relieved," Red said.

We walked down to Danny's and were greeted with the earthy aroma of coffee as we climbed the steps. Sarge was on the back porch with Karl's crew and the guys. Even Dalton was there. A round of good mornings passed about as Kay told us all to take a seat. Travis was there as well, sitting with Ian, Jamie, and Danny. I walked over to the table and told him that Red and Stinness would be down to help him as soon as they were relieved.

"Good deal," said Travis.

"Me and Ian are going to help him as well," Jamie said.

"Even better. We'll have more lumber cut today and we'll have this thing done in no time," I said.

"We're gonna have more help than they have lumber. With me and your Dad, we won't get as much done today," said Danny.

"Stop by Dylan's house on your way to the mill," I told Danny. "I'm going to pop in on my way to town and ask him to help you guys out today."

Danny nodded his approval. "Okay, I like Dylan."

"Let me see what Scrooge over there is up to," I said as I turned from the table.

"Who the hell you calling Scrooge?" Sarge barked.

As I sat down at the table beside him, I said, "If the shoe fits, wear it."

"Hey Morgan, if Travis needs help, I can give him a hand today," said Dalton.

I shook my head. "I'd rather you come to town with us."

Sarge half turned toward me. "You want to put on a show of force or something?"

"No. Yes and no. Just want more people involved in some of this. I'm sure they're going to be issuing grandiose requests today, and we're going to have to start dividing up the workload."

"You don't issue requests, Morgan," Karl said. "That's called an order."

"Oh, I know the difference, Karl. They can order all they want. I will consider their requests. We'll talk them over, and we'll decide what we do."

Karl smiled. "I like the way you work."

"Don't give him too much credit, Karl. His damn head will swell," Sarge gruffed.

"Breakfast is ready," Kay announced, "come in and get a plate."

"Let's hurry up and eat so we can get this over with," Sarge said as he got up.

Breakfast was a quick affair. Jess and Doc showed up as we were eating, and Sarge naturally couldn't resist.

"If you can't get here on time, get here when you can, Ronnie."

Jess came to his defense. "It's not his fault. I was running late this morning."

"What?" Sarge asked. "You scared to walk alone now, Ronnie?"

"Not at all," said Doc. "It's called being a gentleman. Something you wouldn't know anything about," he said, getting a series of snickers out of those there.

"I've forgotten more about being a gentleman than you'll ever know!"

Kay walked out on the porch with a pot of coffee and topped the old man's off. "Linus is the perfect example of a gentleman."

"Thank you, Kay," Linus smiled, then glared at Doc. "See?"

"Why you bringing up old shit? I'm trying to eat here," Doc lobbed back.

CHAPTER 6

"I truly hate my life. I must've been a real son of a bitch in my last life. 'Cause I'm damn sure paying for it now," Sarge muttered.

"Last two," Janet added, getting a look of shock from the old man and laughs from the rest of us.

Sarge shook his head. "Didn't take long for him to rot your mind. Careful, or your head will turn to mush like his."

Janet patted Ted's shoulder. "Oh, I've heard *all* the stories."

Crystal leaned back so she could see Sarge. "So have I!"

"And I'm sure they lied through their teeth. We'll have to discuss these *stories* one day," Sarge said in disgust.

"Hey," Janet quipped, "it's your lie, you tell it." More laughs around the porch from this one.

"Just like I'm sure they did! Enough grab-ass. We got shit to do. Let's load up."

CHAPTER 7

We decided to take the MRAP and Hummer to town. With the potential of Tabor to be around, we weren't taking any chances. It was a large crew this trip with Dalton, Mike, Ted, Doc, Sarge, Thad, Ian, Jess, and Jamie. I rode in the Hummer with Sarge, Karl, and Dalton while everyone else piled into the MRAP.

I told Sarge to go by Gena and Dylan's real quick so I could ask him to help out at the mill today. We made it a quick stop and he naturally agreed. Gena and Dylan were good people that we were lucky to count among our friends. I remembered all those discussions of groups, tribe, mutual assistance, call them what you want, back in the day. How it was hard to find the right people and know where to even look for them. I never thought a group like this would come together after the fact. Fortunately, I was wrong.

"What's the purpose of this meeting?" Dalton asked.

"Not sure," Sarge replied. "That quirtzy ass LT wants to see us."

Dalton's brow furrowed. "They left a Lieutenant in charge of the operation here?"

"No," I interjected before Sarge could say anything, "Mister Personality here is in overall command."

Dalton's head turned to look at Sarge. "Over them as well?"

"That's what it sounds like. But they are in touch with higher, and I was on the horn with Fawcett this morning. Today isn't going to be as bad as you boys think it is," said Sarge with a shit-eating grin.

"You holding out on me, old man?" I asked.

"Just cool yer britches there, princess. Like I said, this isn't what you think it is, and I don't want to ruin the surprise."

"I don't like surprises," I said.

As we passed through Umatilla, I saw Bubba and some of the guys at the old Kangaroo store. They waved as we passed, and I made a mental note to stop by and see them on the way back to give them the charger for the radio. The town was just the way I liked it, quiet, and we made it to the school in short order. The soldiers stationed there were making good use of their time. The school was being fortified with sandbag positions and concertina wire stacked two rows high.

I could see the funky satellite antennas being set up on the roof of the admin building. And there was a large flag hanging from the pole this morning. The place was alive with men and women working. The locals were sitting under trees across the street watching and there were a lot of them. A line of people standing in front of an access point caught my eye, and I wondered what they were doing.

Naturally, people will be interested. If for nothing more than the sight of the machines in use and all the work being done. Apathy is rampant in people whose world revolves around where their next meal comes from. Still, it was reminiscent of a bygone era with kids in trees and adults standing around while others relaxed in folding chairs. The only thing missing was the coolers.

Coming into the administration building, Daniels, the Warrant Officer, saw our procession and muttered, "Uh?"

"What's up?" I asked.

"We weren't expecting so many of you."

I looked back at the group and asked, "Is there a problem?"

"Where's Simmons?" Sarge barked.

"He's in the conference room, but it isn't big enough."

"This is a school, ain't it?" Sarge snapped at Daniels.

"Yes, sir."

"It's got a gymnasium then. Tell them we'll be waiting in the gym."

Daniels nodded. "Yes, sir."

Sarge looked around, then asked, "Daniels, where is the gym?"

"Oh, sure. Go out here and make a right. It'll be straight ahead. We're using part of it right now."

"We don't need much space."

"The cafeteria might be better," Daniels offered. He sealed the deal with, "There's coffee in there."

"To the cafeteria!" Sarge shouted.

I turned to walk out as I knew where it was, and soon we were all sitting in the cafeteria enjoying the Army's coffee.

"That's not bad," Sarge said after taking a sip.

Mike held a cup up. "If it's free, it's for me!"

The door opened, and Simmons was followed in by his staff. "Wow," he said as he entered, "you know something we don't?"

"No, these are just some of the people you will be dealing with," I said, "and I wanted you all to get to know one another. There's more, and you'll meet them all in due time."

"Oh." The look of concern fell from his face, and he added, "Good. Who do we have?"

"This here is Dalton," I said, pointing to him.

Simmons came up and offered his hand. "Good to meet you. And your last name?"

A corporal was with the LT to take notes and was scribbling on a clipboard.

"Just Dalton."

"You don't have a last name?" Simmons asked.

"You will forgive my suspicions of agents of the Federal Government," Dalton said dryly.

"Oh, sure," an uncertain Simmons replied.

"And this is Thad," I said.

"Just Thad?" Simmons asked as he held his hand out. Thad gripped it and shook his hand.

"Just Thad." His deep voice resonated through the cafeteria.

Karl stepped forward and offered his hand. "Karl."

The LT shook his head. "OK then. Let's get to business." He looked back, and one of his staff handed him a folder. Opening it, he laid it out on the table. Looking up, he smiled. "Well, I have some really good news for you." He paused for effect, then checked his watch. "In about half an hour, we have a convoy coming in. In that convoy are some M-ATVs for you guys as well as Hilux trucks."

Shocked, I asked, "Come again?"

"Told you you'd like it," Sarge said with a grin.

Simmons continued, "I was serious when I told you we were here to support you, and I meant it. You can also stop worrying about fuel, as there is a tanker with the convoy as well. There's more supplies on the trucks, such as food, medical, clothing, and much more for the civilian population."

"What is an M-ATV?" I asked.

"It's like our MRAP, only smaller," said Sarge. "They're much better suited for what we're doing."

"The Hilux is a diesel pick-up," Simmons added.

"Hilux?" Karl asked, following it up with, "No shit."

"I know what those are. They weren't legal to import into the US," I said.

Simmons laughed. "That was then. This is now. A lot has changed." Looking at Karl, he asked, "You familiar with the Hilux? You prior service?"

"No," Karl replied with a wave of his hand. "I spent some time working in Africa." Which was technically true. He'd spent some time in Third Group.

I glanced over at Karl, and he caught my eye, giving me a little wink. I was sure this would come up again.

"Oh, right," said Simmons.

"How many of what are we getting?" I asked.

"We're trading the big MRAP in for three M-ATVs, and we're getting …" Sarge looked at Simmons for confirmation. "Is it four Hilux?"

Checking his notes, Simmons nodded. "Yes, sir, that is correct."

"And what are we supposed to do with them?" I asked.

Sarge rose to his feet. "LT, you mind?"

"The floor is yours, Colonel."

Sarge let out a sigh and stood up. "We're going to pair one Hilux with each M-ATV. We'll have two teams to send out at any given time, holding the third back as reserve in case a QRF is needed. The last Hilux is yours, Morgan."

Surprised, I asked, "Mine?"

"You are the acting governor of Florida. You need a vehicle, as things are going to start getting busy," said Simmons. "And, it's a way for us to show that we mean what we said."

"What's that line of people at the checkpoint out there?" I asked.

"We're hiring locals to work for us. We have a lot to do, constructing defenses for this camp."

"That's really good. Getting people back to work," Dalton added.

"It is. It's what we need to do. We need to get more people involved in the recovery," said Simmons. "Which brings me to my next point."

Simmons rustled through his notes, took a page out, and handed it to me. "We need you to conduct a survey of these sites and see what it will take to get them back up and running, or if it's even possible."

I took the paper and looked at it. There were the typical things there you would expect, but I hadn't given any thought to most of them.

"I doubt the hospital will be salvageable. After a year of no power, most places won't be," I said.

"We just need to look at them. You have some engineers here still, correct?" A quick nod from me and he continued. "Press them into service."

"Way ahead of you, LT," said Sarge then asked, "Is my commo on that convoy?"

Taking another page from his folder, Simmons replied, "Uh, yes. Looks like it's there."

Sarge looked back at me. "I requested comms for the militia. You will have your own radios and frequency to operate on."

I had a nagging question in my mind. Something that'd been eating at me. "This is just a thought, but with everything that is about to start happening, do we need to come up with some form of record keeping to keep track of decisions we make and implement? I mean, we're going to start making some rules and coming up with systems for the government, so we should be accountable for those things as well as having a way for the public to learn about them."

"We haven't gotten that far yet," said Simmons.

"Can you guys get me a laptop and a printer, paper, and ink carts for it?" I asked.

"Sure, I can request it. I don't know when or if it will arrive, but I will request it."

With an audible snort, Sarge said, "Just tell them it's for the governor's office."

CHAPTER 7

Daniels slammed the door to the cafeteria open with a bang, startling most of us. "Convoy's here!"

"What the hell is wrong with you? Kicking the door open like you're damn Five-O or some shit!" Sarge snapped.

"Oh, sorry," said Daniels.

"Well, come on out and check out your new rides," Simmons said with a satisfied smile.

We all followed him out and headed back through the school. Looked to me like we were headed to the football field.

As we walked, Thad came up beside me. "New trucks? New armored trucks? Do you think things are about to change?"

I thought about it for a minute. "I think this may be the beginning of the change." Looking over at him, I added, "But I don't know what it's going to look like."

"That's what I was thinking too. It's great someone is finally stepping up, but what are they going to want in return?"

"All this survey shit is going to be a pain in the ass. But it is the right thing to do, and in all honesty, we should have been doing this all along. We should have been out at the start to salvage what we could. "

Thad laughed, the infectious way he does. "Morgan, you a mess. By the time you got home, there probably wasn't much left to salvage!"

With the sound of large diesel engines revving and moving, I looked at him. "You're probably right. Guess we'll find out."

A long line of the modern versions of our Deuce and a half, the LMTV, along with Hummers and a variety of armored vehicles were lined up on Bulldog Lane, waiting to turn onto the football field. Blue smoke hung in the still air as people shouted, engines roared under their loads, and one by one, they pulled in and parked. Most of the armor was moved into positions around the school.

Karl stood watching the show with arms folded over his chest. Sucking air through his teeth, he shook his head. "Brings back memories. But it's good to see the Army acting like the Army again."

"What do you mean?" Dalton asked.

"No traffic vests, none of the completely unnecessary shit the Army is always implementing that doesn't make a shit's worth of difference to combat, just makes it harder. More dangerous."

The soldiers from the convoy were dismounting and mingling with the ones already there. These people had obviously been together for some time from the looks of the greetings. I walked off to stand under the bleachers, kind of out of sight. Dalton and Thad followed. We left Sarge and Karl out there to deal with their kind.

"Look at all that," Thad muttered.

"That is a lot," said Dalton.

"There's the trucks," I said, pointing to where they were being pulled off the road in the lot behind The First Baptist Church.

"Let's go check them out," Dalton said as he stepped off.

Thad and I followed him over to where our new rides awaited us. The Hilux were all white and one beige. Looking at them, I quickly said, "That tan one is mine."

Dalton looked over his shoulder at me. "That didn't take long." Thad chuckled at the comment.

"Just be easy to know which one is mine," I said with a laugh.

Getting in the truck, I was surprised when a soldier shouted at me, "Hey! Get out of the truck!"

We all looked up to see him running in our direction. Not really knowing many of the new folks, we didn't know if he was part of them or part of the convoy. But he had a weapon and was quickly moving our way. His shouting drew the attention of others, and several of them started moving as well.

I climbed out of the truck, and we stood there with our weapons slung, though Dalton took a couple of steps off to the side, and I subconsciously followed his lead so we wouldn't be shooting at one another if it came to it. Crossfire is a thing, and friendly fire isn't. The soldier that yelled at us slid to a stop twenty or so feet away, with his weapon at low-ready.

"Step away from the truck!" he ordered.

Other soldiers arrived on the scene, unsure of what was going on. I raised my hands slightly. "Easy, man. We're just looking them over."

"They're property of the United States government!"

"That doesn't even exist anymore," Dalton calmly said. The statement appeared to confuse the soldier.

"Actually," I explained, "these belong to the governor's office."

I saw Harvey and waved at him. The big PJ walked over and put his hand on the soldier's weapon, pushing it down. "Easy, fellas, this is the acting governor of Florida."

The soldier looked at me, then at Harvey. "Huh?"

"He's been appointed the acting governor. Relax."

"Oh, shit," the soldier said. "Sorry, sir."

I shrugged. "Just doing your job, man. No harm, no foul."

The soldier held his hand out. "Good to meet you, Governor."

I shook his hand and said, "Believe me, it's not my idea."

The soldiers gathered around the trucks, tailgates were dropped, and I watched Dalton, contrary to popular belief, do what he does best, start talking. A lot of people do not know that about him, but Dalton can get anyone to talk and tell him the things he wants to know. I caught onto what he was doing and didn't interrupt, taking a seat on a tailgate.

"So, what's the government look like these days?" Dalton asked.

"You think we know?" one of the soldiers laughed.

"We're under Martial Law," another soldier offered.

"Which means the military is running the country," Dalton countered.

"What have you guys been up to?" Thad asked.

The soldier that first ran up to us said, "Usual shit, really. Patrols, trying to assist where we can. Dealing with bandits, the occasional warlord."

Dalton arched his eyebrows. "Warlords? Do tell."

Some of the gathered soldiers laughed. "It's a loose term. For us, any group that is mobile and armed is considered a warlord."

Dalton looked at Thad and me. The three of us shared a look, and I said, "Well, that describes us."

"Yeah," Harvey interjected, "but you guys aren't running around taking what little other people have. You're not taking prisoners as slaves. There's a lot of really bad shit out there."

"Are you finding many of them?" Dalton asked.

"More than we'd like."

"You said they were taking slaves?" I asked.

"Man," another soldier interrupted, "we've seen some crazy shit."

Another soldier nodded and took a step forward. "Yeah, the good, the bad, and the ugly. We've seen it all. You really can't imagine what people are capable of."

"You wanna bet?" I asked.

Thad added, "We've seen our fair share of humanity."

The soldier that took the step forward looked me in the eye and then Dalton and Thad in turn. He started to nod his head and pointed at us. "Yeah, you've seen it. You know what I'm talking about." Our collective response was to nod our heads slowly.

We sat talking with these men for a while about where they'd been, what they'd done, and seen. It was an interesting conversation, and I noticed Dalton was intently listening to what they said. It was only natural that the old man would arrive on the scene and ruin it.

"What the fuck is this? A sewing circle?" Sarge barked as he approached.

One of the soldiers snapped to attention, shouting, "Aten huh!"

Sarge was immediately in the young man's face. "You do not salute me! Do not ever salute me again, or I will kick you in the nuts so fuckin' hard you'll be wearing 'em on your chin!"

Hesitantly, the soldier dropped his hand. Swallowing hard, he responded, "Uh, yes, sir. Sorry, sir, I thought you were a colonel."

"The only paperwork I have from the Army shows my rank at retirement as Sergeant Major! You will refer to me as Top! Got it, numbnuts?"

The soldier nodded and said, "Yes, s—, I mean Sergeant Major," then added, "Top."

"Better," Sarge snapped, then looked at me. "Can this fuckin' AA meeting do without your presence, *Governor?*" He laid the sarcasm on thick.

I turned to look at the group as I walked away. "Hi, I'm Morgan, and he's an asshole." Thad and Dalton chuckled with a couple of the soldiers. Catching up to Sarge, I asked, "What's up?"

"You need to sit down with Merryweather. He's got some civilian shit he needs to talk to you about. Guess they had some conversations when he was up in Jacksonville."

"Like what?" I asked.

With copious snark, he said, "Not my problem. Like I said, civilian shit."

"Where?" I asked.

"Conference room."

"All right, I'm gonna grab Thad, and we'll head that way."

Sarge stopped. "We're going to load up what we need and head back. You have a truck now, so you can drive back when you're done."

"See you at the ranch later," I said as I waved a hand to get Thad's attention.

>─▟▆▆▆▜─<

The meeting with Merryweather was long. Both Thad and I were surprised at the level of organization finally underway to restore the country. We were informed that Florida was of vital interest because of the ports and the proximity to Cuba. We were shocked to learn that the US Navy had clashed with both the Russian and Chinese navies in a couple of instances.

"The Chinese talk about their hypersonic weapons," Merryweather stated, "but we still have the best sub fleet, and it took a toll on them. There's still a lot of them out west, but nothing that floats or flies can cross the Pacific without being killed."

"That's good news," Thad said.

Merryweather let out a sigh. "Which brings us to our current situation. When you start conducting your survey operations, you will certainly run into them. There is a much smaller amount of Russians in Florida as well. Both are being supported from Cuba via smuggling operations. Your militia will be tasked with finding these elements and destroying them."

"What the fuck?" I asked.

Merryweather looked up, surprised. "What?"

"Isn't that shit your job?" I asked.

Merryweather placed the folder he was holding on the table and looked at me. "As the governor of Florida, this is your job. You've already started to form a militia that will be the nexus for a much larger one. The vision forward is a little different, Morgan. The states will retain their autonomy from the Federal government. The Federal government, once it's fully instituted, will be responsible for defending the borders of the nation and dealing with foreign governments. The bureaucracy that once was the bloated government is over. None of those agencies will return."

I looked at Thad. "Well, it only took a near-death experience for it to happen, but it happened."

Our conversation continued on civilian topics for a while. I was genuinely surprised at the level of effort being made to assist the civilian population. In such times it is obvious that the government will protect itself and, by extension, those involved in it. Thad and I both asked several questions, making notes on paper we had to ask for. Clean sheets of paper were now rather scarce. Something we didn't think about when Little Bit was drawing on so much of it.

"So you will officially know, Thad here is going to be my Lieutenant Governor. Talking to him will be like talking to me," I said to Merryweather.

"What?" Thad blurted out.

Merryweather looked confused.

"I ain't the only one that can get voluntold around here, ole buddy," I said.

"You didn't discuss it with him first?" Merryweather asked.

"No! He didn't!" Thad shot back.

"So, is this a thing, then?"

"Yes, it is," I said and looked at Thad. "I know you buddy. You're a good man and this country needs good men that will do what is best for all of us. I know I can trust you, you have my back and I have yours."

Thad nodded. "Always."

Looking at Merryweather, I said, "It's a thing."

"Good," he responded with a broad smile. "I knew we had the right man for the job."

"I do have one question."

"What's that?"

"Can you put the word out to your people that I'm looking for a music player of some type? MP3 player, an old phone that works and has music on it. Anything like that."

"Sure. I know there are a couple devices like that around. You looking to trade?"

"Yeah, we have some things that might interest folks."

"I'll let my people know."

Standing up, I said, "Thanks. Come on Thad, we have a lot to do."

We left the admin building and walked over to the truck. "You sure about this?" Thad asked.

I laughed. "Man, I'm not sure about anything. But I know I can't do it alone and I know I trust you with my life. You're a smart man, Thad." I stepped in front of him, facing him. "No one can do this alone. I know you don't want this anymore than I do. But it's not up to us. Your fate was sealed that day we met on the side of the road."

Thad ran a hand over his smooth dome. "You right about one thing, I don't want to. But I know you don't want to either, but you doing it. You also right about the day we met. It sure ain't been boring since!"

We got in the truck and I started it up. "This is nice," Thad said, looking around. "Didn't think I'd ever see a new truck!"

I revved the little diesel engine, and with a huge smile I said, "I know, right?" then dropped it in gear and headed out.

CHAPTER 7

We rode in silence to the mill. I knew Thad was turning this development over in his head just as I was. I didn't know what it really meant for him to be my second, but I did know that anything I put him in charge of he would handle. The very idea I was giving out such commands irked the shit out of me. But, if not me, then who?

The guys were hard at work when we pulled up. There was a large stack of two-by material and they were currently cutting one-bys. These would be used for the siding. We were fortunate to have so much seasoned wood lying around to work with. Otherwise, we would have to cut and stack all this lumber for it to dry out, adding considerable time to the job.

Dad was sitting in the grapple with a log already loaded and waiting to go. He waved and climbed down off the machine.

"Man, you guys are moving," I said when he walked up.

"One more day and I think we'll have all we need."

"That's awesome," I said.

"How'd things go in town?"

"Same old shit. Just lots to do, ya know?"

"Just let me know what you need. This is really good."

I looked at Dad. "What do you mean?"

"Just this, out here working. I missed that. Having a goal in mind and the resources needed to actually do it. And the people willing to help. I hadn't realized how much I missed it."

"I know what you mean. Feels like …"

Dad finished the thought. "Progress. Like we're getting somewhere. Not just laying around waiting."

"Exactly."

Thad was already at the mill, tossing the remaining bark slab off the saw from the last completed log. Seeing they were ready for a new one, Dad said, "Back to work!"

"Get after it, see you at home later."

Dad waved as he climbed up the ladder to the machine. It felt good to see him like this. Dad was an equipment operator and could use any kind of machine. I was happy he was back at what he liked to do. A life without purpose is a life without worth. Seeing him—not just him, but all of us—have a sense of worth was incredible.

I pulled up in front of Danny's place and parked. Mel and Erin were on the front porch, each running a comb through one of the kid's hair. Little Bit, Jace, and Edie were running around the yard kicking a ball.

As I stepped up on the porch, Mel spoke up. "Thankfully we don't have a lice problem."

"Finally, some good news!" I said, sounding relieved.

"Everything all right?" she asked.

"Oh yeah."

"Aric is in there." She gestured toward the door. "He wants to talk to you."

"I'll go see him after I get some tea!"

"I was just going over to the house. I'll bring you some back."

"Thank you, baby. Be on the back porch."

I went in and it was obvious Aric wanted to talk so we went out to the back porch and sat down at one of the tables. "What's up?" I asked.

"Morgan, I know you guys are worried about me and are trying to keep me around here so I don't get hurt or anything. But I can't do that anymore. I just can't look at everyone here knowing I'm not pulling my weight. I need to be involved. I need to contribute."

"Your timing is impeccable, Aric. I think you are just the man for the job."

"What job?"

"I need a commander for the Florida Militia."

"What?" he asked, shocked.

"Just that. We need to stand up a substantial militia. We'll need to train and equip them. Establish operating bases across the state. It's going to be a big job."

He was very obviously nervous. "Uh, man, that sounds like a lot."

"It is, no bullshit here. It's a huge job."

"I don't know if I can do all that."

"You'll have help. I'm going to ask Karl and his guys to be your cadre. They will help you with organization and training. But they will work for you. This accomplishes two things: gives you a huge responsibility while at the same time not sticking you in direct action, unless you choose to go. I will never again say no. If you want to go, you go. I'm sorry for not really thinking about you in all this. I can imagine how you feel."

Aric still looked a little shocked. "Uh, thanks."

"So, is that a yes?"

"I mean, yeah, whatever you need."

I stuck my hand out. "Awesome."

He shook my hand as a smile started to spread across his face. "Awesome."

Mel showed up with a glass of tea for me and set it down on the table. Studying us for a minute, she said, "You two look like you're up to something."

"Why, whatever do you mean?" I asked in feigned shock.

"Whatever, I know that look." She turned and walked off.

Aric laughed, then said, "This is crazy Morgan. I mean, really."

Standing up, I said, "Just the new normal, buddy. Just the new normal."

As I turned to leave, Aric said, "I won't let you down, Morgan."

Stopping, I looked over my shoulder. "I know. I wouldn't have asked if I didn't think so, friend."

Miss Kay was sitting on the front porch with Mel and Erin when I came out the door. There was one rocker left and I dropped into it.

"You look tired, Morgan," Kay said.

"*Weary* would be a better description," I responded.

"Is everything ok?"

"Oh yeah, there is just so much to do now. We have an opportunity at the moment to really improve the situation. It's just going to take a lot of work," I paused and looked at the ladies, "from all of us."

"I know one thing, Morgan," Kay said, "if there is a group of people anywhere that can do it, it's this one. There are some truly great people here."

"You are right about that," I said. "We'll talk about some of this tonight at supper. Right now, I'm going to walk down and check on the barn construction."

"I'll come with you," Mel said as she got to her feet.

"Nice." I gave her a wink.

She took my hand in hers as we stepped off the porch. Then Erin jumped up, said, "Hey, wait for me!" then called for her kids to come with her. Naturally, all the kids came along.

We walked toward the pasture and Mel asked, "Is something wrong? You look stressed out."

"Nothing more than usual. I'm just starting to spread the load a bit."

"What do you mean?"

"Thad will be the Lieutenant Governor and will be responsible for some things."

"Really?" Erin asked.

"Sure, why not. I know I can rely on him."

CHAPTER 7

Mel swung our clasped hands. "Good. I'm glad to see you start to rely on others. You can't do it all and don't have to."

"Aric is going to be in charge of the militia. I'm going to ask Karl to assist in that."

"That's great too!"

Looking at her, I smiled. "It is."

The men were hard at work when we got to the pasture. I was surprised to see Aaron there pitching in. All of the posts were in the ground with basic framing up between them. We chatted as they swung hammers and drills whirred. They had a curious energy about them. They were animated by the work and prospect of what that work would bring. It was partly that and partly because this was something new that broke up the monotony of our lives. Not that they were boring, but some days really did feel like Groundhog Day.

"Wow, you guys are moving fast," Mel said.

Erin's little ones ran over to Travis and he climbed down off his ladder to greet them. Picking them up one at a time, he carried them up onto the ladder so they could see the view from six feet higher. God bless the easily impressed.

"Looking good!" I called out.

Travis inspected the work. "It's coming along. These guys helping is making a big difference."

"All you had to do was ask!" Red shouted.

"I have a feeling Travis isn't good at asking for help." I couldn't help but laugh.

"He's not," Erin confirmed. Travis just shrugged.

"We get this done and start feeding her in here for a week or so, we'll be able to start milking her. It'll take a little time to get her used to being handled," I said.

"I don't think that will take too long," Mel called out.

I looked over to see her petting the heifer. The calf was close by as well. Seeing the calf, the kids all ran over and Mel slowed them down on their approach so as not to scare it. It wasn't long before they were all gathered around the two bovines, petting and rubbing on them.

"I think you're right," I said, "shouldn't take long at all."

Hearing a vehicle, I looked up to see the little red pickup bouncing down the road. Audie was behind the wheel, with Baker in the passenger seat. Seeing us, they passed Danny's place and rolled to a stop in front of the gate to the pasture.

"Hey y'all!" Audie called out.

"What brings you guys by?" I asked. Terry and Scott were climbing out of the bed as Baker and Audie walked up.

"Wanted to talk to you about Juniper."

"What's up?"

"I've been told you kind of know about edible plants and stuff like that."

"I do," I said.

"If you have time, might be a good idea to go up there and show those folks some of the plants they can eat. Would really help them out."

"I can do that. There's plenty up there. I'll ride up there tomorrow. Grab someone to ride with me for security."

"I'll go with you," Mel said.

Smiling at her, I said, "Great!"

"Barn raising?" Audie asked.

"Yep. Gonna try and milk this heifer," I said.

"That's one nice thing about the ranch. There's plenty of milk to be had," Audie paused and looked at me. "And it's so good. Not like what you get from the store. Real milk."

"Funny how humanity lived on the stuff for millennia but in recent times it was decided you couldn't drink the pure natural product. For all the talk of organic this and that, they sure were in a hurry to limit it. To put chemicals into as much as they could."

"I blame the funeral industry," Audie said flatly.

"What?" I laughed back.

"I think they were the ones behind it. Putting all the preservatives in food. So they didn't have to embalm anymore."

He said it straight faced and I couldn't tell if he was joking or not. But the absurdity of the statement made me laugh. After a moment, Audie started to laugh as well, and I said, "Remind me to never play poker with you."

Audie shrugged as if to say, *"What are you gonna do?"* then said, "You gotta have fun where you can."

"What do you think about the water wheel? Can you do it?"

Audie rubbed his chin. "I think it can be done. I need some material. I can probably get most of it from the plant."

"That reminds me, there's a metal fab shop in Umatilla. You know where it is?"

"No, that would be a big help. Where it is?" Audie asked, squinting one eye.

It made me laugh, *where it is.* Growing up, Dad and my uncles would talk like this. In public it was hilarious. People would look at us like a bunch of uneducated hillbillies. To us, their reactions were the best part!

"I'm terrible at street names. But I can show you," I said.

"That'd be great."

Looking at Mel, I asked, "You wanna go for a ride?"

"That'd be fun. Of course."

"Audie, let me get my truck and you guys can follow me over. Baker, you need to know where this is, too."

"You should have told us about this a long time ago," she admonished me.

"Sorry, I don't think of everything," I laughed in reply.

"You should be sorry. It's not like you're busy or anything."

"Fornicate thyself, Baker," I shot back, getting a snicker out of her. "Meet you guys up by the bunker." Before leaving, I called out to Red, "How you like swinging a hammer over carrying a rifle?"

He was actually using a drill to run a long lag bolt into one of the timbers. "I'll take this any day of the week and twice on Sunday! Just feels good to be doing something that feels productive."

"Right on, brother. Right on. Catch you guys later."

As Mel and I walked back to the truck, I said, "Let's get the girls. They can ride in the bed. Be fun for them."

Little Bit was following behind, but little ears hear everything, and she quickly reacted to the statement. "I want to go for a ride!"

"That's a great idea, I'll go get them while you bring the truck over," Mel said. Then, calling for Little Bit to take her hand, she added, "Come on sweetie, let's get your sisters."

"Yay, we get to go for a ride!"

We parted ways as I smacked her ass and she headed to get the girls. As soon as I pulled up in front of the house, the door burst open and they came pouring out. I got out and dropped the tailgate and helped them all in.

"Now listen, sit on your butts. No standing up. And hang on to the side, got it?"

"Got it, Dad!" came the droning reply that only teenagers seem capable of. Then I noticed something.

"Hey, where are your weapons?" I asked Lee Ann and Taylor.

"Why do we need them?" Taylor asked.

"You don't leave the house without them. Ever. I'll get them. You stay here." They didn't seem particularly happy at the suggestion, but they didn't complain either.

CHAPTER 7

It was an unfortunate aspect of the current world that we didn't travel anywhere without them. Not that we needed them often. But, like a tourniquet, when you need one, you don't have time to get one. In The Before, carrying weapons was highly frowned upon, going so far as to be demonized. I wondered how all those gun control advocates fared when things started to collapse. I wondered what their views on firearm ownership were now. If they were still alive.

Stepping in the door, I picked the girls' sub guns up from the ready rack I'd cobbled together and put in the living room. It was by the door and was a convenient place to leave them. That way everyone knew where they were.

The girls were carrying on and laughing when I walked back over. I handed Lee Ann and Taylor their weapons. They accepted them without comment, and I was happy to see them both verify the safety and do a quick condition check to make sure the weapons were chambered before setting them aside. Guns were a part of their lives. Just a tool, nothing more. One that deserved respect, not fear. This is what real gun control looks like.

"This is a really cool truck, Daddy!" Little Bit shouted.

"Yeah, I really like it," Tammy said.

"Can you teach us to drive it?" Lee Ann asked. The statement was followed by a chorus of cheers from the other girls.

I smiled. "I sure can! That would be fun. I'll start teaching you all soon, ok?"

"I want to drive too!" Little Bit shouted.

I tousled her hair. "You'll learn to, kiddo. Promise."

Mel had her Minimi with her. Since acquiring it, she was seldom without it. As usual, the muzzle was on the floorboard between her knees.

As I climbed in, she said, "This is a nice truck."

"I know, I really like it."

"We're going to Juniper tomorrow?"

"Yep," I said as I cranked the little truck up. "Show those folks some stuff they can eat out there on the river."

"I remember living on the river." Mel looked out the window as I pulled out. "Really glad we're not there anymore."

"We've been very lucky, baby. Let's hope it holds out."

"What do you mean?" she asked as I pulled out the gate.

"Just that, baby. Nothing is guaranteed today. We have to work for it."

Audie was down at the bunker talking to the guys on duty. I waved at Mary who was sitting on her porch and she waved back. I smiled to myself at the scene of normality. We were doing good. I really did hope it would last.

"You ready?" I shouted out the window when I pulled up beside Audie.

"Waitin' on you!"

"If you're waiting on me, you're backing up!" I shouted back and let the clutch out to spin the tires a little as I took off. This got a string of laughter from the bed, and I looked in the mirror to see the girls all looking out the bed of the truck and waving as we sped away. Looking in the side mirror, I saw the guys waving and laughing at the kids. Again, it made me smile.

We went down Highway 19 into Umatilla. People were already moving toward the school. I should say, more people were. The lawn across the street from the school as well as the parking lot of the McDonalds were always full of people. It had turned into a bit of a festival atmosphere, with a lot of camp chairs and the like spread around with adults and kids filling them. The adults watched the goings on of the Army while the kids mainly played. Someone had produced a set of cornhole boards and there appeared to be a rather intense tournament going on.

"That's a good idea," I said.

"What?" Mel asked.

CHAPTER 7

"Cornhole. We need to find a couple of boards and some bags. Would be a lot of fun in the evening."

"That would be a lot of fun. I'm getting tired of puzzles."

The little metal shop was actually across the street from the plant but one block over, and I never thought about it until it suddenly popped into my head. I turned onto 450A and made a right onto Lane Street and pulled into the yard of the shop. We all got out and checked the doors. The big roll up doors were open, and we walked in.

The girls hopped out of the truck and Mel told them to be careful and not wander off. "Yes, Mom," came the unanimous reply. I always got a kick out of hearing Tammy say it. Such a small word that can have such a big impact on the life of a child. Simply having a mom and dad, whether by birth, or, as in this case, by choice, was necessary for them. All they needed was support, love, and the security of someone who really did care for them.

"Damn," Audie said. "This will be really helpful."

"All this has been right here all this time?" Baker asked.

"Holy shit," Terry and Scott said in unison.

"Yeah, it's been here, I just forgot about it," I said.

"This would have been a big help," Scott said.

"Well, it will be now," I offered.

"Yeah, this will be great," Audie added. Then he looked at Baker. "You think we could get the power back on over here? There's a lot of very useful equipment in here. This is a hell of a fab shop."

"I'm sure we can." She looked at Terry. "What do you think?"

"Just need to check the transformer on the pole and we should be able to get it back up and running. I'll run to the plant and get my climbing gear and we'll check it out. Might be able to do it right now."

"I'll go with you," Scott said.

"Take the truck!" Audie called out.

Terry was already standing in the driver's door. "You didn't think I was going to walk, did you? I've had enough of the sole train, thank you very much!"

"Well, if you guys have this under control, I'll leave you all with it then," I said.

"This is awesome, Morgan," Audie said, then added, "If any other places pop into your head, let me know."

"There is one more, but that's for another day."

Audie cocked his head to the side. "What is it?"

"Well, I'm not exactly sure. It's called Electron Machine Company. It's a big place outside town a little bit. I always wondered what they did there. Some sort of precision equipment, I think."

"Well, I would be interested in seeing it someday."

"We will, buddy. I'll see you guys later."

Mel called to the girls, who were climbing on a stack of large I-beams, and told them to load up. They didn't hesitate and were immediately running toward the truck. Once again, I dropped the tailgate and helped them all in.

Picking up Little Bit, I set her in the truck. "Where's Ruckus?" I asked.

She reached down into her hoodie pocket and produced the sleeping rodent. "Here she is!" Ruckus wasn't interested in playing and headed right back to the pocket.

The girls took their seats, and we headed back toward town. Pulling out onto 19, I said, "We're gonna make a couple of stops."

Mel had her hand out the window, using it to surf the air. "I'm in no hurry."

I shifted the truck, then patted her on the thigh. "Me neither, baby."

She looked over and smiled at me. She was wearing a pair of aviator shades and looked cute as hell. Life was indeed good. It may have been a little harder than it was before. And I know we were the exception and not the rule. Most people had it way worse than we did. But we were working to change that and the thought provided solace.

At times I did feel terrible for living a life of relative comfort when so many were suffering. But who was really to blame for that? Was it my fault that too many people focused on things that, in terms of real survival, just didn't matter, and I hadn't? No, it wasn't my fault. But I still had empathy for them.

I pulled into the market in Umatilla and saw Bubba and Sky there. They waved and started toward the truck before I shut it off.

"Mom! Can we look around?" Tammy called out.

"Yes, just stay together."

As I got out, I said, "And take your weapons." Lee Ann and Taylor both slung their H&Ks without comment and the girls bounded off to check out the offerings.

"Hey Morgan, Miss Mel," Bubba said as he walked up.

"That's a hell of a gun you have, Mel," Sky said.

Mel looked at the machine gun slung across her. "Yes, it is. I like it."

"You look like a badass," said Sky.

"What's up, boss?" Bubba asked.

"Start putting the word out for anyone that wants to join the militia. We're going to start building it up. They'll be trained, provided weapons and uniforms. Just let them know, they will be put to use. They will also be sent out on missions away from town and could be gone for long stretches."

"Really? Where we headed?"

"All over the state, buddy. We have a lot to do. Things are starting to change. It's time to start rebuilding the state. Hell, the country. But we're only worried about Florida for right now."

"I know a few people that have asked about it," said Sky.

"Me too. Seeing the weapons gets folk's attention," Bubba added.

"They fuckin' with you at all?" I asked.

"Dear," Mel said, "I'm going to go look around unless you need something."

"Go ahead. I'll be right here."

"No, not at all. Most say they like seeing it. Like things are changing for the better," Bubba said.

I pointed at the band of blue cloth wrapped around his shoulder. "Glad to see that. Has the Army messed with you guys at all?"

"No. They come out and do patrols on foot around town here. From what we've seen, they're being pretty nice to folks," said Sky.

"Well, that's good to hear."

As we were talking, a man walked up. "Hey Sheriff, when is the Army gonna start providing more than one meal a day?"

"I don't know that they are. It's a bit of a logistics nightmare to get one meal a day."

"Well," he said indignantly, "they sure should!"

"Be happy you're getting one," I said, shaking my head.

The man put his hands on his hips. "Someone needs to step up around here. It's been over a year and all we can get is one lousy meal a day?"

I couldn't believe the guy. "You're absolutely right, someone does need to step up, and that is you."

"What? I've been taking care of myself all this time!"

"Then keep doing so and be happy for the help you get. What's being done here isn't easy. We're lucky to even have the help that's arrived. Stop acting like someone is responsible for riding in here and saving your ass. Those days are over."

"It's not fair," he protested. "They seem to have so much over there." He pointed at me. "Even you and your people have a lot. Everyone knows about you. Your people don't go hungry. You have trucks." He looked at the Hilux. "Shit, new trucks even."

"That's because all of the people you just mentioned all *do something.* They aren't sitting around here complaining. They're trying. I tell you what, you want more? The Army is looking for volunteers. You can enlist and then you'll have all the stuff too."

"What? I ain't joining the Army! I was thinking about joining the militia, though. I heard that one is forming up."

"There's no place in the militia for you. Your attitude is just wrong. We need *can do* people, not bellyachers."

"Who the hell are you to tell me what I can and can't do, Sheriff?"

I looked at Bubba. "Did you hear that?"

With a look of mirth, Bubba said, "Yeah, oh the irony."

"It's my militia."

The man didn't know what to say and just stood there for a moment. "Well, I ain't joining the Army!" he shouted and walked away.

"That was interesting," Sky said.

"Can't please all the people all the time," I said. "Get the word out for me. I've got to get back. How's the radio holding up?"

Bubba held it up. "Fine. Not like anyone is talking on it."

"Don't worry, they will be. See you guys later."

I left Bubba and Sky and walked over to Mel. She was looking at items on one of the tables when I walked up. "Whatcha doin'?" I asked.

She turned to me, holding a bracelet in her hand. "Look at this, it's Tiffany's."

I looked at the diamond tennis bracelet. "Cool, not like it means anything now."

"True, but I do love diamonds!"

I looked at the woman behind the table. "What do you want for it?"

"What do you have?" she asked.

"Give me an idea what you need, and I'll see if I can come up with it."

"Ammunition would be good. I have a pistol, but only have a few bullets for it."

"What caliber?" I asked.

"Nine-millimeter."

"How about fifty rounds?"

She looked shocked. "Deal!"

I took a mag from my pistol belt and asked, "You got something to put them in?"

The woman produced a small purse and said, "Drop them in there."

I proceeded to strip rounds from the mags on my belt until there were fifty in the small bag. "Alright, that should do it."

"It's a nice bracelet," the woman said, "but things that look nice just aren't that important to me these days."

"Thank you so much," Mel said. She'd already put the piece on and was admiring it.

"You're welcome. Enjoy it. Looks pretty on you."

As we walked back toward the truck, Mel wrapped an arm around mine. "Thank you," she said, admiring the bracelet. "I know it's kind of silly in today's world. But I always wanted one and it's so pretty."

"You deserve it, baby."

She rested her head against my shoulder. "Thank you."

I called the girls, who were all gathered around a checkerboard with other kids. They left the game and came running over. As I helped them into the truck, Little Bit said, "All the kids asked if they could go for a ride in the truck."

I laughed. "Not today. But maybe one day we'll come up and take them for a ride."

"That would be fun!"

"Up you go," I said as I hefted her up into the bed. Ruckus was up now and running around on her. The little paracord harness and leash I made for her kept the rodent from getting away.

As we were about to leave, one of the Army Hummers pulled into the parking lot. Daniels was behind the wheel and pulled up beside the truck.

"Hey Morgan."

"What's up?"

"Merryweather wanted me to let you guys know we have a motor pool set up. You can bring your trucks in and get them serviced."

"No shit? That's great. I'll let the old man know."

"We even have some parts and filters and all for the Hiluxes as well. So, when the time comes, bring it on in."

"Awesome, thanks, man."

He waved and put the truck in reverse and backed away. Mel looked over and said, "I guess things really are changing if we can get oil changes."

"It does indeed seem that way," I said as I pulled out.

We headed back toward the house and saw the guys returning from the sawmill turn out on the road in front of us. I knew they had Dylan with them. "Let's stop by and see Gena."

"Oh, that'd be so nice!"

I followed the Hummer as it turned off onto the little lane that led to their house. Dad was driving the Hummer and swung wide to get turned around with the generator attached. I pulled up beside them and stopped.

"Nice wheels," Dad said with a big smile.

"Yours is pretty nice too," I laughed back.

Dad revved the engine a little. "So weird being in a truck again."

"Sure beats walking all to hell!"

Mel got out as Dylan did and walked to the house. Gena was already coming out and the two women met in the yard where they shared a hug. The girls all piled out of the bed and ran over as well. Gena greeted each one with a hug and said something that got them all excited, and they disappeared into the house.

"How'd your day go?" I asked Dad.

"Good. Got a lot cut today. We'll take a truck to bring it back tomorrow."

"Nice. We get that done and get that heifer used to going in there and we can start milking her."

"With all the youngins running around here, milk would be great."

The door to the house burst open and the girls poured out. Little Bit was shouting, "We have strawberries!" Mel and Gena came out, each carrying a bucket. Little Bit ran over with a large berry in her hand and strawberry on her face. "Try it, Daddy, they're so good!"

She handed me a half-eaten berry and I popped the top off and tossed it in my mouth. "Wow, that's a good strawberry."

"They're so yummy!"

"We're gonna get back. See you at the house," Dad said as he put the truck in gear.

"Alright, see you there," I said.

Mel and Gena talked for a few more minutes as I got the girls into the truck. They had a small bag of berries they were sharing, which kept them happy. Mel hugged Gena and I waved at Dylan. He was sitting on the porch taking his boots off. Seeing him in shoes was unusual in the first place, as he was usually barefoot. The relief on his face was obvious and it made me laugh.

When Mel started toward the truck, I waved bye to Gena, and we headed home.

"Look at all these berries," Mel said as she inspected the bucket in her lap. Another was in the backseat.

"They're really sweet," I said.

"Gena grew them in her greenhouse."

"What are we going to do with them?" I asked,

"I'm going to talk to Kay and see what we can do. Shortcake would be nice, but we don't have any whipped cream."

"Still be good without it."

Taking a bite of a berry, she said, "Yes it would. We'll make a dessert for everyone."

Back at home, the girls settled into the living room to watch a movie. After a long day out, they were ready to do what kids do best: nothing. Mel took the berries over to Danny's and I dropped into a chair on the porch to relax for a bit. The dogs were lounging in the yard in patches of sunlight that made it through the thick canopy of trees above. Then I realized something was missing and quickly went inside.

Returning with a glass of tea, I took my previous position and put my feet up on the rail. Now this was relaxing. Since The Day, our world had become quiet. All the noise that had filled the modern world was wiped out for the most part. All that was left were the sounds of the natural world, and the natural world is pretty quiet. I'd become accustomed to the silence and enjoyed it. In The Before, I didn't like the quiet and sought out noise, so much so that I even slept with a white noise generator.

Now, however, I did seek the silence. After a day of being in a truck or in town, I was ready to get back out here to the oasis of tranquility this little place had become. Humans had developed a world full of overstimulation. Our senses had been constantly bombarded, and this had caused our brains to adapt to the new environment. We had begun to lose our primal senses as a result of it. Removing the stimuli allowed our brains to reset. To get back a little of their capabilities.

With this in mind, I sat and listened to what I could hear. Closing my eyes, I laid my head back. The wind sighed lightly in the trees. Oak leaves fell like a quiet rain, making more of a ticking sound than a drop splashing. The shrill call of a blue jay added to the rhythm. Somewhere in the distance, a dog barked. Opening my eyes, I looked at Meathead and Drake. Both raised their heads and looked lazily around. If they weren't bothered, neither was I.

A rustle in the trees got my attention and I watched a squirrel make its way through the canopy of one of the oaks. Other than man, all of nature's creatures lived an existence of absolute freedom. They could go where they wanted, do as they pleased. Of course, this came with a price tag. They were solely responsible for their lives. For continuing them and for sustaining them. If they did not acquire the food they needed, they died. If they weren't aware of their surroundings, they could be killed and consumed by another beast. This was an immutable fact for all life. Except humans decided none of that applied to us. We rejected the notion that we're nothing more than another beast walking the face of this Earth. We were better than that.

Terry stood under the transformers with a long telescoping insulated pole in his hand. The top of the pole had a simple hook on it, and he'd managed to catch the small eye on the top of the fuse holder hanging from the switch. He looked over at Audie and got a thumbs up. Terry gripped the pole and, using his knees, slammed the switch closed. There were two more to do, as this was a commercial three-phase service.

Turning the power back on a circuit is a difficult job. The entire circuit needed to be inspected to make sure it's complete and there are no downed wires. All transformers on the circuit needed to be opened. When the power went out, people didn't go around turning things off. Lord only knows what was left running, and where. The possibility of fire was huge, so a great deal of effort went into making sure everything was ready before a circuit was reenergized.

In this case, the primary (or high voltage) cable running on the power poles was actually cut just past the fab shop. There was nothing past it that would need to be energized, so it was faster to cut the cable and roll it up against the next pole downstream, thereby eliminating the possibility of an accident.

Terry slammed the last switch closed and gave Audie a thumbs up. Audie walked around the outside of the shop to the main disconnect located by the power meter and flipped the big breaker on. Then he went inside to the distribution panel and turned the main there on as well before flipping two breakers labeled "Lights." The metal halide lamps in the fixtures over his head sparked and popped, and he could hear the transformers in them start buzzing as they heated up. The lamps slowly grew in intensity until the shop was filled with bright light.

Audie flipped a couple more breakers, then walked around the shop testing equipment. Everything he tried worked and a sense of relief washed over him. Turning, he looked at Baker. "Looks like we're good!"

"Fantastic!"

Scott came in and looked at the panel, then flipped another two-pole breaker on and went back outside. He returned a moment later. "Water is on."

"The well pump works?" Audie asked, even as the sound of the toilet in the shop's bathroom started to gurgle and chug as the tank filled.

"Sure does!"

Audie looked over his shoulder into the bathroom and laughed. "Guess so!"

He walked into the admin office for the shop and looked around. The office area was large and had a bathroom in it that included a small shower. Against the back wall of the shop was a small kitchen area with a little apartment-sized range with an oven. Standing in the middle of the room he turned in a slow circle, taking it all in.

Walking back out to Baker, he said, "I think I'm going to move over here. I'm gonna be here all the time anyway. There's a small kitchen in there and another bathroom with a shower. This will be perfect for me."

"Works for me. Be good having you closer."

"I'll bring Kim out here and let her see it. We like it at the ranch, but having our own space would be really nice."

Baker looked over her shoulder at Scott and Terry. "Tell me about it."

Supper that night was a joyful experience. Everyone was in a good mood. Maybe it was the supplies coming in. Maybe it was the strawberry shortcake we had for dessert. Maybe it was both of these and more. A sense of change was growing stronger and stronger, and everyone felt it. I sat across from Mel with my back to the screen enclosing the porch and could see nearly everyone.

CHAPTER 7

Slowly chewing a mouthful of food, I looked around at the people gathered there.

Aric and Fred were there. The babies were sleeping peacefully in a portable crib in the living room. The voices were all mindful of the infants just inside the house and kept low. Thad was smiling broadly. Mary was saying something to Fred and Thad listened intently. Mike and Crystal sat with Ted and Janice, Doc and Jess. The three couples talked and laughed. Mom and Dad sat at a table with Danny, Sarge, and Miss Kay. Dalton sat with Karl, Imri, and Chad. Travis and Erin sat their kids at our table. Smiles were on all the faces.

"What's the matter?" Mel asked me.

Snapping back to the moment, I said, "Oh, nothing. Just watching everyone have a good time."

Mel turned around as Little Bit let out a loud laugh. Sarge had her cradled in his arms like a baby for a moment before he put her upright on her feet, announcing, "That's all the play an old man has, sweetheart."

Mel looked back and smiled, then reached across the table and gripped my hand and winked. I smiled back and returned to my meal. After finishing a wonderful meal, coffee was brought out and our usual informal planning session kicked off.

"Mikey!" Sarge barked. "You and Crystal find a place yet?"

"We're still looking."

"I have an idea on that. Would make things easier for all of you," Kay said.

Sarge looked at her. "What is it?"

Kay smiled and slid a little closer to him. "You could just move in here. Then they could stay in the house with the girls."

"That's a great idea!" Mikey called out.

The look on the old man's face was priceless. He certainly hadn't expected that. For a moment, no one said anything. Then

Thad spoke up. "Come on Linus, make an honest woman out of Miss Kay!" The comment was greeted with a chorus of cheers.

Sarge dropped his chin and shook his head. When he looked up, Kay was staring at him.

"Well?" he asked, "Is that what you want?"

Her eyes welled up with tears as she nodded a yes.

He leaned over and kissed her, a rare public display, and said, "Then of course I will."

The dam broke and the tears fell. Kay wrapped her arms around the old man's neck and hugged him tight as the porch exploded in shouts, hoots, and cat calls. The cheering was interrupted by the cries of a baby from the house.

Sarge jumped to his feet. "Now you've all done it! Woke them babies up!"

Fred and Aric quickly got up and headed for the house. Fred stopped and patted Sarge on the shoulder, then leaned over and kissed him on the cheek. "It's ok. It's for a good reason, and they need to eat anyway."

"Hey, Sarge," I said, and he looked over. "Merryweather has a motor pool set up and says they can service our trucks. Might want to run them down there one at a time and get that done." I was tossing him a bone to get the attention off him.

"That's good news. They sure as hell need it!"

Fred and Aric came back out on the porch, each holding a squirming infant. Fred sat down and started to nurse one of the babies and I waved Aric over, motioning to the table where Karl was sitting. He took a seat with the baby over his shoulder as he gently patted its back.

"Karl, Aric here is going to be in overall charge of the militia. I was hoping you guys would assist him. No offense to you, you're just new to me and I've known him for some time now."

"No problem, Morgan. I wouldn't want to be in charge anyway. But I will be happy to help you form the militia. Anything we can do to help, we're ready."

"You guys will have to provide the training for them and help him with forming it all up. We essentially have to build this from scratch."

Karl laughed. "No we don't. The government spent a lot of time and money teaching me how to go into a country and do this very thing. I already have the plan."

"Awesome," I said. "Then I'll leave you alone to discuss this."

"Is there some strawberry shortcake? Thought I heard something about shortcake," Chad asked, looking around and rubbing his belly.

"I'll check on it," I said as I got to my feet.

"I'm gonna pitch in with them," Dalton said.

"Sounds good to me. You guys let Aric know what you need, and we'll do what we can to make it happen. We'll pull weapons from the commie armory for now. Unless DOD wants to send us a bunch."

"We've got a lot to do until then," Karl said.

"I'll leave you to it, then."

I walked over to where Thad was sitting and stopped behind him, putting my hands on his shoulders. He looked up at me and smiled the way he always does. It faded quickly when I started to speak.

"Can I get everyone's attention, please?"

The porch quieted down and all eyes were on me. "Just want to let everyone know, Thad is now the Lieutenant Governor of Florida."

The reaction was animated, though muted. The smile that faded from Thad's face had returned as everyone began to congratulate him. People were getting up and going over to shake his hand and pat his back. Mary sat beside him just beaming, though I thought I detected a little uncertainty in her. Sarge walked over to stand beside me, taking in the scene.

He slapped me on the back, saying, "Damn good call, Morgan."

"Looks like the lazy days are behind us now," I said.

Sarge laughed. "Lazy days? Where the fuck have you been?"

"Hey man, I think you and Miss Kay living here together is a really good thing."

"It's time," he said, then looked over at me. "Trust me, not the first time she's brought it up."

"What took you so long, then?"

"I wanted to make sure Danny was ok with it first. This is his house, after all."

"I don't mind," Danny said from behind us.

We looked back and Sarge asked, "You sure?"

"Of course. You two can have the master down here. Your own bathroom and all."

Sarge smiled, another rare public display. "Thanks, Danny."

Danny shrugged. "We're family, man."

"We are, aren't we," said Sarge.

"Tomorrow I'm going up to Juniper," I said to Sarge.

"What in the hell for? We were just there."

"Audie mentioned their food situation. I'm going to go up and show them plants they can eat, how to collect and process them."

Sarge grunted. "Well, you did a lot to keep us in groceries when we lived on the river. They could probably use the help."

"That's what I thought. Mel is going with me."

"I'm sending someone out tomorrow to recon the group at the lake. I want to get that handled and soon."

"Who's going?" I asked.

CHAPTER 7

"Not sure, might just send Dalton and Karl."

"If Karl goes, Imri will go as well."

"That's fine with me. He is a lot like Dalton. There's a lot of unanswered questions to that story."

I looked over at Imri, then said, "I like him. Seems like a nice enough guy."

"That's not what I mean. He's a good man, I have no doubt about that. But like Dalton, I sense an incredible capacity for violence in him." He looked me in the eye. "I can just feel it. And it makes me happy. Glad to have him here with us."

Kay came out of the house with a large pan and placed it on a table. "Anyone want shortcake?" The reply was unanimous and immediate.

Mel laid out a stack of bowls and Mom brought out a tote full of silverware. People began to line up and Kay served them. I guess all those years in school cafeterias made for some hard to break habits.

When Sarge got to her, he asked, "Is this all of it?"

"I have a smaller one inside for the men at the bunker as well."

Sarge smiled. "You're a good woman, Kay."

Kay looked at him, arching her eyebrows. "About time you realized it."

He leaned over and kissed her on the cheek. "Oh, trust me, I've known all along."

Dad was right behind Sarge and said, "Tell me we have coffee to go with this."

Sarge spun around to face him. "Butch, we always have coffee!"

Dessert was enjoyed by all. It was the perfect ending to a good day.

CHAPTER 8

I'd made plans with Mom the night before so Mel and I could sneak out early. Today was going to be rather routine around the ranch. The old man was moving his things into Danny's, and Janice and Crystal were moving their things into the house with the guys. Other than a recon of the group on the lake, there wasn't anything special going on.

I grabbed the bottle of tea I poured the night before from the fridge as Mel came out of the bedroom. We were quiet as we stepped toward the door. Mel leaned over and dropped a note onto the couch telling the girls to go see Grandma when they woke up. But Mom would probably be there before they did.

In silence we rolled up Highway 19 in the cool early morning air. The sky was clear and bright. The sun was just getting up over the trees on our right, and as Mel looked out, she shielded her eyes with her hand.

"It's so pretty," she said.

"It is. I see it almost every day."

"How can you under all the trees? There's really nowhere you can see the sky."

"I don't know. I didn't mean I see the sun every day. Just that I see the sun rise every day."

She laughed again. "Isn't that the same?"

I shrugged. "Perspective."

She laughed once again and reached across the bench seat and took my hand. I squeezed hers and looked at her. She was enjoying the scenery as it zipped past. I looked down and saw I was doing nearly seventy. Not that there was a speed limit, I just didn't want the moment to end. If it wasn't for the body armor and weapons, this little ride would feel perfectly normal.

However, all good things must come to an end, and it wasn't long before we were pulling through the gate. The same woman came out of her kiosk/house and rang the old bell as we passed by. Vincent was waiting in the parking lot when I pulled in, a look of mild confusion on his face.

"Hey," he said, "didn't think we'd see you again so soon."

"Audie said you guys could use some instruction on edible plants around here. Sorry, I didn't think of that before."

"No, no, you're fine. I'm just really happy you came out here to do it! We really could use some advice."

"We can take a couple of canoes and go down the river and I can show you what I know."

"That'd be great. Let me grab a few of my folks that really need to be there."

"We'll meet you guys down by the boats."

As we walked down to the water, Mel took it all in. "This place is so pretty. I miss coming here."

"Looks a little different now," I said, looking at a group of people thatching in the side of one of the pavilions.

"Yeah, but what a place. To have all this and call it home."

"You remember living out there, right?" I asked.

"I'll admit, it wasn't as comfortable as being at home."

"We even had little houses. These guys, some of them are sleeping in these pavilions. Not exactly comfortable."

Vincent's people made their way down to the launch. Canoes were slid into the water and soon we were gliding out into the crystal-clear springs. The surface was almost perfectly flat. The only visual way to even know the water was there was because of the swaying of aquatic plants below the surface.

Mel looked back over her shoulder. "This is really nice. I miss being on the water."

"What? You hate canoes!"

"Well, I haven't done this in a while."

"Shit, I'm surprised we're still in the damn boat! You used to be able to turn one of these over just by looking at it!"

"Yes, yes I could," she said.

We glided up beside Vincent and I asked, "Are you guys harvesting anything from the river?"

"Clams and mussels. No one knew about plants, so we didn't want to make anyone sick."

I pointed at a patch of cattails. "Let's get everyone over there."

There were four boats all told and we gathered together in front of a thick stand of the long thin green leaves. "You all probably know this is cattail. It can provide several kinds of food."

I went on to describe how to collect the roots and process them for starch. How to find the rhizomes and what to do with them, as well as how to collect the hearts as a potherb. The last part of the discussion covered the flowering head and how it can be eaten.

A woman was looking at a dried brown flower head and asked, "You're supposed to eat this like corn on the cob?"

I laughed. "No, no. You can eat them like that when they're green. Right now, you can collect the pollen. You need a bag or something. Just pull them over and stick the head in the bag and shake them to knock the pollen off. No need to cut the heads off. Then sift the pollen for any foreign debris and it's ready to use."

"So, could we mix this with the starch from the roots?" a man asked.

"Yes, mix it with cattail starch or even ground acorn meal."

"Ground acorn meal?" the woman asked.

"I'll show you that when we get back. Right now, paddle over there towards that palm tree," I said, pointing across the river.

I worked the boat in between the rest of them, with one side against the high bank. "Ok, you see this plant with the arrowhead leaf?" I didn't wait for a reply. "The leaf is the big giveaway and so is the white flower. This is called Wapato and is a lot like potatoes."

Stabbing a paddle down into the mud, I explained the process. "The native tribes would wade into the river and use their feet to dislodge the tubers. I like to use a paddle. These will be really productive later in the fall." I raked the paddle around in the mud, stirring it up.

Some small tubers began to float to the surface and were collected. Seeing my success, the others began using their paddles to grub for tubers as well. The patch was productive and there were tubers floating all around in no time, all of which were carefully collected.

"There sure are a lot of them," Vincent said, using a paddle to scoot some tubers within reach.

"Just don't hit the same spot over and over," I said. "With wild edibles you can completely wipe a colony out. So make a mental note of where they are and kind of when you hit them. Give it some time to recover."

"That's a good idea," Vincent groaned as he leaned over and scooped up some taters. "Look at all this. Between these and the cattail, what did you call it?"

"Cossack's Asparagus," I replied.

Vincent held up the growing inner heart of one. "Doesn't look like much."

"Maybe not, but you can eat it. Has kind of a peppery taste. I like it."

Tossing it back into the boat, he asked, "What else can we eat?"

"Let's head down the river and I'll look."

Easing over to the edge of the bank, I waved the others over. "This is a good one," I said as I reached down and lifted some stalks of the plant from the water. "This is watercress and a very good potherb. You can cook this like you would any other leafy green. Just remember what I said about overharvesting; you can wipe it out quickly and it won't return."

At a wide spot in the river, just past the bridge for the county road, I spun the boat around to face those coming downstream. "See these two plants?" I pointed them out. "You can also eat the lily pads. Every part of them is edible. If you dig up the roots you can process them like you do cattails, but the flavor isn't very good."

"No, it ain't!" a woman called out. "We tried to bake one, couldn't even chew a single bite of it!"

"They're pretty bitter, that's for sure," I laughed back.

"I ain't eatin' it. That bite of the root was enough for me."

"I promise, the leaves and flowers don't taste like that. That's another thing, you can make a good tea out of the flower. But this one," I pointed to the other, "is Hemlock. As in Poison Hemlock. While every part of the lily is edible, every part of this—the leaves, stems, flowers, and even the roots—are very poisonous. And this isn't the only poisonous plant around. Be very careful what you attempt to eat."

"Other than what you have shown us, how can we tell if something is edible?" Vincent asked.

"There's what's called the 'universal edibility test,' but I don't recommend it. It takes a long time, and you can still get sick."

"Is there anything out here you can smoke?" a man called out.

Turning to see him, I replied, "Actually, there is. It's not here but it's in your camp."

The man's face fell. "In our camp? It's been there the whole time?"

"Sorry," I chuckled, "but yeah."

"Well Sheriff, just as soon as we get back, you gotta show me."

We paddled a little further until I saw an orange tree like the one on the Alexander Run. "Have you guys tried the oranges?" I asked.

The same woman that wasn't a fan of lotus roots spoke up again. "They're *sou-ar*. They don't never get ripe."

"No, they're sour oranges. Think of them like a lime or lemon. We found another one on the banks of the Alexander Run. These are truly wild oranges."

"I ain't never heard of sou-ar oranges, Sheriff."

"Well, they're a thing. You can use them to season food. Like that rice we brought you, use it on that. Or you could make ceviche, catch some fish and filet them out and add juice from the oranges, cover them in it. The citrus juice basically cooks the fish."

"I don't eat no raw fish," a man called out from another boat.

"It's not raw, the juice—," I waved him off, "never mind."

"I'm sure you all know about the cabbage palm?" I asked.

"If it wasn't for that, we'd have starved to death over the winter," said the cantankerous woman.

We ventured ashore and I showed them more plants that they could use, like green briar.

Using a digging stick, I was at work uncovering the rhizomes and setting them out. "Process this just like you would cattail. This starch turns pink when exposed to the air, so don't let that throw you."

"Where'd you learn all this, Sheriff?" a man in his sixties asked.

"I got into this stuff when I was a kid. Making baskets and waterproofing them, making traps and snares. Learned how to make fire with nothing but what I could find on the land."

"Not for me," the woman interjected. "I don't want to be rubbing sticks together."

"Look around you," I scoffed. "The entire world is that way now. There are no more grocery stores. Just like every other animal on this planet, you have to go out and earn your food now. And these things I've shown you will help. Shit, a hundred years ago, every child in this area would know these things."

She swatted at a bug on her calf. "This isn't the life I want to live."

"We'll it's the life you have. What are you gonna do? Lie down and wait for it to all go back to normal? I have a mantra I live by: Ain't dead, can't quit."

She was rubbing at a welt on her leg where a deer fly had bitten her. "No, it's just this shit! Damn bugs everywhere. Not enough to eat. No place that is really dry." She vigorously rubbed at the bite. "And then this shit!"

We were standing in a small clearing that was part of a habitat transition area. On our left was a low oak hammock with cypress trees closer to the river. On the right were sparsely spaced sand pine with palmettos choking the ground beneath. I looked down in the little clearing and spotted a broadleaf plantain.

Pulling it up, I stripped the leaves from it and held them out to her. "Here, chew these up into a paste and put it on the bite."

"That's disgusting," she recoiled.

"It'll stop the pain, promise."

With a great deal of undue suspicion, she brought the leaves up to her mouth, giving one a tentative lick. Finally putting them in her mouth, she chewed them like a two-year-old might a brussel sprout. After chewing it, she messily took it from her mouth and propped her foot up on a stump and pressed the mass to it.

As green juice ran down her leg, she asked, "How long do I need to hold it there?'

"Take that bandanna off your head and tie it around it. It'll stop hurting." I looked around at the group. "This plant," I'd pulled another one and held it up for everyone to see, "works on any kind of a bite or sting. You can eat it too; the leaves are just a little stringy."

"Let's head back, Sheriff," one of the men said. "You still need to show us what we can smoke!"

As we paddled back, I was in no hurry and let the rest of the boats get ahead of us. Mel leaned back with her feet up on the bow, dragging the fingers of her right hand in the water. It was so peaceful on the river. Only the raucous call of the occasional blue jay broke the cadence of the paddle dipping into the clear water.

Without looking back, Mel asked, "Can we stop at that wide spot where it was so shallow?"

I nosed the canoe into the old beach that was in constant use before The Day. But it was empty, and the Ocala Forest was working to reclaim it. I had to use my knife to cut some limbs out of the way just so we could get out.

We slipped our boots off and rolled our pants up. Holding hands, more to steady one another than anything, we stepped out into the cool water.

"Shit!" Mel shouted, "That's cold!"

"Feels good, quit yer bitchin'."

Mel leaned over to dip her hands in the water and the Minimi slipped from her shoulder and dunked into the river. She gasped and quickly pulled it out.

CHAPTER 8

"You don't have to worry about that thing, baby. Little water isn't going to hurt it."

She looked at the weapon. "I guess that's true. Not like there's anything on here water can mess up." Then she looked around as she wiped the cool water on her face. "We need to bring the kids down here for the day. I think they would really like it."

"Why don't we just take them to Alexander? It's closer and there may not even be anyone there."

"That's true. Can we go look on our way home?" she asked.

"Sure, let's get back up the river though. It's gonna be a whole lot harder in a couple of places."

We made it back to camp and I was happy to see Vincent's people unloading a large mass of cattail roots as well as other plants. The old fellow that asked about what he could smoke was waiting at the takeout when the canoe ground into the sand.

After helping Mel out, I looked at him and said, "Come on. I know what you want."

"I haven't had a smoke in months. Got lucky a couple of times and found one or two here or there. But it's killing me not to be able to smoke," the man said.

"Well, this was actually proposed as a cash crop back in the sixties. And it makes a good tobacco substitute."

I walked out toward the parking lot as I knew what I was looking for grew in disturbed soil. It didn't take long to find it either. Pointing it out, I said, "There it is."

"Spanish needles?" he asked, surprised.

"Yep, you can also eat it. Cook it like spinach and it's very good for you. The Latin name is Biden's Alba."

"How do you smoke it?"

"Just dry it out, grind it up and smoke it."

The man pulled a few leaves off and twisted them in his fingers, sniffing it suspiciously. "You sure about that?"

"Yes, sir, I am. It's not going to be like regular tobacco, but it'll scratch that itch."

Gesturing with it suspiciously, he asked, "You ever smoke it?"

"I only smoke cigars on occasion."

The man dropped to his knees and began stripping the leaves from the small bush. "Well, I'm about to find out!"

With that task out of the way, I looked around for Mel and found her sitting near the swimming area with a few ladies. They were watching several kids swim. Walking over, I sat down beside her on the low stone wall.

"I can't believe you carry that thing," one of the women said.

Mel looked at the machinegun. "I like it. Makes me feel safe."

"Have you had to use it?" another woman asked.

"No, not yet, thankfully. Only in training."

Seeing me take a seat, one of the women said, "Thank you for showing us what you did today. That will really help. We knew you could eat some stuff, like the cattail, but no one here knew how or what."

"I hope it helps. Should have done it sooner is all."

With a dismissive wave, she said, "Don't worry about it. We appreciate what you've done. You brought food, bullets, even brought doctors out."

"Don't forget about the shoes!" another woman announced.

The only one not to speak up did so. "You have no idea how much those shoes mean to us. My boys haven't had shoes in months."

"We're trying to get more help out here for you folks."

"You think you'll be able to get us power?" one of the women asked.

"We're working on it. It'll take a while. We have to completely engineer it and see if we can even find the parts we'll need."

"I don't really miss it," one of the women said.

The woman with the two boys added, "It is nice they are always outside now. Not sitting in the house playing video games."

"Yeah," another said, "because we live outside now!"

"That's how it is in most of the world," I chimed in. "People live outside and only sleep inside. It's only in the West where we live our lives inside—in boxes."

"In boxes?" one of them asked.

"Yeah," I replied and pointed at the pavilion being covered in thatch. "Look at that. It's a box." I pointed to the concession stand. "That's a box too. Now, look around at the woods, see any right angles? Any squares or rectangles?"

"I never thought of that."

"Right angles, perfect right angles, just don't happen in nature. We humans build with the method because it's easier. Look at the old Roman aqueducts, all the supports were arches. It's naturally stronger but harder to construct. We're not meant to live in boxes."

"Sheriff, you mentioned acorn meal earlier. Can you elaborate on that?" one of the women asked.

"Oh, sure. It's pretty easy, actually. Simply collect a bunch of acorns and put them into a cloth sack, a pillowcase is perfect, and put them in the spring. Leave them there for several days. This will leach out the tannic acid that makes them so bitter. Then you can put them into a container and pound them into a mush. Pour water into it and stir it around. The shells will float to the top and you can remove them. Pour off the water and let it dry in the sun. You can then pound it into a powder or store it however you like. Use it kind of like flour. You can make a decent bread from acorn and cattail meal."

The woman sat there, her mouth open for a second. "That is amazing. I mean, they're everywhere and we had no idea how to eat them. We tried—," another woman cut her off. The one that wasn't a fan of her current lifestyle.

"And they were awful!"

"No one could even get one down," the first woman added.

I laughed at the thought. "Yeah, they are pretty rough until you soak them." Then I remembered something I probably should share with them. "One more thing, before putting them into the sack to soak them, put them in a bucket or something and fill it with water. Any that float you'll want to discard. They have a small larva in them, acorn weevil grubs."

"That's disgusting," the complaining woman replied.

I shrugged. "They're good protein."

She was horrified. "What!" Shaking her head, she added, "No way in hell I'm eating a worm."

"They're not worms. They're just larvae."

"It's the same thing!"

I looked her in her eyes and said, "Then you have never been truly hungry. Because you will eat the bark off the trees when you're starving." Looking at the ladies, I added, "Don't forget the hickory nuts. You can treat them just like acorns, it's called Pawcohiscora and is a valuable source of fat, one of the hardest things to find in nature."

One of the women was shaking her head and with a raise of my eyebrows I asked her, "What?"

"How in the world do you know all this weird shit?"

"Well, there was a time when you had access to the answer to literally any question you could ever have. That and books."

"Lots of books," Mel added.

We sat and chatted with the ladies for a while. I watched as the old fella dying for a smoke laid the leaves he'd collected on a grate over a smoldering fire. He wasn't about to wait for them to dry. After chatting a little longer, we said our goodbyes and headed back for the truck.

"Can we take the road through the forest on the way home?" Mel asked. We were holding hands as we walked.

"Sure. Haven't been out that way since we hit the camp. We'll take a look at it on our way by."

We headed east on Highway 40 for a little way before turning right onto Forest Road 37. It runs straight north-south through the forest just to the west side of the bombing range. I couldn't help but think of my walk through the area as we drove.

"When I was on my way home, I walked through here," I said.

The truck hit a particularly large rut and bounced both of us out of our seats. Hitting my head on the roof, I rubbed the knot.

"Slow down!" Mel shouted as she tried to get the Minimi back between her legs.

"Ya think?" I asked, laying the sarcasm on thick.

With the truck now crawling along, Mel asked, "You walked through here?"

I laughed at the memory. "Yeah, met a bear on the trail in the dark. That was interesting."

"What is with you and bears? There was the one in the house and now one out here? How many times have you crossed paths with a bear?"

I thought about it for a minute as I counted them off on my fingers. Looking at five fingers, I replied, "Looks like five."

She laughed. "Oh yeah, the one at Grasshopper Lake with the kids."

"And the one that climbed up to my tree stand while I was hunting."

"That's four. Where was the fifth?"

"Oh, that one came out of a dumpster. Scared the shit out of me. It had a ripped open trash bag in its mouth and strung garbage all over the place as it ran away. I think by the time it got to the tree line, all it had was the bag."

"Imagine the disappointment when it realized all it could do was lick the bag."

Her reply made me laugh as I imagined a bear lying in the woods licking God knows what off a trash bag from a dumpster.

"That is a disgusting thought," I said, shaking my head.

She was getting a kick out of it. "Yeah, hot garbage juice!"

I waved my hand in front of my face as if I was trying to keep the smell of the thought from assaulting my nose. "That's enough of that."

I can handle strong smells. Even very unpleasant ones. I knew what burnt flesh smelled like. It's an aroma that will stay with you. But the worst thing I ever smelled was a drowning victim that had been in the water for several days. Just the thought of that made me gag, physically. Naturally this made Mel laugh.

"Oh, come on. It's only garbage!"

"Not every time."

This part of the Ocala Forest in particular is a rather hostile place to live. There isn't much in the way of food sources. The soil in the area is almost universally sand that in places is pure white and would be a great resource for masonry or use in cement. For growing food, however, it just wasn't in the cards. Early pioneers called it The Big Scrub, among other less pleasant things—a name that stands to this day.

The predominant tree in the forest is the sand pine. Long of trunk with a natural curve, depending on wind direction and angle of growth, with short evergreen needles, they are perfect for log construction. The bark is paper thin, and the cambium layer was a food source for natives of the area in times of hunger. Today, however, well, in The Before, they were harvested for pulpwood for paper mills. The seeds of the small papery cones are food for birds and to a lesser degree, squirrels.

The sand pine was a prime example of how the Federal Government would take advantage of *public* lands. It was illegal to cut any living plant in a national forest. You had to have a permit to harvest firewood and could only collect downed wood from the ground. Meanwhile, the feds contracted with timber companies and sold off thousands of acres of timber from public lands.

The timber companies would come in and decimate an area. It was terrible to see the results of an area that had been cut. Everything was destroyed. Of course, they would quickly return to plant seedlings so they could get another harvest in a few years. But it really demonstrated the lunacy behind federal laws like simply cutting plants in a national forest.

Under the tall canopy of the pines are scrub oaks. This broad name contains several varieties, with the dominant being the turkey oak. These are small trees, with a tall one being twenty-five or so feet. The leaves of this red oak variety have extreme points, giving them the appearance of a turkey track, as opposed to the lobed leaves of the white oaks. The acorns it produces are very high in tannic acid and extremely bitter. Nonetheless, they are an important food source for deer and other wildlife.

"I remember the days we would take the girls out here for rides in the woods," Mel said, then, with a sly look, added, "and when we'd come out here."

Smiling, I said, "Yeah, the good ole days."

I had to drive rather slowly. Forest roads were a challenge even in The Before. After a year without even the meager maintenance that was provided for them, they were rough to say the least. Before, the roads would be rutted after rains by the locals running out to the woods to splash their trucks through the mud. Now the rain itself did all the work. Deep washouts were everywhere, making for slow going.

I slowed the truck to a stop in front of a substantial washout that cut diagonally across the road about two feet deep. Getting out, we looked into it.

"Can we cross that?" Mel asked.

"Maybe. But I'm not going to try it. If we get stuck, it's a long ass walk home, and I don't feel like doing it again."

We were just below the crest of a hill that the road ran over the top of. Slinging my rifle over my shoulder, I held out my hand and said, "Come on. Let's walk over this and see what it looks like."

We walked through the washout and to the crest of the hill. The road dropped away on a long gentle slope. At the bottom of the hill was another washout. "We're just going to have to turn around, baby," I said.

"We tried," Mel said.

Just as we were turning around to leave, we heard a pop. "What was that?" Mel asked.

I turned and looked back. "Don't know."

Then there was another pop, this one much louder. I saw a splash of dirt in the road about forty meters in front of us, followed by the unmistakable whir of a tumbling bullet passing through the air. Reflexively I crouched, grabbing Mel's arm and pulling her down with me. We were forced to our bellies as more rounds began to crack around us. I raised my rifle, looking through the ACOG.

"Where are these fuckers?" I asked.

Mel already had the Minimi's bipod deployed and had the weapon tight to her shoulder. Glancing over at her, I smiled. She was serious, there was no mirth or sarcasm on her face. Scanning the long road ahead of us, I spotted a figure at the side of the road five hundred-or-so meters away.

"I see him."

"Where?"

Rolling to my side, I dropped the mag from my rifle and pulled one with red electrical tape wrapped around it from a mag pouch on my pistol belt and inserted it into the rifle and chambered it, ejecting the ball round already there.

"Watch where this goes and open up on it. Remember, controlled bursts."

"I'm ready."

Shouldering the rifle, I looked through the optic again. Now there were several people in the road. Mel said she thought she could see them. I took a sight picture, using the hash on the reticle for five hundred meters and fired a shot. The tracer looked like a laser shot from Star Wars as it streaked away. The round missed, impacting behind the people in the road, several of which were standing in the open, firing at us.

"Five hundred meters, aim just over their heads," I said.

No sooner did the words leave my mouth than the Minimi opened up. Damn! I forgot how loud that little bastard was. But Mel was unphased as she sent six round bursts down the road.

"Come up a little higher," I said, and she adjusted her aim.

She was really into it, focused. I was surprised when, between bursts, I heard her talking. With her ears ringing as loud as I'm sure they were, she was talking louder than she probably thought.

"I have," another burst, "the ability to send your ass to the Trinity," another longer burst, "like death when it's after a Kennedy!" More bursts.

The people in the road were no longer running toward us. Instead, they sought the imaginary safety of the bush. I was firing at individual targets as they presented themselves. In less than twenty seconds it was over. There were no more people to be seen and all the firing had stopped.

Mel ceased firing, as there were no more targets, and we sat in silence watching the road. The only sounds, besides the ringing in my ears, were the raucous call of a mockingbird in a nearby tree and the ticking of the barrel on Mel's baby as smoke rose from it.

"Let me have that thing," I said, reaching out for the machinegun.

Mel came off the weapon and I handed her my rifle, which she immediately shouldered and began scanning the road. I shouldered the weapon and sent several long bursts of fire into the woods on either side of the road where we saw the people.

"Looks like they all got away," Mel said.

"Fine by me. They're not shooting at us anymore. I don't care where they went."

"Who do you think they are?"

"Probably people from the camp. Don't think we'll be stopping by today. But we're going to come back, in force, and see what's going on. Let's get out of here."

We crawled back from the crest of the hill before standing up to cross the washout and got back to the truck.

"Get in and reload that thing before we move. I want it ready," I said.

I pulled security while Mel reloaded her weapon, which didn't take long. She was pretty handy with the weapon system. Once she called out she was up, I climbed in and performed a ninety-seven point turn on the narrow, rutted road to get us headed back the way we came.

CHAPTER 8

Making our way back out to Highway 40, I looked over at Mel. "So, uh, what was all that?"

Innocently, she looked over at me. "What?"

"That '*send you to the Trinity*' shit. I thought Karl told you to use '*die motherfucker die.*"

"I don't know. It's a Rob Bailey song that just popped into my head. Why? Was it fucked up?"

Laughing, I said, "No, baby. I was actually very surprised. You didn't panic, freak out, or anything. You simply got to work and did what needed done." I reached over and squeezed her shoulder. "I'm proud of you."

"Thank you," she said, pride painted on her face. "I wasn't really scared to be honest."

"Well, this was a minor thing. They were far away and didn't have any heavy weapons. Trust me, it can be terrifying. But you still did awesome."

"I told you I could do it."

"I know you *can*. I just don't want you *to*." She cut her eyes at me, and I added, "But I gotta admit, it was kinda hot."

She looked down at the weapon between her legs. "This thing is hot!"

"Oh yeah, don't let it get on your leg."

Mel looked out the window for a second, then back at me. "It was such a rush. I mean, it's hard to explain it."

"I know exactly what you're talking about. Terrifying yet exhilarating. The adrenaline dump is a hell of a rush."

As the intersection of Highway 19 approached, I said, "We're going to have to pass the main entrance to the camp. Get your weapon pointed out the window. If anyone shoots at us, it's up to you to suppress them so we can get past."

While maneuvering the weapon, she asked, "Have you ever been shot at out here?"

"No, first time."

I was a little tense as the sign for the Pine Castle bombing range came into view. I moved over into the left lane to give us some distance from the cover of the bush on the right where I felt ambushers would be lying in wait.

"Alright, keep your eyes open," I said, the tension in my voice obvious as I accelerated. But we passed without incident. No shots were fired, and we didn't see anyone.

"I wonder how many people are in there?" Mel mused.

"Don't know. There were quite a few when we pulled out. But I can't imagine there are many still there. There's nothing to eat. This forest," I indicated to either side of the road, "is a very harsh place. Also, we're skipping Alexander. We need to start moving in force, more than one vehicle at a time."

"I totally understand."

We were approaching the turn onto our street when I said, "When we get back, let's get the Suburban. I want to give it to Audie. He's doing so much work he needs wheels."

"That's a good idea. It's just sitting there."

"It's beat to shit but it runs, and he's smart enough to keep it that way. That guy can build anything from nothing."

Mel sat with her head cocked to the side for a moment. "We have some really interesting people around now."

We drove past the bunker and waved at the guys there. As I turned into our gate I said, "Jump into the Suburban and we'll run it over to the ranch."

I dropped Mel by the Suburban and was turning around when I saw Sarge stomping toward me. He was saying something, but I couldn't make it out over the sound of the truck. He stopped where I would have to pass him, hands on his hips, shaking his head. I stopped in front of him and looked at him, saying nothing.

"Where the hell's your radio?" he barked.

I pointed at my plate carrier. "Right here."

Pointing his chin at his chest, he keyed the mic clipped to his carrier and asked, "Where's your radio?"

My radio was silent and I pulled it from its pouch and looked at it. The screen was blank and I tested the power knob. "Guess it's dead."

"Start carrying a spare battery; been trying to get in touch with you for over an hour."

"We were up at Juniper, probably wouldn't have been able to get me up there."

"We're going to fix that. We need to put up a tower to get our antennas on."

I immediately knew where to get them. "I know where there are several. Plus, the power company has one that's two hundred feet tall. If we had a repeater, we could put it up on there."

Sarge shook his head. "If the world hadn't gone to shit, we wouldn't even need it! But it did, so let's work on solutions to our real problems."

As he spoke, Mel pulled up behind me in the Suburban. Sarge looked at her and asked, "Where the hell are you going?"

"Taking the Suburban to Audie. He needs a set of wheels."

"That's a good idea. He's at the metal shop now. Baker said he was going to set up shop there, move in."

"Ok, good spot for him. By the way, we were going to go by the camp today but took some fire on our way in."

"What?" Sarge nearly shouted.

"I was taking a forest road to the back side of the camp. Some people started shooting at us. We returned fire and they ran off. No big deal."

The look on Sarge's face told me he knew something I didn't. "It *is* a big deal. That freak circus is missing from the lake. They moved on and we don't know where."

"Shit."

"Yeah, shit. But we're going to find them."

"We were going to go by Alexander Springs today as well but didn't after that little incident. I think we should pay the camp and the springs a visit in the very near future."

"You have a masterful grasp of the obvious. Must be why you're the governor."

"And you're still a smartass."

Mel honked the horn. Sarge's head snapped up, and he gave her the stink eye.

"Well, I'd love to continue this chat, but some of us got shit to do." Without waiting for a reply, I put the truck in gear and pulled away, leaving the old man fuming. Mel blew him a kiss as we drove by, insult to injury. I know I'll pay for it later.

It was a quick trip to the shop. Audie was inside at work with a broom when we pulled up. Pausing his sweeping, he walked out to greet us.

"Hey Morgan, Mel!"

"Hey Audie," I said.

"What's up?"

I pointed at the Chevy. "Thought you could use some wheels. It's a little beat up, but it runs good, and that Cummins is nearly bulletproof."

Audie walked toward the truck and Mel held the keys out to him. Taking them, he opened the driver's door and looked in before walking around it. "This is awesome, Morgan. Thanks!"

"I figured with all the work you're doing you'll need it, and it's just sitting at the house not doing shit."

"I'm going to kick the rest of that windshield out, if you don't care."

"It's yours now, do what you want with it."

Audie scratched his head. "Where the hell did you find a Suburban with a Cummins?"

CHAPTER 8

I told him the story of finding it on the side of the road for four hundred bucks. He didn't believe me until Mel chimed in, backing my claim.

"Four hundred? That's insane! The motor alone is worth more."

"Yeah, the guy had it under a little carport. Said he wanted to turn it into a chicken coop and needed the space. He got it from an old doctor who ordered it with the Cummins and used it to take his family on road trips."

"Whatever he used it for, good on him." Audie looked the truck over, walking around it. "I'm going to pull the back seats out. I also have a little trailer I'll hook to it. This thing will be a mobile shop in a week." He looked at the Hilux. "That's a damn nice truck."

"The Army brought some in. I got one, somehow."

Audie smiled at me. "You know damn well why you got it." Looking back at the truck, he said, "Nice little 2.8-liter Toyota diesel. Take care of it and it'll run forever."

"It'll give us more mobility, so I'm happy. Hey, uh, don't go out to Juniper until I give you the all clear. We'll be providing an escort for you out there moving forward as well. We went out there this morning and took some fire from the forest on our way back."

"Who was it?"

"Don't know. We were going through the forest to check on the old camp. Never made it there. Might just be people from the camp. But the group out at the lake is gone and we don't know where they went. So no running around alone right now. We should have had an escort ourselves, to be honest."

"I appreciate the truck, Morgan. It will make my life a lot easier."

"You ready to head back?" I asked Mel. She gave me a quick nod and I asked, "Wanna drive?"

"It's been a while since I drove a stick."

"Yeah, decades!"

"Bet I still can."

With a smile, I said, "Let's find out."

"Don't burn that clutch out, Mel!" Audie called out as he got in behind the wheel of the Suburban.

After starting the engine, Mel didn't hesitate and put the truck in reverse, looked over her shoulder, and backed out with ease. Out on the road she put it in gear and went to pull away. But the truck shuddered and stalled. She looked at me and I laughed at her.

"Don't know why, but reverse is always easier. Go ahead, give it another shot."

She got it moving on the second try, and we headed home. As with many skills allowed to go dormant, shifting through the gears came back to her rather quickly. Her efforts became more fluid as we went, and by the time we passed through Umatilla and the market, she was driving smoothly. People waved as we passed, and kids waved and would run as though they were going to chase us. It was humorous and made me think of movie reels of long ago when cars were a new invention and how people would react.

Turning on our road, we stopped at the bunker where Red and Wallner were on duty.

"How do you like my new truck?" Mel asked.

Red whistled. "That *is* a nice little truck."

"How do you like it?" Wallner asked.

"I like it. Smoothest ride I've been in for a long time."

I patted the dash. "It's a great little truck. One thing we don't have to worry so much about breaking down."

"I hear the wait for Triple-A is long as hell," said Red.

"I heard it can take forever," I said with a smile.

CHAPTER 8

"A little bird told me you guys were shot at out in the forest," said Wallner.

"Yeah, they were pretty far away." I patted Mel's leg. "Mel got her Minimi on them pretty quick, and they didn't want any of that."

"Also heard that Tabor's group left the lake," Red said.

"I heard. Don't think it was them, though. We didn't see any vehicles. But the roads were pretty rutted. We were actually stopped and looking at the road when they started to shoot at us. They were about five hundred meters away."

"We'll have to find those assholes," said Red.

"We will," I said, "Next time we won't wait. When we find them, we'll deal with them right away."

"We'll keep an eye on the road," said Wallner. "I'm keeping the burned-out armor on the road manned at night. Just to give us a few additional seconds if someone is coming."

"Good deal. You guys need anything?" I asked.

"We're good," Red answered.

We said our goodbyes and Mel pulled off. We were met in the yard by the dogs, who eagerly wagged their tails and nosed our hands as we got out. I gave them each a little love before heading to the house. The girls were sitting on the living room floor with a mountain of makeup spread out before them.

"Where did you get all of that?" Mel asked.

"We went through houses today and found all this!" said Tammy.

"I'm going to go find Thad," I told Mel.

"Ok," she said as I headed for the door.

I walked over to Danny's and found Sarge's Hummer sitting in front of the porch with the doors and the rear hatch open. Looking in, I saw personal items stacked inside. Sarge came out the door as I walked up the steps.

"You moving in?" I asked.

Sarge stopped and pulled his hat off, scratching his head. "Yeah. That'll give the house to Dumb and Dumber so they can move the ladies in."

"And keep you closer to Miss Kay."

A sudden burst of laughter announced the arrival of a passel of kids that came running around the side of the porch. Jace and Edie were playing with Erin's kids. They screeched and screamed as they ran past us on whatever adventure their little minds had conjured.

"To be a kid again," I said as they passed us.

"Shit, I wouldn't want to be one now," said Sarge.

"Yeah. But you know, they might end up on the best end of all this."

"Maybe."

"Things are looking up for us. With the Army here now, we may really get support and be able to start moving forward."

"We just got to find that asshole Tabor and kill him. Again."

I snorted. "If you'd have done it right the first time, we wouldn't be in this position."

Uncharacteristically, Sarge's reply was subdued. "I know, Morgan. And it bothers me more than I can tell you. If someone gets hurt by them, I don't think I'll be able to forgive myself."

"I'm only fucking with you. It's not your fault."

"The hell it ain't!" He was angry now. "If I sent a squad out with orders to terminate with extreme prejudice some asshole that needs terminating, and they come back and tell me the job is done and then the fucker pops back up? Heads would roll. I have to be accountable as well. It won't work any other way."

I put my hand on his shoulder. "You'll get him this time. Of that I have no doubt. Look at the help you have now. Karl and his guys, Dalton. Tabor's ass doesn't stand a chance."

"They're out looking for him right now."

CHAPTER 8

I hadn't even noticed the two M-ATVs missing. "You send them out in the new trucks?"

Sarge nodded. "We're not going out after that dickhead in soft trucks."

"I'll need two of them tomorrow and another pickup."

"What are you up to?" Sarge asked as he sat down in a rocker.

I dropped into one beside him and said, "I'm going to go check on Alexander Springs. Last time we were there it was empty. I want to see if anyone has moved in. After that I'm going to check on two other springs. They would naturally draw people for the resources they offer and are a logical place to look for people."

"Who are you taking?"

"I wanted to talk to you about that. I was thinking Thad, Danny, Dad, and maybe Red."

"I'll give you Mikey, too." Before I could say anything, he added, "I'm not doing it to get rid of him. I'm doing it because you need him. He's an annoying little shit, but he's damn good at what he does." I could see he was visibly thinking. "You need more people. Good call to take two trucks. But you only need one pickup. We need to establish some SOPs on things. If trucks leave here, they need a minimum crew of three, driver, navigator and gunner. Pick-ups can get away with two but never less."

"Ok, I like that. So, I need eight people then."

"Take Ronnie and Ted too, so you have a doc. This is the first mission like this. I want you to have all the help you might need."

"Agreed."

"Where are these other springs?"

Standing up, I said, "Come on, I'll show you."

We went into the house and I grabbed the gazetteer and sat down at the table. I flipped through the pages until I found what I was looking for and showed Sarge.

"This is Rock Springs." Flipping to another page, I said, "And this is Wekiwa Springs."

Sarge studied the pages for a minute. "Looks awfully crowded around there."

"You are getting into the burbs around Wekiva. But we haven't had any contact with areas outside of the immediate area and we need to start branching out."

"I agree. Just pointing it out. You'll have to be damn careful."

"That's why I want the trucks."

Sarge studied the map a little more, flipping between pages and rubbing his chin as he did. "I'll get with Ted and have him stock the trucks. We'll send you with some extra ordinance in case you come up against a hard target."

"I'm hoping this will be a boring recon."

Sarge looked at me. "Hope is not a plan. Speaking of plan, make one for this. I want a PACE plan in place before you leave. I want primary, alternate, contingency, and emergency routes, and the same for comms."

"Comms might be tough at this distance."

"I'll take care of that on this end. I'll also send you out with an antenna that, should we have problems, you can put up in a tree for a better signal. If we can't stay in communication, then you can't go. Comms are mandatory."

"We're going to have to switch to HF eventually," I said.

"I'm already working on the antennas for it."

"Di-pole?" I asked.

"No, same sloper I sent you home with. You'll also have a NVIS antenna in case that doesn't work."

CHAPTER 8

The sloper antenna is a single strand of wire that is "sloped" in the direction you want to send your message. It's quick and easy, and can be cut to match any frequency so there is no need for a tuner. The NVIS is a near vertical incidence skywave antenna in the form of an inverted V that sends the signal nearly straight up where it bounces off the ionosphere. The reflected signal allows communications inside the *skip* zone of HF. Comms requires a little magic, chicken blood, and tobacco smoke at times.

"That should do it," I said.

"You planning on being gone overnight?"

I shook my head. "No. Not for this."

"Have it in your plan, just in case. Make sure you take plenty of chow and water as well." Sarge sat rocking for a moment, then looked at me and said, "Tell you what. You go to Rock Springs in the morning. I'll have the guys check out Alexander. They're going to be out that way anyway. I want them to check the forest for Tabor and stop by Juniper. So going to Alexander isn't far."

"That would speed things up for me."

"Go knock out your plan so we can go over it after supper tonight. I know this kind of stuff isn't in your wheelhouse, Morgan, but you're putting together an OPORD, or operational order. We need to start doing things the right way. Have you told anyone they are going out tomorrow?" I shook my head. "You need to do that as soon as possible. That's called a WARNO, or warning order. So the men have time to get their gear together and take care of anything they need to before you head out."

"I'll go tell them."

As I stood up, Sarge said, "Some of them are down at the barn. I'll tell my guys." Rising to his feet, he said, "Here, I have something for you."

I followed him into the house, and he went into the downstairs bedroom he would share with Kay. It was a master suite with a full bathroom. Coming out, he thrust a brown canvas covered notebook at me.

"Here, use this for notes and such. I have more notebooks as well. You'll need something to keep notes in."

"Ok, thanks. Good idea."

I walked out the gate and headed the short way down the road to the pasture where the cow was kept. I could hear the guys as I approached. It sounded like they were having a good time. When the barn came into view I was surprised. The construction was nearly done. Not that the structure was complicated or anything, but I thought it would take longer to build than it had.

"Damn you guys are fast!" I said as I opened the gate.

Dad was up on the roof with Travis screwing down the tin. Thad, Aaron, and Danny were on the ground either passing the sheets up or finishing the nailing of the siding. Since plywood was no longer a thing for us, we had to go back to older methods of construction. Clapboard siding is how things used to be done and was the method we employed now.

Starting at the bottom of the wall, the first board was nailed onto the framing. Subsequent boards were nailed above with about a one-inch overhang of the board below. While not airtight, it would shed the rain, and with the tin roof, provide a dry shelter.

"Perfect timing," I said.

"What for?" Danny asked.

"We're going to take a little ride tomorrow to check out some of the other springs. With people congregating at them, we need to check them out. Plus, we're going to start hitting hospitals and places like that as well."

"Sounds good to me. I'd like to get out of here for a little while."

As Danny spoke, Jace and Edie came running through the gate with Erin's kids in tow. Travis looked down at his little ones as they ran about shrieking and laughing. Danny grabbed Edie as she ran by him. Swinging her up into the air, she squealed with laughter. Jace grabbed Danny by a leg and held on for life. Danny dropped Edie to her feet, and she wrapped herself around the other leg. I laughed at Danny as he took exaggerated strides with the two kids hanging on.

"Who all is going?" Thad asked.

"It'll be you, Dad, Danny, Red, Mike, Ted, and Ronnie. That gives us three men per truck and someone riding with me in the Hilux."

"I'll go too," Travis said.

"Cool, giving us a third guy in the Hilux would be good."

"Can we go?" Travis's little girl called out.

"No, baby," he laughed back.

"Where are you going?" she asked.

"For a ride. But you have to stay here."

"I'll have some info for you guys at supper tonight. Route, comms plan and all that," I said.

"You say supper?" Thad asked from the roof where he knelt.

"You hungry, big man?"

He patted his belly. "Am I awake?"

Looking at my watch, I said, "It's getting close to that time. I'll get with you guys at supper."

I left them to get home and try to put this plan together. It annoyed me that I had to actually sit down and put this shit on paper. But at the same time, I knew we needed to start working smarter. We had so much to do now that we couldn't waste time with fuck ups. With that thought in mind, I stopped by Danny's and grabbed the map book.

CHAPTER 9

The house was empty when I got back, and I opened the maps up on the dining table and unzipped the notebook Sarge gave me. Inside, there were two Rite in the Rain pens, a five-inch by seven-inch spiral bound notebook, a clear plastic protractor, and a small plastic ruler. Considering the contents, I added a mechanical pencil I found in a drawer, along with spare lead and a container of red leads as well. Finding a yellow highlighter that seemed to be good, I added it to the pouch.

Sitting down at the table, I started to study the map. The route was pretty easy, and I knew it well. Nonetheless, I wrote it all down, laying the path out, and going so far as to even indicate which direction each turn was—north, south, and so on. I plotted the route to Rock Springs and from there to Wekiwa Springs. Then I simply reversed the track to come back.

Looking it over, something was tickling my brain. Then I remembered the return route should be different. But did it really? We're not fighting a war. We're civilians out looking around. Granted, we won't look like civilians at all. But there were no indications there's a military force, or anyone for that matter, with the ability to take out an armored vehicle. With that thought in mind, I took another look at the map and picked out a quick route back. Well, kind of quick.

With my planning done, I poured myself a glass of tea and went out to the porch. Since sitting in anything with a plate carrier on is profoundly uncomfortable, I took it off and set it in one of the chairs before sitting down. It was late in the day and a haze hung in the air. The dogs were off somewhere, as were Mel and the girls. So it was quiet and I sat enjoying the silence.

But it wasn't long before I heard voices. From the sound of it, it was the guys coming back from the barn. My suspicions were confirmed when I saw Aaron walk into the yard. He went over to his tent and dropped into a camp chair he'd come up with somewhere. There was a folding chair in the corner of the porch, and I grabbed it as I stepped off. Walking over to his tent, I opened the chair and sat down.

"How's it going, Aaron?"

He looked around, then at me. "Good. I guess. I'd like to leave."

"I know and I'm sorry. That radio really messed things up for you."

"Wish I never touched it," he said, shaking his head.

"Hey, this isn't a bad place to be stuck. Good food, don't have to worry about anyone messing with you or your camp. Pretty safe."

"I know, and you're right. I just, I'm just not really into hanging around a lot of people. I like to be on my own."

"Just as soon as we can, we'll get you out of here. I promise."

"I believe you. From what I've seen about you, you keep your word and try to do right. It's not that I want away from you personally. I just want away from people in general."

"I get it, people do suck. And I really am sorry you're stuck here. I know you can see our position."

Aaron sat picking at his fingers. "I know you are." He looked up at me. "We're both kind of stuck, I guess."

We sat chatting about nothing for a little while. Then the sound of the girls came drifting across the yard. Looking over at Danny's, I could see Mel and the kids coming down the drive. I left Aaron, who wasn't much of a conversationalist, and cut through the fence to Danny's.

"Where have you guys been?" I asked as I approached them.

"We went to see Fred," said Mel.

"How are the babies?" I asked.

"They're so cute!" Little Bit shouted.

Tammy sounded excited when she said, "I got to change a diaper!"

I laughed. "Kiddo, I bet Fred will let you change all the diapers you want. I know Aric will!"

She wrinkled her nose. "It was kind of gross. Baby poop really stinks."

"I think poop in general stinks there, kiddo," I said with a smile.

I took Mel's hand as we headed for the house. The kids said they were hungry, and Kay should have supper ready by now. As we walked, she asked what I'd been up to. I told her about the recon mission for tomorrow and she said she wanted to go.

"Really?" I asked, surprised. Not that I should have been. Mel had made it clear she wanted to take a more active role in things. It scared me to think she would be exposed to danger. But then, she probably felt the exact same as I did, only about me.

"If you want to come, you can come," I told her.

"Where are you going?"

"To Rock Springs and Wekiva."

"Then I'm really coming. I want to see The Rock."

The Rock was the Rock Springs Bar and Grill just outside the gate of Rock Springs State Park. When Mel and I met as teenagers, we would hang out there from time to time as her dad was a big fan of the place. It was a small juke joint with a single pool table, rectangular bar, and a small kitchen. It was a dive bar. But it was a good dive bar.

"I doubt they are still in business, babe."

"I know. I just want to see it."

As the kids thundered up the steps of the house, I answered her. "Well then, you're gonna."

When the door to the house opened, the sound of happy voices could be heard. The kids ran into the kitchen and gave Mom and Miss Kay hugs. Kay talked to the girls about their visit to Fred's and they were more than happy to chatter away about the babies. Leaving the girls to their gossip, Mel and I headed for the porch.

Most everyone was out here, with the exception of Karl and his guys. Seeing Sarge, I moved over to the table where he sat with Dad and took a seat, asking, "Where's Karl and his crew?"

Sarge looked up, perturbed, in the middle of saying something. He looked at Dad and asked, "Didn't you teach him any damn manners?"

I held my hand in front of his face and snapped my fingers. "Hey, Old Man, over here. I know you need a nap, but let's try and pay attention."

Sarge's head slowly rotated to face me. He stared, not saying a word. I was looking at him, eyebrows raised, expectantly.

After a moment he said, "You ever snap your fingers in my face again, I will break them off and shove them all up your ass. We clear?"

"Ok, but now that I have your attention, where's Karl?"

He didn't answer right away. Glaring at me just a little longer, then taking a drink of coffee before speaking. "They're out looking for Tabor. I already fucking told you that!" He took another sip from his cup, eyes locked on me. "Besides, it's none of your business. It's my problem. Let's talk about your problems. You have OPORD ready?"

Taking the notebook from the cargo pocket of my pants, I handed it to him. Snatching it from me, he dropped it on the table with exaggerated indifference. I rolled my eyes and turned my attention to Mel, who had sat down beside me.

"Make sure your ruck is packed tonight. After dinner let's get you a plate carrier as well," I said.

"I guess that's a good idea," she replied.

"We don't know what we'll come across and our truck isn't armored. And trucks are bullet magnets."

"As much as I hate to admit it, he's right, Mel," Sarge added.

I turned to look at him. "You finally awake?"

He pretended not to hear it. "Everyone that goes out in a vehicle needs armor from now on. Especially the patrols that will be going out."

I tapped the notebook. "What do you think?"

Sarge flipped the book open. In contrast to his usual asshole ways, he was serious this time. I took the cue, this wasn't the time for jokes. "You did pretty good, Morg," Sarge said. "You even did an exfil route that was off your infil." He looked at me and nodded. "Good job."

"I have to be honest; it was an afterthought. I really didn't think I needed to. It's not like we're fighting against another organized force. Shouldn't really need it."

"You always need it. And how do you know what you will find out there? We have no idea what's going on ten miles from here. What you're doing does have a significant element of risk to it. Remember that and don't get comfortable. You need to always be thinking of the ambush that's waiting just around the corner for you."

A hand landed on my shoulder, and I heard Mikey's voice. "Don't worry, Boss, I'll take care of them."

Sarge jabbed a finger at me. "I know you're in charge of this patrol," he then pointed at Mike, "but you listen to the snot nose there." Sarge's head dropped, and he shook it side to side.

Looking back up, he added, "He's a giant pain in the ass, but he's damn good at what he does."

Mikey beamed. "Thanks, Top!"

"Don't let it go to your head, shit bird! Ted's going too," Sarge said before looking back at me. "You tell your people yet?"

"They know we're going out, but not where exactly yet. I was going to go over it after supper. You get me a comms plan?"

Sarge took a piece of Rite in the Rain paper from his pocket and unfolded it, laying it on the table. Then he produced a pair of reading glasses and put them on. Naturally, this got Mikey started.

"Holy shit, you really are getting old!"

Without looking up from the paper, Sarge said, "Live long enough and it will happen to you." Then he looked up at Mikey. "But I don't think you need to worry about that."

"Pfft, whatever." Mikey gestured with a wave of his hand.

"May I continue?"

"Oh, yeah, sure. I'm gonna get some grub."

Sarge looked at me and shook his head. "Here are the freqs we'll use. VHF for as long as it lasts, then we'll switch to HF. There really are no other forms of communication that will work for us, so all you have is your primary and alternate. You may have to make stops and set up an antenna to get back to us. The antennas are already in the truck and Mike knows how to use them."

I looked at the sheet. It had check-in times as well as waypoints with code names. The old man chose old country western singers so we had waypoints like Cash, Waylon, and Willy.

"You have us checking every half hour? Seems excessive."

"Maybe, but this is the first such patrol we're doing. If an hour and a half passes and we haven't heard from you, we will come looking for you. This way we know where to start looking. Got it?" I nodded and he said, "Go brief your people."

I looked across the porch and saw Aric and Fred at a table with my girls all there helping with the little ones.

"I'm adding two more to the trip, Mel obviously, but also Aric."

Sarge looked over at where he sat and nodded. "If he's going to be in command of your militia, he needs experience in the field. Good call."

"Cool. I'm going to trade Thad and Dad out for these two. I want them to get started on the antenna tower. I'll show them where they are. Right now, let me get with everyone and we'll go over this." Looking at Dad, I asked, "You cool with that?"

"Yeah. I'm just happy to be here. Besides, I like all the projects you guys are working on and a radio tower sounds fun."

"Good deal. I'll tell Thad." I hopped up and stepped over to the table Thad was sitting at and took a seat beside him.

"Hey man, not gonna need you tomorrow."

Thad's brow furrowed. "Why not?"

"I want to take Aric out. He's been stuck here for so long and feels useless."

"I can see that. You need anything from me?" Thad asked.

"Yeah, you and Dad will follow us out in the morning, and I will show you where some radio towers are that we can take down and move over here so we can get some altitude for our transmitters."

"SLAP!" Thad shouted and started to laugh.

"Huh?" I was totally confused.

"Sounds like a plan!" Mary shouted from across the porch.

"I love that!" Mel called back to a smiling Mary.

"Yeah, ok, you can slap the shit out of these towers," I returned.

Thad slapped me on the back, still laughing. "I been waiting for a chance to say that to you."

"Where the hell did it come from?"

Thad stretched out his arm, pointing at Mary. "She said it to me last night. I laughed so hard."

"What was last night's plan?" Mikey asked from the next table over.

Thad stopped laughing, wiping the tears from his eyes and said, "One you ain't a part of."

Of course, this got a round of laughs and I saw Sarge get up and walk over. He leaned over the table, looked around conspiratorially, and said, "When it comes to Mikey, SLAP means, stupid little asshole punk."

The table broke into a chorus of laughter as the old man spun on his heels and headed back to the table he came from.

Even Mike was laughing. "That's pretty good, Grandad, pretty good."

Sarge responded with the finger.

I got up and called out for everyone going out the next day to join me at one of the tables. As I did so, I called Red on the radio and asked him to join us. The porch was crowded but folks moved to give us a table to ourselves. As we all took a seat, I looked at Aric, who was looking at me, and waved him over. He practically jumped from the table he was at, stumbling and nearly falling on his ass. When he sat down beside me, he felt as though he were vibrating.

"What's up?" Aric asked.

"We're going out on a recon tomorrow. Should be out and back on the same day," I said.

We chatted around the table for a few minutes while we waited on Red. It was just good-natured banter, jokes, and kidding. Red showed up, announcing, "I'm here now. You may begin."

With everyone present, I went into the ops plan. Laying out the map, I traced the highlighted route with my finger as I explained how we would get there and then how we would get back. I covered the comms plan Sarge prepared. Then I explained the purpose of the mission was a recon to check out the other springs to the south of us as the Juniper had become a magnet for people, and that these may have as well. Also, it would be our first venture outside our own area.

Ted asked to see the notebook and I handed it over. He studied it for a minute, then said, "Ok, Mikey is in one truck, I'm in the other. We can divide everyone else up accordingly." He looked around the table before continuing. "Everyone needs a ruck packed for this trip. Plan on being out for three days; pack accordingly."

"I thought you said we were coming back tomorrow," Travis interjected.

"We are, but we always plan for the worst." Ted looked at Ronnie and Mike. "Let's make sure we have some rockets. RPG should work."

"I'll throw the mortar in a truck too," Mike said.

"Nothing says hello like indirect," Ronnie added.

"I'll have a fifty on the trucks as well. Well, one fifty and one DShK."

"What's that?" Travis asked.

"It's the Russian version of a fifty. Big-ass bullets!" Mike replied.

"This should be pretty simple," I said, "just in and out. We're not hanging out or anything. We will be doing a lot more of these kinds of missions moving forward, so this is a good shake down for everyone."

"Get some sleep tonight," Ted instructed, then looked at me. "What time do you want to leave?"

"Eight."

"Alright, everyone meet here by 0730."

"I'll have breakfast ready for you all in the morning," Kay said from where she sat with Sarge.

The rest of the evening was spent having supper and the cutting up and laughing that generally came with it. I was just finishing up my food when Thad came over and knelt down beside me.

"After we look at these towers you want to get, I'm gonna start getting things ready to slaughter a hog. We could use the meat, and I'd like to cull a couple."

"How many?" I asked.

"Just two. They ain't real big. The way we're keeping them they don't get too much fat on them."

"We could supplement them with corn."

"Finishing them with corn would be nice," Thad said as he thought about it. "We could get them into the paddock behind the barn and feed them corn for a couple weeks."

"They'd taste better for sure," I said.

"Alright, after the tower thing we'll run by and see Cecil. Get a load of corn."

"Need any help getting them into the paddock?"

Thad smiled broadly. "Nah, they pretty easy. I go out there with a bucket of corn and they'll all want in!"

I slapped him on the back. "If you need anything, just let me know."

The smile faded from his face. "You be careful tomorrow. I don't know where you going, don't sound far, but we ain't been nowhere around here really. Just be careful."

"I will buddy, promise. This should be no big deal, really," I said, and Thad nodded and patted my shoulder again as he stood up.

Little Bit was sitting across the table from me. Finishing a long, messy drink from her cup, she banged it down, wiped her mouth with the back of her hand, and asked, "Daddy, can we play Legos tonight?"

"Sure, kiddo."

"I love Legos!" Tammy shouted.

"We have bunches of them!" Little Bit shouted.

Tammy looked at me and asked, "Can we go home and get them out?"

I nodded. "Of course, go and get them out and I'll be there shortly."

"I'm not playing with blocks," Lee Ann said.

"I will," Taylor said as she got up from the table. "Party pooper."

Lee Ann shrugged. "I just don't like blocks."

Taylor leaned over as she passed behind her sister. "They're Legos, not blocks."

"Look like blocks to me."

"You don't have to if you don't want to," Mel said.

"Yeah," I added, "you don't have to. I mean, I know you have no building skills and will just be embarrassed by my magnificent creation."

"Pfft," Lee Ann spat back.

I shrugged and with a smile said, "It's true and you know it."

Lee Ann quickly got up from her seat and picked up her plate as she headed for the house. "Now I have to show you."

Mel leaned over and bumped my shoulder. "Nice job."

"Oh, I knew I'd get her," I said with a laugh.

Since supper was done, we decided to head home. I was tired but had some Lego construction to do first. The girls had already left and were, no doubt, in the process of covering the living room floor with Legos. Mel was holding my hand as we walked through the cut in the fence to our house. She wasn't saying anything and looked like she was thinking.

"What's up?" I asked.

Quickly looking up at me, she said, "Oh, nothing. Just thinking about earlier today and what tomorrow could be like."

"Let's hope nothing like what happened today happens tomorrow."

"Of course. I don't really want to do that anymore."

Surprised, I asked, "Do you not want to go?"

"No, I want to go. What I mean is, I hope we don't have to do stuff like that … in general. I wish we could just live our lives and not deal with it."

We were nearly to the house when I said, "Let's sit on the porch for a minute. It's really nice out."

We both took a seat on the porch, with the dogs close at hand begging for attention. Mel is an animal lover and was more than happy to pile it on them. Drake was the biggest ham in the world. He'd been an attention hound since we found him. That weird fucker I put a well-deserved bullet in must have spent a lot of time with him. Meathead, on the other hand, just didn't give a shit. About the only time he wanted attention was when Drake was getting it, and that didn't last long.

"You need to go back over there and get yourself a plate carrier. You're going to need it. Find a helmet that fits you too," I said.

"We should have done that before we left."

"I know, just forgot. I need to go in here and get my Lego on. There's plenty of help over there if you need any."

Mel stood up and Drake dropped onto his haunches in a perfect begging position. Not that they ever were around when we ate, but I guess old habits die hard. Mel smiled at him and patted his head.

"I'll go over. You go in there and play Bob the Builder," Mel said, then looked at Drake and said, "Come on, Drake. I think we can find you a snack."

While I didn't think Meathead possessed the intelligence to understand what she said, he was immediately on his feet looking very anxious and wagging his tail.

Standing up, I said, "If you create a monster, it's your problem."

"What?" Mel asked as she stepped off the porch.

"Taking them over there around dinner time. Don't want them to get in the habit."

Mel patted Drake on the head. "It's not gonna hurt. They don't bother anyone and are never in the way. They're good dogs and deserve a treat every now and then."

"I'll tell you *told you so*," I said and laughed as I went inside.

CHAPTER 10

It was dark when I opened my eyes. Fumbling around for my watch, I looked at the time: quarter to five in the morning. I groaned a little and dropped back onto my pillow. Mel stirred but didn't wake up. Before putting my watch down, I wound it. This had become a part of my daily routine since The Day. I wound it every morning.

The watch I wore was made by a company called Maratac. It was a true mechanical watch, no batteries, no need for an atomic clock or any of that nonsense. Just wind it and it keeps time. It also wound itself through natural movement during the day. I like things like that. Low tech, while not always convenient, works.

Since I knew there was no way in hell I was going to go back to sleep, I got up quietly. Mel had time to sleep, no sense waking her up. I padded out to the living room in bare feet, which I should have known better than to do. In the dark I stepped on a Lego which elicited the same response as stepping on a damn sand spur! Cussing under my breath, I rubbed the ball of my left foot as I held the back of the couch.

While leaning over the couch, I saw Mel's plate carrier. She'd brought it back last night, telling me Sarge had approved it. A helmet sat beside it. I was happy to know hers had side plates in it. (Vehicles are bullet magnets. That's been a universal truth for as long as they have existed.) Mine didn't have side plates because I wore it every day, almost, and they're just hotter and uncomfortable.

In the kitchen I pulled the tea jug out, only to discover there was barely enough for a glass. Pouring it into my cup, I took out the kettle and filled it. Time to make tea. I wasn't about to go on this safari without tea! I'd have to put it in the freezer when it was done. Maybe it would only be warm when I left. With tea taken care of, I put on a pot of coffee for Mel. We kept a can around because she liked it. I did too, on occasion. Especially in cold weather, and that time of year was fast approaching.

I left the top open on the kettle so it wouldn't whistle and wake everyone up. But as they say, a watched pot never boils, so I decided to leave and make a head call. By the time I returned, it was a rolling boil. Shutting off the gas, I dropped the bags in and left it to steep then returned to the bedroom and grabbed my ruck. I carried it out to the shop so I could go through it before we left. My best friend in the world once told me, *if you stay ready, you ain't got to get ready.* Those words stuck with me and I kept the ruck packed at all times and with me. But it was good to go over it from time to time.

Unpacking it all, everything was in good shape aside from the normal abuse a kit gets when in a ruck that's been tossed around and lives in a vehicle. But I decided to change out the MREs for fresh ones. I pulled a case out from under the workbench and went to work rat-fucking it.

For those unfamiliar with the term "rat-fucking," let me elaborate. Rat-fucking a case of MREs means you're going to go through it and take all the best stuff. Not whole meals, no. Every meal will be opened, all the good shit taken, and the undesirable shit left behind. When you're with any kind of a crew, this is one of the dirtiest things you can do. It leaves them with no alternatives, and they have to eat the veggie lasagna or go hungry. It's also a sport to see who gets to them first. In this case, they were mine, so I rat-fucked away.

CHAPTER 10

Keeping MREs in your ruck is a double-edged sword. While you have food that requires no prep, it's heavy and bulky. You can only carry so much. But for the purposes of this ruck, that was fine. I didn't plan on carrying it unless things went tits up and the weight was well within what I could carry. Let's just say, I had some insight into that.

Once I had everything I wanted, I added three loaded rifle mags to the bag before closing it up. I rummaged around and found a fifty-caliber ammo can and filled it with mags. With everything in order, I carried the ruck and can out to the truck and put them in the bed. Going back to the shop, I grabbed the now-ravaged case of MREs and my empty glass and went back inside.

I left the case on the dining table. The girls would make short work of it. They loved MREs and would take them at any opportunity; they wouldn't make it through the day. The best part is they don't know how bad some of them are and will happily eat them because they're *cool*. Kind of a win-win for me. I get rid of them, and the girls get a treat. Kind of.

The sky was going from black to cobalt and I went back into the bedroom and sat down on the side of the bed. Giving Mel a little slap on the ass, she rolled over and looked at me.

"What?"

"Time to get up. We have shit to do today, remember?"

Sitting up and rubbing her eyes, she groaned, "Oh yeah. What time is it?"

"Six-thirty."

"Oh, good. There's time for coffee." She looked around, confused, "Do I smell coffee?"

I laughed. "The power of suggestion, baby. It's ready. You want a cup?"

"Please. I'm going to take a shower."

"I'll bring it in to you."

I went out and got her a cup and placed it on the counter in the bathroom and left her to do her thing. Going back outside, I grabbed a few things I'd taken from the Suburban, like a tow strap, a couple of full fuel cans, and a set of jumper cables.

Back in the shop, I grabbed a small twelve-volt compressor I'd scavenged from a house as well as a tire plug kit. I had a couple Zarges aluminum cases I'd had for years and I put one in the bed and all the recovery stuff in it. Trying to think of anything else I could do, I decided to drop the spare tire out from under the truck and put it into the bed as well.

Vehicle operations add a layer of complexity to things. You have to take the vehicle itself into account when you're thinking about sustainment. Your vehicle is always your closest resupply, but it too requires inputs and forethought for things that could go wrong. I would have liked a spare fan belt as well, something to ask Merryweather about. With the tire now in the bed, I went back out to the shop and found a four-way lug wrench and carried it back out to the truck with a full five-gallon jerry can of water. That was about all I could do. I was as ready as I could be.

Mel was out of the shower and dressed when I came back inside. My last-minute preparations had made me a little sweaty, so I ran through the shower real quick as well. Never miss a chance for a hot shower. Once I was dressed, I found Mel in the kitchen pouring coffee into a thermos. I took my tea from the freezer and poured it into a stainless double wall Yeti bottle and added ice.

"You go through your ruck?" I asked.

"I did. It's ready to go."

"You ready?"

She looked around a little apprehensively. "As ready as I'm going to be."

"Alright, let's grab your stuff and head over to Danny's."

CHAPTER 10

Walking outside, we tossed Mel's kit in the truck and walked next door. People were already at Danny's and busy getting things ready. The M-ATVs were sitting on the road in front of the house. Mike and Ted were on top of the trucks loading the weapons mounted to them. One had a fifty cal and the other had the Russian equivalent, the DShK. It fires 12.7 millimeter, or fifty caliber, projectiles.

One of the major differences is that it uses a continuous belt of links that separates at twenty-five, fifty, or one hundred rounds, whereas the Browning fifty has disintegrating links that come apart with every round fired. I prefer the disintegrating links, as they fall away and you don't have half a spent belt swinging from the weapon.

Everyone was loading their things into the trucks when Jamie walked up to me. She was smoking a cigarette and made me think of Perez. Taking a long drag on her smoke, she looked at me, and when I looked over, blew it in my face.

Fanning the smoke away, I said, "Sorry, Jamie."

"This is bullshit."

"I know you want to go, but I need some of these other people to get some time outside the wire as well."

She took another long drag before blowing it in my face again. "This is bullshit!" she repeated as she walked off.

Ian stepped up beside me and was quiet for a minute. "Well, I guess she's pissed," I said.

"Just a little. She still wants to kill someone, anyone, to make up for Perez."

"There will be more opportunities. We have to get everyone up to speed and that won't happen if they stay here all the time."

"I know," Ian sighed.

"Well, have fun with that today," I said with a laugh.

Ian looked at me. "Yeah, thanks."

Travis walked up carrying a ruck and his rifle. I'd never asked him about weapons and didn't know what he had. The M1A he carried surprised me.

"You bring enough gun?" I asked. Travis is a small guy. Maybe five-eight or nine, and thin. The M1A looked enormous in his hands.

"I like it. I know I can hit whatever I'm shooting at."

"You got enough ammo for that thing?"

"I only have three clips for it."

"Go see Sarge. He has one as well, and I'm sure he'll loan you some mags for it. And we have ammo for it, too."

"Ok, I'll ask."

When Travis walked away, I had an idea. Plucking the mic from my plate carrier, I keyed it and spoke, "Hey Bubba." It took a couple of tries before I heard a groggy Bubba reply.

Go ahead.

"What size boots and pants do you wear?"

What?

"Did I wake you, princess?" I smiled at the image of him sitting on the side of his bed in utter confusion.

Yeah, I'm up. What do you need?

"What size pants and boots do you wear?"

Uh, thirty-eight inch waist. Boots are size eleven.

"Find Sky and Ron and find out what size they wear. You guys need to get ready and meet me at the market. We're going on a mission."

Suddenly the sleep was gone from Bubba's voice. *Really? Ok, I'll go tell them. We'll be at the market waiting on you.*

"Hurry up on the sizes. We're about to head out."

When Bubba came back over the radio it was obvious he was running. *Ten four! I'm almost to Sky's house!*

CHAPTER 10

Aric rode up on his four-wheeler with his gear. I intercepted him before he got off. "Go over to my house and put your stuff in the truck. You're riding with me." With a nod, he sped off.

"You people got your shit together yet?" Sarge barked from the porch where he sat in a rocker drinking coffee. "Looks like a damn Chinese fire drill for special needs kids!"

Mike stood up on the roof of the truck, "Calm down, Grandad. You're not even going."

"You're as useless as a white crayon, you know that?"

Mike smiled. "Come on, it ain't a dick, don't take it so hard." The comment got a round of laughs from everyone there.

Sarge sipped his coffee. "You're not the dumbest son of a bitch I've ever met. But you better hope nothing happens to him!"

"Oh! Burn!" Crystal shouted at Mike.

Jess stomped up to me and poked me in the chest with her finger. "Hey!"

Surprised, I stepped back. "What?"

"Why am I going on this? Ronnie is going. I want to go too!"

"Look, everyone can't go. This is a short mission, in and out—" I was cut off by Mikey.

"Like sex!"

"Shut up, Mikey!" Sarge barked.

"Oh, come on, man! That was funny."

Sarge stood up. "You really need to start listening to me. You're too damn ugly to be this fucking stupid!"

Crystal laughed again. "That's two!"

Sarge smiled and winked at her.

"Look," Jess jabbed her finger into my chest again, "you're not going to keep me here. I can do this too."

"I know and that's not it, I promise. Aric has never been out on a mission. Danny hasn't really either. And I'm picking up some of the militia guys to go with us as well. You'll go out. Just not this time."

While not happy with my response, Jess relented. "Alright. But I better go out on the next one."

While all of this was going on, Bubba called back and gave the sizes Sky and Ronald needed. I went into the house and upstairs to see what we had in our inventory. It didn't take long to find three pairs of pants for each of them and a pair of boots. I grabbed a few pairs of socks as well and carried it all downstairs. Sarge was in the kitchen refilling his cup and asked what I was doing.

"Taking these to Bubba, Ron, and Sky. I want to take them as well."

Sarge smiled. "You'd make a good officer, Morgan. You're always looking to take care of your people."

"Just think they need to start being involved. We have all these resources, let's use them."

He saluted me with his cup. "Good job." Then he looked out the front window. "Looks like they're ready." He sat there in contemplative thought for a minute, then said, "It's time for us to give out callsigns."

"What do you mean?"

"We have too many people involved in things now. Like today, we'll have people scattered all over. We need to assign a callsign to each person individually."

"Okay. What do we use?" I asked.

"Don't worry, they come rather naturally. Let's get everyone rounded up and we'll do this."

Sarge grabbed his radio and made a call for everyone to gather up. Most people were there already. Aric called and said he was next door and would be right there and Sarge decided not to wait for him. When everyone was gathered up in front of the porch, Sarge produced a notepad and a pen.

"Alright folks, we need callsigns for everyone. This will be your callsign from now. It is the only way you will refer to each other on the radio." He paused for a moment to let that sink in. "So, let's get started. Morgan."

I looked at him. "What?"

"Are you even listening? Didn't we just talk about this? Fuckin' airhead."

Mike laughed. "Oh, that's a good one for him!"

"No, not that," Sarge said.

"What else are you gonna call that cracker ass cracker?" Mike asked, jokingly.

Sarge started to scribble. "Morgan's callsign is Cracker."

I looked at him. "You've got to be kidding."

Sarge didn't reply, he just surveyed the crowd. "Mel."

She looked surprised to hear her name. Sarge looked at her for a minute. "Minimi," he announced, getting some giggles from the crowd.

"I like it," she said, adjusting the weapon's sling.

"What about you?" I asked.

"I have one, dip shit." Sarge replied and looked around. "Stumpknocker. You all know it."

"Teddy, what's your callsign?"

Before Ted could make a sound, Mike shouted, "Mooseknuckle!" Then looked at Ted and said, "You know why."

"Oh my God, Mooseknuckle?" Jess laughed.

"Nice try, shit bird," Ted said.

Sarge smiled and started to scribble. "Mooseknuckle it is."

"Oh come on!" Ted shouted.

"Does it bother you, Teddy?"

"Fuck yeah it does!"

"Good. Every time you hear it, you'll know it's payback for being such a little shit!"

"This is bullshit," Ted replied. Then suddenly said, "If he gets to give me mine, I get to give him his!"

"Oh, this ought to be good!" Mike said, rubbing his hands together.

Sarge stepped down off the porch and walked over to Ted. Putting a hand on his shoulders, he said, "You know I love you like a son, Mooseknuckle. But that pleasure is all mine."

Sarge turned and looked at Mike. As the smile on Mike's face faded, the most genuine smile began to contort the old man's face in a way I'd never seen. No wonder he didn't smile a lot. It's fucking scary.

Sarge stood in front of Mike, rocking on his heels for a second. "You know, I've waited a long time to be able to call you this over the radio. Lord knows I've shouted it enough times after releasing the mic. Mike's callsign from now on is Shithead." The moment the words left his mouth the old man started to laugh hysterically. And he wasn't alone. Everyone was doubled over.

For his part, Mike's response was classic. Pumping his fist in the air, he shouted, "Hell yeah!"

Sarge walked back up on the porch. "Doc!" he shouted.

Ronnie raised his hand and Sarge looked at him. "You're still Doc."

Ronnie just shrugged as Jess hugged him. Looking at Sarge, she asked, "What about me?"

"Seminole!" Sarge called back.

Jess smiled from ear to ear. "I like it. Thank you." The old man had no idea what to do with the *thank you* and looked genuinely confused for a moment.

"Yeah, OK. Thad!" he barked out, and everyone started giggling.

"Right here, Sarge," Thad said, raising his hand.

"There's really only one option for you. Snake," Sarge said as he scribbled.

Thad started to laugh. "Snake! You crazy as hell!"

"Jamie!" Sarge barked and naturally looked toward the trucks. Jamie was sitting on the hood of the Hummer.

Before the old man could speak, Jamie stood up, taking a drag off a cigarette before flicking it away. "Perez."

Sarge's face was impassive. "Perez."

"Ian? Where's our resident Jarhead?"

He was standing right beside Jamie and looked around, as if to say, *I'm right here.*

"There's only one name for you too. Crayola."

"Oh, of course. Marines eat crayons. I get it," said Ian.

"At least it's not Mooseknuckle!" Ted shouted.

"Danny!" Sarge barked.

Danny was sitting off to the side on the porch and stood up. Sarge looked at him for a minute. "You're a hard one, Danny. You're never around it seems unless you're needed, then you're always there." Sarge jabbed the pen at him. "I got it. Kilroy!" Danny's response was to sit back down.

Sarge scanned the crowd, "Butch? Where you at?"

"Right here," Dad said, raising a hand.

"You got a preference?"

"In Vietnam, my callsign was Smokey."

Sarge smiled. "Smokey it is."

"Lastly, Dalton!"

Dalton snapped to attention, in the British manner. Holding his weapon at present arms, vertically in front of his chest. Lifting his left foot, he stomped it hard on the ground and shouted, "Present!"

Sarge watched, shaking his head. "You really are one of a kind, Gulliver."

"That would be good for him!" Mary shouted. "Gulliver!"

"Negative," said Dalton. "I already have a callsign." Taking a step forward, he raised his weapon into the air with one hand striking a He-Man pose, then, in the voice of Michael Buffer, shouted, "Vanilla Thunder!" He then started to mimic techno music and went into an imitation of a stripper, gyrating his hips and dancing, with eye contact and all, to rousing catcalls and whistles from those gathered there.

Looking down at his notebook, Sarge muttered, "For fuck's sake."

In a thick hick accent, Dalton said, "Hustlin' ain't easy, Sarge."

"That's it. For those not here, we'll get with them and give them one as well," Sarge said. Then he had another thought. "One more thing, home base here will be Adelaide and the Army in Eustis will be Cheyenne."

Sarge motioned for me, and I followed him into the house. He poured us each a cup of coffee and sat down on a barstool at the counter.

"I talked to Merryweather this morning and he's got a couple of people over there in the infirmary he's worried about," Sarge said.

"Worried about what?"

"They have two cases of suspected malaria."

"Malaria? Where the hell did that come from? I mean, there's the occasional case, but it's damn sure not common."

"Well, it looks like it might be here. They're requesting drugs for it. We'll have to see if they get it."

I took a sip of coffee and thought for a moment. "There isn't much we can do, but we should probably post a notice or something."

"That's what I was thinking. We'll have to make some signs or something."

"Or, let's just have Merryweather's people type it up on one of their laptops and print it out. We can post them in a few places."

"That's a good idea. I'll handle it."

Taking a drink from my cup, I set it down and turned to leave. "We'll be in touch."

Sarge looked down into my cup. There was still a little shot of coffee in it. He picked it up and dumped it into his. "Let's do a comms check before you head out."

"We'll do it from the end of the road before we pull out. I'm taking Thad and Dad to a house with some towers. We can take them down and bring them here so we can get some antennas in the air."

"I'm going too. I want to see what's there."

"I'm headed to the truck now."

"Here you go, Linus," Miss Kay said, hanging him a thermos of coffee.

"Thank you," he said with a smile, then leaned over and kissed her on the cheek.

I didn't say anything in front of Miss Kay, choosing to wait until we were on the porch. "You getting soft?" I asked.

He smiled at me. "It's been a long time since I've had the care and attention of a woman. My life just wasn't conducive to it. It's really nice."

I bumped him with my shoulder. "I'm happy for you. Both of you."

"Thanks, Morg. I'm happy too." Then his tone changed and he got serious. "You be careful today. Don't take any risks. If you make contact, break it and get out. Remember, this is a recon. Not a movement to contact. Do not get into a gunfight."

"We'll do our best."

"Alright, let's get this damn gypsy troop on the road."

Everyone mounted up and I ran over to the truck Ted was going to ride in. Danny was driving it and I climbed up on the side to talk to him. "We're going to go to a house over on 439. But I need to go to Umatilla first to pick up Bubba and Sky."

Danny nodded. "I'll follow you."

Seeing Mel, I called to her, and she walked with me back to the house. I tossed the pants and boots into the back seat of the truck and we loaded up. Mel and her Minimi sat in front, Aric insisted, while he sat in the back. Aric was obviously excited. He was organizing his gear, finding a comfortable place for his weapon and other kit.

"You ready?" I asked him as I started the truck.

When he looked over, the smile on his face was so big I thought it would crack in half. "Yes, I am! *Damn*, I've been waiting for this for so long."

"Well, it's here now and will be from now on."

"Thanks, Morgan!"

I waited on the road for the trucks to start moving and pulled out in front of them. As we passed the bunker, I made a call on the radio using the callsigns Sarge gave us. "Convoy, radio check."

Mosseknuckle, copy, I heard Ted call back. You could hear the disdain in his voice.

Shithead, copy, Mike called.

Stumpknocker, copy, Sarge called.

"What's with all these callsigns? Mooseknuckle?" Aric asked.

"The old man handed out callsigns this morning," I said.

Mel turned in her seat and looked at Aric. "I'm Minimi."

"What's mine?" Aric asked.

I looked at him in the mirror. "We don't know yet. You're lucky. He's not picking yours."

CHAPTER 10

In the mirror I could see Thad and Dad in the little red pickup. They were at the tail of the convoy, with Sarge's Hummer in front of them. Just a quick run to town, then we'd get this show on the road.

"Man," Aric nearly shouted, "I am so glad to be here!"

Glancing over, I said, "Glad you're here too. We're going to town to get a couple of militia folks, then to a house with radio towers. I want to see about taking them down so we can move them to our place."

We found Bubba, Ron, and Sky waiting at the market. As soon as they saw the trucks, they started walking out to the road. I rolled up to them and stopped.

"Jump in where there's room back there. This is just a recon mission. Should be pretty boring. Hopefully," I said.

"We don't care what we're doing," said Bubba.

"Just the idea we can get out of here for a little while is enough," Sky added.

"In a truck!" Ron shouted.

"Now that you are here, we need to come up with callsigns for you all," I said.

"Callsigns? For what?" Bubba asked.

I laughed. "What do you think a callsign is, Bubba?"

"Just didn't know we were gonna have 'em is all."

"You're Bubba in every way," I said. "Callsign, *Bubba*."

"Not very original," Bubba moped.

"But accurate, big man," I said with a laugh.

"What about me?" Sky asked.

"How about Storm?" Mel said. "You know, they happen in the sky and you look like you could wreak havoc if you put your mind to it."

Sky smiled. "Storm, I like it."

"What about me?" Ron asked.

"Mangnum," I replied.

He smiled and nodded.

"You three hop in. We have things to do. Aric, we'll figure yours out later," I said.

They ran back to the trucks and were quickly onboard. As I pulled off, I said over the radio, "You guys just follow me. We'll go look at the towers real quick."

"Hurry up every chance you get!" Sarge barked into the radio.

I drove up to Cassady Street and took a left. This route would take us by Caldwell Park and eventually out to Wiygul Road which dead ends into 439. It was interesting to be on these roads. I don't think I'd been on them since before The Day. There were people visible as we passed through the neighborhood of houses that made up the east side of town. However, that changed when we got to Wiygul.

There weren't many houses on this road and the few that were there looked empty. I eyed Ruff's Saddle Shop as we passed it. The gate was closed and the lime rock road leading to the store, usually so well maintained, was a mess. With all things considered, I doubted maintenance of the driveway was a big priority. The next thing that got my attention was the sod farm.

I never knew who ran the farm or even the name of it. But I'd seen them cutting sod so many times it was obvious what they did. The pastures they cut on were like pool tables, perfectly flat with no trees. Well, they had been. Now, without the constant spraying of weed killers, they were a tangled mess of weeds. Thistle, beauty berry, mullein, and many others were now growing prolifically.

"That's sad," Mel said from the backseat.

"Yeah, they used to look so good," I said.

Aric was looking at the fields as we passed them and asked, "What was it?"

"Sod farm," I said.

CHAPTER 10

"Ah, they grow yards."

Mel laughed. "That's one way to put it."

It was a short run down 439 to the house. The gate was open, and I pulled in. I could hear Sarge telling the guys to keep the trucks on the road. They pulled just past the gate and stopped in the middle of the road. The Hummer and Thad's little truck pulled in behind me. I tooted the horn as I got out.

Thad pulled up beside me and looked at the house. "Looks empty."

"About to find out," I said.

Dad and Thad climbed out of the truck as Sarge walked over. "Anyone home?" Sarge asked.

"Doesn't look like it," I said, "let's go see."

"You go see," Sarge said, "I'm goin' around back."

Thad followed Sarge as I started toward the porch with Dad, Aric, and Mel. The house looked abandoned from the outside. The yard was overgrown and weed-choked. A layer of dust on everything gave the place the feel of general decay. When I knocked on the door, it moved.

Gripping my weapon in my right hand, I opened the door with my left. Swinging the muzzle up, I clicked on the Surefire light mounted to it. The dark room was filled with brilliant white light, gotta love lithium batteries. The living room was trashed. It had obviously been searched a couple of times. With Mel covering the door, Aric and I cleared the house. Every room was in disarray, but no one was home.

Grabbing my mic, I called, "House is clear."

Come out back, I heard Sarge reply.

We went out the backdoor of the house and saw Sarge and the guys gathered around a block building. It had a very sturdy metal door with no knob that showed very obvious signs of abuse. Someone had tried, very hard from the looks of things, to breach the building. The door had clearly been assaulted with a sledgehammer as well as the walls in a couple of places to the point rebar was exposed. The structure was concrete block construction reinforced with rebar, and the cells poured with concrete. Someone was serious when they built it. We walked around it to see if there were other doors and there were none.

"Looks like someone tried to burn them out," Dad said as he inspected soot marks that ran down the walls.

"Doesn't work so good with concrete," said Sarge. "All the antennas route into there. I'm willing to bet that place is full of radios."

"How the hell we going to get in there?" Dad asked. Then, pointing at the wall, added, "Someone tried to get through the wall with a sledge and couldn't."

"That's why I think it's all in there. No one got in."

"So how are we getting in?" I asked.

Sarge shook his head and let out a sigh. Grabbing his mic he said, "Shithead, bring your breaching toys and come around back."

What kind of breach? Mike asked.

Still shaking his head, eyes closed, Sarge said, "Explosive."

We heard Mikey's reply without need of the radios. He was shouting like a kid as he ran across the yard. He rounded the corner carrying a pack in one hand and his weapon in the other and skidded to a stop. When he saw the building, a smile spread across his face. He walked over to the door and dropped his pack.

"This one?" Mike asked, pointing at the door.

"Get it open, Ricky-tick!" Sarge barked.

Mike stepped up to the door and ran his hand over it. Laying his face against it, he said "Hello, gorgeous. Oh yeah, we're gonna have a blast."

Mel laughed. "That's funny! A blast!"

"Knock it off, Shithead! Get it open!" Sarge barked.

CHAPTER 10

"Calm down," Mike said and patted the door, "breaching is an art."

"I can shove a blasting cap into a block of C4! A fuckin' monkey can do it!" Sarge shot back.

"Yeah, and blow the entire place up! Just step back, let me do what I do."

Mike rapped on the door with his knuckles and gave it a push. Kneeling down, he opened his ruck and rummaged around. Looking back at the door, he considered his options. Gripping his radio mic, he made a call.

"Hey Doc."

Goatheaaad.

Mel looked at me. "Did he just say 'goat head'?"

"Yeah, kind of a play on 'go ahead.'"

With a knowing nod, she responded, "Right."

"How many bags of saline do you have?" Mike asked.

Looks like about six.

"Can you bring two back here to me?"

We have wounded?

"Negative, need them for the breach."

Roger that. On my way.

While Mike waited for Doc, he prepped his charge. He used a small amount of C4 that he formed into a little donut. He then took out a roll of tape and peeled a piece off.

"What kind of tape is that?" I asked.

"Breacher's tape," he said as he worked. "It's double sided and really fucking sticky. It will hold the charge to the door."

Mike placed the donut on the piece of tape then took a roll of green cord and began laying it on top of the donut in a figure-eight pattern.

"What the hell are you doing, Mikey?" Sarge asked.

"Breaching a door," he said without looking up.

"Hurry up every chance you get, Nancy."

"I didn't have prepped charges so, I have to make it now. This shit takes a minute. Explosives are not very forgiving. Chill the fuck out." Mike never looked up when he replied. He was focused on what he was doing. Sarge took the cue; Mike was being serious.

Doc showed up with the saline bags and handed them to Mike. Once Mike had the correct amount of det cord configured on the charge, he cut another piece long enough to leave about a foot of it on either end of the charge and wove it through the coils. Then he laid one of the IV bags on top of it, flipped it over, and removed the liner of the breaching tape and stuck the other IV bag to it before wrapping the entire thing in duct tape so that it was like a sandwich.

Once it was all secure, he cut another piece of breaching tape and stuck it to the bottom of the charge. Taking the two ends of det cord on the charge, he brought them together and taped the ends to one another with electrical tape. With the charge ready, Mike pulled out a roll of time fuse.

"The burn rate on this is three seconds per inch. I want a ninety-second fuse. How much do I need?" Mike asked.

"Thirty inches," I offered.

As he was crimping a blasting cap to the fuse, Mike looked up and smiled. "Look at the big brain on Morg!"

With the detonator crimped, Mike used a seamstress tape measure to measure out the thirty inches of fuse.

"Why don't you have a regular tape measure?" Mel asked.

"We like to keep metal away from explosives so there's no chance of a spark," Sarge quickly replied.

With the fuse cut, Mike took out a little green tube and removed a plug from the end, loosened a cap, shoved the fuse into it, and tightened the cap to hold it securely. The M81 fuse igniter is a spring-loaded device with a primer charge inside. The operator simply removes a safety pin, places their finger into the ring on the end of the igniter and pulls in a quick, sharp motion. The spring-loaded pin strikes the primer, igniting the fuse.

Now that the charge was armed, Mike removed the backing on the breacher's tape and slammed it to the door. To no one in particular, Mike said, "I should have had a piece of wood or something on the bottom of this to keep it flat. That's why I added the C4," looking at us, he added, "gives it a little more kick."

"That's not going to destroy whatever is behind the door, is it?" Sarge asked.

"No, this charge will cave the door in, kind of fold it up. Alright, everyone get around the corner." We all moved and lined up against the wall.

I tapped Mel on the shoulder. "Plug your ears and open your mouth."

She clearly didn't understand why, but did as I said. Then we heard Mike.

"Fire in the hole! Fire in the hole! *Fire in the hole!*"

There was a *pop* and I looked at the second hand on my watch. Mike ducked around the corner and checked his watch.

"Twenty seconds!"

He counted down in ten-second intervals until there was a crashing explosion. The concussion was impressive. The air was filled with smoke and dust and smelled of cordite. We walked around the corner to see the door lying on the ground in front of the building. Inside was pitch black, so I pointed my rifle in and clicked on the light. What we saw was unimaginable.

There was a large bench running across the end of the room opposite the door. A swivel chair sat in front of it with the skeletal remains of a person in and about the chair. The most disturbing thing about the scene, to me at least, was that the skull still had headphones on. Though the lower jaw had fallen off.

"Oh, that's disgusting," Mel said.

Doc looked at the remains, then at Mike. "Should have saved those two bags. This guy is seriously dehydrated."

"What is wrong with you two?" Mel asked. "That is a person."

"No," Mike replied, "That *was* a person."

"Holy shit," Sarge said as he stepped in. "It smells like two trash cans were fucking in here!" Then he looked around. "Look at all this shit!"

The room was packed with radio equipment. There were numerous radios mounted into a wood panel on the bench. Dials and gauges of several types looked out as well. There were antenna switches, power supplies, microphones, speakers, and computers.

I walked over to the bench and picked up a notebook. Flipping through the pages, I was surprised to see so many notes were made about people transmitting and not using callsigns. Whoever this was had even gone so far as to use a directional antenna to determine the azimuth of the transmitters. He'd written down names of people he spoke to that didn't have a callsign. It appeared from the notes that the operator was far more concerned about nonexistent FCC rules than he was about what was happening to people.

The notebook didn't contain any notes on the unfolding events. Only hate-filled comments on the people he'd talked to. I couldn't believe what I was reading.

Lincoln Nebraska: Steve, wouldn't give last name, no callsign, no 73's

Near Austin: Debra Banks, no callsign, foul language, no 73's

The book was replete with such notes. I just shook my head.

"What's that?" Sarge asked.

"Station log."

"Anything interesting in it?"

"No, just a sad ham, man."

"Sad ham?"

I looked at Sarge. "Yeah, you know, those old fucks on the radio that act like the RF police. When they're not talking about their radios, they're bitching and whining about other people not utilizing the air waves in a manner they approve of."

"Oh," Sarge laughed. "I know what you mean. Annoying fuckers."

Thad stepped over to Sarge and asked, "What do you want us to do?"

"Take it all, everything. Every meter, cable, connector, every damn thing. I want it all. We'll come up with a plan to get the towers down as well."

"Baker has that boom truck," I said.

Sarge snapped his fingers. "Damn, that's right. That'll do it." Then, looking at me, said, "We've got this under control. You guys get the hell out of here."

As we headed out, Mike said to Sarge, "What'd you think of that?"

Sarge placed his hand on Mike's shoulder. "Damn good job, Mikey, damn good."

Mike looked surprised, almost unsure of what to say. "Oh, uh, thanks?"

"Mike, there's a time and a place for fucking around. But every place isn't every time. You did good. Despite the fact you're a terrible human being, I'm proud of you."

Mike looked at me. "Was that an insult or a compliment?"

"Just call it a win, man," I said as I walked out.

CHAPTER II

Karl sat at a picnic table in Alexander Springs and studied the map. They'd made their way to the spring in search of people, but the spring was empty. It was obvious people had been there. The remains of fires and feeble attempts at brushing in the side of one of the pavilions were all that remained.

"What are you thinking?" Imri asked.

"Well, we're going to ride over to the bombing range and look around," Karl said as he folded the map. "We could ride around out here for days and not find them."

"Morgan said they were shot at on the west side. You want to ride out there and take a look?"

"Yeah. We'll do that then head back to the hood."

"Good. I need a shower," Imri said, looking at his shirt.

Karl laughed. "You hadn't had a real shower in months until we got here."

"I know. Then we found a place, not only a place with showers, but a place with hot showers! And I intend to take full advantage."

"Yeah. When you don't have something and there is literally no way to get it, you learn to live without it."

"But as soon as the opportunity presents itself to have it, you'll take it."

Karl stood up. "Let's get going. I want a shower too." He looked around and asked, "Where's Chadster?"

"I have no idea."

"Chadster!" Karl shouted.

"I'll walk down to the spring and see if he's down there."

"He needs to carry a damn radio. I'll go see if he's in the snack bar up there," Karl said as he started up the hill.

And Karl was right. Chad was in the old snack bar. He was going through cabinets and looking through the detritus left by countless others that had come before him.

"Chad, what the hell are you doing?" Karl asked.

Chad looked up to see Karl leaning against the door to the small space. "Just seeing what's around."

"You know there's nothing there. How many people you think have been through this place?"

Chad rose to his feet and dusted his knees off. "Lots, I would imagine. But you know, out here in the middle of nowhere, never know what you could find."

"And what did you find?"

Chad looked around. "A mess."

"Come on. Let's ride out by the camp and see if the people that shot at Morgan want to shoot at us."

"We get to kill people today?"

"Only if we're lucky, Chad. Only if we're lucky."

They walked back down to the Jeep, which was parked right in the middle of the park. Karl had driven almost down to the water.

"Where the hell you been?" Imri asked when he saw Chad.

"Scrounging," Chad answered.

"Tell him what you found, Chad!" Karl shouted.

Imri looked expectantly at Chad, who said, "Nothing. I was just looking around."

"Dammit Karl," said Imri, "I thought he actually found something."

"Karl said we're going to hunt some fuckers," said Chad.

Imri perked up. "We get to kill someone today?"

Karl laughed and jabbed a thumb in Chad's direction. "He said the same thing! Come on, load up!"

CHAPTER 11

We left Sarge and those with him to drool over the radio equipment. I don't know why he was so excited, we had more radios than we needed at this point. But I guess in this world, there's no such thing as enough.

As I was turning onto Mill Creek Road, the radio crackled. *Keep the speed at fifty, Cracker,* I heard Mike say.

"Roger that."

"Man, this feels so good!" Aric said from the backseat.

"You glad to be out for a bit?" Mel asked.

"I'm glad to be doing my part for a change."

"You've always done your part, buddy," I said.

"Yeah? Well, it doesn't feel like it when you never get to help. I just can't tell you what it means to me. Thank you."

Looking at Aric in the rearview mirror, I said, "We were just looking out for you, Fred, and the kids. The thought of you getting hurt right as you're starting a family is scary."

Aric sat forward on his seat to lean in between Mel and me. "I get what you're saying. But you have a family and it hasn't stopped you from putting your ass on the line."

"He's got you on that one," said Mel.

"You are correct. I know it doesn't make sense. However, I also do not see the need to put people in harm's way that don't need to be."

"Morgan, you're a good dude. But you can't do it all on your own and you've been trying to. Everyone sees it. As a matter of fact, you shouldn't even be here. You're the acting governor, for crying out loud."

Glancing over at him, I said, "Not something I wanted either. I don't even know what to do. There's no real direction other than a list of places they want us to look at."

"Are we going to one of them now?" Aric asked.

"No, this isn't on their list. But I want to go there and see how many people might be there."

"What about Orlando? Or Sanford, Altamonte, or any of the bigger cities?" Mel asked.

"We're going to have to go look at them. But we need a real plan for that. We'll need a much larger force to do it. I don't want to be anywhere near a large population center without a detailed plan."

"We should start planning on it."

I looked at Mel. "Hey, I have enough people piling shit on my plate. Stop helping."

She gave me a dismissive wave. "You'll do it eventually."

We were rolling down Route 44A when the radio crackled again.

Cracker, what's Rafiki?

"It's a Christian NGO that works in Africa. They have a school there and prepare their missionaries to go overseas."

Ever been in it?

"Negative. Only looked at it from sat photos."

What's it look like?

"A school campus. There's probably a dozen buildings back there. I don't see any reason to drive back. It's a narrow road in with brush right up to the edge. It would be a great place to hole up, though. Pretty isolated."

I think we should look at it at some point.

"Roger that."

"Why would he want to go back there?" Mel asked.

"He's probably thinking that as an NGO they'll have supplies there that could be useful. But it would have to have been searched by now."

"Or," Aric added, "someone is living back in there. Maybe a lot of someones."

"That could be the case too," I said as we turned onto Highway 437.

Grabbing my mic, I said, "Heads up. We're coming to an intersection with a couple of stores. There's also a shopping center on the southwest corner that had a grocery store and restaurants."

Roger!

We hadn't seen a soul since leaving. Like the land was simply devoid of people. But then we came to Circle K at the intersection, and it was much like the ones in Umatilla and Altoona. People congregated there, and this one was no exception. The newer of the two Circle K stores at the intersection was the first one we came to. Catty-corner across the intersection sat an older store. The pump island wasn't nearly as large as the newer one and was empty.

Keying my radio again, I said, "Let's pull in here."

You go in with him, Mikey. I'm going to stay out here on the road and provide cover, I heard Ted say over the radio.

Roger.

I pulled into the parking lot to looks of amazement from those gathered there. Some of them were obviously fearful, with two people taking off running. The majority of people, however, appeared genuinely curious as they shaded their eyes with their hands to see the circus that was pulling in. The truck Mike was in stopped in the parking lot as I pulled around in front of the store and climbed out.

"Keep your eyes open," I said as I closed the truck door, pocketing the key.

Mel was out with the Minimi slung, muzzle down. Aric and I were as well, with our weapons slung as we approached a group of people standing under the fuel canopy. I waved and smiled as we walked up.

"Hey, how's it going?" I asked. The moment I did, I knew it was a stupid thing to say.

"How the hell you think it's going?" a large, bearded man said. He wasn't fat, just big all over. He had a bolt-action rifle slung over his shoulder.

"Yeah, that sounded stupid when I said it."

There were maybe a dozen people lounging in a collection of chairs that ranged from folding camp chairs to a recliner. The usual accoutrements were present: a chessboard and an upturned bucket with a checkerboard.

"Who the hell are you guys? The Army?" the man asked as he studied the M-ATV.

"No, we're not Army. But we are working with them."

"Working doing what?" he asked suspiciously.

"Trying to get things back together."

"We haven't seen anyone from the government since things fell apart. No one has come around. No one has helped. We're just left on our own to figure it out."

"So were we. And yet, here you are. I know it hasn't been easy. But you made it this far and things will only improve from here."

The man looked around. "How exactly are they going to improve? I don't see shit going on that's going to help us."

"Well, for now, the Army is serving one hot meal a day at Umatilla High. I know it's far from here. But you can walk there in a couple hours."

The man looked furious. "You expect me to walk to Umatilla every day for one meal?"

"Not at all. You don't have to go. But you can. There's also doctors there and the chance for work."

"Work?" The man sniggered. "What the hell are they going to pay us with?"

"Food, clothes. There's lots of ways."

"Well," the man started and looked around at those gathered there with him. "I'm not working for anyone!"

"And you don't have to," I said. Then I looked at the people behind him. "If any of you want what I mentioned earlier, just go to Umatilla High."

"What's with the star?" the man asked.

"It says sheriff on it," I answered.

"I don't remember any election," the man said, then looked back at those behind once again. "Any of you vote for this guy?" Looking back at me, he said, "I know I didn't."

I let out a sigh. "That's irrelevant to this discussion. I just am for the moment. Look, all we're trying to do is help. The country is finally on a path to repair. While it may never be like it was before, it will get better."

"If you can just proclaim you're the sheriff, then I'm the governor of Florida!" the man shouted, getting some snickers from those in the crowd.

Aric stepped forward. "Um, actually, he's the acting governor as well." His words chilled the snickers.

"Who the hell are you?" a woman from the crowd asked.

"No one you know. Just in the wrong place at the wrong time. None of this shit was my idea. But someone needed to step up, and it came down to me," I said.

"So that's why you have all this security?" the man asked, then looked at Mel. "I got something she can secure."

As Mel and Aric both started to protest, I stepped forward and quickly struck him in the sternum with the muzzle of my rifle. When he started to crumble, I landed a butt stroke to the top of his head, knocking him out. There were gasps and a couple of shouts from the crowd. At the same time, I heard truck doors opening and boots running toward me. The crowd shrank in the face of the show of force.

"What's up?" Doc asked as he ran up.

"He insulted Mel." I turned to address the crowd. "While things are getting back together, we need to remember our manners. It's a different world now. You insult someone, you very well could pay a price for that." I pointed to the man on the ground who was just starting to come around. "This man insulted my wife. He paid for it. That's all. He's still welcome in Umatilla for hot food. Just bring your manners as well."

"You OK, Mel?" Sky asked.

Mel shrugged. "Didn't bother me any."

The man was in a sitting position now, holding his head. "What the hell happened?" he slurred.

Reaching down, I unslung his rifle and opened the bolt. "You insulted my wife."

"What are you doing to my rifle?"

Looking in the chamber, I said, "It's empty. Why are you carrying an empty rifle?"

"Empty?" someone from the crowd shouted.

Looking up, I asked, "Is that a surprise?"

"Hell yes!" a woman shouted. "He struts around here like he's King Shit on Turd Island because he says he has a rifle with bullets!"

I showed the empty chamber to the crowd. "Doesn't look like it," I said as I tossed the rifle to the ground.

The crowd started to close in on the man. There were angry shouts. It was obvious what had occurred. The man thought he could bluff his way around with an empty rifle. Now that everyone knew the emperor had no clothes, the balance of power had shifted.

"Well folks, remember Umatilla High for medical care and hot food. There are also a couple cases of suspected malaria. I would take precautions." Then I told my people, "Let's get on the road."

From what I was hearing, the man was about to have a really bad day and he knew it.

"You can't leave me here. They'll kill me!" he shouted.

I stepped over to him and knelt down. "And what did you do to them to make them want to kill you?"

He was a typical bully. Now that his victims were no longer afraid of him, and he didn't have the upper hand, he was terrified. From the looks of some of the people there, he should be.

A woman stepped up and spat on the man and said, "You're not such a badass now, are you, Rob?"

Looking from her back down to him, I asked, "Was he a problem?"

The woman crossed her arms over her chest and rubbed her nose that was starting to run. With tears in her eyes, she said, "Yes," and her voice cracked. Then she lunged at him, kicking him. She screamed, "You son of a bitch!"

Grabbing her, I pulled her back. "Calm down, calm down."

No!" she screamed back as she fought against me. "You don't know what he did!"

"Shut up, Paula," another man from the crowd interjected. "All he did was try to keep the peace around here."

I looked at the man, then at the woman. "He on this guy's side?" I asked.

She nodded. "Yes. Those two." Her eyes narrowed and she screamed, "You know what you did!"

"What did he do?" Mel asked.

The woman looked at her. "You know what he did."

"Say it," I said, "Say it and I'll deal with it. Right here, right now."

Wiping her nose again, she said, "He said, if we wanted to eat, we had to fuck him!" Then she looked at the other man. "You too! You did it too!"

I looked at the crowd. "Was anyone else here forced by these two to do things against their will?"

"Shit, he's the only one with a gun around here now," another man said.

"It was empty," I said.

"We didn't know that. He always said he'd shoot whoever didn't do what he said."

Looking down at the man, I said, "Is that so?"

"He did it to me too," another woman said. She walked through the crowd up to where we stood. "Both of them. They're sick, sadistic." Then she broke down into sobs and dropped to her knees on the ground, muttering, "Lily."

I knelt down beside her. "What did you say?"

"Lily is my daughter," she looked up at me as tears ran down her face. "She's only thirteen."

A rage began to build in me. "Did he …" I couldn't even say it.

She nodded and I rose to my feet.

"Aric, get that asshole over there and put him in a truck. Secure his hands."

"What the hell is this?" the man protested. "You can't do this to me! Just because you have a badge doesn't mean you can come in here and tell us what to do!"

Aric was trying to get his hands secured with zip-ties as I stepped over to him. With an open hand, I slapped him in the nuts, hard. He crumpled, his knees buckled, and he went to the ground. Leaning down, I grabbed his chin and lifted it.

"And you don't have the right to force yourself on a thirteen-year-old girl." Then, thinking, I said, "Don't put them in a truck. Take them over there," I said, pointing to the rear of the parking lot.

Bubba and Danny pulled the first man to his feet. He was still recovering, and they had to drag him for the most part. His partner wasn't going quietly, and Aric was using quite a bit of force on him before finally getting him into a submissive position. Pain, properly applied, will yield compliance. They still had use of their voice, though.

"These fuckers won't be here tomorrow!" he shouted. He had no idea what lay ahead.

We put them against the block enclosure for the dumpsters as the crowd made their way over. They were held at gunpoint as I turned around to address the others.

"There will be no aspiring warlords or," I turned to look at the two, "bullies." Looking back at the group, I said, "While there may not be much in the way of law, organized law, at the moment, we all have the right to defend ourselves." Looking at Lily's mother, I added, "For rape, the penalty is death. There are no jails. We no longer coddle criminals. For people that will rape a woman or a child, there is no reforming them."

"What?" Rob asked, suddenly catching on to what was unfolding. "You can't just line us up against a wall and shoot us. We have rights!"

I laughed at him. "What about Lily's rights?"

"That little bitch is a whore, just like her mother," the bigger man shouted.

I heard Mel say, "Move, Aric."

Looking back, I saw she had the Minimi level, hanging from the sling with the grip in her right hand and the left supporting the front of the weapon. Aric, seeing the weapon leveled in his direction, quickly stepped aside. The two men were unsure. Their eyes darted from the weapon to me, then to Mel.

Nothing was said for a moment. Then the Minimi erupted with a thunderous report. Cement dust was blasted from the wall along with small pieces of the two men. Mel shot them to the ground and was still shooting them when Ted ran over and grabbed her.

She let off the trigger, the weapon smoking, spent links and brass scattered around. Mel's eyes were fixated on the two bodies. I watched, waiting for a reaction. But there was none. She simply put the weapon on safe, dropped it onto the sling, and walked over to the truck. She pulled the case of MREs out and walked over to Lily's mother.

"Take these. Don't share them. Go home and give one to Lily." She paused and looked around before adding, "If anyone tries to take these from you, I will be back and I will deal with them."

The woman took the case and looked at it. Still sobbing, she said, "Thank you! Thank you so much!"

I took a step forward. "You all heard what I said earlier. There's a hot meal every day in Umatilla. There will be more locations later. But for now, it's what we have. There is zero tolerance for taking advantage of anyone. We all have it hard enough. We need to be working together." Pointing at the bodies, I added, "This is what will happen to those that prey on others. Everyone clear?"

The radio suddenly crackled, *Thunder One, Thunder One, Rhino one-one.*

"Go for Thunder One," I called back. Merryweather was going to love our new call signs.

Rhino one-six needs you to come to the TOC.

"Negative, I am indisposed for the day."

Wait one, came the reply. *Uh, roger that Thunder One. Rhino one-six requests your presence at your earliest convenience.*

"I'll come see him when I'm free."

Copy. Rhino one-one out.

"Who were you talking to?" a young man from the crowd asked.

"The Army."

CHAPTER 11

"So, you're serious when you said the Army is in Umatilla?"

I turned to look back at the M-ATVs. "Where do you think we got those? Yes, I'm serious. If you want to go to Umatilla High School, you can get a meal. See a doctor and maybe even get some work through the Army."

"You can also join the Central Florida Militia," Aric said. "Just tell the soldiers at the gate you want to talk to the militia." Aric then looked at me.

I smiled, saying, "Good job, man. Good job."

"What do we get in the militia?" the young man asked.

"Food, training, weapons, uniforms. But it isn't free. You will work for it," said Aric.

With a jut of his chin, the young man asked, "Who are you?"

"Aric Vonasec. Commander of the militia."

The young man turned and started to walk away. One of his friends called out to him, "Where you going?"

Looking over his shoulder, he responded, "To Umatilla! I'm joining the militia!"

A couple of people shared looks, then called out, "Hey man! Wait for us!"

I looked at Aric and said, "Look at you, already recruiting."

Aric just smiled. But there was a change in his demeanor. It was clear he'd found purpose. Something he'd needed for some time.

Mel was still looking at the bodies of the two men. Dark rivulets of blood were snaking away from them and toward the storm drains. I walked over in front of her. With the view blocked, she looked up.

"You OK?" I asked.

"I thought I'd feel different."

"How do you feel?"

"I don't know. Justified? I don't really know."

I put my arm around her and turned her away from the scene. "Well, you may feel differently in the next couple of days. If you want to talk about it, I'm here."

As we walked, she asked, "How many people have you killed?"

I shrugged. "I ... don't know. Don't keep track. I don't think I'd want to know. Don't start counting, baby."

"I'm not. Was just curious."

We loaded back into our trucks as the people hanging out at the Circle K gathered around the bodies of the two men. None of our people had any issues with what was just done, and it appeared as though the others didn't either.

As I started the truck, Aric said, "Well, that was intense."

"Shit happens," I said.

"What do you think those Army guys are going to think of our new callsigns?" Aric asked.

"That should be interesting," I replied with a chuckle. "They don't know yet."

***

"You missed that one!" Imri shouted as he tried in vain to hang on inside the Jeep as it bounced down a rutted and washed-out forest road.

Karl was hunched over the wheel, his tongue protruding just a little as he concentrated on the road ahead. "I'll go back for it! Just keep an eye on the tire tracks, those are Morgan's. We'll be able to find the ambush site."

Chad sat in the rear seat, one hand on either side of the roll bar. "There's no way there's anyone out here."

"We're the only ones that really have wheels. They can walk in," Karl said.

"Why the hell would they want to?" Imri asked, staring out the window. "Look at this God-forsaken country. There's nothing out there."

CHAPTER 11

"Check the map, Imri. How much farther to the camp?"

Imri did his best to read the map as he was repeatedly slammed back and forth by the violent rocking of the Jeep. In exasperation, he said, "Just slow down for a sec. I can't see shit."

Karl eased up a little. "Hurry up!" he shouted.

"What's up your ass?" Imri asked as he inspected the map.

Karl laughed. "I want a shower."

Imri looked at him. "What? All that shit about a shower earlier and suddenly it's cool when you want one?"

"How much farther?"

"Looks like it's about a mile."

"I don't think my kidneys can take another mile," Chad announced.

"Don't worry, Chadster, we'll be there soon!" Karl assured him.

Before heading out on this mission, Karl had prepped the Jeep for the job. The top and doors were removed to provide a better view. The normal things were there: water, chow, a SAW, ammo, and recovery gear. It didn't leave much room for them, but it was enough.

They continued down the road that nature was quickly recovering. Weeds and even small trees were taking root in the road, and it wouldn't be much longer before it would be impassable by a wheeled vehicle. For now, though, the brush only came up to the hood in most places, save the occasional sand pine that found purchase in the soft sand of the road.

Suddenly Imri shouted, "Karl! Stop!"

The Jeep skidded to a stop in a cloud of dust. Looking around anxiously, Karl asked, "What is it?"

Imri's head was hung out the window, looking down. "Tracks," was all he said as he got out.

Karl quickly exited the Jeep as well. It took Chad some effort to extricate himself from the backseat.

Karl and Imri studied the tracks before Karl spoke. "Looks like three people."

Imri nodded his agreement. "Look at this track. There's barely any tread left on the shoe."

"Same with these boots here. Looks like everyone is wearing out their shoes."

Chad came around and looked at the tracks as well. "What do you see?"

"Three people," Imri said.

"Men," Karl corrected him. "Look at the size of the tracks."

"If it's a woman, she's a big bitch," Chad said.

"The tracks just lead down the road," Imri said.

"Can you follow them from the Jeep?" Karl asked.

"Yeah, if your driving doesn't give me a TBI."

"Chad, get that saw out and see if you can prop yourself up to see over the windshield. With Imri watching the road, we need more eyes looking for threats," Karl said.

"I'll get the sling out. It'll help," Chad said.

The sling was an invention of Chad's. It was made from nylon webbing and crudely sewn into a seat of sorts. The ends had loops that were wrapped over the rollbar and secured back to itself with two carabiners. When set up, the shooter sat on the three straps of webbing that made up the seat, with another one that ran past the small of the back. This way the shooter basically sat in it, keeping rearward pressure against it.

Karl waited for Chad to get his impromptu bosun's chair set up before pulling away. He proceeded slowly this time, listening to Imri as he tried to make out the tracks. The sand helped a lot, but Mother Nature was hard at work and weeds were quickly covering the road.

"I can see where they turned around," Karl announced.

Imri looked up. "I see it. The tracks are coming and going right here."

"They probably came up to look at the scene after Morgan left."

Pulling his head into the Jeep, Imri said, "Let's go see."

Karl stopped the Jeep in front of a large washout and stepped out. "This is the spot for sure," Karl said.

Imri made his way through the washout with a pair of binos in his hand and his rifle slung over his chest. Approaching the crest, he dropped down and crawled up. Chad remained in the Jeep with the SAW. He was scanning the sides of the road and to their rear. Karl and Imri were looking forward; someone needed to watch their six.

Karl made his way over to Imri, taking up a prone position beside him. Picking up a link, he said, "Well, this is where they were shooting from. You see anything down there?" Karl asked, squinting to look down the road.

"I can see some tracks in the road. Nothing else."

Karl sighed. "Well, we can't make it down there on this road. Not even the Jeep will get through that washout."

"What do you—" Imri was cut off by an announcement from Chad.

"Guys, I got contact back here."

Karl and Imri both immediately rolled to their sides to look back. "Where?" Karl asked.

"Two hundred meters or so. On the right."

"How many?" Karl asked as he got to a crouch and started to move back to the Jeep, with Imri bringing up the rear.

"I only saw one. They act like they're trying to hide and doing a really shitty job of it."

Imri was leaning on the Jeep glassing the road with the binos. "Sit still, Chad. I can't see shit with this thing moving."

"I'm not moving!"

"Then stop breathing."

Karl had his rifle up to his cheek, looking through the optic down the road as well when Imri said, "Got 'em!"

"Where?" Karl asked.

"About a hundred meters out. See that really bright green pine tree on the right?"

"The one leaning over? Oh, I see 'em."

"You tracking, Chad?" Imri asked.

"I can't see them but I see the tree."

"They're moving in the tree line," Karl said.

"What do you want to do?" Imri asked.

"They're too close to try and ambush now. Let's just wait and see what they want. Chadster, come on down from there. Let's move down into this wash and watch."

The three men moved down into the wash and took up positions. Chad had a clear field of fire to the right side of the road while the Jeep obscured a lot of the left. Imri moved to cover the left side of the road. The men whispered back and forth as they waited for whoever was stalking them to make themselves known.

It didn't take long before they could hear movement forty-odd meters from them in the wood line. Chad flipped the safety off the SAW, holding it tight to his shoulder and looking down the barrel. The sound stopped for several long seconds. Then they heard a loud *snap* and all sound once again ceased.

Karl was getting impatient. Cupping his mouth, he called out, "We know you're out there! Make yourself known!"

The woods were quiet. Only the slight noise of a breeze swaying the sand pines could be heard. Karl and Chad kept sweeping the woods, trying desperately to see something, anything. Their careful attention was broken by the sudden rapid report of Imri's M4.

"Contact left! Two men, twenty meters, five o'clock!" Imri shouted over the rifle as it barked and spewed fire.

As soon as Karl shifted, Chad opened fire and the SAW's thunderous report added to the cacophony of noise. Karl started to fire into the woods on the right, then shifted to the left.

"Check!" Imri called out as he pulled a fresh mag from his chest rig.

"OK!" Karl called back and slowed his cadence of fire. Once Karl heard Imri firing again, he called *check* and performed a combat reload, just dropping the mag in the weapon. They could be collected after the shooting was done.

Chad kept up a steady rate of fire in short, controlled bursts. Machine guns go through ammo quick, though, and it wasn't long before he also called *check*.

Karl shifted position to fire on the right side of the road, shouting, "Covering!"

Chad slid down into the washout and opened the weapon's cover. Running a gloved hand through the feed tray, he looked under it before placing a new belt on the tray and slamming the cover closed. Turning his head to the left, he gripped the charging handle, palm up, and pulled it to the rear before pushing the handle forward to its detent. The SAW, like most machine guns, fired from an open bolt, meaning the bolt was held to the rear until the trigger released it.

With the weapon reloaded, he called out, "Up!"

While the three men had thrown a couple hundred rounds downrange in mere seconds, the return fire was a trifle in comparison. Only a couple of rounds were fired back at them, and none of them had even come close.

"Cease fire! Cease fire!" Karl called out.

The shooting stopped and the men listened as they scanned the woods around them. Imri was reloading again with his weapon up in his workspace, scanning the area as he mechanically performed a reload without looking until he was ready to drop the bolt. He quickly glanced at the chamber as his left thumb hit the bolt release, slamming a round home. He closed the dust cover unconsciously.

"You guys see anything?" Chad asked.

"No," Karl said. "We're going to have to go out there and look for them."

"Do we really?" Imri asked. "That's just an ambush waiting to happen."

"I don't want to either. But you know we have to."

"I'll cover you guys," Chad added.

"Which side do you want to do first?" Imri asked.

"Since Chad's over here, let's do the left side first. How many did you see over there?" Karl asked.

"Two," Imri quickly replied. "I think ..."

"On you," said Karl.

The two men moved through the bottom of the washout until they were off the road before climbing out. With their weapons at low ready and crouching, they moved into the woods parallel to the road. With Imri in the lead, Karl took up a position about five meters to Imri's seven o'clock. This way, one bullet wouldn't come from anyone ahead of them and hit both men.

They moved for about forty meters, stopping to listen occasionally, before Imri held up a hand. Karl looked at him expectantly. With two fingers, Imri pointed at his eyes, then at the ground. Karl moved over as Imri continued to scan the woods. Reaching Imri, he could see the patch of blood-soaked sand.

Karl studied the area for a minute before saying, "They went that way, to the west, deeper into the woods."

"How many?"

Karl studied the tracks again and followed them a short distance. "There's two of them. One is helping the other."

"They're probably not a threat at this point."

"I hope not. But we can't stay here all day and we damn sure aren't wandering off into the woods to look for them. Let's

CHAPTER 11

go check the other side. Back the way we came so we can use the washout to cover our movement across the road."

"Moving," said Imri as he returned the short distance to the washout.

"What'd you see?" Chad asked when they got to him.

"Blood trail. Two sets of tracks, one helping the other," said Karl.

"You going out there now?"

"Yes we are, Chadster. Cover us."

"I'm on it," said Chad, lying against the wall of the washout.

As Imri passed him, he planted his palm into Chad's back, using it to push himself out of the wash.

"Get off me, asshole!" Chad ordered through clenched teeth. "How much do you weigh?"

"I won't tell," said Imri as he cleared the obstacle.

"Yeah, most women won't," Chad said with a smile.

In reply, Imri looked back and blew Chad a kiss before following Karl into the bush. Once into the woods about ten meters, the two took a knee to look and listen.

"You hear that?" Imri asked.

Karl looked at him, incredulity painted on his face. "I haven't had batteries for my hearing aids in a year. You know I can't hear shit. What is it?"

Imri strained to listen again. "Almost like someone crying. Or whining."

"We have someone wounded out here then. Let's find them. You can hear it, so you take point."

Imri didn't reply. He simply rose to a crouch, shouldered his weapon at low ready and moved past Karl. Taking the rear position, Karl kept an eye on their six so no one could sneak up from behind. The fact that Chad was still back there with the SAW reduced the tension a bit.

Stalking a wounded human is the most dangerous kind of hunting. Hunting an armed and wounded human takes it to a terrifying level. As a result, the two men moved slowly and cautiously. Sweat built up on Imri's brow, ran down his forehead, and dripped from his nose. It wasn't because of the physical effort. It was the stress and adrenaline.

Every two or three very cautious steps, Imri would stop and listen and scan the surrounding woods. The low growing scrub oaks made seeing anything low to the ground challenging. Often they would need to take a knee to check the ground ahead. It was on one of these kneeling pauses that Imri's body went rigid and his weapon swung to the right just a little.

"What?" Karl whispered.

Imri stretched his left hand out, pointing to the base of a pine tree with a clump of young scrub oaks growing around it. Sticking out of the clump was a dirty sneaker that rocked back and forth rapidly. It was the movement that caught his eye. In nature, horizontal movement is the key indicator of an animal. Vertical movement is common. Things fall from trees. Gravity is always at work, and everything that goes up must come down.

Horizontal movement, in most cases, is something living. Something waving back and forth is certainly caused by an animal. The only exception to that being the occasional leaf fluttering in the breeze. In this case however, the sneaker was an obvious indicator they'd found a human.

The hunting of humans had been hard for untold numbers of people after The Day. Not that most people wanted to. However, when the law of the jungle supersedes that of man, one either adapts into the hunter or simply remains the prey, victims the old society molded them into.

Modern humans have a natural aversion to killing other humans. The ones that couldn't overcome this deeply ingrained taboo perished, often horrifically. Karl and Imri possessed no such repulsion. Quite the contrary, they were of a small but persistent warrior class that accepted the killing of others as necessary at times. Neither of them relished it. They just didn't hesitate when it needed doing.

Using hand signals, Karl indicated he would circle behind the person as Imri approached on his current track. Scanning nonstop, Imri watched Karl as he moved out, all the while watching that wagging sneaker. As Karl moved, so did Imri. He was now close enough to hear the pathetic sniffling and crying. It was obvious at this point it was a young woman.

They were very close now. With hand signals, Karl indicated he would approach and go hands on with the person. Imri would cover Karl. Imri nodded and Karl started to move. The stalk had been slow. This last part, closing to contact, happened quickly and dynamically. Karl rushed the position as Imri also closed the short distance.

There was a cry, stifled midway through, followed by thrashing in the bushes along with pleas and more cries. When Imri got to Karl, he had a young woman face down on the ground, a knee in her back as he patted her down for weapons. Finding one, Karl picked up a heavily worn Browning Hi-Power and tossed it to Imri.

"She's wounded," Karl said over the woman's cries as he ripped open the IFAK on his rig. This was violating a cardinal rule, your IFAK was for you. You should never give yours to someone else leaving you without. But the Jeep was right there, as well as Karl's medic ruck. He could replace what he used.

"Please, please, please, don't kill me!" the young woman pleaded in a shuddering voice. Her hands trembled as well, and it was obvious she was going into shock. She'd been shot twice in the right leg and the wounds were terrible. Karl applied a tourniquet to her thigh as high up as he could. Then he pulled a pack of Z-fold gauze out and started to pack the wound.

"This is going to hurt," he said to the woman, "but it's necessary."

She howled in pain. In their travels, Karl had managed to acquire some scarce supplies. He had bottles of ketamine, morphine, and propofol. He could relieve her pain for her, even sedate her to make her more manageable. But those meds weren't for someone who, only moments ago, was trying to kill him. No, she would have to tough it out.

The woman screamed and cried out as the wound was packed. Karl was holding the gauze in place with his thumb as Imri opened a pressure dressing to cover it when she finally passed out. Karl checked her pulse and made sure she was breathing.

"She's lost a lot of blood. We need to get her out of here," Karl said.

In reply, Imri knelt down and pulled her up. Karl helped and Imri quickly had her over his shoulders in a fireman's carry. Karl now took security as they moved quickly back toward the Jeep.

Getting close to Chad, Karl called out, "De oppresso libre!"

"Mortem tyrannis!"

It was an easy code to use. Not many people spoke Latin so the chance they would even know what was going on was small. For those that did know, the odds of knowing the reply to the challenge was slim as well.

"Holy shit!" Chad said when he saw the girl. "How bad is she?"

"Two to the right leg. We need to get her to town," said Karl.

"You want to take her to Morgan? They don't have a surgeon."

"No, to the school. They have more resources."

CHAPTER 11

Imri made it to the Jeep and put the girl in the backseat. Karl came over with a stethoscope and checked her heartbeat and respiration. "She needs fluids."

"You have any?" Imri asked.

Karl nodded. "In that ruck, there's Ringers in there. Hand it to me."

Imri handed over the ruck. Karl quickly got out an infusion set and a tie, which he quickly wrapped around her arm and secured. Holding her arm out, he tapped at the inside of the elbow joint. Finding the vein, he stuck the needle cap in his mouth and pulled the needle out. He hit the vein on the first stick and removed the sharp, leaving the cannula in place. Using the same rubber tie Karl used to get the IV started, Imri wrapped it around the rollbar of the Jeep and secured the bag of Ringers to allow gravity to do its job.

With fluid now flowing into the girl, the men quickly loaded up and Karl got the Jeep turned around and headed back the way they came. No self-respecting Green Beret would ever go out the way they came in. But in this case, there was no alternative. They simply couldn't pass the washout.

"Hang on back there, Chadster. This is gonna be rough," Karl said as they hit a big bump.

"That's what I like about you Karl. Nothing gets past you!" Chad shot back.

>≡∭≡<

Audie lifted the rod from the weld he was doing. It died in a brilliant flash and Terry opened his eyes.

"Looks good, Audie. You sure as shit can weld," Terry said.

"I like to weld. Always enjoy it," said Audie as he picked up a chipping hammer and knocked the slag from it to reveal a beautiful weld beneath.

"You think this gear will do it?" Terry asked.

"I timed the wheel, well, the axle. Based on that RPM, this should be able to turn a gen head fast enough to carry a load."

As Audie spoke, Sarge's Hummer pulled into the parking lot. Both men looked up as the old man got out of the truck.

"Hey Sarge," Terry called out.

"How are you fellers doing?" Sarge called back.

"Working on this power unit for Alexander," said Audie.

"Looks good. Nice welds." Sarge then turned to Terry. "I need that boom truck. We've got some antenna towers we're going to take down and relocate."

"It's over at the plant. You want me to go get it?" Terry asked.

Sarge nodded. "Yeah. If you see Baker, bring her too."

Terry was already headed for the door when he shouted, "Roger that!"

"You're going to need some concrete to get those things put up," said Audie.

"For some of them. I think one or two won't, but we'll see."

"I'll have to ask Morgan if there's a cement plant around here. All we really need is the Portland Cement. We can get the sand and aggregate."

"Grab some hand tools, whatever you think we might need," said Sarge.

Audie pointed at the Suburban. "Everything we'll need is in there."

"You get it set up?"

"Yeah," said Audie. "Come on, I'll show you."

They walked over to the old truck and Audie showed Sarge how he installed toolboxes, a torch set, and various other tools. For all intents and purposes, it was now a mobile workshop.

"Looks good, Audie. You're ready to get some work done."

"I like having things organized. Knowing where your tools are will save you time."

CHAPTER 11

Hearing the boom truck approach, Sarge said, "Just follow me."

Audie pulled the bay door down and locked it before leaving. He liked his new place and keeping it secure was important. Not that he'd had any issues. But in this world, possession was ten tenths of the law. If you can defend it, it belongs to you.

When they got back to the house on 439, Baker walked up to Sarge. "Well, now I see why you needed the truck."

"Yeah, we'll need it for sure. "

"Where are you going to put these?"

"One back at our place. One for you. The other two I'm thinking of putting on either side of town, one on the north and one on the south side, and put repeaters on them. That is *if* we can find batteries and solar panels to run them."

"That shouldn't be hard. You don't need much power for that, do you?"

Sarge shook his head. "Not at all. A single twelve-volt battery and small panel and charge controller to keep it going. The coax and power wire will be the hardest thing to come by. We need to be real careful with the coax when we pull it out here."

"Who's going to climb up there?" Baker asked.

Sarge looked at Dad. "Butch, you wanna climb up there?"

Dad laughed. "Shit, in my day I would. But my tower climbing days are over."

"Don't look at me!" Thad shouted. Then with a laugh, added, "I don't do heights."

"I'll climb it," Audie said. "I don't mind heights. Hell, it'll be fun."

"Audie," said Thad, "if you think that's fun, you is crazy!"

CHAPTER 12

Kay watched Mary fidget with her coffee cup. Smiling to herself, she said, "You're gonna be fine, Mary."

Mary smiled meekly and looked up. "I know you keep saying that. But there's something I never told you."

"What's that?"

Mary took a deep breath, letting it out slowly. "I never wanted to have children. I mean, I loved the idea of it. I wanted a child, I just didn't want to *have* a child."

Kay gave a little laugh. "It's not that bad."

Mary looked away, and as she began to speak, her voice cracked. "I know it's usually pretty routine." She wiped a tear away and looked at Kay. "My mother died when I was young."

Kay reached across the table and took Mary's hand. "Oh, you poor dear, I had no idea."

"It's okay, I don't talk about it. Mother died giving birth to my sister, Michelle."

"That is so terrible. I didn't know you had a sister. You never talk about your family."

Mary looked down into her cup, then back up to meet Kay's gaze. "I don't have a sister."

Kay covered her mouth with a hand. "Oh, no."

Mary nodded. "Michelle died three days later. Complications, they said. But that's what they always say."

Kay got up and walked around the table to sit beside the younger woman. Putting an arm around her, she said, "That won't happen to you."

"That's what everyone says," Mary replied, then looked Kay in the eye. "That's what they told Momma too."

"What happened to your mother and sister is not normal, you have to know that."

"I do. But it happened and she was in a hospital."

"Look, I'm going to take Fred some lunch. Come down with me and see those two beautiful babies. They were born right here, not in a hospital, and Fred is fine and so are the babies. Everyone is healthy."

Mary straightened up, wiping her face with her hands. "You're right," she said, then smiled. "I want to go see Fred."

"I'll go get the food for them and we'll walk down there," Kay said as she got up.

Mary took a deep breath before exhaling. "Okay," she said as she rose to her feet.

We continued on our route to Rock Springs. The ride was quiet, there was no chatter. Before leaving, I put an antenna up in a tree and made contact with the old man. We really needed repeaters. Having to stop and put up an antenna was a pain in the ass. I just used the opportunity at the Circle K to knock out a contact. Next time we will be stopping to make contact.

The thought of stopping to put up an antenna to make a shot was a sign of the old world still lingering around. What did it matter if we stopped? We had no schedule. No timetable we were working from. We'd just become so used to convenience, anything that was even a mild inconvenience was looked upon with spite. Things took longer to do today. Everything was a little more difficult. Now, you actually had to work for what you wanted.

We were rolling down 437 headed toward Sorrento as my mind wandered. I should have been paying attention, but I was relaxed and let my mind poke around in the darkness. I was thinking of all those people with skills that were essentially useless in this new world.

Tech people came to mind. Along with human resources folks. There were countless others that fit into this as well. They dedicated their lives to skills that were utterly useless except in a technologically advanced society. They worked on things that didn't exist physically. Sure, the computers they used were real. But their work only existed in the virtual world. Just bits, 1s, and 0s. But then they didn't really exist either. Virtual reality is kind of cool. But unlike the world of VR, humans have basic needs that must be fulfilled.

In a world where Grubhub will deliver to your door anything you wish to eat at any time day or night, most people never considered what it would take to feed themselves or their families. They chose pursuits that didn't require hard skills.

Most would have guffawed at the idea of learning what plants are edible or ways to process water so it was safe to drink or build a fire without a lighter and gasoline (which never ends well). These are skills that will keep you alive. The modern world, however, disincentivized this kind of knowledge over useless soft skills that rewarded only money.

In the modern world, money was king. You couldn't exist without it. All your needs had to be provided for with money. Useless paper that arbitrary value was attached to. You couldn't eat it. It made for shitty tinder. But it was absolutely essential. That is one thing I do not miss. I thought about money for a second. I had a couple hundred in cash still. More as a souvenir of The Before than anything else.

Then I thought about the Internet and how I hadn't missed it at all. The repository of human knowledge, always at your fingertips, and it just vanished in the blink of an eye. And I didn't miss it. Sure, I missed being able to look up something. While that was part of the original intent of the Internet, it had turned into a behemoth that no one ever expected until it infiltrated every aspect of life. The Internet was a time sink that consumed millions of hours of people's lives a year. Even though it was gone, it was still wasting my time at the moment.

It was kind of surreal being out on roads I hadn't seen since The Day. We were approaching Highway 46 in Sorrento and I slowed as the intersection drew near, not because of the approaching turn, but because there was a large oak tree down blocking most of the road. I moved to the right and went off the road through the open shoulder. Looking in the mirror, I saw the trucks were following and made the turn for the short ride on 46.

JJ's Package Lounge was now a charred ruin. The structure had obviously caught fire after The Day and was completely burned.

"That's a shame," Mel said as we passed it.

"Nice place?" Aric asked from the backseat.

"No," I laughed, "just a dive ass bar."

"You know I love dive bars," said Mel.

"Dive bars can be fun," Aric added.

It wasn't just JJ's. The liquor store next to it was also burned out, as was the Ace.

"Looks like there's a firebug in the area," I said.

"Yeah, someone burned them down for sure," said Aric.

"I bet people have burned down lots of places," Mel said.

"I would say that a lot of bad shit was done by shittier people after The Day," I said. "When the thin veil of civility falls, it removes the restraints that hold people back."

The First Baptist Church of Sorrento was still there. The arsonist left it for some reason. In the parking lot were a couple of oaks with large canopies, and a group of people were sitting in an assortment of chairs in the shade. Hearing the trucks, they

CHAPTER 12

were quickly on their feet and walking toward the road. When they saw the trucks, they pulled back a bit, stepping back from the road.

Mel waved at them as they stared in apparent shock. They didn't wave back, just stood there slack jawed as the convoy passed. Looking in the mirror, I could see Mike waving at them from the turret. There were more people as we came into the small town. I don't quite know what the attraction is to convenience stores, but at the Circle K on the corner was another group of people.

"They look rough," Aric said.

The people were filthy. The two men had long unkempt hair with shaggy beards to go with it. One of the women there looked as though she had dreadlocks.

"Bet they're crawling with lice," Mel said.

"Probably so," I agreed.

"You gonna stop?" Aric asked.

"No. We're not going to stop and talk to every person we see. Let's see if we can find large groups of people."

"We have the ability to feed people in Umatilla," Mel said. "But what about other areas? Is there any way we can get help out to more places?"

As we turned back onto 437, which was a small jog in the route, I said, "We need to, and it's a priority. But before we can even think about that, we have to have the manpower to secure an area to be able to do so. The Army just doesn't have the bodies to do it, so we'll have to do it with the militia."

"We're going to need a lot of people," said Aric.

"We are," I said and looked at Aric in the mirror. "You have a lot of work to do!"

We were now entering an area predominated by greenhouses. The small city of Apopka is known as the foliage capital of the world. A large variety of plants were grown there and shipped around the globe. These facilities typically covered large acreages with both outdoor grow beds as well as the greenhouses. The area sits on the Central Florida Ridge and is some of the highest land in the state. It was once dense oak forests with scattered sinkhole lakes, and these were the only water sources in the region.

I wasn't surprised at seeing a few people. They would naturally have to migrate to water, which is why we were on this mission. In the forest, the springs were remote and would take a lot of time to get to. Rock Springs and Wekiva, however, were in close proximity to a denser population, and therefore would have a higher likelihood of being occupied.

We were passing through an area of growers when I slowed. "Damn."

"Wow, that's a lot of people," Aric said.

Keying my radio, I called out, "Mikey, you seeing this?" His callsign just wasn't stuck yet.

Tracking, he called back.

"What are they doing?" Mel asked, trying to discern what was going on.

The sign on the road announced this was the van Hoekelen Greenhouses. From what we could see from the road, it was a large operation and appeared to still be running. Our convoy was spotted and soon people were standing in the road gesturing at us. There wasn't panic, but there was definite concern, as I could see some people gesturing wildly and a couple of people running off.

On the radio, I said, "They look pretty nervous. Let's be very careful and very friendly."

Roger that, said Mike.

Shithead, you go up with them. Stay close. We're going to stay on the road and provide security, I heard Ted say.

Copy, said Mike.

I approached at a crawl with the two trucks behind me until we were within thirty or forty feet of the people gathered there. They looked at us anxiously. Then a group of people ran out from the greenhouses armed with an assortment of weapons. I stopped the truck and shut it off.

"Let's get out. Keep your hands where they can see them. Let's see if we can talk," I said.

Mel was hesitant. "You sure? They have guns."

"So do we," I assured her.

"Bigger ones, too," Aric added.

Stepping out, I waved to the people and made sure my badge wasn't covered by my sling.

"Hello!" I called out.

The group shared glances and seemed to look to two men for guidance. Both of them were armed but not doing anything threatening.

"You see that?" I asked quietly.

"Yep," Aric confirmed.

"What?" Mel asked.

"Those two guys seem to be the honchos around here. The blonde one with the AR and gray-headed old guy," I said.

I was relieved to see them using hand signals telling their people to calm down or something to that effect. The older man I estimated was in his sixties with the younger in his late thirties. I raised my hand in a wave again and called out, "*Hello!*"

The two men shared a look and a couple of words before taking a few steps forward. With a slight wave and a nod of the head, the older man started to walk slowly toward us. We stopped a short distance from one another and I began to speak.

"How are you guys doing?" I asked.

The two men shared a confused look before the older one replied, "As good as can be expected."

I gave a little laugh. "Isn't that the truth? I'm Morgan Carter, acting sheriff of Lake County." I hated to say acting governor. "You mind having a word?"

Now the confusion on the men's faces was obvious. Tentatively, the older man said, "Sure."

I walked over to him and offered my hand. "Morgan. Nice to meet you."

"I'm Dale," he said, "this is my son Brian."

"Nice to meet you both."

"You really the acting sheriff?" Brian asked.

"I am. Wasn't my idea."

"Who made you acting sheriff?" Dale asked.

"The Army."

The two looked at one another, astonishment clear on their faces. "The Army?" Dale asked. "I didn't think it even existed anymore."

"It does. We're essentially under Martial Law at the moment. They're running the country."

"What about the President?" Dale asked.

"Arrested."

Dale snorted. "Well, maybe there is hope after all."

The comment relieved me. Anyone who can find a little humor is my kind of people.

"Well, we're trying."

"We haven't seen any help from anyone at all," Brian said. "Where the hell have they been?"

"They're trying to set up distribution points. Right now the only one is in Umatilla."

"Umatilla? What the hell did they set up shop there for?" Dale asked.

"Couple of reasons. The biggest being we have the power on in town and some of the surrounding area."

"Power? How the hell do you have power?" Brian asked.

CHAPTER 12

"The juice plant in town has a small natural gas turbine. It makes enough power for what we're doing right now."

"Then how the hell do you have natural gas?" Dale asked.

"That, I don't know. It comes in from the west coast somewhere, but we can't really go over there and look around, what with Tampa glowing in the dark."

"I reckon not," said Dale.

"So, what's all this?" I asked, nodding toward the people behind them.

Dale looked back, then back to me. "Just a group of folks trying to survive is all."

"I'm curious why here. There's no water around. Not close, anyway. What's made you all stay here?"

"We have water," Brian replied.

"The nursery has an artesian well. It provides more water than we need," Dale said.

"Oh, nice. I would kill to have one of those at my place. How in the world are you feeding everyone?" I asked as I'd estimated there were thirty or more people here just in what I could see.

Dale squinted and looked at me. "You really the sheriff?" I nodded. "I'm guessing you're telling the truth. Not like you can just find those armored trucks lying around."

"I'm telling you the truth, Dale. We're out conducting a survey to see where there's large groups of people so we know where to set up next. We're no danger to you at all."

Dale and Brian spoke quietly for a minute before Dale said, "Then come on. I want to show you something."

I waved for Mel and Aric to come with us. As they walked up, I said, "This is my wife, Mel, and this is Aric. He's the commander of the Central Florida Militia."

Dale looked surprised. "We have a militia?"

"We do."

Dale looked at Brian and said, "Imagine that. This morning we didn't have an Army. Now we not only have an Army, but we have a militia too." He looked at me and asked, "What other surprises do you have in store?"

"He's also the acting governor," Mel said, nodding in my direction.

Dale looked shocked. "What? You didn't say you were the governor. You said you were acting sheriff for Lake County!"

"Yeah, not my idea. I wasn't asked. I was voluntold," I said.

"Let me get this straight," Brian said, "you're a sheriff and the governor right now?"

"It looks that way. The Army put it all on me. I didn't want anything to do with it."

"Why you? I mean, who the hell are you?" Dale asked.

"Just someone who tried to make a difference. I was just looking out for my people and anyone we could help. It's a long story. Maybe one day I can tell it all."

"Sounds like a hell of a book!" Brian said.

"Well, come on, Governor or Sheriff, or whatever you like to be called," Dale said.

"Morgan. Just call me Morgan."

We followed them back into a very large complex of greenhouses. There were dozens of them and they were at least a hundred feet long. There were people everywhere, all busy. These folks were not idle. They weren't waiting for someone to help them; they were helping themselves.

As we approached one of the greenhouses, a man and a woman emerged pulling a nursery cart loaded down with vegetables.

"Oh, wow," Mel said. "Are you growing all this?"

Dale stepped into the large opening at the end of the structure and turned. "Yes, we are. After things went to shit, I started growing at my house. But there were more people than we could feed that way. I started looking around and when I found the artesian well here, I knew this was the place. Most of these people live here or very close. They had to leave their homes. No water, no food. Nothing. So we slowly built a community here."

"Where did you get all the seeds?" Mel asked.

"I was a rather intensive gardener before. I had a large stock of seeds and liked to experiment," Dale said.

Brian laughed, adding, "Dad doesn't have a green thumb, he's all green on the inside. I remember as a kid helping package seeds for storage. Some of those we're eating now."

"How do you handle security?" I asked.

Dale turned and walked into the greenhouse and we followed him. As he walked, he said, "So far we haven't had too many issues. No one knows we're here and we like it that way."

"We've dealt with those that wanted trouble," Brian said.

Stepping into the greenhouse, the temperature was notably higher as well as the humidity. Greenhouses always have the same smell to them, and this one was no different. It was a combination of chemicals, earth, and greenery. It brought back memories of my youth. When I was a kid, we had a neighbor who had a large greenhouse, and I would play in there with his grandson. Then in my teens, I worked in one. Miserable job, don't miss it one bit.

Inside the greenhouse were elevated beds bursting at the seams with produce. They were growing all manner of veggies and the abundance was impressive.

"Holy shit," Aric said when he saw it all.

Dale turned and smiled. "Beautiful isn't it?"

"Dale," I asked, "how many people do you have here?"

Dale looked at Brian for the answer. "Fifty-two, including children and some elderly who cannot work. We feed them all," said Brian.

"What are you doing for protein?" I asked.

"Whatever we can find. There isn't much in the way of meat anymore," Dale answered.

"Fifty people cannot possibly eat all this. Are you storing any?" Mel asked.

"We dry some. We've made some dehydrators and they're better than nothing."

"How many of these are in production?" I asked.

"Nine of them," Brian answered.

They gave us the tour. All of the greenhouses in production were full of plants of all kinds. They were growing a wide variety of produce, even some exotics.

My radio went off. *You all good in there?* I heard Mike ask.

"We're good in here. Be out soon."

"That them boys in the trucks?" Dale asked. I nodded and he added, "You got some serious hardware."

The tour continued and they showed us the artesian well that made all this possible. They'd made a manifold with a separate pipe running to each greenhouse to provide water. There was a central kitchen, and they ate communal meals like we did. They also showed us a small building used as a school for a handful of kids. It looked like they were making a real effort at living as normal a life as they could.

"This is impressive," I said.

"Thank you. It's hard work and there are no free lunches, but everyone eats," said Dale.

"Would you be interested in working together?" I asked.

"In what manner?"

"Well, trade for starters."

Dale cut his eyes toward me. "Trade for what?"

"How about beef?"

Dale laughed. "Beef? Where the hell you gonna get beef?"

"We have cattle. I can trade actual beef with you or cattle. What I'm thinking is, we keep you in beef and you keep us in veggies."

"Cattle would be nice, but they'd be a huge target," Brian said.

"What if I stationed militia here?" I asked.

Dale rubbed the back of his head as he thought about it. Then he said, "I have an idea. How about you make us part of the militia?"

"How many people of fighting age do you have here?" Aric asked.

"'Bout thirty," Brian said.

"Let's do this then," I said, "let us get some people over here in the short term. They will bring some equipment with them, radios, weapons and the like. I will have our instructors come out here and train your people. Is there anything you're in real need of?"

Brian laughed. "What *don't* we need?"

"Ammunition is in short supply," Dale said.

"We'll handle that. I'm thinking more along the lines of a doctor, clothes, that kind of thing," I said.

"We could definitely use a doctor," Dale said as he visibly thought about things. "I guess the basics, ya know, batteries, hygiene stuff."

A woman was walking out of the greenhouse with a large tub in her hands. "Soap would be nice," she said, then leaned over to Mel adding, "and tampons," before continuing on her way.

"You have anyone in immediate need?" I asked.

"We've got one old woman here that's in pretty bad shape," said Dale.

Pulling the mic from my plate carrier, I called Ted. "Hey Ted, can you send Doc, Sky, and Bubba down here? Tell Bubba and Sky to bring their shit. They're going to be staying a while here." I knew as soon as I was around Sarge he would remind me of callsigns. But Ted nor Mike probably cared in the least.

Roger that. They're on their way.

Looking at Dale, I said, "I have a Ranger medic coming in and two militiamen. They will stay here with you until we come back. Might take a day or two to get everything together, but we'll be back. Bubba has a radio and we'll put up an antenna before we go so we can communicate."

"What are they supposed to do?" Brian asked.

"Security. They have weapons and ammo and can get in touch with us. But they're good people and will do whatever they can to help out."

We talked small talk until our people came in. Brian took Doc to see the woman and Aric went with Dale to find a place to quarter Bubba and Sky, leaving Mel and me alone.

"What do you think?" Mel asked.

"I can't believe no one has come in here and taken this over."

"Let's walk," I said, and we started down the long row of greenhouses.

"They seem happy enough," Mel said.

"They do. I want to talk to a few of them without Brian and Dale there."

In a greenhouse that wasn't in production, we found several people sitting and cutting vegetables and laying them on large screen trays for drying. Mel and I walked over and knelt beside a woman who looked at her in shock.

"Who are you?" the woman asked, eyeing the machine gun with suspicion.

"I'm Mel. We were passing by and saw your place here. This is all incredible," she said, picking up a yellow squash.

CHAPTER 12

"It's a lot of work. Everyone here works. We got no time for freeloaders."

"That is the way things are now. Is it safe here?"

"Safer than most places. When there's trouble, everyone helps to fight off whoever thinks they can take what's ours."

"That's the way it should be," I said.

The woman looked back over her shoulder. "Who the hell are you?"

"I'm Morgan," I said, then reluctantly added, "Acting Governor."

The woman's mouth fell open and she dropped the squash she was cutting up. Standing up, she walked over to me. "You're the governor?" She looked past me as though she expected something. "Where's the help? We've been on our own for so long. I gave up hoping someone would come."

"Things are just now starting to improve. That's why we're here, to help you folks. We're going to work with you."

With a look of utter distrust, she said, "How are you going to help us?"

"For starters, provide security for you. Second, I have a doc here to check on anyone that needs it. We're also going to supply you with beef in the next couple of days."

"Beef! I haven't seen a cow in a damn year! Where the hell you gonna get beef from?"

"We have a herd. Another group of folks like you that worked hard to keep them. They're good people and we support them and they us. That's how things have to work today."

"So, you're the governor, you're not going to … I don't know what you call it … come in here and take everything?"

I laughed. "No ma'am. We execute people for things like that."

The woman wasn't sure what to say to that. "Execute?"

"There are no jails. We're all in a hard spot and anyone looking to take advantage of the situation will be dealt with. Permanently."

"We executed two men on our way here for rape," Mel said. The woman looked at her, pain on her face. "Women and young girls."

"I wish you would've got here sooner," the woman said in a low voice.

"We're here now," I said.

Leaning over, hands on her knees, Jess took a ragged breath and blew a few strands of loose hair from her face. "This is a hell of a lot harder than I thought it was," she said.

Dalton was leaned against an oak tree inspecting the training knife he'd carved from the stalk of a cabbage palm. "It's not easy. The best training you can get is with an uncooperative partner. Makes it real."

Jess straightened and stretched. "You are certainly uncooperative. Where did you learn all this?"

"Started when I was young. Discovered I had a talent for it. It's been a part of my life since."

Jess turned the training blade in her hand around, grip forward and motioned to Dalton. "Again."

Dalton stepped forward, leaving plenty of distance between them. Holding the blade out in front of him, he moved it back and forth. "Remember the arc of the weapon. With a blade you want to be either outside it or inside it. You can't do any damage outside, so try to get inside it. Whenever you're ready."

Jess swayed back and forth for a moment, planning her attack. Blade in her right hand, forward grip, she rushed in. Dalton deftly stepped into her attack, parrying her thrust with his left hand while stepping even closer to her and trapping the wrist of her blade hand in his armpit. Wrapping his left arm under hers, he grabbed her by the neck, his fingers on the back and his thumb pushing her chin upward. He never deployed his blade.

Still in the hold, Jess shouted, "Shit!"

As Dalton released her, he said, "Try not to thrust. It's easier to get your blade trapped. Slash, cut. There are times for stabbing motions, but you have to be in really close."

"This is nothing like it is in the movies."

"No, it's not. In the movies you can't smell the breath of your adversary, his sweat. In the movies, no one gets tired, and they fight forever. In real life you have less than two minutes of real fight in you. Maybe more, depending on your cardio level and the strength of your opponent."

Jess leaned against the oak tree they were using for shade. "Reality is never like the movies."

Dalton kicked a five-gallon bucket over onto its top and sat down. "Why are you wanting to do this?"

Jess shrugged. "I don't. Thought it might come in handy someday, and I just want to be more capable. I really wanted to go out on this mission, but Morgan wouldn't let me."

"I don't think it was because he didn't want to. Think about who went out. Several of them have never gone out."

"Yeah, like me. It's boring."

"From what I've heard, you've done plenty around here."

"What about you?" Jess asked. "It doesn't bother you to be left out?"

"No. I've been involved in enough bad shit in my day," Dalton replied, then looked around. "That's why I like it here. It's quiet. Safe. There's good people with a plan. There's food, hell, there's power. Trust me when I say, boring is good. Boring lives are usually much longer than exciting ones."

"I guess."

Dalton rose to his feet. "The tree. Let's go."

"Again?"

"On your feet. This is where you get better. Faster. Boring is also necessary in training. These drills are monotonous, but you build speed. You ever hear the term *muscle memory?*"

"Yeah, it's like doing something enough that your body just knows what to do."

Pointing his knife at her, Dalton said, "No. It's a myth. It doesn't exist. What you are doing is creating neural shortcuts in your brain. It's like driving your car. Being as you're a young college age woman, I would assume you've texted and drove before."

"Stereotype."

"Tell me I'm wrong."

With a dismissive wave, Jess said, "Whatever, continue."

"The point is, you can still drive your car while you're texting because you have so many repetitions of driving your car, your subconscious can handle it while you focus on texting."

"But people get in accidents all the time."

"True. Because you cannot literally focus on two things at once. But you can still *do* two things at once. One is just running in the background."

Jess considered the statement for a minute. "I see. So, if I get this, what you're saying is, in normal life, I'm focused on whatever I'm doing and if a threat comes up, I'll react to it faster?"

"Faster and with more precision. You won't just fumble for your knife or gun. Your brain will know exactly how to do it and will do it quicker subconsciously than your conscious can. It's like getting a head start."

"Ok, I get it now."

"Want to know how many repetitions it takes to get to the basic level?" Jess rolled her eyes. Dalton took it as a cue to continue. "Five thousand. It takes five thousand repetitions just to be competent at it. How many times do you think you've hit the tree?"

"Not even five hundred."

Dalton pointed at the tree. "Let's go. One."

Jess stepped back from the tree, gripped her palm blade, and made a high to low, right to left slash.

"Two," Dalton said, and she made the opposite strike. "Three."

><////><

Karl took the turn onto Highway 40 at a higher speed than he wanted, fishtailing the Jeep as he did.

"Slow down, boss. We aren't doing any of us any good if we roll this thing," Imri said.

Shifting through the gears and gaining speed, Karl asked, "How is she?"

"Still alive!" Chad shouted back.

Karl pushed the Jeep hard, but it was still over twenty miles to the school. In trauma cases, there is what is known as the golden hour. This is the timeframe that provides the best chance of someone surviving a trauma injury. But the golden hour is predicated on the fact there is a higher level of care available. That an ambulance with paramedics or, better yet, a Life Flight helicopter will swoop in and rescue the victim and fly them to a hospital with specialists in the fields of trauma care. None of that existed anymore. The golden hour was no more golden than any other at this time.

"What the hell happened back there?" Chad asked from the backseat.

"We were ambushed, what do you think happened?" Imri asked.

"They started shooting?" Chad asked.

"No, I saw them first. Hate their fucking luck."

"Don't worry about it, Chadster. We came out on top and if we're lucky, the girl will live," Karl said.

"Probably gonna lose the leg though," Imri added.

"Not my problem," said Karl.

The Jeep was making good time and as they raced past home, Imri made a radio call.

"Stumpknocker, Stumpknocker, Lightning."

Stumpknocker is out of comms right now, this is Adelaide. Send your traffic, Lightning.

"We are en route to the school with a casualty. We were ambushed in the same spot Morgan was."

Wallner's voice came back over the radio. *Uh, copy all Lightning. Who is the cas?*

"OPFOR. Female, early twenties."

Lightning, this is Rhino six, we copy and will have medics waiting. Come in through the rear gate near the stadium. SITREP on casualty.

"Rhino six, cas is critical. Two rounds right thigh," Imri paused and looked at the girl's forehead where Karl wrote the time the tourniquet was applied, then his watch. "TQ applied forty-seven minutes ago. ETA, ten minutes."

Copy all, Rhino six out.

The little red Jeep drew a lot of looks as it came in fast, turning in front of the McDonalds. With only the few cars used by the crew and Army on the roads, pedestrians simply didn't look at them the same. Walking across or even right down the middle of one was now normal. The asphalt strips were no longer the domain of the machines. Now they belonged to people.

And there were lots of people milling about Bulldog Lane. Seeing the Jeep come around the corner nearly on two wheels, most people ran immediately. Those that froze at the odd sight were quickly pulled out of the road by others. Karl drove around

CHAPTER 12

to the rear doors off the ball field and turned in. Harvey was there with several others waiting for them with a stretcher.

They quickly unloaded the girl from the Jeep and placed her on the stretcher. Harvey ordered them to get her inside quickly and she was picked up and carried away. Imri fell against the side of the Jeep and let out a long breath. Karl leaned back against the fender, arms crossed over his chest.

"Well, that's done," Karl said. "Wonder if they have any coffee."

"I could eat," Chad said, patting his belly.

"Coffee does sound good," Imri added.

The three men made their way to the cafeteria where there was indeed coffee. As they came in, there were a couple of soldiers on duty.

Seeing the guys walk in, they said, "Sorry guys, we're in between meals right now."

"What? No mids?" Karl asked.

The young soldier smiled. "No sir. No mids here."

"You got coffee?" Imri asked.

"Right over there," the soldier pointed. "The Army runs on coffee."

Karl headed for the coffee station. "No truer words have ever been spoken."

><·IIIII·><

Audie leaned back against the Swiss Seat that kept him secured to the tower. The Swiss Seat is a ten- or twelve-foot-long piece of rope that is tied in such a manner as to become a repelling harness or similar. They are a great thing to know how to tie, as you never know when you could find yourself needing to be secured to something in an emergency.

In this case, Audie was having fun. Looking down at the ground, he shouted, "The view is amazing! You sure you don't want to come up here?"

"We ain't got all day, Audie! Hurry the fuck up ever' chance you get!" Sarge shouted back.

Audie was unfazed. He was one of those guys who was always in a happy mood and took the time to notice and enjoy the little things. Like being a hundred feet up in the air with an unobstructed view. So he enjoyed it for a moment before returning to his task of removing the bolts from the topmost section of the tower. This would be the most difficult section to remove, as the boom on the truck wasn't tall enough to clear it.

"Butch, you sure about this rigging?" Sarge asked.

"It's the best we can do with what we got. It's going to swing out pretty hard, but Audie agreed it's the only way to get down. After this it's a piece of cake."

Sarge shook his head. "I don't like it. But if you two say so."

"Looks like he's about ready. Let me get on the controls," Dad said.

Dad climbed up in the seat and looked up through the window in the roof. He could clearly see Audie, who also had a radio. Hand signals and the radio were the methods of communication, with hand signals being primary. They're just faster, and with a good operator, he should be anticipating your moves anyway.

Watching a good operator and signal-man work together is impressive. So much is done without communication and the level of trust between these two cannot be overstated. If the operator misunderstands the intent or simply isn't paying attention, people can get hurt or killed. Seeing it done so smoothly makes it look easy.

CHAPTER 12

Audie held his hand out, palm up, pinching his thumb and first two fingers together. Dad slowly took up slack on the hook until he saw the line was under tension and let off at the same moment Audie's hand collapsed into a fist. Audie started to climb down the tower so he would be below the section when it finally separated.

Dad watched him climb and waited. Audie got into position and secured himself to the tower with carabiners. Then he stuck a leg and his arms through the structure and held on. He looked as though he was scared to death and clinging to the tower for dear life. But he was just making sure he didn't get slingshotted off if the tower did anything unexpected.

Keying his radio, Audie said, "Give her a shot, Butch!"

"Here we go."

Audie was looking up and watching as the tower suddenly groaned and moved. Nothing extreme, but any movement is nerve-wracking. Dad applied more power to the hoist and the top section broke loose and moved up. It was still connected to the other section, but it was now clear that it was going to come off.

Dad keyed his mic. "Audie, you want to come down? No telling just how that thing is going to swing when it comes off."

"No, I know it'll shift. But I'm far enough down. It can't hit me unless it falls, and it ain't heavy enough to break those chokers."

"Ten four, here we go."

Dad applied power to the hoist again, watching the section move ever so slowly. When one of the corners separated from the one below it, the section rocked unsteadily, but was still under control.

"I hate watching this," Baker said.

"You can tell we aren't in the old Army," Terry said. "No way in hell they'd allowed some shit like this."

311

"That's why nothing ever got done," Sarge retorted.

Just as Sarge stopped speaking, the section separated. There were two chokers attached to the section, one higher than the other, but still below the top. When the section finally cleared the tower, it shifted to distribute the weight onto the nylon straps. It shifted quickly and violently. But Dad was ready for it and already had the machine in a swing, preventing it from hitting the tower.

Audie let out a whoop. "Damn good stick work, Butch!"

"I don't know about you, Audie, but my ass was puckered for that. Think it tore a hole in the seat," Dad said over the radio.

"You couldn't have drove a BB up my ass with a jackhammer!" Audie called back.

"That's a hell of an operator," Terry said as the load was being lowered to the ground.

Dad leaned out of the cab and asked, "You want to just put it on the truck here?"

"Yeah," Sarge said, "just lay it on here."

"Glad we started on the tall one," Thad said.

"It'll be easier from here on out," Danny added.

And it was. The only hard part with completing the takedown of the towers was getting the guy wires off, and that wasn't much of a challenge. By late afternoon, all three were on the ground. The group sat around on the bed of the boom truck and the scattered sections of tower when the job was complete.

"Only thing that would make this better is a cold beer," Sarge said.

"Now why'd you have to go and say that?" Terry asked. "I haven't thought about a cold beer in a long, long time. Now I am."

"I sure could use a cold one," Thad said, "or six."

"Yep," Audie said, laying back on the bed of the boom truck. "I love me some box beer."

CHAPTER 12

"What the hell is box beer?" Sarge asked.

"You know, twelve packs and cases."

Dad laughed. "Never heard that one, Audie, that's funny. But right now, I'd be happy with a flat top and a can of beans and motherfuckers."

Sarge immediately started to laugh as the others looked on in confusion.

"Uh, sorry Butch, did you just say *beans and motherfuckers?*" Thad asked.

"Oh yeah. They were terrible. In C-rats from Vietnam, one of the menu items was lima beans and ham. I don't mean like grandma made. I don't know how you make something taste so damn bad." The response got several laughs.

"Better than beans and dicks," Sarge added.

Thad waved a hand. "I don't even want to know."

"What's a flat top?" Baker asked.

"Canned beer in steel cans," Sarge answered.

Dad smiled and nodded. "Yeah, and you needed a church key to open them."

"A John Wayne or a sharp knife," Sarge said.

"You had to cut the can open?" Baker asked.

"More like punching a couple holes in the top. Like you used to do to motor oil," said Dad.

"Why wouldn't you just screw the top off?"

Dad, Sarge, and Audie really got a laugh out of that one.

CHAPTER 13

Once Bubba and Sky were settled in, we left. I worked with Ted to get an antenna up and we made contact with Wallner back at home. The signal was in the weeds, but we could communicate. We ended up not leaving Doc there. The woman he checked was very ill, but there wasn't much he could do for her. He wasn't sure what it was other than the fact she was very sick and weak.

"It could be another malaria case," Doc said as we walked back to the trucks.

"How the hell does something like malaria get started?" I asked. "We haven't seen that in many years."

"Who knows. Maybe mosquito control kept it away," Doc suggested. "Hard to say, really."

I saw Travis standing beside one of the M-ATVs and waved at him. He looked like a little kid holding that big ass rifle and it made me smile. He waved back and looked like his usual happy self.

As we were getting in the truck, Mel asked, "You think Rip is still there?"

"I don't know. Maybe. Don't know what The Rock could possibly be doing right now though," I said.

"What's The Rock?" Aric asked.

"It's a little bar right outside of Rock Springs called the Rock Springs Bar and Grill," I answered.

"Can't imagine a bar doing any business today."

"Guess we'll find out when we go past it."

"I wish they were," Mel said. Then she reached over and put her hand on my leg. "Remember going there?"

I laughed. "How can I forget!"

"You two meet there?" Aric asked.

"No, we met in a little neighborhood up the road from it when we were sixteen."

"Damn. Sixteen. That's a hell of a long time."

"Only seems longer," I said, looking at Mel.

"Uh huh. You say that but you know you couldn't live without me," she shot back.

"Oh, I could," I quickly said. Then looked over at her and added, "But I wouldn't like it much."

Looking at Aric in the mirror, I said, "I'll show you the neighborhood in a few minutes."

I made a left-hand turn onto West Kelly Park Road headed east. Kelly Park Road, as it's known locally, runs straight as an arrow east/west and ends up at Rock Springs State Park. As we made our way east, I pointed out a small dirt road on the south side.

"There's a nursery back there I worked at over one summer when I was in high school. Worst job I ever had," I said.

"I imagine it's hard work," said Aric.

"Hard, hot, underpaid, really any negative you could think of. I remember there was an old black man that worked there and one day I found him using a backhoe. Went over to see what he was doing, digging such a hole in the middle of a field for no reason. He told me he was digging a gopher turtle out to eat it. A highly illegal act at the time."

"Really?" Mel asked, "A gopher turtle?"

"I bet there aren't that many left now," I said. "Slow and easy to catch meat doesn't stand a chance. There were only so many of them because they were protected by the State."

CHAPTER 13

"Wonder how many species will be extinct after this?" Aric wondered aloud.

"Hard to say, really. Hungry people don't generally care how many of them there are. Only with the one they may have found at the moment. Pretty sure the day of the granola-crunching tree huggers is over."

"Hey, there it is!" Mel announced as the entrance for Kelly Park Hills came into view.

It was a typical cookie-cutter subdivision built in the late 80s with as much imagination as anything built back then had.

"We moved in there my freshman year of high school from Seminole County. But I managed to buy a motorcycle from a guy down the street and rode it to my old school. I wasn't going to Apopka High in the 90s!"

"Was it rough back then?" Aric asked.

I laughed. "It was either '88 or '89 that the Klan wanted to have a *Meet the Klan* event on city property. The city had a requirement for anyone using their property to get an insurance policy. They threatened to sue the city. So, yeah, it was pretty rough back then."

"The fucking Klan? Wonder what happened to people like that?" Aric said.

"Same thing that happened to the rest of us. The Day was the epitome of equity. It didn't care who you were or what you thought. The crash was just a little softer for those who tried to prepare for such an event."

It wasn't far from Kelly Park Hills to The Rock and it came into view quickly. Even from a distance, it just didn't look the same. Just like the block and stucco sign at the entrance of the old neighborhood that was nearly hidden in a thicket of weeds, the area around the old bar was too.

High weeds, young trees, creeping grass, Virginia creeper, poison ivy, and numerous other plants were quickly reclaiming their right to the land and everything on it. Grass was encroaching from the sides of the road out onto the asphalt. Taller weeds sprouted from cracks in the road surface. In some places, small trees did as well. All of these worked to destroy the patches of petroleum and rock that man laid down to make travel faster and more comfortable.

In a decade, the roads would probably be nothing more than overgrown forest trails. The very intricate yet barely maintained world we created for ourselves and often took for granted was so incredibly fragile and the forces of nature were unrelenting. In the end, Nature would prevail.

"It looks so different," Mel said.

"Does and doesn't. But then, so does everything these days," I said.

Aric leaned up between the seats to get a better look. "Doesn't look like much from here."

"Are those horses?" I asked, straining to see.

"It looks like it," Mel said.

"It is!" Aric added.

As we got closer, our observation was confirmed. There were indeed a couple of horses tied up out front, like something out of an old western. They stood lazily on three legs with one foot raised to the tip of the hoof. Occasionally their tails would whip at their flanks to drive away flies.

Grabbing my radio, I said, "This is the place."

Shithead, you go in with them. We'll stay back and provide cover, I heard Ted say.

Roger that, Mike replied, finishing with, *Mooseknuckle!*

"Let's check it out," I said as I drove slowly toward the little bar.

There were a few people outside and when they saw the trucks, they began gesturing wildly and a man ran toward the open door. He stood in front of it, shouting inside while pointing at us. It didn't take long before three other people ran out. Two men and one woman appeared, all carrying AR-type rifles. They were clearly apprehensive and looked about nervously.

Passing by yet another defunct convenience store, I stuck my hand out and waved to the people watching us. The wave appeared to confuse them and they spoke quickly amongst themselves. I slowed even more as we pulled into the parking lot.

"That's Rip!" Mel said. Looking closely at the group, I saw she was right.

Rip was one of the men holding a rifle. Mel leaned out the window and waved. "Hey Rip!"

Shading his eyes, he looked closely, his mouth hanging open. It quickly turned into a smile and he waved.

"Holy shit!" he shouted. "What are you doing here?"

Rolling to a stop, I shut the truck down and we stepped out. I was looking at Rip when he made eye contact with me. The surprise was very obvious on his face. He smiled broadly as he stepped toward us.

"Damn! Morgan and Mel? What the actual fuck?" Rip said.

Reaching him, I stuck my hand out. Laughing, I said, "Damn man. What the hell are you still doing here?"

Rip shook my hand and pulled me into a hug. Slapping my back, he said, "Where the hell else am I going to be?"

Stepping back from him, I said, "Gotta point. We all have to be somewhere."

Rip looked at the trucks. "What's all this? You in the Army or something now?"

Mike's M-ATV pulled to a stop behind my truck and Travis and Danny stepped out in full kit. Seeing them, Rip's eyes darted to mine. "What the hell is going on?"

I looked over my shoulder. "It's a long story." Looking back at Rip, I said, "You don't have to worry about us, though." I looked around at The Rock for a minute. "What do you have going on here?"

"Is Deb here?" Mel asked, before Rip could answer me.

"Mom's inside. Dad stays at home to keep an eye on the place."

"I'm going to go in and see her," Mel said and went to the truck for her weapon.

When Rip saw it, he said, "Holy shit! Where the hell did you get that?"

"Oh this little thing?" Mel asked. "We have a lot of stuff."

Rip looked at me and pointed at the M-ATVs. "What's all this?" He looked at me closely. "Where did you guys get all this? Weapons, radios? Fucking trucks? That means you have fuel! Where the hell are you getting all this shit?"

"We'll get to it. What about you?"

Rip looked at me and pointed to the sign that read: World Famous Rock Springs Bar and Grill. But "Bar and Grill" had been painted over and now read: Trading Post.

"We're a trading post now."

I laughed. "Always hustling, huh?"

"You said we all have to be somewhere," said Rip. "Well, we also all have to do something."

"What the hell are you trading?"

"Whatever we can find. We work with some farmers for vegetables. We have people with chickens for eggs. Firearms and ammo are the hottest commodity. Fuel was a really good business for a while but that's getting really hard to come up with now." Rip pointed at me. "The stuff you have would do great." He smiled, rubbed his chin and said, "Wanna do a little business?"

"Well, I can't do that."

"Why not?"

"It's not mine, technically."

"Who's it belong to?" Rip asked.

"Well, short story, I'm the acting sheriff of Lake County as well as, I hate to say this, I'm also the acting governor."

Rip howled in laughter. "No really, what's with all this?"

Looking down, I noticed the sling of my weapon was covering the badge. I pulled it aside so Rip could see it. He laughed again and said, "I've got a couple of them inside. Nice try."

"Not a joke, buddy. I mean it."

The smile faded from his face. "You serious?"

"As a heart attack."

Rip laughed loudly, leaning over and slapping his knees. "You're serious? You're really fucking serious?" I nodded, and he continued to laugh. "OK, OK," he said, wiping his eyes. "Wow. I mean, wow."

"You should try it from this side."

"How the hell did that happen? I mean, what the hell do you even do? I guess that explains the trucks and shit."

"It does explain the trucks. I don't really know what I do just yet. This is really the first trip out of our area."

"You still live in Umatilla?"

"Yeah. We have power over there. For a small area anyway."

"What? How?" he asked.

"The juice plant there has a small gas turbine power plant. We found some folks that knew how to run it and they got it spun up."

"Where's the gas come from?"

"The west coast someplace. We don't know. But the gas is still flowing."

"Well shit. Maybe I need to move to Umatilla!"

We moved over to a picnic table under the porch and sat down. We spent a while talking, catching each other up on what we had done since The Day. From what I gathered, things were rough for them at first. The bar was a natural target once people figured out things weren't coming back.

"In the beginning it was pretty cool. Kind of like block parties out here. I'd fire up the big grill and people would bring whatever they had to cook. We had a pretty decent stock of beer, but it didn't last long," Rip said.

He went on to describe how once the realization sunk in that things were not coming back anytime soon, people changed. They'd abandoned the bar for several months, retreating to the family place out west. The idea of the trading post came about naturally. The Rock was kind of the gathering place for locals. Not to mention all the people that took refuge at the springs just up the road.

"That's why we're here. I thought the springs would attract people. We're starting to look for concentrations of them," I said.

"Ohh sheeit, do they attract people!" Rip said.

He went on to explain that the springs drew people from far away. He told me there were probably a couple hundred people in the park. Not to mention the locals that used the spring as well. It was the best source of potable water in the area, and anyone living in the greater area knew about it. So it only stood to reason that when they ran out of water and the situation became desperate, they would move to the closest source of clean water they knew about.

I asked how things were going in the park. How it ran, that sort of thing. I was not really happy to hear the reply.

"It's fucking rough in there, man."

"What do you mean?"

Rip did his best to lay it out for me. The spring was split in half by two groups, and they maintained a very shaky relationship. There was the spring head area that extended down the run to the swimming area and stopped. Then there was the swimming area group that controlled everything past that. The two sides constantly fought a low-grade war for control of the spring head.

"Which doesn't make any fucking sense," said Rip.

"There isn't much in the way of fish on the upper side," I said.

Thrusting his hands out, Rip exclaimed, "Exactly!" It was pretty obvious he'd had this discussion before. Then he said, "But that ain't all."

He continued to tell me that there was also a larger group at Wekiwa Springs. That park was located in a densely populated area. More people knew about it, and it was far more accessible than Rock Springs.

"So, the Wekiva group and the two Rock Springs groups fight each other on the river for control," he said.

"They fight for control of the river? To what, control the fishing?"

"To control everything. Access, the fishing, anything to do with the river. If you want to get to the river, you have to go through one of these groups. Who you have to talk to depends on what you want to do and where."

"Damn," I said as my mind wandered. Then I looked up at him. "What about you? Do these people mess with you guys? Or with anyone?"

"They tried in the beginning. But," Rip held up his rifle, "we have ammunition, they don't. So, they're all really nice to us because they need us." Rip twirled a finger around. "This little trading post does pretty well. I can get almost anything you need."

"You in the horse business too?" I asked.

"If that's what you want! But I don't have any. Too much trouble. You got to feed the big bastards."

"How do you get all the way out here from your place then?"

Rip jumped up. "Come on, I'll show ya."

I followed him into the building. It looked exactly like I remembered, with a couple small exceptions. The beer coolers were gone and the bar top was covered in various wares for sale. Mel was with Deb, Rip's mother, behind the bar and waved at us when we came in.

Deb started out from behind the counter, holding her arms open. "I can't believe you two just walked in here. This is amazing!"

Mel and I had been going to The Rock for over twenty years before The Day. We knew them as good friends we'd see on Wednesday nights for steak night. Or on the weekend if we were passing by, we'd stop in for a fantastic burger and a beer. I hugged Deb and we chatted for a few minutes before Rip tugged at me to go out back with him.

"I use these!" Rip said, standing proudly in front of a couple very nice electric bikes.

"Oh hell, those are nice," I responded instinctively. "But how do you charge them?"

"Like I said, I can get about anything. So, I got myself a real nice solar power system cobbled together. It charges the bikes, runs the well and a small fridge, and I can run a window unit AC at night."

"Running water is a damn nice thing to have," I said with a laugh.

"You ain't shittin'! And, I don't have to walk. Charge this baby up every two days and I'm golden."

"That's a hell of an idea," I said.

"Beats walking," said Rip.

"Walking is for suckers!" I laughed back.

CHAPTER 13

As we walked back through the bar, I asked about the group at Wekiva. Rip said that group was much larger according to the people he talked to. And there was fierce combat at times where the two rivers met. Then there was Wekiva Island, a nice riverfront bar with a seawall just downriver from where the Rock Springs Run and Wekiva Runs merged. That area was generally controlled by the Wekiva group. They essentially had a throttle hold on the river. From the island you could go all the way to the St. Johns River.

"How are these groups operated?" I asked.

"Whatcha mean?"

"Who's in charge, how do they treat people, that sort of thing."

"Well, depends on who you ask," Rip replied.

I pressed him to elaborate, and he did his best, starting off with, "You gotta understand, I don't really know. I can tell you what I'm told."

The way he explained it was like this. Anyone could join the groups. Each had their own way of handling that and none of them were really all that bad short of general hazing. The problem came when there was conflict between the groups. Prisoners were essentially slaves. Kept as trophies and abused by the captive community in a general way. Anyone could tell them to do anything. If they refused, they'd be beaten or tortured. They could also face torture if their previous tribe conducted a successful raid against their captives. Or if the captive tribe lost a skirmish to their previous tribe, they could face retribution.

"They take slaves?" I asked, making sure I heard him.

"Yeah, but it's not like that. It's more like being held until an opportunity to profit from returning them. I mean, it is fucked up, but it's not like they're being forced to perform heavy labor or something. I don't know, it's hard to explain."

"Ok, so kidnapping then."

"Yeah, I guess."

"Well, these people are not free to leave, are they?" I asked.

He shook his head and said, "They are held against their will and violence can be committed against them by anyone."

"That's not cool."

"I know, but like I said, it's hard to explain. I mean, they don't just grab people off the street. It's only when they're fighting with one another. They're all really just normal people doing their best to get through a shitty situation."

"There are better ways," I said.

"You wanna go in there and have a look?"

"I don't know. That's what I was thinking about doing but now I'm not so sure."

"Look, I know these cats," Rip said, and jabbed a finger over his shoulder. "They see all this shit roll in, they're going to piss themselves. You ain't gotta worry about them. They don't have any ammo. They fight with bows and spears and shit."

I grabbed my mic and made a call. "Hey Ted, you and Mike come over here real quick."

Their reply was the door popping open on Mike's truck and hearing Ted's start to move. In a couple minutes, both were sitting at the picnic table opposite us.

"Sup," Mike asked with a gesture of his chin.

I made introductions and then told them what Rip had told me. They knew the plan was to go into the springs and I didn't even need to say anything else.

Ted looked at Rip and asked, "How hairy is it?"

"Oh, like I told him, they don't have any guns. They fight with bows and arrows. You guys will scare the shit out of them."

"Fuck it, let's go for a ride," Mike said.

Standing up, I looked at Rip and said, "You ride with me."

"Oh, come on. I can't ride in one of those bad bitches?" Rip grumbled, pointing at an M-ATV.

"Another time, sport. Come on."

Ted was still sitting and held his hand up. "Hold on. I don't think we need to rush into this."

"What's up?" I asked as I sat back down.

"They may," Ted started, then looked at Rip, "or may not have weapons. But they certainly do have fire and that is a hell of a weapon. We could very easily be enveloped by a crowd, and it isn't a stretch to think they could light the trucks up. I say we come back with a real force, infantry, to protect the trucks. We can bring in supplies for them, so they'll see it as a supply mission. They won't be as eager to fight that way."

I nodded. "I see what you're saying. It is risky, especially knowing they are a little on the militant side."

Aric had been sitting at another table listening to our conversation and asked, "Do you know any of the honchos in there?"

"Yeah, know them all," said Rip.

"Can you send someone in there and ask them to come up here for a little chat? Don't tell them why, just try to get them up here."

"Sure." Rip looked around. Finding who he was looking for, he held a cupped hand to his mouth and shouted, "Tommy!" and waved the young man over when he looked up.

He came over and Rip told him what he needed. The young man nodded and went over to the two horses, mounted one, and rode off at a trot toward the park.

"What's this guy like?" Ted asked.

"Who? Tommy? He's ok."

"No, whoever Tommy went to get."

"Oh, Andy. He's ok. He's the less, I guess, less aggressive one than some of the others."

"Good," I said as I stood up. "We'll try and coordinate with him to return and distribute some supplies. Maybe even bring in a hot meal."

"Skip that idea, Morgan," Ted quickly replied. "Too hard to do and would open us to having to deal with a riot. The supplies are going to be hard enough to distribute without causing a damn shit show."

"You could just bring the supplies here," Rip said.

I laughed and looked at him. "So you could sell it to them?"

"No, I mean, have them come up here to get it. So you're not trapped in there and can control the crowd."

"That's actually a really good idea. We can set up a control point down the road there with a couple of gun trucks. Let them through a handful at a time," Mike said.

"But I want to get in there and get a look at what's going on. See how the people are treated. How they're living," I said.

"After we hand out supplies, we could probably get in pretty easy and they wouldn't be so interested in rushing the trucks if they've just been given stuff. That's the best way to do it," Ted said.

"We could also put some people into the line," Aric said.

"What do you mean?" I asked.

"Put some of our people in the line. No one knows who we are. They'll look like everyone else and can talk to people freely."

I turned that over in my mind. "That's a brilliant idea, Aric. Stick some of our people in the line. They'll have to look like everyone from the park."

"Yeah, but they know everyone in there. Everyone knows everyone. They'll know they are strangers," Rip said.

"Ok, then," I said, "They'll just say they live in the area and heard about the supplies and came to get some. They can then ask questions about the park, how to join, what it's like. All that."

CHAPTER 13

"There you go, Morgan," Ted said, nodding at me. "That's how to do it. We can provide overwatch for our people. They can't carry long guns but concealed pistols. They'll never be out of our sight so there isn't much to worry about."

We discussed the plan a little more until Rip pointed down the road. We looked up to see Tommy approaching with another man on the horse with him. They rode up and climbed down. As Tommy tied the horse up, Andy walked over.

"Who the hell are you guys?" he asked.

Standing up, I offered my hand. "Morgan Carter, acting governor for the state of Florida."

He looked surprised. "Acting governor?"

"You gonna shake my hand or leave me hanging?" I asked.

"Oh, yeah." His grip was firm as we shook.

"Yes, acting governor. We're trying to get things going on the path to recovery. It's going to be a long and slow process. But it's begun."

"Damn," Andy muttered. "We haven't seen a single soul that was with any sort of government. Where have you guys been? What took so long?"

"This is a recent development for me. I live over in Umatilla. The Army has set up a base there at the high school. Supplies are starting to be brought in and we're looking for concentrations of people so we know where to take them."

"We certainly have a concentration of people."

"How many do you have in there?" Aric asked. Andy looked at him and Aric introduced himself. "Aric Vonasec, head of the State Militia."

"No shit? A militia too?"

"It's just getting going as well. So, how many people do you have in there?"

"I don't have an exact count. But it's around three hundred, probably."

The statement shocked me. I knew there would be people here, but never imagined there would be that many. But then, it only made sense. Water is life and people certainly need water. A source that was safe to drink right where it appeared out of the ground was worth its weight in gold.

"Damn, that's a lot of people. How about Wekiva, how many do they have?" I asked.

"More. I don't really know, but it's definitely more."

"And you and they do not get along? You're in conflict with one another?"

"It's just about resources. Or access to resources. We both have large groups of people that need to eat. It's really over food. It's just turned into the us versus them thing."

"Every war ever fought was over resources," I said. "With that thought in mind, if we removed the need to fight over food, we could eliminate this then, correct?"

Andy looked at me. "Probably. But you know things are never black and white. I have some inside who will want to continue the fight because that's what they are focused on now. The ones who see security as their jobs are going to push back."

"How about you?" I asked.

"Man, I just want things to go back like they were. I mean, I know that's not going to happen. But it's what I want. I have three kids. It's not been easy. My wife had a nervous breakdown, and it took a long time to get her to where she is now. I just want to live my life. Have enough to eat. Watch my kids grow up in a world with a future."

Reaching out I gripped his shoulder. "I'm really glad to hear that. That's what I want as well. Here's what we're going to do …"

We talked for nearly an hour. I told him what we would be bringing, just basic supplies at the moment. Food and hygiene being the top priority. He thought that was great and certainly needed. I also told him when we returned, we would set up a clinic here at The Rock and people could be seen by a doc. This really excited him, too. We discussed how we would do this, using Mike's idea of a control point and allowing them in a handful at a time. Since it would take a little time to get this put together, we agreed that when we returned, Rip would send someone in and let them know we were ready, and they would come out.

"This is pretty crazy. All this time, nothing, and just like that, here you are. People are going to be really excited," Andy said.

"On that note," Ted interjected. "Stress to your people, especially your security folks, that this isn't the time or place to try any shit. They wouldn't stand a chance." Ted motioned to the M-ATV with the fifty mounted in the turret. "This is only a small example of the weapons we have. We will destroy anyone who makes an attempt on us."

"We only have a couple of guns with ammo. Don't worry, we're not suicidal. Plus, you're here to help. Why would we attack you?"

"Some people see us as a threat. They've lived a year answering to no one but themselves. So when an authority figure shows up, they think we're trying to come in and take over. We are not doing that. We're trying to get help to people. We don't interfere in local operations unless they're doing bad shit."

Andy cocked his head to the side. "Like what kind of bad shit?"

"Anyone, and I do mean anyone, being held against their will. Any sort of sexual violence. Both of these are capital crimes and will result in summary execution. You need to share that with your people. That's very important. Not to mention, any crime against others will also be dealt with. We're all in a hard spot. We don't need to be worried about someone taking what little we have. Law enforcement may not be everywhere like in The Before. But it is here, and everyone has the right to defend themselves and their property. Period."

Andy slowly nodded his head. "I like you, Governor. I like you a lot. I'll be honest with you. We do have some people held against their will. They were taken prisoner during skirmishes on the river. But they aren't really mistreated, and we usually end up just swapping them for our people that were also taken. As for sexual crimes, there have been some for sure. But we police that ourselves very well. We take the same view on it."

"Ok, good. When we return, I want to go out and meet with the people in Wekiva. We're going to offer them help as well. But I want a full prisoner swap conducted and the taking of prisoners to end. If either side continues, they will deal with us, and I've already told you what the consequences are. Also, I want you to keep this conversation low key. There is no telling how your people will react. Let's not give them days to think about it and get worked up. Likewise for the other group. Don't say anything about it."

"Then how am I supposed to manage a full prisoner swap?"

"Keep things business as usual," Ted said. "When we come back, we will handle the prisoner swap and make sure everyone understands the new situation."

"Good idea," I said, then looked at Andy. "What are the other leaders in your group like? Is there anyone that is going to be a problem?"

Andy looked at Rip. Rip gave him a *better tell him* look and Andy looked back to me. "Yes. We have a group of three guys and their followers that are going to be a problem. They're the ones that really keep the fighting going on. They're always raiding Wekiva and attacking their people on the river. If it wasn't for them, we would probably get along."

CHAPTER 13

"You're three hundred strong," Ted said. "Why don't you just take them out?"

"They do have weapons. A couple rifles and pistols and ammo. They don't use them except as a threat. But since the rest of us don't have guns, they kind of get their way."

"Have they harmed people in your group?" I asked. Andy looked down and nodded. I asked, "Capital crimes?" He nodded again, without looking up.

"We will deal with them for you," Ted said.

"What are you going to do?" Andy asked.

"Put them on trial," I said.

Surprised, Andy asked, "What?"

"Just that. We will put them on trial. Your people will be the jury."

Andy looked stunned. "Really?"

Nodding, I replied, "How do you think that will go?"

"For them? Not good. They've done a lot of dirt to a lot of people." He looked me in the eye. "They have a lot of revenge coming at them."

"In that case, it is even more important that you not tell a soul about this," I said, then looked at Rip, "and that goes for you as well. No one other than those of us sitting here right now can know about this."

"I ain't saying anything," said Rip.

"I won't say anything to anyone," Andy added.

"Not even your wife. Not your kids. 'No one' means just that: fucking *no one*," Ted said. "This is not a joke."

"I can see you mean business," said Andy. "I won't say a word. Just try and get back as soon as you can."

"We will. We have others we need to get back to out this way as well. It's a priority," I said.

With the mission as complete as we could get it today, we decided to load up and head back. Ted stressed once again the importance of keeping their mouths shut. When I went inside to get Mel, who was still talking to Debbie, I told Deb to keep quiet about our visit as well, telling her we would be back in a couple of days with food and other supplies. Naturally, this really excited Deb and she assured us she would keep quiet. Saying goodbye, we walked out to the truck.

Ted was waiting for me and said, "We need to get an antenna up and let Adelaide know we're headed back."

"I was going to," I said as I grabbed my ruck with the antenna and throw line.

I got the antenna up in a tall pine tree and made the call home. The signal was surprisingly good, and I made a mental note of the fact. After letting Wallner know we were headed back, we loaded up. I called on the radio asking if everyone was ready, got an affirmative from both trucks, and we pulled out.

CHAPTER 14

There were visitors with Fred when Miss Kay and Mary arrived. Mom was there with Jamie and Ian. Pleasantries were exchanged between them all and they settled into the living room. Kay brought a basket with scones made from blackberries picked by the kids out behind Danny's pond. Mom went to the kitchen and set a kettle of water on the stove. Hot tea would be nice with them.

The babies were awake and content as they were passed around to be held. They cooed, burped, and farted as babies will do.

"Have we heard from them?" Fred asked.

"Who?" Kay asked.

"Morgan and them. Have they called in?"

"Oh, they have. From what I heard, everything is fine."

Fred relaxed a little. "Good. I'm just a little nervous with him leaving."

"It's understandable," said Mom. "You're a new mother. Lots of new emotions."

Just then the front door burst open and the girls came through with Tammy in the lead. She carried a box in her hands and was smiling from ear to ear.

"Hey Fred!" Tammy shouted as she walked in. "Look what we found!"

Tammy went over to the sofa where Fred was sitting and placed the box on the floor in front of her. She started talking as she opened it.

"We were going through one of the houses looking around and I found this." Tammy removed a small electrical device from the box and held it up. "It's a pump. For you, know, milk for the babies."

"It's a breast pump," Taylor added. "Mom used one when we were little."

"Oh, wow," Fred said as she took the pump. "I never thought about this."

"And there's more stuff too!" Little Bit shouted.

Lee Ann handed over an unopened box of bags for the pump. "There are a lot of these too. You can pump a lot of milk for them."

"Even better," Jamie said, "Aric can feed the babies. It'll be his first time."

Fred's face lit up. "You're right! I didn't even think about that." She looked up. "This is amazing, thank you girls!" Fred leaned out and hugged them all.

"As soon as I saw it, I thought about you," Tammy said.

"Thank you for that, Tammy. It's very sweet."

Tammy shrugged. "You're family. It's what you're supposed to do."

"Oh, that is the sweetest thing," Kay said and held her arms out. "Come here and give me a hug!"

Tammy smiled and wrapped Kay in a warm, genuine hug, resting her head on Kay's chest.

Taylor handed Fred a plastic shopping bag. "These are pads for your bra. You know, so if milk is leaking out."

Fred looked into the bag before looking up at Taylor. "You girls are amazing! I would have never thought of this."

"We watched Mom growing up. She breastfed all of us, so I kind of know how it goes. She was still breastfeeding Ashley when I was ten."

"Oh, wow," Kay laughed.

CHAPTER 14

>―▬―<

With the towers loaded onto the boom truck, Sarge took the lead to head home. They'd agreed to unload them in the field behind the bunker, which was also Thad's front yard, so they would be sort of centrally located. Pulling in, Terry parked the truck where Sarge indicated, hopped up on the controls, and unloaded the sections.

While the truck was being unloaded, Sarge walked over to the bunker to talk to Wallner. "How's it going, Wallner?" Sarge asked as he approached.

Wallner was waiting outside, knowing the old man was probably coming over. "Good. Everything is going smoothly."

"You heard from Morgan?"

"Yeah, they're on their way back now."

"How'd it go? You got any coffee?"

Wallner gestured to the bunker with his head. "Yeah, come on in. They've made all their check-ins without issue. They did find some people."

Sarge poured himself a cup of coffee and walked back outside. "That's good to hear. This was his first real mission."

"He did good. Is he going to be doing more?"

"Hell yes he will. Why?"

"I don't know. Just seems strange for the governor to be out running around on missions like this."

"The job is a little different now. He's not sitting in Tallahassee using ten pens to sign his name on useless shit. We've got a state to get back up and running and we need every swinging dick we can find to get out there and make it happen."

"I agree, trust me. I just wonder how long before the Army brass decides he shouldn't be out there like that."

Sarge sipped his coffee for a minute to think. "I see what you mean. But if I know Morgan, he'll tell them to shove that idea up their collective asses if they suggest it."

"What if it's not a suggestion?"

"We have more weapons than they do at the moment. I don't think that will happen. Aric is already at work building the militia. It will start growing soon and will answer to us, not the Army. Besides, I don't think they would do anything like that. It would appear we have a pretty good working relationship with them."

Wallner nodded. "We do indeed. So far. You know the Army though, if it can be fucked up, they can do it."

Sarge grunted. "Yeah, if there's a hard way to do it, they know it." He finished his coffee and returned the cup to the bunker. "Thanks for the coffee, buddy. I'm gonna go see what's for supper. I'm getting hungry."

"Sounds good. I could use a bite myself."

Sarge walked back over to the truck where the unloading was done, and Terry was storing the boom so the truck could leave. Audie had gone back to his shop when they finished the loading. He said he had a project he was working on and wanted to get it done. Dad was talking to Baker and Scott. Thad said he was going to see if Mary was home and wandered off.

"Butch, you ready for some supper?" Sarge asked.

Dad patted his belly. "I could stand to eat."

Sarge looked at Baker and Scott. "You guys come on down to the house for supper too. Been a while since we had y'all over."

"Hell yeah!" Scott shouted.

"Thank you. A real home cooked meal would be nice," said Baker.

"You hear that?" Scott shouted at Terry. "We're eating dinner here tonight!"

CHAPTER 14

"Hot damn!" Terry shouted. "That Miss Kay is one hell of a cook!"

"We'll see you all up there," Sarge said. "Come on, Butch. Let's see if we can find our women folk."

"Let's do it. I need some coffee," said Dad.

"I stole a cup from Wallner," said Sarge as he walked over to the Hummer.

"When do you want to start putting the towers up?" Dad asked as he climbed into his seat.

"Soon. Like tomorrow," said Sarge. "At least one of them. Just have to decide where to put it."

Miss Kay was in the kitchen with Mom and Fred. The babies were on the floor in the living room with the girls and the gaggle of kids gathered around them. A cartoon movie of some sort was playing on the TV and the kids were all quiet and content. Jamie and Ian sat on the front porch while Jamie had a smoke. Jess was walking up the driveway of the house when Sarge turned in. She looked over her shoulder and stuck her ass out toward the truck. Sarge honked the horn at her, and she looked back and smiled.

"How'd it go?" Ian asked as Sarge started up the steps.

"Good. Only one problem with the whole thing."

"What's that?" Jamie asked.

Sarge turned his empty cup upside down. "Ran out of coffee."

"Thankfully we made it back before anyone succumbed to the effects," Dad added.

Jamie laughed at them. "You old fuckers and your coffee."

"It's proof God loves us!" Sarge fired back.

Dalton's deep voice filled the air from behind them. "No, this is proof God loves us."

They all looked up to see him holding a Mason jar. He spun the lid off and took a tug. Swallowing it, he let out a breath. "Could use a little more time in the wood, but it's not bad."

"Where the hell did you get that?" Sarge asked as he stepped down and reached for the jar.

"I made it."

Sarge sniffed it. Letting out a whistle, he took a pull from the jar. Shaking his head, he swallowed it. "Shit! That's hot!"

"Little raw yet," said Dalton.

Sarge turned to Dad. "Butch, you want some?"

Dad held his hands out. "Naw, I gave that stuff up years ago."

Ian jumped to his feet. "I didn't. Give it here."

Sarge handed it over and Ian started to raise it to his lips when it was snatched away.

Jamie had a hold of it, saying, "Ladies first." Still holding her cigarette, she turned it up and took a big drink. Sarge giggled watching her, thinking she couldn't possibly swallow it all. But Jamie looked at him, her cheeks puffed out like a Gerbil with a mouthful and swallowed it, finishing with a loud, "Ahhh," and wiping her mouth with the back of her hand.

Sarge grunted, "Lady my ass."

"Lick my ball sack. I'm not a lady," Jamie shot back. Sarge's eyes went wide and he didn't know what to say. Jamie chuckled at his obvious discomfort.

Finally getting the jar, Ian turned it up. His eyes went wide and he choked it down. "Holy shit, that's terrible! What the hell is that, methyl ethyl ketone? Good grief!"

"You people have no taste," Dalton said, taking the jar back. "This is some fine corn liquor."

"It hasn't mellowed one bit," Sarge said, then smiled and added, "It's awful but it *is* wonderful!"

CHAPTER 14

As Danny was taking a sip of the liquor, Karl's Jeep came bouncing down the road and turned into the gate. Pulling up behind the Hummer, they climbed out and joined everyone on the porch. Seeing the jar, Imri looked at Dalton with a *is that what I think it is* look, to which Dalton nodded.

Sarge was screwing the lid back on when Imri said, "Let me get a shot of that."

Imri took a mouthful, winced, and swallowed. "Argh! That's still pretty rough."

"Let me have it, Imri," Karl said. He took a drink and handed it to Chad.

"It's not bad actually," Karl said. "It's not Aunt Helen's finest, but it's not bad."

"Y'all ain't shit," Chad said and turned the jar up as though he was going to chug it. But suddenly white liquor came gushing out the side of his mouth. Coughing and gagging, Chad tried to get his breath. Standing up straight, he tried in vain to get air into his lungs but only managed a ragged wheeze.

Imri snatched the jar from his hand. "You pussy! Get your shit together, man! You're embarrassing yourself!"

Chad bent over, resting his palms on his knees and coughed, hacked, and gagged. Straightening up, his eyes were red and watering profusely. But he still couldn't get a breath.

"Karl, how'd it go today?" Sarge asked.

"Come on, I'll tell you over supper."

>―※―<

Our route home would be different. Not that I really thought we needed to engage in all this cloak and dagger shit, but it was SOP for the old man, and it did make sense. Leaving The Rock, we headed south on Rock Springs Road. This area used to be dominated by greenhouses and equestrian ranches, but in recent years, development found its way out here and most of the land was being consumed with shitty track house communities.

I hate these places. I cannot imagine how anyone would want to live in one. Preplanned hell on Earth in my opinion. Zero lot lines, HOAs, and nosy neighbors that can hear when you take a shit. No way, no how. All the development followed the construction of the 429 expressway. It's a toll road that connected Orlando to the *country* and allowed those Orlandoites a fast and easy route into our neck of the woods.

These people wanted out of the city and moved to the country bringing with them all the shit they left behind. I like the fact there isn't a Starbucks within ten miles of my house. I like that there aren't a lot of the amenities most people need. It saves you money and keeps you from getting caught up in whatever is the new *thing* at the moment. If you have to drive forty-five minutes for a mocha frappa what the fuck ever, you probably aren't getting one.

When Ponkan Road came into view, I made a call on the radio.

"We're going to hang a right here. There's a laydown yard for the power company just past the turn. I want to swing in there and see what's lying around."

Both trucks confirmed and we made the turn. The yard was originally a Florida Power facility. But Duke Energy took them over in the recent past. I worked for Florida Power many years ago in the line department at the Jamestown yard in Winter Park. I loved the work, hard as hell. Physically demanding is an understatement. Climbing poles wearing a set of hooks is not for the faint of heart. I'd been to this facility before. It's where I actually filled out my intake paperwork.

Turning into the yard, I wasn't sure what to expect. As it was the power company, I almost expected it to be operational. Most people do not fully appreciate just how much capability power companies have. They have immense resources in both machines and manpower and can accomplish incredible things.

It turned out to be like everywhere else. Abandoned. There were a few cars in the parking lot. The doors stood open on some. I wasn't interested in the parking lot. I was interested in the warehouse and laydown yard. I wanted to see what was left of the wire, transformers, switches, and fuses. Things we needed.

Passing the warehouse, I parked between two big concrete pads with transformers lined up on them. There were both pole and pad mount versions. Good news already. Getting out, I looked the transformers over, took out my notebook, and started an inventory.

"Hey Aric, can you go over there and count the poles for me?" I asked. "I want to inventory what's here."

"Sure," he replied and headed off.

Mike and Danny came walking up and Danny said, "This is a good idea."

"There's more of these around and we will inventory them all. Maybe even come back and collect it all and relocate it."

"That's what I would do. When power starts coming back on, this stuff will disappear quick," Mike added, then pointed at the warehouse and asked, "What's in there?"

"That's the warehouse. Full of all manner of shit. Or at least it was."

"You want to search it?" he asked. I gave him an affirmative nod and he offered, "We'll go clear it."

"I'll be done out here by the time you do that," I said and went back to counting.

Mel was with me and looking at the equipment as I inspected it.

"I remember when you did this stuff," she said.

"The good ole days." I leaned over a transformer to read the nameplate.

"You would come home all hours of the night. You worked a lot of hours then."

"It was a good job. Kind of miss it. I liked the work."

"Yeah, but you didn't like the people."

I grunted. "It wasn't the people. It was the damn union."

"Oh, that's right. Didn't they file some kind of forms against you?"

"Yeah, they're called grievances. Said I was doing too much work. I would go out and do something, something very simple, but the book said that job took three men. Which is ridiculous. And they would file one against me. I just got sick of it and quit signing them. I wasn't in the union so union forms didn't mean shit to me."

Mel looked around, adjusted her Minimi and said, "No union around here now."

I counted all the transformers, rolls of wire, switch arms, bucks, and everything else that was out there. With the big stuff counted, we headed for the warehouse. Aric came over and gave me the count of the poles and their sizes. I added it to my list as we walked. Danny and Mike were waiting on the loading dock for us.

"How's it look in there?" I asked.

"Fucking mess. There's shit everywhere. But they didn't mess with the hardware really. Looks like kids were in here, busted shit everywhere," said Mike.

I followed them inside, clicking on my weapon light as I did. The warehouse wasn't pitch black. There were skylights of a muted yellow that allowed some light in. But the shelves remained dark.

I walked the high rows of shelves, inspecting the insulators, clamps, fuses, automatic couplers called pickles, and the rest of the hardware. Bolts, washers, screws and the like were plentiful. What was missing was all the stuff linemen would steal every time we came in. Flashlights and batteries were obviously gone. So were gloves, rain suits, hard hats, safety glasses, basically anything a person would need to do this kind of work. None of that shit mattered, though. The hardware is what was important, and there was plenty of it.

"This is great," I said. "We'll need to come back here and load all this up and take it back."

"That'll be a hell of a job," Mike said.

"That boom truck will make all this a lot easier," said Danny.

"Hell yes it will," I said. "We need to go look behind that building over there. There should be trucks parked back there. I'm sure they don't run, but we might be able to get them running. A line truck or a bucket truck would be one hell of a score."

"I'll go look," Danny said.

"I'll go with you," Mike said as they walked off.

Mel and I continued to wander through the warehouse. She pointed to a bunch of shattered light bulbs.

"Kids got in here, it looks like. Why break shit for no reason?" she asked.

"They make a loud pop when they bust." I bent over and picked up the carcass of one of them. Taking out my Leatherman Tool, I cut the element off its mount and held it up. "These are great for sharpening knives. We always cut these out."

"What is it? Glass?"

"Kind of. It's a sintered aluminum oxide material. Very hard and really good for knives. When we come back to load all of this stuff up, I'll get them all. Good to have."

Mel shook her head. "Now I remember those. I would find them in the laundry."

"Hmm, must have been like the money you found in the laundry. I never got that back either," I said with a smile.

"Hey, if it's in the dryer, it's mine. Finders keepers and all that."

"So, do you have a box full of high-pressure sodium elements someplace?"

"Pfft, no. I threw that shit away. You didn't miss it."

"Uh, actually I did."

Putting my arm around her shoulder, we started for the door when Aric showed up. He'd been wandering around on his own.

"Find anything?" I asked.

He shrugged. "I don't know what half of this shit is."

"Well, I do. And there's a lot here we can use."

"I'm glad *someone* does."

"Baker, Terry, and Scott will love this place," I told him.

Walking toward the truck, we could see Mike and Danny coming back from behind the building. We waited for them, and I asked what they found.

"There're two bucket trucks back there. Nice looking ones and two of the crane trucks," Mike said.

"Line trucks," I corrected.

"Whatever. There's two of each. But they look like they've been sitting a long time."

"I'm going to get Audie to fuck with them and see what he can do. We'll have to tow one of them back to his shop at some point."

"I'll help him," Danny offered.

"You guys ready to get home? Getting late and I want to be home before dark."

"It's time to put out the fire and call in the dogs," Danny said. "I'm getting hungry."

"We're burning daylight, let's go," Mike said as he headed for his truck.

"We done here?" Ted called out.

In response, I twirled a finger in the air and truck engines rumbled to life. We continued down Ponkan Road until it intersected with Plymouth Sorrento Road where we turned north. In a behind-your-back-to-get-to-your-elbow move, we took it back up to Kelly Park Road and turned west for the short drive to the 429 on ramp.

We hadn't seen many people on our route. I did see one young boy, maybe ten or so, run out toward the road when he heard the trucks. But he immediately fled when he saw them. The odds of seeing anyone on the expressway was slim and I mainly focused on getting home. We took the 453 split toward Mount Dora and exited on Highway 46.

From there it was a short drive to Round Lake Road where we turned north again. I was beginning to feel like I was home getting out here. But not quite yet. Round Lake dead-ends into Wolf Branch Road but there's a small road that continues north into a small subdivision. I crossed over Wolf Branch and continued.

Keying my mic, I said, "This road is going to dead end up here in a cul-de-sac. One of you needs to come around and take the lead. Just continue due north and break any fences we come to. We'll eventually hit a dirt road that will lead to forty-four."

I saw Ted's truck swerve out from behind me and accelerate. It passed me and took the lead. We drove through the yard of the last house on the street. None of these places looked occupied and we didn't stop to inspect them. It was a small community of McMansions with lots about an acre in size. Still too crowded for me, though.

We went off road for a while, winding our way through patches of trees and bush until we hit the dirt road, Grand Champion Lane. From there we were about fifteen minutes from home. I started thinking about the communications tower for the local power company. It was just to the west of where we were. By far the best place to put a repeater for us. It would provide a huge footprint. It sits on a hill and is two hundred feet tall. The only issue would be power for it.

I mulled over the tower as I drove and, before I knew it, I could see the burned armor sitting in the road that announced our arrival back to Adelaide.

As I turned in, Mel asked, "Weren't you supposed to go to the school and talk to them?"

"Yeah, tomorrow. I've had enough for one day."

"Me too. I'm ready to see my youngins," Aric said.

Mel looked over the seat at him. "You have two of the cutest babies I've ever seen, Aric. I can't wait to see them too." Turning back around, she added, "It's kind of funny what their presence has done around home. Everyone loves them and they seem to make everything a little brighter, I think."

"Thanks, Mel. I honestly thought the chances of me having a family were nil after The Day. But then I met Fred and I thought about it, but realized it still wasn't possible. I mean, at the time I was working for DHS and they damn sure wouldn't allow it."

Mel looked at me and smiled. "Then Morgan showed up and changed that."

Aric laughed. "Yeah he did!" He reached up and slapped me on the shoulder. "I cannot thank you enough, Morgan. You quite literally gave me my life back. I'm forever in your debt."

"You don't owe me shit," I said, looking at him in the mirror.

Turning to look out the window, he said, "Yes I do. More than you will ever know."

The porch was packed when we showed up and everyone was excited to hear about our adventures. As we made our way out to the back porch, I saw Dad and stopped. We did our usual greeting and he asked how things went.

"Pretty good. When everyone gets out here, we'll tell the story."

Mel came out and brought me a cup of tea. God, I love that woman. I thanked her and chatted with Dad and Dalton some while everyone settled down. Dalton slid the jar to me and I took a sip. The raw liquor burned all the way down.

"Sheeit!" I said.

Dalton grabbed the jar, took a swig, and swished it around in his mouth before swallowing. "Everyone's a critic. I'll save you all from it and drink it all myself."

I grabbed the jar. "I'll help."

The shit was pretty raw. But it had the desired effect. Quickly. And that was all I really cared about at the moment. Not that I was going to get shitfaced. But I could really use a buzz right now. Everyone was finally out on the porch and Sarge stood up.

"Alright Morgan, the floor is yours. Time for your AAR."

An AAR is an after action report used in the military to cover what you did, how you did it, what went right, and what went wrong, along with discussions on how to improve.

I got up and sat on top of the table with my feet on the bench so everyone could see me.

"Those of you that were out on this mission, feel free to jump in if you think I missed something. I made some notes as well."

I started into our trip and the first encounter at the Circle K store on 437. There were a number of looks at Mel as I explained what went down. Several people nodded or spoke words of affirmation about the actions taken. People close to Mel reached out and patted her back or arm.

"That's a hell of a baptism to it, Mel," Sarge said. "There is no easy way. At least in your heart you know why and that it was necessary. That will help."

I continued and explained about the farm we found and Dale and Brian. I told that we left Bubba and Sky there and would need to get back to them soon. Sarge and I discussed Dave and how we needed to go over and talk with him. Sarge said he would handle that for me.

"They growing that much?" Thad asked.

"More than you can imagine. It was shocking," said Mel.

"They dry some of it. They don't have any meat so they're living off a vegetarian diet. We can work with them and get them some protein and they'll share the veggies," I said.

"The kitchen in town can surely use it," Sarge said.

"That's what I was thinking. Get this set up and they will be able to provide more and better meals," I said.

"Good work," said Sarge.

"They may also have a case of malaria there as well," Doc offered. "An older woman there was pretty sick. Fever, aches, the usual symptoms for it. When are those meds getting here?"

"I'll check on it tomorrow. Continue," Sarge said as he scribbled a note in his book.

I got to the part about The Rock and explained what took place there. There was a lot of chatter amongst everyone, and they seemed very interested in this part. I gave a brief background on Rip and his family, how we knew them, and for how long. Then I explained the situation in the parks.

"You didn't go in?" Sarge asked.

"No," Ted answered. "They estimate there's over three hundred people in there. I didn't want the trucks to get enveloped. They may or may not have firearms, but they do have fire and I didn't want to even think about the possibility. We'll need to go back in force."

"I'll talk to Merryweather and we'll coordinate a mission. We'll go in hard and make a show of it," said Sarge.

"We came up with a plan on how to do it," Ted said. "We'll make them come out of the park to the trading post to get supplies. Set up a choke point with a couple of gun trucks to keep them back and let them in a handful at a time."

Looking at Sarge, I said, "I was also thinking of putting some of our people in the line with them to talk to folks and get a feel for what it's like, how it's run, the good, the bad and the ugly, you know? It was Aric's idea."

"Good idea. Anything there we need to worry about?"

"There's a small subset there that will be an issue. From what Andy told us, they do have some guns but no one knows about ammo. He said they use them to threaten people and get their way. These are also the same people keeping the fighting alive on the river. They appear to be the muscle inside. There's three main actors and some supporting cast. I don't have exact numbers on it."

"We'll have to figure out who the hell they are and separate them from the rest somehow," Sarge said.

"Andy will point them out to me and we will detain them. We're going to hold court with the people from the park acting as the jury. Let the people that have had to deal with them all this time decide what to do," I said.

"Good call," Sarge said with a nod. "So, you didn't even go to the other park?"

"No, once we heard what was going on and that there were even more people at Wekiva, we decided it wasn't worth the risk. When we return, we will go meet them. I want to end the fighting on the river and make them release any prisoners. Those days are over, and they need to understand that."

"Alright. Anything else?"

"Yeah, we stopped at a Duke Energy laydown yard. There's a lot of stuff there we need to get. Poles, transformers, fuses, switches, wire, lots of stuff. We need to bring it all back to town here. I'm sure Baker can use it and we can get power out to a few more areas."

"I don't know how much more we can actually power up," Baker said. "The Army is using quite a bit of power and that little turbine wasn't designed to run the whole town. It's about maxed out."

"There's a little juice left in it though," Terry added.

"We shouldn't push it," I said.

"Agreed. We don't need to stress it to the point of failure. Most folks have become accustomed to not having power, so there's no real need to push our luck," Sarge said.

"I think it would be best," said Baker.

"It was a successful mission for your first real one, Morgan," Sarge said. "There's going to start being a lot more of these as you well know. Thinking of things like the power company laydown yard is a big deal." Sarge paused and looked around the porch. "We all need to think about things like this. Any time there is a facility or a place that could have things we need, we need to check them out. Think outside the box. Get creative. Never know what you'll find if you just look."

"We need to have a talk with Merryweather," I said. "We need to come up with some kind of framework for what we're doing. What are the priorities, and develop missions to deal with them. Like, how are we going to help all these people we found today? Are we going to start shipping food to them every week? Every month? Can the Army even pull that off? Do they have it? There's a lot we need to find out."

"We'll go have a powwow with him tomorrow. We do need to get some organization." Sarge spun around to look at Karl. "Karl, you wanna give your AAR?"

"Sure." Karl stood up. "We went out to Alexander Springs. Place was empty. Then we went down the same road Morgan was ambushed on behind the bombing range."

CHAPTER 14

"You get ambushed?" Mel asked.

"No, we stopped at the washout, like you did, and conducted surveillance. They weren't down the road this time. They were actually behind us when Imri saw them." Karl paused and looked at Imri. "You want to tell it?"

Imri stood up and cleared his throat. "Yeah, we uh, were on a halt, like Karl said, when I heard a sound in the bush behind me. I turned and looked, searching for it when I saw movement about thirty or so meters away, which surprised me that they were that close. I called out contact and opened fire."

"Imri was on the right flank at the time," Karl said. "Then we were engaged from the left. Chadster opened up with the SAW and I did as well with my rifle. Return fire was sporadic and ineffective and quickly died off. We decided to investigate the right side first and I went out with Imri. We found a blood trail and that was it."

"You engaged them first?" Sarge asked.

Karl nodded. "Of course. Soon as we knew they were there. I wasn't going to wait for them to start shooting."

"I wouldn't either. Go on."

"We returned to Chad and went out to search the left flank and there we found a young woman, maybe twenty or so. She'd taken two rounds into her right leg and was in pretty bad shape. We got a tourniquet on her and I started an IV. We loaded her up and took her to the school. Harvey was waiting for us and they took her into the infirmary."

"What's her condition?" Sarge asked.

"Don't know. We had a cup of coffee and headed back."

Sarge looked at me. "We'll follow up on that tomorrow as well." Sarge looked around the porch. "Anyone got anything else?"

"We really need to butcher some hogs," Thad said. "I'd really like to do it in the next day or two. We also need to go get some corn and bring it back here to start training the heifer to milk."

Sarge nodded. "Alright. Whoever wants to help with hog butchering, get with Thad. As for the feed, we'll figure that out."

"I was just going to take the red truck up there and load it in the bed. We'll have to figure out some way to protect it, but at least we'll have some here." Thad paused for a moment, then added, "Now that I think about it, let's get the corn here and separate out the hogs we want to butcher. I'll finish them out on corn for a few days. Won't hurt none and will clean 'em out a little."

"We need to find some way to store the corn," Sarge said.

Still sitting on the tabletop, I said, "Drums."

"What's that?" Sarge asked.

"Let's put it in fifty-five-gallon drums. With lids and rings, they'll be air tight. We can store them outside if need be."

"Where we going to find clean drums with lids and rings?" Thad asked.

I winked at him. "I know a guy. On the way to town tomorrow we'll stop by and talk to him."

Mike raised his hand and Sarge eyed him suspiciously. "What is it?"

"I'm going to mount one of the Kornet rocket launchers to one of the trucks. I was thinking about it today. With Tabor still out there and possibly even Cubans and Russians, even though we haven't seen any in a while, I think it would be a good idea to have some anti-armor capabilities when we're out running around. Never know when we just might need to blow something up."

Sarge considered the statement for a moment. "Good idea, Mikey. I like it. Make it happen."

Mike sat back, looking pleased with himself. Crystal rolled her eyes.

"We also need to pick a spot for the first tower to go up," Sarge said and turned to look at me. "That reminds me, we need concrete. Do you know of anywhere that might have Portland cement?"

"We can try the hardware stores. If that doesn't work out, there is a cement place out the other side of Tavares, headed towards Howey-in-the-Hills."

"Who in the hell names the towns down here?" Dalton asked. "Every place should be called something like Alligatorville. Or Tick Station."

"You done?" Sarge asked. "Can the adults talk now?"

Dalton rolled a hand in front of himself. "Inshallah."

Mikey busted out laughing.

Confused, Jess asked, "What's that mean?"

"If God wills it," Sarge answered. "And he does. So, let's pick a spot and get to work on the footer for it."

"We can get grounding cable from the laydown yard," I said.

"Glad you thought of that, thank you. Hadn't considered it," Sarge said.

"I saw some cad weld molds there as well as some shots for them. Guess people didn't know what they were."

"Hell, I don't know what it is," said Sarge.

"It's basically small charges of thermite that you use to weld copper cable together or to something. They use molds that you put the cable through, pour the thermite in, and there's flash powder in the bottom. The flash powder in the shot ends up on the top of the mold when you're done. You light it with a striker, and it flashes over. Then you can remove the mold and it's welded."

"I'll let you handle that shit," said Sarge.

"I'll help," Mike said, "I want to see this."

Ted raised a hand. "Me too. I want to see it."

"Anything else?" Sarge asked.

"I have something," Fred said as she stood up. Everyone looked over to see her carrying little Wyatt over her shoulder coming out of the house onto the porch. She was walking toward Aric with a big smile on her face. "Today Tammy and the girls found something and brought it to me."

She got to Aric and handed him his son. He took the infant and cradled him in his arms as he spoke quietly to him. Then Wyatt started to squirm and fuss.

Looking up at Fred, he said, "I think he's hungry. When did he last eat?"

Fred looked down at him, a smile still on her face. "He is hungry. But you're going to have to feed him."

Aric looked shocked and asked, "What?" Naturally this got some laughs from people. "How do you expect me to do that?"

From under the baby blanket, Fred produced a small bottle. It was one of those designed for the bags, no bottom with a locking ring that held both the nipple and the bag in place.

"What's in it?" Aric asked.

"Milk. My milk."

Aric was genuinely confused. "How?"

Fred turned and looked at Tammy. "Well, today, Tammy and the girls found a breast pump in one of the houses and brought it to me. So now you can feed your son," she said and handed him the bottle.

Aric took it as a peaceful look came over him. He looked down at little Wyatt and asked, "You hungry buddy?"

Aric put the nipple to his son's mouth, and he greedily took to it and began to suckle. Aric smiled and looked up at Fred. She smiled back and ran her hand through his hair.

"This is so cool," he finally said.

CHAPTER 14

The porch was an emotional scene, with many of the women tearing up and even most of the guys feeling it. But it didn't last long. Sarge broke the moment up like only he could.

"I think Wyatt's the smartest one out here. Let's eat!" There was a round of claps and catcalls.

Mom, Miss Kay, Erin, and Taylor all headed for the kitchen with Kay saying, "All right, calm yer horses. We'll get it ready. Line up!"

"It's about to get western in here," Dalton said. "You little 'ins bunch up and us bigguns line up."

CHAPTER 15

I was rattled awake by something running across my face. Instinctively reaching up, I grabbed a hold of something soft and warm. Opening my eyes, I saw it was Ruckus. She didn't struggle in my grip and just stared at me, nose twitching.

"Guess you didn't make it to your cage last night, huh?" I said as I sat up.

"What?" Mel muttered from under the blanket.

I patted her ass and said, "Go back to sleep."

Getting up, I went out to the living room where the cage was, then detoured into the kitchen. Opening the fridge, I looked to see what was there. It was pretty bare. Not much for a squirrel for breakfast. Carrying her over to my plate carrier, I took out a pack of MRE crackers that I keep there with a cheese pack in case I need a little snack. Then I put her in the cage with half a cracker. She was quite happy with it and settled onto her haunches to enjoy it. I checked to make sure her water bottle had water 'cause those crackers are dry as hell.

Now that I was up, I got myself some tea and got dressed. It was six-thirty in the morning and I knew the old man would be up, so I slid into my plate carrier and slung my rifle as I headed out the door. The dogs were sitting patiently on the porch when I came out and fell in behind me as I headed for the cut in the fence. Aaron's tent was dark when I went by, and I could hear him snoring softly. I really wanted to get him out of here. But it was just too risky.

The lights were on at Danny's when I came around the front of the house. I expected to see Dad and Sarge on the porch,

359

but the rockers were empty. Stepping up on the porch, I could see the door to the back porch was open and went in. Sarge and Dad were sitting at one of the tables with Dalton having coffee.

Sarge looked up when I came in, then at his watch, then back at me. "What's wrong?"

"What do you mean?" I asked.

"You're up, dressed, and moving around, and it's not even seven. Something must be wrong."

"No. Was woke up by a limb rat running across my face. It's a little startling. Since I was up, thought I would come over and see what you guys were up to. Knew you'd be up."

"Of course we're up. We're adults, for cryin' out loud!"

Dad got up with his cup and asked, "You want coffee?"

I held my cup up. "I'm good. Not the right time of year for that shit yet."

"Blasphemy!" Sarge barked.

"Coffee is as necessary as air and water," Dalton added.

"Look, you all drink brown water. I drink brown water. Same same."

"It's not the same! Men drink coffee! If you can't drink hot coffee on a hot day, you're weak! I can't believe you survived this long," Sarge shot back.

"Do you guys get a prize or something for getting converts? Is this some kind of cult?" I asked, taking a drink of tea.

"You'd think," Dad said with a laugh.

"So, what's on your plate for today?" I asked.

"You and me need to go see Merryweather, for starters," Sarge said.

"On the way we'll stop and talk to Mario. He's got lots of drums, rings, and lids. We'll get some from him to put the corn in. Be the best way to store it."

"We'll need machinery to move them with," Dad said.

"We can load them with Cecil's tractor and use Thad's to unload them," I said.

"We were discussing where to put the tower up," said Sarge. "It needs to be someplace central."

"We need to establish a TOC," Dalton said.

"We're not going to be able to have HF rigs everywhere," I said. "We should set up a TOC and run all the radios into there. We can put up repeaters for VHF. I still say we should put one on the power company tower. It's the tallest thing around here. There's already an antenna up there. We just need to come up with a repeater and install it. Don't need to climb that tower."

"How tall is it?" Sarge asked.

"Two hundred feet."

"That would give us a hell of a footprint. Let's go look at it today if we can."

While we talked, Karl and Imri came through the door. They were both looking for coffee as well.

"Fresh pot in there," Dad said. "Help yourself."

After getting a cup, they came out to the porch and took a seat.

"Morning, gents," Karl said as he sat down.

"What's on the menu for today?" Imri asked.

"We have to run to town," said Sarge.

"We're getting a lot of interest in the militia," I said. "We're going to need to start training people again soon."

"I'm down," said Karl. "Easy work. Just let us know when you're ready."

"You going to check on that girl?" Imri asked me.

"Yeah, I was going to check with Harvey and see how she was doing. See if she's awake. Maybe we can talk to her."

"Karl, you got anything going today?" Sarge asked.

"If you guys don't have anything for us, I wanted to do a little more recon. See if we can find these guys," said Karl.

"Fine by me. We need to locate them."

"I'll go with you," Dalton said.

Imri looked at Karl and smiled. "We'll leave Chad here today. Let him have the day off."

"Where are you going to look?" Sarge asked.

"I was thinking about riding around that lake they were camped on. They have to be near a water source somewhere," said Karl.

In an aristocratic British accent, Dalton said, "Right! I'm positive they will be located near a body of water."

"That's what I was thinking," said Karl as he stood up to go fill his cup.

"There's a lot of bodies of water around here," I said. "They call it Lake County for a reason."

"That's an understatement," Sarge added.

"If we don't look, we definitely aren't going to find them," Imri said.

Karl returned with a full cup. "You two ready to go?"

"Now?" Imri asked.

"Why not?"

In the same accent, Dalton said, "But I haven't had me rations yet, Leftenant!"

"OK, OK," Karl said as he took a seat. "After breakfast."

"Better," Imri agreed, "much better."

"When do you want to go to town?" I asked Sarge.

"After we eat. No sense getting up there too early."

"We need call signs for you guys," said Sarge.

Karl laughed. "Ask Imri what his is."

Sarge looked at Imri expectantly.

"Nope," said Imri.

"Shitty call sign," I said.

"It's Rambo," said Karl. "He was so violent the IDF almost booted him. They gave it to him."

Sarge laughed. "If the IDF called you Rambo, I'm damn sure calling you Rambo." Then he looked at Karl and asked what his was.

"Charlie Zero Three."

"That's no fun at all," I said.

"Come on Tinkerbell," Imri said, "you can do better than that."

"No, that was my call sign," said Karl.

Sarge reached into his pocket for his notebook. Opening it, he started to write, saying it as he did. "Imri, Rambo. Karl, Tinkerbell."

"What?" Karl laughed.

Sarge slapped the book closed and smiled. "You know you don't get to give yourself a call sign."

The front door opened and Thad and Mary walked in along with Doc and Jess. I could hear Kay in the kitchen now and Jess joined her. After getting coffee, the guys came out to the porch.

"Where are your retarded brothers?" Sarge asked Doc.

"They're at the house fucking around with that Kornet."

"They get it mounted up?"

Taking a drink of coffee, Doc said, "Yeah they got it. They were out there most of the night."

Sarge slapped the table. "I don't even know why I let him do that."

"It's not a bad idea," said Karl. "I'd take one on my Jeep if I could. Those Soviet rockets are pretty damn good."

While this discussion went on, I went to the kitchen to see if Miss Kay had scraps for the dogs. She handed me a bowl that the plates were scrapped into the night before.

"Waste not, want not," she said with a smile.

"Agreed. They'll be happy."

I took the bowl out the back door of the porch and whistled. Drake and Meathead came running around the side of the house, tongues lolling. Using my folding knife, I divided the scraps between the two bowls we fed the dogs from. They were just outside the door and any leftovers went into them. We used two bowls, so they didn't have to compete. But they never seemed aggressive toward one another.

Putting my knife away, I heard Little Bit and the girls. I watched as they came through the hole in the fence. Seeing me, she ran over and wrapped me in a hug. I rustled her hair.

"Hey kiddo. Where's Ruckus?" I asked.

"She wouldn't come out of her house this morning."

"Because she was up all night running around the house. She ran over my face this morning and woke me up."

She giggled with much enthusiasm at the statement. "No she didn't, Daddy!"

Reaching down I scooped her up. "Yes she did. Did you see some cracker crumbs in her cage?"

"Where did she get a cracker from? I want a cracker."

I pulled the open pack from my plate carrier and handed it to her. She laughed, throwing her head back. "An MRE cracker!"

"What other kind of cracker do you think we have?" I asked as I bounced her up and down.

"Daddy!" she giggled.

Mel walked up while I was playing with Little Bit and leaned in for a kiss. As I tried to give her a kiss, Little Bit was pushing both our faces away.

"Eeww! Stop it!" she protested.

I carried Little Bit and held Mel's hand with the girls following behind us. They were chattering away like young girls will. They seemed to have an unending level of enthusiasm when they talked. I will never figure that out. How they talk so fast, loud, and much but can't seem to muster the energy when there are real things to be done.

I held the door open for the girls as they stampeded through. Little Bit wanted down, seeing that Jace, Edie, and Erin's kids were all now on the porch and it sounded like it. The porch, so quiet only a few minutes ago, was now loud and bright. The sun was up and people continued to arrive.

Breakfast this morning was simple egg burritos, scrambled eggs in a tortilla. That press we bought so many years ago had more than proved its worth. We were running low on sausage. When pigs were butchered, we ground all of it into sausage. Spices were getting harder to come up with and there was a never-ending search for more. As a result, the sausage of late had been little more than ground pork. We were nearly out of it now though, and we needed to butcher hogs.

I walked over to where Thad was sitting. "Hey buddy. I'll get you some corn today. We'll get a couple drums and I'll fill them at the plant."

"Good. I'll use it to separate the ones we'll butcher and feed them up for a couple of days. Then we can process them. I'll start getting things ready for it."

"Good deal," I said and walked back over to where I was sitting.

Mel arrived with a burrito for me, and it didn't take long to eat. Guess I was pretty hungry this morning. I talked with Mel for a bit, telling her I needed to go to town. She opted not to attend this trip.

"Sounds boring to me," she said.

"Probably will be. But we need to do it."

Aric and Fred arrived with the babies, and the girls were lining up to hold them. I went over and talked to Aric, telling him after breakfast I wanted him to go with us to town. He needed to be included in any discussions about militia.

"I appreciate it," Aric said with a nod.

I laughed. "You say that now." And I patted his shoulder as I walked away.

As soon as Aric finished his breakfast and kissed Fred and the babies, we headed out. We were going to take Sarge's truck to town. Fine by me; he could drive. I said bye to Mel and the girls on my way out the door.

Mike and Ted were pulling through the gate when we came out. Mike opened his door and leaned out. "You guys headed to town?"

"Leaving now!" Sarge shouted.

"We'll follow you!" Mike called back and the old man gave him a thumbs up.

"Two trucks all the time now?" Aric asked.

"In most cases, yes," said Sarge, "but not always. Karl, Imri, and Dalton are going out on a little recon in the Jeep. Want to keep that small so they can sneak around."

As we passed through the gate, I looked at Sarge and asked, "Weren't you supposed to give this back to Merryweather?"

"Oh, about that. I'm not," he replied.

"Why not?"

"Mainly, I don't want to. Second, Aric back there needs a set of wheels. Let him have the Hilux."

"Really?" Aric asked.

"You do need a set of wheels," I said.

"He does. They don't need this truck and we need more trucks," Sarge said and looked over at me. "You're the governor. You need to start telling them what you need. Start pressing them for more supplies. Otherwise, we're just wasting our time with this playacting."

With Altoona approaching, I pointed toward the market. "There's Mario. Pull in so I can talk to him about drums."

Sarge wheeled in and I hopped out.

CHAPTER 15

"Hey, Morgan," Mario greeted me as he placed a case of Mason jars full of honey on a folding table. "You guys are out early."

"Just need to run to town but I wanted to talk to you real quick."

"What's up?"

"You have empty drums that are clean?"

Mario laughed. "Oh yeah. I have them. Lots of them."

"Can we get some with lids and rings?"

"Sure. How many do you want?"

"Well, we have a mountain of corn we need to get stored in something before the rats get to it. I figured the drums would be the best option. Nothing can get in them, and they can be stored anywhere."

"I have seventy or seventy-five of them right now. Used them to transport honey to the co-op but those days are over. You can have as many as you need."

"Awesome. What do you want for them?"

"Is this whole corn going in them?" I nodded and he said, "How about a drum of corn then? That would last us a long, long time."

"Hell, you can have two! Thanks, man. This will help out a lot. Now we can move it around and get it to people that could use it."

"Come out to the house later and we'll get you what you need."

I shook his hand. "Thanks, buddy. Really appreciate it."

Getting back in the truck, Sarge asked, "We got drums?"

"He's got about seventy-five of them. Said we can have all we need."

"That's a hell of a lot of corn for sure," Sarge said as we pulled off.

"How many do you think we can fill?" Aric asked.

"All of them, probably," I said.

"You're doing a hell of a job, Morgan," Sarge said.

I looked at him sideways. "And?"

He cut his eyes at me. "And what? I can't just say you're doing a good job?"

"I don't know," I replied. "Can you? It's highly uncommon."

"See, this is why. You shitheads don't know how to take a compliment."

As we turned onto Bulldog Lane, I said, "Let's get this shit over with."

"Oh, it won't be that bad," said Sarge.

"I don't know. They called me yesterday and wanted me to come up here and talk to them. Told them I was busy, and they asked me to come by soon as I could. I don't even want to know what the hell they want."

Parking the truck, Sarge said, "Let's go find out."

LT Simmons was waiting for us at the security point that we entered through and waved us over.

"Morning," he said with a nod.

"How's it going, LT?" Sarge asked.

"Oh, you know, just trying to rebuild the nation. Nothing much."

"So, you're saying you have lots of free time, then?" Sarge said with a laugh.

"We'll be in the cafeteria," Ted said as we followed Simmons.

Simmons laughed at the comment as he turned to lead us to our meeting. It was in the conference room in the admin building and we all took seats around the table. Merryweather showed up with Warrant Officer Daniels and the three men took seats.

CHAPTER 15

"Morning, Governor," Merryweather said with a broad smile, and I nodded in reply. "We have a mission we need you to do as soon as possible."

"And what is that?" Sarge asked.

"We need to conduct a survey of the port at Canaveral. I've brought this up before, but it's becoming more critical. It's the closest port we can bring large vessels into and it will allow us to get more aid and supplies in."

"Isn't that the Navy's job?" I asked.

"Under normal circumstances, yes. But as you well know, we're not working under normal circumstances. So we need you to do this."

"I'll work up an OPORD and get it to you," Sarge offered.

"Good." Merryweather smiled.

"Is that what you needed yesterday?" I asked.

"Yes, this is a high priority, and we need to get it done as soon as possible. Where were you guys yesterday?"

"We were checking some places I thought would hold large numbers of people."

"What did you find?" Daniels asked.

I gave them the bullet points of what we found, telling them about the farm and the groups fighting to control the Wekiva River. We discussed several options, but in the end, I was surprised when Merryweather said it was our call on how we handle it.

"I have a question," I said.

"Shoot," said Merryweather.

"What is your capacity to supply people? How much can you move, how fast, and what do you have?"

Daniels and Merryweather shared a look before Merryweather, looking uncomfortable, leaned forward and cleared his throat. "Well, that's why we need to look at this port. We simply do not have the ability to transport the amount of supplies needed by truck from the Pan Handle. We need the port. Basically, I was told we can support this outpost and bring in extra with each trip. But to get more here will require the port."

"You know how far it is from here to Canaveral?" I asked.

Merryweather looked at Daniels, who checked his notes. "It's about ninety-seven miles to the port from here." He looked up for emphasis before continuing. "It's about three-hundred and ninety miles to Eglin from here."

"The logistics of it just don't work out right now. We are going to get one supply convoy every two weeks," Merryweather said. "The trip is so far they have to bring a fuel tanker as well. It's just costing too much. We don't have it to waste. The port is the answer. The way it will work is like this. Trucks will be loaded onto a RORO ship."

Sarge glanced over at me, saying, "That's a roll on roll off transport." I gave a little nod, and Merryweather continued.

"The trucks will unload at the port and convoy here. Unload and return to the ship to be returned to Jax."

"You're bringing all of this out of Jacksonville?" I asked.

Merryweather nodded, and I looked at Sarge.

"Jacksonville is only about a hundred miles from here. It will take just as long to get there as it will Canaveral. Why are we doing this dumb shit?"

"This isn't the only place we will have outposts. We will be setting up more of them," Daniels said. "This will allow us to forward deploy men and material a lot faster."

I rolled my head to the side and looked at Sarge. "You said if there was a hard way to do it, the Army knew it, and you weren't shitting."

"Trust us, Morgan," Daniels said. "There's a lot of thought went into this. We all just need to do our part."

"You have enough personnel to set up these new outposts?"

"Where are you on your militia?" Merryweather asked.

CHAPTER 15

I looked at Aric. "This is Aric Vonasec. He is the commander of the militia. This is a recent development, and we'll need time to get people to join, train, and equip them. It will take time."

Aric nodded at the men.

"Good to meet you, Aric," Daniels said as he leaned across the table to shake his hand. He then made introductions to the others. Then he suddenly remembered something and looked at Sarge. "We also have your repeater up. That should help in our comms."

"Did your people fuck with it at all?" Sarge asked.

"No, why?"

"It was programmed the way I wanted it, and if your nerds started fucking with it, I'll have to do it again."

"Nope. We just installed it on an antenna and powered it on. Seems like it's working. We don't have a radio for it, so we couldn't test it."

"Your radios won't talk to ours?" Aric asked.

"They will," said Sarge. "The repeater is set up so we can talk to them on one frequency and only to our people on another they don't have access to."

"We're ready to test it when you are," said Daniels.

"We'll do it when we leave here," said Sarge.

"Where are we on the malaria meds? We think we found another case," I said.

"They will be on the next truck. In limited supply," said Merryweather.

"How limited?" Sarge asked.

"To treat cases but not enough to use as a prophylactic."

"How about that girl Karl brought in?" Sarge asked.

"She's stable at the moment," Simmons answered. "But she lost the leg, and she may not survive it. We don't exactly have a surgical suite. Joiner did what he could for her."

371

"If she wakes up, we want to talk to her," I said.

The discussion shifted to the militia, and Aric was the center of the conversation. There were many things discussed that he had no answers for and he made furious notes. Aric had a lot of work ahead of himself and I kind of felt bad for dumping it on him. Simmons told us that there were many people showing up asking about joining the militia and that they were making a list of prospects.

I was listening, making the occasional note myself, when our radios crackled to life.

Stumpknocker, Stumpknocker, Rambo!

Sarge jumped in his seat and quickly called back, "Send it, Rambo."

We've found two MRAPs in Mad Max paint schemes at their last known POS, back at the boat ramp!

We all jumped to our feet and headed for the door. Sarge was on the radio talking to Imri as we ran out.

"What are they doing?"

Looks like they're getting water. It's not the entire group. Two trucks and six or eight men. We have the Goose and are going to engage.

"Rambo, you are weapons free! Take them out. We're on our way from Cheyenne!"

Copy! Imri called back and before he released the PTT we heard him say, *Let's move!*

Ted and Mike were already sprinting across the common of the school toward the trucks.

From behind, Simmons called out, "What do you need from us?"

"Nothing. This will be over before we even get there!" Sarge answered.

We tore out of the parking lot headed toward Eustis, pushing the trucks as fast as they would go. It didn't take Karl and the guys long to engage. We hadn't even made it to Lake Shore before the radio came to life again.

Stumpknocker, Stumpknocker, Vanilla Thunder!

"Answer him!" Sarge barked as he maneuvered the truck.

"Send your traffic!" I shouted.

Both targets have been engaged. We've got their people pinned down against the lake shore. ETA?

"Less than ten," I said and looked at Sarge. "You better hurry the fuck up!"

Ah, Stumpknocker, we have a problem! MI-24 inbound from the south! I say again, MI-24 inbound from the south!

"What?!" Sarge barked and cranked his neck to look out the window.

"Where is it?" I asked.

Due south from us. Coming in hot! Like Baskin Robbins, it's thirty-seven flavors of fuck you!

"Turn here!" I said and pointed to a road on the left, then looked back to make sure Mike and Ted were still there and they were. Right behind us.

"Where's this going to take us?" Sarge asked.

"To the hospital. We may be able to get an eye on it from there."

I pulled into the parking lot on the north side of the hospital and stopped. We all jumped out and started looking. It didn't take long to find the enormous aircraft. The sound of the rotor beating the air into submission was unmistakable.

"There it is!" Sarge called out, pointing.

Mike was in the turret of the M-ATV rotating the ATGM, anti-tank guided missile, mounted to the turret into firing position. Sarge looked up at him and shouted, "What the hell are you doing?"

Mike looked up. "What?"

"That's not an anti-air missile!"

"No, well, you always said the Hind was a flying tank!"

"Just relax! Don't do anything stupid!" Grabbing his mic, Sarge called the guys.

"Vanilla Thunder, Vanilla Thunder, SITREP!"

We're keeping them pinned against the shore. But that Hind is coming right at us!

Just then the Kornet came alive with a thunderous flash of flame and smoke as the rocket hurtled skyward. We all watched in awe as it flew a herky-jerky path toward the lumbering Hind. The Kornet is a wire guided anti-tank weapon meant for killing armor on the ground. However, since it is wire guided, it can be shot at anything the operator can see. Visual contact must be maintained throughout the flight until the warhead impacts the target.

The Hind was out over the lake now and settled into a hover. Sarge was incredulous and looked at Mike.

"You gotta be shittin' me!" Sarge barked. "What the fuck is Ivan thinking?"

"He's thinking there's nothing here that can kill him. That's what he's thinking!" Ted said as the white trail of smoke from the rocket got closer and closer to the huge machine.

It was surreal to see the little trail of smoke merge with the helicopter. The impact shot a geyser of yellow smoke, flame, and debris out the other side of the machine. It looked as though the pilot made a feeble effort to climb as flames licked out the sides. Then the rotor blades struck the tail boom, severing it, and the ship folded as it simply fell from the sky trailing thick black smoke, landing in the lake with a massive *splash*.

Mike was on top of the truck now, howling for all he was worth. Hands clenched into fists, he pumped them and jumped up and down on the roof. We were all shouting and high-fiving. It was an impressive feat and something Mike would talk about forever more, I'm sure.

CHAPTER 15

The radio brought us back around.

Was that you?

"Damn straight! Roger that, splash one Hind!" Mike called back.

We could use some help over here. They're tucked in tight to the shore. If you can come in from the east, we can persuade them to leave their cover.

We were already getting back into the trucks when Sarge said we were on our way. We went out the way we came and made the turn onto 441 headed west. This would allow us to hit the flank of their position. It wasn't hard to see where it was, as there were two thick columns of black smoke coming up from the two burning vehicles.

"Aric, get up on that gun!" Sarge said. The old man kept a 240-machine gun mounted to the turret of his truck at all times. We knew Tabor and his people were around and there was no such thing as *enough gun.* Aric scrambled into the sling seat in the turret and I heard him charge the weapon.

"Soon as you see bodies, open up!" Sarge shouted.

As soon as the ramp came into view, the machine gun over our heads started to rattle. Ted was in the turret of the M-ATV with his carbine firing. Then he dipped down and came back up with an M320 single shot grenade launcher and started throwing 40 mike-mike rounds at them. As we closed, Karl and the guys broke cover and started closing in as well.

When we met in front of the two burning trucks, all return fire had ended and the survivors were cowering in the water with two trying to swim away. A burst from Aric into the water around them followed by stern orders from the old man convinced them to swim back. In all, we took four prisoners.

They were a sad looking lot, honestly. Dirty, shaggy hair and beards. The mismatched weapons they had were a wreck. None I would want to go into a gunfight with. Karl, Imri, and

Dalton were securing the prisoners and searching them. Sarge checked the bodies of the dead looking for Tabor. Not seeing him among them or the captives, he went over to the prisoners.

Grabbing a man by the hair, he wrenched his head back. "Where's Tabor?"

"He doesn't go out on supply runs. He's at camp," the man groaned as he strained against the force being applied to him.

"Where's camp?"

Before the man could say another word, the radio once again crackled to life.

Stumpknocker, Stumpknocker, Cheyenne!

"Send it, Cheyenne!" Sarge spat into the radio.

RTB ASAP!

"Cheyenne, we're in the middle of something. We just splashed an MI-24 into Lake Eustis!"

Copy! We have a serious fucking problem inbound! RTB! RTB!

ABOUT THE AUTHOR

CHRIS WEATHERMAN, also known as ANGERY AMERICAN, is the author of 23 published works (and counting), including USA Today Best Sellers *Forsaking Home* and *Resurrecting Home*. His books include the Survivalist Series—a sensational hit that began with the Book 1, *Going Home*—and has now sold more than one million copies worldwide.

Book 11, *Engineering Home*, reached #1 on the Amazon New Releases Charts in Dystopian Fiction and Dystopian Science Fiction at its debut and climbed to the #2 spot on the Amazon Best Seller Chart, only behind George Orwell's *1984*.

Chris appeared in season one of History Channel's *Alone* series. He has been involved in prepping for over 30 years and practices primitive skills as well as modern survival that focuses on being prepared with the proper equipment.

Chris worked as a tradesman in the power industry for nearly 20 years building power plants and performing line work for power companies. He worked his way up to be the commissioning and start-up supervisor for many of these projects and has a solid understanding of power generation and distribution.

Although he currently makes his home in Florida on the edge of the Ocala National Forest with his wife Mel and his daughter Little Bit, Chris travels the country appearing at expos and prepper-focused events to meet with readers, sign books, and occasionally speak. His travels allow him to meet and train with instructors and students all over the country on preparedness and homestead design, covering everything from food production to security.

In 2023, Chris started the *Angery American Nation Podcast*, addressing the issues affecting America today with humor, insight, and unabashed honesty. Covering a wide range of topics including politics, social issues, current events, survival, and self reliance, he challenges conventional wisdom and encourages listeners to question the status quo. The *Angery American Nation Podcast* aims to contribute to a more informed and engaged citizenry.

ANGERY AMERICAN ONLINE

Facebook	AngeryAmerican
YouTube	@angery-american
Twitter/X	@TheAngeryAmeric
Instagram	@angeryamerican
TikTok	angeryamerican
Amazon Author	author/angeryamerican
Amazon Store	shop/angeryamerican
Goodreads	goodreads.com/author/show/7122142.A_American
Bookbub	bookbub.com/profile/2530946551
Rumble	rumble.com/angeryamerican
Patreon	angeryamerican
Podcast	Angery American Nation Podcast

ANGERYAMERICAN.COM

Printed in Great Britain
by Amazon